Also by
NIGEL BALCHIN

★

LAST RECOLLECTIONS OF MY UNCLE CHARLES
SUNDRY CREDITORS
A WAY THROUGH THE WOOD
THE ANATOMY OF VILLAINY
A SORT OF TRAITORS
THE BORGIA TESTAMENT
LORD, I WAS AFRAID
MINE OWN EXECUTIONER
THE SMALL BACK ROOM
DARKNESS FALLS FROM THE AIR
LIGHTBODY ON LIBERTY

THE FALL OF THE SPARROW

"A blessed companion is a book"—JERROLD

THE FALL
OF
THE SPARROW

*

NIGEL BALCHIN

THE COMPANION BOOK CLUB

LONDON

*Made and printed in Great Britain
for The Companion Book Club (Odhams Press Ltd.)
by C. Tinling & Co., Ltd., Liverpool,
London and Prescot.*
S.457.UA

"Be a man laden with sick women, children, brothers, sisters or servants, or be he sick himself, then let them lie where they be, and we praise him too if he would burn himself or the feeble person."

Medieval German Law.

"Are not two sparrows sold for a farthing? and one of them shall not fall on the ground without your Father."

St. Matthew. Chapter X, v. 29.

CONTENTS

OCP/911—A*

PROLOGUE

If I had kept to my original plan I should have missed the whole affair. But the weather was vile and the river in spate, so I came back a week early, intending to spend the last few days of the vacation pottering about in London.

I knew that my housekeeper would still be away, so there was no point in going to the flat till bedtime. I went straight from the station to the club, was given half a dozen letters which I put in my pocket unopened, and went and played billiards. It must have been after eleven when I reached the flat.

I heard a telephone bell as I came up in the lift, and somehow knew at once that it was my telephone. The flat had been empty for three weeks, and the telephone must have gone unanswered a good many times, but as usual it seemed vital to get the door unlocked and answer before the ringing stopped. I shot out of the lift, took what seemed to be several minutes unlocking the collection of locks on the front door, and then had some difficulty in getting the door open because of the mass of newspapers and letters on the floor inside. But the telephone was still ringing. I went to it and said "Welbeck 1183" rather breathlessly. A voice said, "Is that Mr. Payne?"

"Yes."

The voice said, "This is Ted Law," and paused. At least, that is what I thought it said. This seemed to be my cue to say something, but as I had no idea who Ted Law was I just said "Yes?" politely and waited.

The voice, which had a slight trace of north country accent, said carefully and rather coldly, "I'm sorry to bother you, but I rang up on the off-chance that my letters had miscarried. Have you received them?"

I said, "Well, I may have or I may not. I've been away and there are a lot of letters here. I haven't looked at them yet."

"I wrote to your club as well."

"I haven't opened those either."

The voice said, "Ah, I see," in a tone that meant it didn't believe me. "Well, I only wanted to say that if you didn't want to be involved, I should quite understand. It seems to be the general attitude."

"Involved in what?"

"I realize that it isn't a pleasant business, though personally, I should have thought. . . ."

I said, "I don't think you quite understand. Not having read your letters, I haven't the faintest idea what you are talking about."

". . . to me, friendship has certain obligations. But that's only a point of view, of course. . . ."

There was something familiar about the phrase and the tone, and suddenly I realized that "Ted Law" was Laidlaw. There was only one thing that he would be writing to me about, and I said quickly, "I didn't realize it was you, Laidlaw. Is it something about Jason?"

"Of course."

"He's in trouble?"

"Yes."

"What sort of trouble?"

Laidlaw said, "I don't want to talk about it on the telephone. It's all in my letters."

"Well then, can you hold the line while I find them and read them?"

"I can't, I'm in a telephone box."

"Then can I ring you back?"

"I'm not on the telephone. I only wanted to know if you were coming tomorrow."

12

I took a deep breath and said, "Laidlaw, I think perhaps you'd better ring me back in half an hour. By then I may have some idea what this is all about."

The letters were there, four of them in all, the two to the club being copies of the two to the flat. Heaven knows how Laidlaw knew my club. The first was dated three days after I had left. It said:

DEAR PAYNE:

I have had a most disturbing letter from Jason Pellew. He is in serious trouble and is under arrest. He gives no details, and merely asks me to send him some cigarettes, but I feel something more should be done, and hope you will agree, and co-operate. I am trying to contact a legal acquaintance of his named Bryce about it.

Yours sincerely,

ARTHUR LAIDLAW

The second was dated three days ago and ran:

DEAR PAYNE:

I do not know how to interpret the absence of reply to my letter about Jason Pellew. Perhaps it did not reach you. He has now been remanded in custody on a whole series of charges. The solicitors who are representing him don't appear to know him at all. I have been in touch with Bryce, whose interest, like that of everybody else, seems lukewarm. However, I am meeting Bryce at his chambers at noon on the 25th if you cared to join us. But perhaps you are too busy.

Yours sincerely,

ARTHUR LAIDLAW

PS. People's attitude to friendship seems very singular. For my part I regard a friend in trouble as an inescapable responsibility.

A. L.

That was all. I sat up till one o'clock waiting for Laidlaw to ring up again, but he never did. He explained later that he had no more coppers for the telephone.

*   *   *   *   *

Bryce had very pleasant chambers looking out towards

13

the Embankment. I had not seen him for ten years, and he was stouter, and the thick black hair was beginning to grey slightly at the temples. But it only made him more completely the successful barrister, and as I looked at that handsome face and cool smile, felt the firm handshake, and heard myself greeted in that lovely deep voice, I reflected that it was silly to dislike Bryce, and that perhaps I was merely jealous of him.

Bryce sat down at his desk, waved me to a chair, handed me a box of cigarettes and said, "I take it the subject is Jason?"

"Yes."

Bryce shook his head and said, "Yes. Well our dear little Jason certainly seems to have been very naughty. Not, as you know, for the first time. But this time very much on the wrong side of the law."

I said, "Can you tell me what it's all about? I had a lunatic conversation on the telephone with that ass Laidlaw which told me nothing, and two letters from him that didn't tell me much more."

Bryce said, "Yes, poor old Laidlaw. He's coming here this morning."

"I know. That's why I came early. I gather Jason's in jail?"

"Charged with what?"

Bryce smiled at his fingers. "Well, the dear boy doesn't appear to have *murdered* anybody—or if he has they haven't found out about it. But apart from that he seems to have tried his hand at a fair range of things. There are half a dozen main charges—dud cheques, false pretences, stealing while bailee, stealing a car, and so on."

"All money things?"

"Oh, yes. All various illegal methods of raising the wind. There's about a couple of thousand pounds involved altogether."

14

"When did all this happen?"

"In the last six months. You know his wife left him?"

"Yes. I saw him after that quite a lot. Then about a year ago he disappeared and I've never heard from him since."

Bryce said, "Well, it appears that after that the dear boy, finding himself a little short of cash perhaps, set out to write quite a few cheques. When they began to bounce, he started to get things on tick in the name of his godmother, old Lady Peasmore, and sell them."

"Good God!"

"He then borrowed a flat from an unsuspecting character named Archer and proceeded to flog everything in it that was floggable, even down to the furniture. He then stole a car, drove to Edinburgh, and was eventually picked up by the police there, wearing military uniform and calling himself Major Stegler."

Bryce shook his head. "There's no doubt about it that for a few months he had what is normally called a high old time. Every cent of the money's gone, of course."

"What on?"

"I've no idea. Wine and women and horses, I should guess. That's where that sort of money usually goes."

"But Jason doesn't drink much and doesn't gamble."

"I don't think you and I know just what Jason *does* do, Henry."

I said, "Of course, the man's as mad as a hatter."

Bryce shrugged, "Maybe," he said. "But not, I'm afraid, in the legal sense."

"He's been hopelessly unstable for years. You know it. I know it."

"People who do these things usually are," he said rather coldly. There was a long pause.

I said, "Well, what's being done about it, Bicycle? If I'd been here, of course, I would have done something before. But obviously I want to help if. . . ."

Bryce spread out his hands. "How *can* you, Henry? How can anybody? Of course this chap Laidlaw's been rushing round enjoying himself immensely in his favourite role of the Faithful Friend. I gather that wet nurse to Jason is a job he always wanted, for some obscure reason. He's written to or been to see everybody whom he thinks might help, and he's very bitter about the absence of response. But as I said to him, most of these people have befriended Jason in one way or another over the last twenty years, and they've had all they wanted of it. He's never been exactly a *rewarding* person to help."

"Which people do you mean?"

"Well—his godmother. And this chap Archer whose furniture he stole. And ourselves, if it comes to that."

I said, "I didn't know you'd ever done anything for Jason. At least, nothing that exactly *helped* him."

"You may remember a small matter during the war when you came to me for help on his behalf."

"Personally, I've never found him unrewarding."

"Then you're an exception, my dear fellow. But in any case, what can anybody do? Jason's committed these offences, some of them very unpretty ones. He's confessed to them and he'll plead guilty."

"He will?"

"Of course. After that, there's nothing to be done but the speech in mitigation."

"Are you appearing for him?"

"No. I have a case that day."

"Who is?"

"A chap named Arnold. Quite good, I believe."

"Laidlaw says his solicitors are no good."

Bryce sighed.

"That's pure Laidlaw. I've seen the solicitor and he's quite a sensible little man."

I was beginning to be really angry. I said, "It's all quite

good and quite sensible, but I gather that the end of it is that Jason will go to jail."

"Almost certainly," said Bryce coolly. "There's an outside chance that he might be bound over, but I should say it's a hundred to one against."

"But surely if evidence is given showing that the man was invalided out of the army on psychiatric grounds, and that he was under treatment only a few months before all this happened . . . ?"

Bryce held up a hand. "Ah now, Henry—this is where you'll have to talk to his solicitor and counsel. It's not my case, you see. But I think they'll tell you that sort of plea is one you've got to be awfully careful about nowadays."

I said, "In God's name why? It's true."

"So it may be. But I warn you that the Courts are very tired of having people like Jason before them with the plea that the poor dears can't help it, and are more to be pitied than blamed."

"Well, aren't they?"

Bryce hesitated. "I don't know," he said sombrely. "In my profession, Henry, you come across a lot of people in trouble. Sometimes you feel that it's just bad luck, and that a worthwhile person has gone wrong. But attractive little man as he is in some ways, I can't say that Jason's ever struck me as being much good to anybody—including himself. After all, society hasn't treated him badly—far better than it treats a lot of people. I don't know that he's ever done anything in return." He shook his head. "You can't put Jason forward as a person who's never had a chance—not if you know some of the people I've defended in my time, who *really* hadn't. He's had plenty of chances and he's mucked them every time. That's all."

I said, "And no one else is in the least to blame?"

"Well, my dear man, we all have to take *some* responsibility for ourselves."

17

There was a pause. I said, "You've known Jason for twenty-odd years. You may remember him when he was a pretty little boy of twelve at school—and some of the things that happened then. You'll remember a lot of things since. Do you tell me that Jason's just a crook, who deserves no sympathy?"

He didn't say anything, but just sat there looking handsome and smiling, so I went the whole way and smiled back at him sweetly and said, "Not even *your* sympathy for example?"

Bryce stared at me for a moment quite expressionlessly and then looked out of the window and said, "I wasn't saying anything of the sort. I was only warning you of what a Court may feel. . . ." He stopped as the door opened and his clerk showed in Laidlaw. Bryce got up and said, "Ah, here you are, Laidlaw." I thought he seemed relieved.

I had not seen Laidlaw for years, but he had hardly changed at all. He had been going slightly bald at twenty and he was still going slightly bald. He was still immensely tall and very thin, and he stooped no more and no less than he had always done. Even the spottiness which might have been a sign of late adolescence was still with him. He peered at me through the thick glasses that magnified his eyes and said, "This is a terrible business, Payne."

I said, "It sounds a first-class mess."

"I'm glad that you found time to come along, at least. I was beginning to feel that friendship meant nothing nowadays." He turned to Bryce. "I've seen his godmother."

"Yes?" said Bryce rather wearily.

"Her attitude," said Laidlaw with great bitterness, "is, 'I don't want to talk about it. It's all too painful.' Too painful for *her*, mark you."

"What did you want her to do anyhow?"

"Not to press the charges of using her credit."

"*Is* she pressing them?"

"Not particularly, I suppose. Anyhow her attitude's better than the man Archer, who's positively vindictive."

18

"Well, Jason sold his furniture. You'd probably be vindictive if you lent somebody your flat and he sold all your stuff. It was a mean thing to do."

Laidlaw sighed. "Perhaps," he said softly. "But you see, all *I* know is that the man who did it was my friend."

Bryce said, "Well, he doesn't appear to have been *Archer's* friend. Archer had only known him six months." He waved a hand towards me. "That's going to be one of your main difficulties, you see, Henry. Practically all these charges, except stealing the car, are things where Jason has let down somebody who had been good to him. You can't expect much sympathy from the Court for that sort of thing "

I said, "I don't expect any sympathy for what he's done. I haven't much with it myself. What I want is some understanding of why it all happened—why an otherwise honourable man should suddenly act like a criminal cad."

Laidlaw goggled at me and said stiffly, "I cannot allow you to apply those words to Jason."

Bryce smiled at his fingers. I said, "Oh, for God's sake, cut it out, Laidlaw. I've known Jason longer than you have and I'm probably as fond of him. But it's no good just sentimentalizing and talking about friendship. The plain fact is that he's always been slightly off his head, and now something's pushed him over the edge. The only thing that can possibly save him is to convince the Court that he wasn't responsible for his actions."

Laidlaw smiled bitterly, "In the course of my sentimentalizings," he said sarcastically, "and whilst you were wherever it was you have been for the last month, I have been endeavouring to gather evidence to establish that." He fumbled in his brief-case. "I managed to trace Pinnock, the psychiatrist who treated him during the war. . . ."

"Pinnock? I doubt whether that will have got you far. The man who *could* have helped is dead."

"I arranged for the solicitors to write to Pinnock to see if he would be prepared to give evidence for Jason. Here is his reply." Laidlaw put on another pair of spectacles and read, "Dear Sirs, re Jason Pellew. I have your letter concerning the above, but regret that I do not feel that any evidence that I could give would be likely to help your client. I remember him as a plausible and untruthful person of poor moral fibre and neurotic tendencies, who, like a good many others, felt that it would be more comfortable to take no further part in the war. I could not honestly say that he struck me as a person of any social value. Yours faithfully, Eustace Pinnock."

There was a pause. Bryce shrugged his shoulders and said, "You see?"

I said, "I knew Pinnock was a menace, but he really wrote that about a man who had been his patient?"

"Here's the letter if you want to see it."

Bryce glanced at his watch and said, "Well now, can we get down to brass tacks. He comes up for trial on Thursday?"

"Yes."

"And I'm seeing Arnold and the solicitors tomorrow afternoon?"

Laidlaw said, "I should like to be here if I may."

"Well, frankly, Laidlaw, I should prefer you not to be. You've done all you can. I think it's far better now if you leave it to the legal types."

I said, "I should like to get Stephen Parsons to give evidence. He treated Jason for a while."

"He's another psychiatrist?"

"Yes."

"All right. I'll put that to them and see what they say. They may want it or they may not. Anyhow, I can promise you that everybody will do their best. But don't expect miracles, will you?"

We went down the narrow stone stairs in silence. It was a brilliant sunny day.

20

Laidlaw said, "I've never really been sure whether you are on Jason's side or not, Payne."

I said, "Then you're crazy."

"You spoke very harshly of him a moment ago. But it's the general attitude. People whom he thought were his friends. . . . It's a thing I don't understand—a thing that's foreign to my nature."

"If it's any satisfaction to you, I think you're the only friend, in your sense, that Jason's got."

Laidlaw's spotty face flushed with pleasure. "That's handsome of you, Payne. I don't suggest, of course, that you aren't fond of him, or like Bryce and these other people. But. . . ."

I said, "Is it possible to see Jason?"

He turned and peered at me anxiously. "He's particularly asked that people shouldn't visit him. I haven't even seen him myself, though of course I've written and sent cigarettes and so on."

I did not say anything. After a while Laidlaw said, "I do feel it's important that Jason's wishes over this should be respected, Payne. After all, I myself should have liked nothing better than to see him. But he did say *most* emphatically that both before and after the trial. . . ."

The river was high, and a brisk wind from the north-east was blowing it into little waves which slopped against the buoys. A big barge that looked like some sort of tanker was just coming under Westminster Bridge. I said, "All right, Laidlaw. Don't worry. I won't see him. After all, what good would it do?"

*   *   *   *   *

In the cab on the way to the Court I said, "I've almost certainly brought you on a wild-goose chase, Stephen. I've heard nothing from the solicitors, so I don't imagine they're calling either of us. I know Bryce was all against it."

"It doesn't matter," said Parsons. "I'd like to see what

21

happens to him. Anyhow, Bryce may be right, you know. The Courts are very tired of psychiatrists. And if it comes to that, psychiatrists are very tired of the Courts."

"I find that completely terrifying. Here's a case where the only possible line of defence is the psychiatric one, and nobody dares to use it because it may annoy the judge."

"It *is* terrifying, but it's true. And you can see why. Supposing they call me, and I say that Pellew is a psychopathic personality, which is a pretty vague bit of jargon anyway. That may or may not mean anything to the judge, depending upon whether he's an ancient diehard who's still living in the days of hansom cabs, or a man who is interested in these things. But in either case it means nothing to him legally, because the law makes no provision for that sort of person. To the law, people are either mad or sane. I can't say that Pellew is mad, in the legal sense. And if I did, half a dozen prison doctors would swear he wasn't. Ergo he is sane and responsible. The fact that he finds life more difficult than some people is neither here nor there. It isn't so much a matter of annoying the judge as of confusing a nice clear-cut issue."

"But we're in the middle of the twentieth century, Stephen."

"We are. And far worse off in this than we were twenty years ago." Parsons sighed. "It was the war, you know. Psychiatrists did a fine job for the Services in getting a lot of people discharged who were useless, and much worse than useless. But since most people didn't realise how dangerous these chaps were, and how necessary it was to get rid of them, it looked as though the wanglers and the weaklings were getting away with it. They often thought so themselves, and used to boast about how they'd deceived the simple 'trick cyclist.'"

"But even so. . . ."

"Then we've had the people in the profession who simply can't understand that they and the law are talking about different things, and will keep rushing into the witness box and getting themselves shot to pieces. The result is that, whereas twenty-five years ago nobody knew anything about psychiatrists, and was prepared to treat them as experts of a sort, nowadays everybody knows that a psychiatrist means a gullible sentimentalist. Hence, of course, people like Eustace Pinnock. He was quite a good man before the war. But he was very insecure and couldn't bear to be thought a simpleton. So he started to talk about people of weak moral fibre and no social value. It made him popular with commanding officers, but it didn't help the army much. Nor, of course, his patients."

I said, "So on the whole you think they're right not to call you?"

Parsons shrugged. "I've given evidence a good many times. I've never yet got a man off. I doubt if I've ever reduced anybody's sentence by a day. Twice at least I think what I've said has done a person harm—when one has got that sort of judge." He frowned. "You see, Henry, the law doesn't want to know the truth about people—not the *whole* truth. Its job is difficult enough coping with what's lying about on the surface."

In the big, square, pillared hall I saw Laidlaw. He was talking to a small fresh-faced, boyish-looking young man in wig and gown, and an even smaller grey-haired one, and he was stooping almost double as he peered into their faces in turn. He waved me over and introduced them as Jason's counsel and solicitor, and I introduced Parsons. From that day to this I have never been able to remember the solicitor's name or what he looked like, except that he was small and grey. The young barrister said, "It's frightfully good of you to come," very earnestly, and then gave a curious nervous

23

giggle as though to apologise for having said something foolish.

I said, "I gather you won't be calling Parsons or me."

"Well, no. I don't think so. It's terribly good of you. . . ."

"Parsons thinks you're probably right."

"Does he?" said the young man. "Does he *really*? I am awfully glad." He giggled again, and then, half turning aside, he said in a low voice, jerking his head towards Laidlaw, "I think his obvious sincerity . . . you know?"

I didn't see what he meant, but I said, "Yes," vaguely.

"We shall be on early," said Arnold. "That's one good thing. They'll take the undefended cases first. There'll be a bit of a hooh-hah first because the judge is new and has to be welcomed. It's a bit tricky for me, that, because one doesn't know what he'll be like. I knew him when he was a silk, of course, but that's no guide."

I said, "What's going to happen to Pellew?"

He looked very serious and shook his head. "I don't know. It's not an easy wicket. Too much money involved. Two hundred pounds and we might have got him bound over. But two thousand's—well—two thousand. You know?" He giggled briefly, stopped suddenly and said, "Of course, I shall do my best."

Laidlaw said, "Well now, if you and Dr. Parsons would like to find yourselves some seats, Payne. . . ."

The court was rather big, and it seemed to be practically full of jurymen, who were answering a roll call. Parsons and I found ourselves seats at the side. Laidlaw did not sit with us but went and sat down below beside the little grey solicitor. Parsons looked round and said, "I wonder whether it's entirely by accident that they always make these places look like chapels? The little solicitor chap thinks he'll get about a year."

The usher called "Stand," and we rose as the judge came

in. He was a tall man with a big-featured swarthy face and thick black eyebrows—rather a fine face. He seemed to be half-smiling, and it was some moments before I realised that the half-smile was a permanent expression, produced by a large scar at the side of his mouth. When he did smile the result was quite different and far less pleasantly whimsical.

I was glad I had been warned about his being new and having to be welcomed because I found it rather trying. Not that anybody said or did anything that was not entirely correct. A barrister—presumably the senior one present— rose and offered the congratulations of the bar, and said what a good appointment it was and how glad everybody was about it and how they all looked forward to pleading before the judge; and the judge replied very quietly and modestly that he hoped to uphold the proper traditions, etc., and ended by saying that he hoped to show a proper consideration for the convenience of members of the bar. All of which was entirely as it should be, and said pleasantly, with the sort of smile on everybody's face that one uses when addressing an old friend formally in public. But I wasn't their old friend, or a member of their tight little fraternity, and nor was Jason, and I knew that he must be waiting somewhere while all these pretty compliments and courtesies and smiles were passing, and that soon all these faces would set into a hard, dispassionate professional gravity and then they would bring him in—the man who wasn't a member of their club—nor of anybody's now.

But if they were members of a club, it was a club with decent, civilized rules, and after all the compliments the Court was adjourned for five minutes before the business of the day began. The judge went out and I was still wondering idly whether he occupied the five minutes in prayer or in drinking a whisky and soda, when he was back again, and Jason had popped up in the dock like the assistant in a conjuring trick.

I was sitting at the side of the court and could only see his face in profile, with the turned-up nose and the rather pouting cherub mouth. He was dressed neatly in a grey suit. The mop of tow-coloured hair was tidier than usual. I think he must have plastered it down with water. He looked very small in the dock—I always tended to forget how small he was—and at first glance he might have been sixteen instead of thirty-six. He was rather pale, and the expression on his face was one I had never seen before. It was not the usual expression of careful solemnity and penitence that one had seen so often when he was in hot water, but had a sort of strained calmness. Even from where I was sitting one could see the slight trembling of his arms and shoulders and the twitching of his scalp.

He made a slight, rather hesitant bow to the judge, and then stood there at attention while the clerk read the charges. There seemed to be a tremendous number of them, and at the end of each one Jason gave a little bob and said, "Guilty," quietly but quite audibly. It was the only word I heard him say that day.

As the clerk sat down and the prosecuting counsel rose, the judge stared for a moment at Jason and then flapped his hand slightly, and Jason sat down, which meant that I could only see the top of the tow-coloured head. I was grateful for that curt flap.

Jason had pleaded guilty, and there was not much for the prosecutor to do, except state the facts. He managed to get himself into a slight tangle at one point about the dates, and the judge made him go back and untangle himself, though it didn't seem to me to matter much. Apart from the policeman who had arrested him and the one who had taken his statement, there were no witnesses for the prosecution, and there was only one moment of interest. That was when the policeman was explaining that when arrested Jason was wearing a major's uniform with the ribbons of the Military Cross and other decorations. The judge looked up and said, "He was wearing the ribbon of the Military Cross?" He said it rather sharply, as though it mattered to him.

The prosecutor said, "Yes, m'lud. I should say that I am instructed that the accused *was* a major in the late war, and was awarded this decoration."

"And the other ribbons? Were they ones to which he was entitled?" Counsel hesitated and glanced at his brief. "No, m'lud," he said in a faintly puzzled voice. "They appear to have been decorations awarded at various points in the war, to members of the Italian forces by the German and American armies."

There was a moment's pause and then a very faint titter in court. The judge looked at Jason for a moment with the curious scarred half-smile which was not a smile at all, and then nodded briefly without comment.

They were very fair to him. There was no attempt to make it all any blacker than it was. They only proved, quietly and dryly, what everybody knew already; and when counsel came to the really nasty bits, like selling Archer's property from the flat, he mentioned them with what seemed to be almost a sigh and a shake of the head. They were so fair that when they came to read Jason's statement, I could be sure that somebody else had helped him to put it into words proper to the occasion. For the words were very proper, though scarcely in Jason's normal style. They explained how, finding himself "financially embarrassed," he had "embarked upon a course of conduct" which he "now realized was both foolish and criminal." It then went on to confirm the charges, and after a rather formal expression of regret and apology to those who had suffered "loss or inconvenience," ended "I now see the foolishness of my conduct, and whatever the decision of the Court, have resolved henceforth to strive to rehabilitate myself in the eyes of my friends and of society by honest work." Instinctively at this point I glanced at the dock, but there was nothing to be seen but the top of Jason's head. I heard Parsons make a slight noise which may have been a sigh or a chuckle.

That was all there was in the statement. No explanation, no excuse, and a perfunctory apology that sounded as deeply felt as a vote of thanks to the Mayor. From the point of view of defending Jason, the prosecutor's speech had been far more valuable; and from the judge's face it looked as though he thought so too.

That was the end of the case for the prosecution. Then Arnold got up to open the defence. I turned to say something to Parsons, and before I knew what was happening Laidlaw was shambling into the witness box and being sworn, and I realized what Arnold had meant by that reference to his "obvious sincerity . . . you know?"

I had not bargained for their calling Laidlaw, and for a moment I was so bitterly angry with their fumbling silliness that I nearly walked out of the Court. But Parsons said quietly, "It can't do any harm now," and I sat back and watched.

Arnold said, "Your name is Arthur Percy Laidlaw, of 36 Marlowe Crescent, S.W.8?" Laidlaw said, "It is." He was leaning with his hands on the front of the dock, and with his curved spine he was the shape of a carelessly made question mark. As he spoke his Adam's apple shot up and down convulsively in his stringy throat.

"You are an accountant?"

"I am."

"You have known the accused for many years?"

"For many years." Laidlaw shot a wan smile towards the dock. "We were at Cambridge together."

"At where?" said the judge gently, Laidlaw's wan smile

toward the dock having left him with nothing but the back of Laidlaw's head.

"At Cambridge, m'lud."

The judge said, "Ah, yes, Cambridge," and made a note of it as though he meant to remember the name.

Arnold said, "You have done what you could to help the accused in the past?"

"He is my friend," said Laidlaw with simple heroism.

The judge looked a trifle puzzled. "You mean you *have* done so, Mr. Laidlaw?"

"Yes, my lord."

"In all his dealings with you, you have found him honest and honourable?"

"Completely so."

"These proceedings came as a shock to you?"

Laidlaw drew himself up with a jerk and gazed round the Court as though the shock had just been received.

"I was *dumbfounded*," he said in a hushed voice.

"You have tried to help him even since these proceedings started?" Arnold went on.

"I have done my best to."

"And whatever the result of this case you are prepared to stand by him and to help him further?"

Laidlaw's Adam's apple jumped violently, "I am prepared to do absolutely anything that lies in my power," he said quietly. "That is what I think friendship means."

It was probably the supreme moment of his life, but it was over.

Arnold said, "Thank you, Mr. Laidlaw."

Laidlaw hesitated and turned hopefully to the judge, but the judge merely bent his head courteously in dismissal, and Laidlaw turned and descended from the box, kicking the side of it loudly as he did so.

Arnold gave his wig a slight prod of adjustment and said, "M'lud—I am sure your Lordship will agree with me that this is a tragic case. Here is a man of previously unblemished character and an excellent war record, who through folly, and worse than folly, finds himself in the dock on these charges. . . ." He went on in this strain for about five minutes, at the end of which what he had said was that it was all very sad, with an underlying implication that it would have been far less sad if Jason had not been the son of a general, nor been to a public school and university. He then went on to explain the agony of soul Jason felt in finding himself in the dock and the firmness of his resolution not to find himself there again. This took another five minutes. During all this time the judge was listening with what seemed to me peculiar intentness—leaning slightly towards counsel, and never taking his eyes off him. I thought of the phrase, "Incline thine ear to my prayer." It may have been a mere mannerism, but I had a feeling that he was genuinely waiting and hoping for Arnold to say something sensible in Jason's favour.

And then Arnold began to get himself into a real tangle. He said, "Moreover, m'lud, I would point out that the prisoner is a man who has many good friends, which is not a thing to be lightly discounted."

I saw the judge's eyebrows go up, and at that moment Arnold seemed to lose the thread of what he was saying and paused. I muttered to Parsons, "The bloody fool! Which side is he on?"

The judge frowned slightly and said, "Can you expand on that, Mr. Arnold? I don't want to interrupt you, but to me one of the most difficult features of this case is that the accused *has* had excellent friends who have treated him very well, and whom he has treated very badly. You see my difficulty?"

Arnold looked confused and said, "Quite, m'lud. I quite see that. I merely meant that his ability to inspire affection must . . . must. . . ."

"But it is possible to inspire affection without deserving it, surely?"

"But hardly to retain it, m'lud—as the accused has done in the case of Mr. Laidlaw, for example."

The judge shook his head doubtfully, "I grant you Mr. Laidlaw," he said, "who is certainly a very good friend indeed. But you must remember that Mr. Laidlaw has not been plundered by the accused. Others in whom he undoubtedly inspired friendship and affection—Mr. Archer, for example—have had a more unhappy experience."

Arnold said, "I quite agree, m'lud."

"But please go on, Mr. Arnold. I only mentioned this because I didn't altogether follow your line of argument."

After that there was clearly nothing more to be done with it. Arnold went on for a few minutes more without saying anything of value, and then sat down rather abruptly. The judge went on staring at him for a moment or two and then nodded slowly and looked down at his lap in silence. After a few moments he raised his head and gave a little flap towards the dock. Jason stood up. The arm and shoulder that I could see were shaking violently, but his face was still the calm, strained mask.

The judge said, "Jason Pellew, on your own admission you are guilty of a long series of offences. Not only are these offences serious crimes, but many of them have about them an element of meanness and ingratitude which makes them particularly distasteful. Not only have you stolen and misappropriated and cheated, but you have not hesitated to do these things to friends who trusted and believed in you." He paused for a long second and stared at the prisoner, the handsome big-featured dark face at once contemptuous and troubled.

"Your counsel has said that it is a tragic thing to see a man of your type and record in such a position. With that I agree. You were born the son of a distinguished soldier. You were given a first-class education. You served your country gallantly during the war, and had the honour to hold His Majesty's commission. Yet with these things behind you, and every opportunity before, you chose, for the sake of money which you put to no sensible use, to enter on this career of sordid crime, which has brought shame to the honourable name you bear, and deep distress to good friends who have helped you. . . ."

The judge paused and sat again for a long moment with bent head, staring down into his lap.

In that moment of complete silence I looked round the big courtroom—at the two policemen on either side of the small, yellow-haired figure in the dock—at the crowd of bored jurymen in the public seats—at the line of wigs and black gowns on the front benches—at the coat of arms above the large and splendid figure of the judge, sitting there with silver-wigged head lowered, it might have been in sorrow, or thought, or even prayer. Somehow it all seemed very big and impressive and powerful for the miserable pettiness of the job in hand—so big that one could almost see its huge shadow darkening the figure in the dock.

> *The hills like giants at a hunting lay*
> *Chin upon hand to see the game at bay*
> *Now stab and end the creature . . .*

★ I ★

"THE SON OF A DISTINGUISHED
SOLDIER . . ."

IT MUST have been in 1923 or '24, for I know I was about nine and had just gone to my preparatory school. I think we were coming home from church, for there was a feeling of formality which I associate only with the walk to and from church. My father said, "Is it tomorrow that we're going to the Abode of Bliss?"

My mother frowned at him and shook her head in a way that meant that he shouldn't say things like that in front of me. My father was always saying things that he shouldn't have said in front of me.

I said, "What is the Abode of Bliss?"

My mother said, "Nothing, darling. We're going to tea with the general, that's all."

"What general?"

"General Consternation," said my father, giggling.

I knew he had made a joke because he giggled, but I could not see it. I said rather sulkily, "I don't know what consternation is."

"Then look it up in the dictionary," said my father briskly. "Whenever you come across a word you don't know, look it up. That's what a dictionary is for."

When we reached home I went and found the dictionary and looked up consternation. It said, "Consternation, con-ster-na'shon n. (L. consternatis, from consterno—con, and sterno, to throw or strike down) Astonishment; amazement or horror that confronts the faculties and incapacitates a person for consultation and execution; excessive terror, wonder or surprise." I took the dictionary to my father and read this out to him. He roared with laughter and said, "Exactly. Particularly the bit about being incapacitated from consultation and execution. I always am."

I said, "Why are we going to tea there?"

My mother said, "Phil, do stop it. You'll drive the child crazy."

"Bunkum," said my father. "He's crazy already. I never knew anybody who talked such nonsense." He caught hold of my hair and started towards the door, tugging me after him. "Come on. Let's go and play tennis."

My mother said, "Darling—it's Sunday."

"All right. Then we'll play French cricket instead. The Continental Sunday. Come on—*you* come and play French cricket, Sue."

My mother hesitated and then, with a sigh, followed us on to the lawn. It was entirely surrounded by high hedges and completely private, but she kept looking round nervously to make sure that no one was watching. During the game my father came very close and was making terrifying feints with the ball to make me move my feet. I dabbed out with the bat and hit him in the face, raising a large lump over his eyebrow. As my mother was bathing it she chuckled and said it was a judgment on him for playing on Sunday. My father said, "Well, I think it's a bit much if God is going to start biffing me in the eye with cricket bats." My mother frowned at him and shook her head, meaning that he shouldn't make jokes about God in front of me.

That night, when I was in bed, I said, "Mummy, where *are* we going to tea tomorrow?"

She said, "Only to General Pellew's, darling. He's got a little boy just a bit younger than you. His name's Jason."

I said, "His name's a sort of mixture of John and James isn't it?"

"Or Johnson and Jameson."

This pleased us both and I went on chuckling about Johnson and Jameson for a long time after she had gone.

The next day the lump over my father's eye was smaller but blue. About half-past three we set out for the Pellews'. It was apparently only about a mile away, and my father wanted to walk, but my mother insisted that we should go in the car. This was a mistake, for turning in the rather narrow drive in front of the house my father brushed against a bush and broke some twigs off it. At that moment a rather short, very thickset man appeared on the front steps and shouted angrily, "Hey—steady there. Be careful, man."

"I beg your pardon."

"That's all right," the thickset man said grudgingly. "But those things cost money." He came forward as we climbed out of the car and held out his hand to my father and said, "Hallo, Payne." They shook hands. The general turned to my mother, bowed briefly and said, "Good afternoon, ma'am. Hallo, boy." He then turned his back on all of us, and went and examined the bush, while we stood in a hesitant group on the steps. After a moment he gave a short grunt, turned, said, "Well, come in," and started into the house ahead of us shouting, "Mary—they've come."

We stood in the hall for a moment, and I had time to look at General Pellew. He was, as I have said, a stocky little man with faded red hair peppered with grey. His eyes were small, and of a curious hot brown colour, with colourless lashes, which gave him an angry pop-eyed look. The rest of his face was the colour of old bricks. He was wearing a tweed jacket with leather inserts at the elbows, which was a thing that I had never seen before.

The general made no effort to take our coats, or to show us where to put them. We just stood in the dark, stone-flagged hall in silence. After a while he let out a roar of, "Mary—what the hell are you doing? Your guests have come." He

35

turned to my father and said, "Manners," bitterly. Mrs. Pellew appeared on the stairs. She said, "Oh, I'm so sorry. . . ." The general said, "Keeping people standing about." Mrs. Pellew greeted my father and mother and then turned to me and took my hand and said, "And this is little Harry?"

I disliked being called Harry, as I do to this day, and I disliked being called "little Harry" even more. I said, "Good afternoon," stiffly. I did not care for the look or sound of Mrs. Pellew. She was a tall woman—considerably taller than the general—and years later I was to realize that when younger she must have been a rather beautiful woman. She had very large grey eyes and a delicate, slightly upturned nose. But her cheeks had fallen in, leaving her with prominent cheekbones, her neck was thin and scraggy, and her brownish hair was wispy and lifeless. But it was less her appearance than her voice that I disliked. Mrs. Pellew whined. Whatever she was saying, even if it was only "Good afternoon," had a note of complaint and martyrdom. My father once remarked that wherever he was with Mrs. Pellew he always wanted to get up and let her out before she actually began to scratch at the door.

Shortly after Mrs. Pellew arrived we positively got rid of our coats and were taken into the drawing-room. All I remember about the room is that it was very cold, though it was quite a warm day outside. The general said, "Where's Jason?" Mrs. Pellew said, "Out in the garden."

"Well, what's he doing out there? He ought to be on parade with people here. Probably be covered in mud and muck."

"But George, it doesn't *matter*," said Mrs. Pellew in that high, droopy voice. "The child must play."

"He can play when it's his playtime. But if there are people here he ought to be on parade. Somebody's got to show some elementary manners if you can't."

"How old is Jason?" said my mother gently.

"Seven," said Mrs. Pellew.

"You wouldn't think it," said the general bitterly. "Still wets his bed like a baby. Can't read properly. Of course it's the way he's been coddled." He turned to his wife and said viciously, "I'd be obliged if you would carry out my wishes and go and get my son." Mrs. Pellew looked at him for a moment with a sort of weak hatred, and then rose and went out without a word.

The general turned to my father and said abruptly, "Were you in the war?"

"No," said my father politely. "I was a shirker."

"Oh," said the general, staring at him with the hot little eyes. After a moment he grunted, looked away and said, "Well, anyhow, you're frank about it, which is more than most of them are."

My mother had gone rather pink. She said, "My husband's joking, General Pellew. He volunteered in 1914 but was rejected because of his heart."

"Oh—you've got a heart?"

"So they tell me," said my father gravely.

The general grunted and shrugged his shoulders in a way that suggested that it was rather worse to have a bad heart than to have been a shirker. Mrs. Pellew returned and said, "Here's Jason. Say good afternoon, darling."

He was very small—much smaller than I, even allowing for the difference in age. But even then he was not spindly or weak-looking. He had his mother's large grey eyes and turned-up nose, but those were the only ways in which he resembled either of them. For his mouth was very full and red and pouting, and he had a tangled mop of very fine, silky, light yellow hair. In nearly thirty years I have barely known anybody meet Jason without discovering, sooner or later, that he was very like a cherub.

My mother smiled at him and said, "Hallo, Jason," and

he went across and shook hands with her silently and gravely, and then with my father and then with me. As we shook hands he looked down at our hands, not at me.

The general said, "Hands are probably filthy, anyhow. Go and wash them."

Mrs. Pellew said, "I *have* washed them, George."

The general said, "Go and do as I say, Jason." Jason went silently out.

My father said, "It's a good name for him, Jason. Carries the golden fleece round with him."

"What?" said the general. "Oh, yes. Damn' silly name for a boy if you ask me. But there it is. Mary wanted it. What have you done to your face?"

"That is where my wife struck me," said my father quietly. "With—with a rolling-pin."

My mother was only just over thirty at the time, and very pretty. She went scarlet and tugged at her skirt, which, in the fashion of the day, was very short. She always tugged at her skirt when agitated. She said, "Phil—how *can* you. . . ."

I said, "I did it with a cricket bat. We were playing French cricket."

"Oh, did you?" said the general. "Well, *I* was taught not to interrupt when older people were talking."

I whispered to my mother, "I want to go home." She did not say anything, but patted my hand and made a funny face at me.

The general said, "Well—is there ever going to be any tea?"

Mrs. Pellew sighed and said, "But George, it's *only* five to *four*!"

Jason had come back now. She turned to him and said, "Darling, wouldn't it be nice if you were to show Harry the garden?"

It was not a large garden, but it was long and narrow. Jason and I walked right to the other end of it in silence.

Then he stopped and pointed and said, "Those are peas."

I said, "We've got some peas, too."

"I expect yours are bigger than ours," said Jason politely.

This was an unusual gambit and I did not know the continuation. I said, "Oh, I don't know."

Jason said, "Do you like peas to eat?"

"Not much."

"I do," he said with quiet satisfaction. We started to walk slowly back in silence.

After a while I said, "Have you got a dog here?"

"No," said Jason. "I had a rabbit but it died."

I said, "Our dog was run over, but we're going to have another. I'm going to have it for my birthday."

"When is your birthday?"

"November the thirteenth."

"Mine's December the thirteenth," said Jason.

We looked at one another and laughed. It was the first breaking of the ice. Jason said, "Did you really do that lump on your father's face?"

"Yes."

"Did you get a good hiding?" said Jason hopefully.

"Of course not," I said, puzzled. "I didn't do it on *purpose*. We were playing French cricket."

"How do you play that?"

"You try to hit people's feet with a ball."

There was a shrivelled potato lying on the ground. I picked it up and said, "You have that stick and try and hit it away when I throw this at your feet."

Jason hesitated and then picked up the stick. I saw him give a quick glance towards the house as he did so. I threw the potato gently at his feet. He made a feeble pass at it with the stick and missed, and the potato hit his toe. I said, "That's out. Now you throw it at my feet."

Jason's eyes went to the house again. "I don't think we'd better," he said nervously.

39

"Why not?"

"It might go on to the garden."

He took the potato and put it carefully back where we had found it. I said, "I go to school now."

"So do I," said Jason.

"Yes. But not a proper school. You're not old enough. I only went last term. It's at Eastbourne."

"Where's that?"

"A long way away. It takes two hours to get there."

"I go to Miss Chinnock's," said Jason. "But I don't expect it's the same," he added with the odd, submissive politeness.

"No, it isn't. I used to go to one like that. It's not a real *school* like Boars Drive."

"It's lovely though," said Jason rather wistfully. "I like Plasticine best."

There was an old apple tree beside the path. I said, "I bet I can climb that. I can climb every tree in our garden except one."

"No, you mustn't," said Jason quickly.

"Why not?"

"They'll see."

"I don't care."

I started to scramble up the sloping trunk and found an easy foothold, and reached the lowest branch. It was only about three feet from the ground. I sat on it and said, "It's an easy tree to climb."

Jason said, "Come down. Oh, *do* come down. They'll catch us." He held out his hands in entreaty and I saw that he was going to cry. I hesitated for a moment, but there was such terror on his face that I was frightened. I slid down and said rather huffily, "Oh, all right, if there's going to be such a fuss. But what *can* we do? I'm bored."

"I don't know," said Jason helplessly.

"What do you do when you're by yourself? Just stand about like this?"

He just stood and gazed at me in dumb misery. The big grey eyes were full of tears. I realized that I was not behaving well and said awkwardly, "There's nothing to blub about. Come on, cheer up for Chatham." I smiled at him and he made a great effort and smiled back.

I said, "What was your rabbit called?"

"Bun," said Jason. His face lit up. "I could show you where it was buried," he said tentatively.

I said, "That would be nice." I was not used to being entertained by a sensitive and nervous host, but I was beginning to get the hang of it.

It was nearly five o'clock when they came to call us to tea, and we were immediately sent to wash our hands by the general, and then sent back to wash them again because we had not done them properly. During the meal my mother and Mrs. Pellew talked about domestic affairs, while the general lectured my father on some subject which I did not understand at the time, but which I realize now was the measurements of the Great Pyramid and their prophetic significance. (Years later a regular soldier told me that practically all retired Sappers became a little odd, and that the Great Pyramid was one of the most common things for them to be odd about.) My father listened gravely, or at least appeared to be listening. The general never spoke to Jason, except once to tell him to sit up, and he never spoke to me at all.

I did not mind the lack of conversation, for it was an excellent and varied tea. In fact, it was its very excellence that led to the final disaster. There were, amongst other things, a jelly with sliced banana in it, and a large apricot flan. Mrs. Pellew asked me which I would have, and after a severe inward struggle I chose the jelly, of which I was particularly fond, hoping that the meal would go on long enough for me to get back to the flan later. Mrs. Pellew then asked Jason, and it was clear that he, too, was torn

41

by indecision. After a moment's hesitation he whispered something to his mother. The general looked up and said, "Don't *whisper*, Jason. I've told you about it before. Speak up and say what you've got to say, for God's sake."

Mrs. Pellew said, "Oh *no*, darling, you can't have *both together*."

"Why can't he if he wants it?" said the general sharply—and even at the time I knew that if she had given Jason both he would have been angry about that.

"Well, they don't go together, George," said Mrs. Pellew in her high whine.

"Nonsense," said the general. "Give the child what he wants."

"But they're not *meant* to be eaten together, George. He can quite well have jelly first and flan after."

The general said, "Who pays for the food in this house?"

"Perhaps . . ." began my mother gently.

"And who makes it?" said Mrs. Pellew, bursting into tears.

"Will you do as I tell you?" said the general loudly, rising to his feet. His wife did not move, but just sat staring at him with her face puckered and the tears running down her cheeks. There was a moment's awful silence. Then the general pushed back his chair so violently that it fell over backwards with a crash, and rushed round the table. I shrank towards my mother in terror, and she put a protecting arm round me. The general seized a spoon, grabbed Jason's plate, and ladled half the jelly on to it, spilling a large piece of it on the tablecloth. Picking up a knife, he sawed the flan in half, added that to the plate, and dumped it in front of Jason with a bang. He shouted, "There. Now get on with that." He whipped round, glared at me, and said, "And you, too," and dumped the other half of the flan on my plate.

"I don't think Henry wants it, thank you," said my mother very quietly.

The general took no notice. He was staring at Jason with his angry pop-eyes. Jason had shrunk down in his chair till his head was only just above the table, and he seemed half hidden behind the huge mound of food on his plate. His face was very pale, and even his lips, which were usually particularly red, were now a yellowish pink. He was staring at his father with the same wide-eyed terror that I had seen when I climbed the apple tree.

The general gave a sort of ghastly caricature of a smile and said, "Well, what do you want now, old man? Some cream?" He grabbed for the cream-jug and then suddenly Jason hid his face in his hands and started to scream—awful rhythmic screams that came with each breath. I think I started to cry, too. The general stood glaring for a moment, and then, leaning across the table, he picked up Jason's loaded plate, hurled it at the wall, and rushed out of the room. The plate did not break. It just bounced off the wall and fell messily on the carpet.

My mother had caught me to her. Jason had stopped screaming and there was complete silence for a moment. Then my mother said, "Come along, darling," very gently, and got up. Mrs. Pellew had Jason on her lap and was holding him tightly. I don't remember anything else about our going, except hearing my mother say, "Is he all right?" and seeing her gently pass her hand over the yellow mop of hair as he lay with his face hidden. On the way home my father and mother hardly spoke at all, and when they did it was to say very commonplace things in rather low voices. As soon as the car was out of the Pellews' drive and on the road, I saw my father take his left hand off the steering wheel and take my mother's hand, and after that we drove home in silence, my father driving with one hand.

That night when my mother said good night to me she held me for a long time in silence and she said, "I'm sorry that wasn't a very nice tea party, darling."

I said, "I like banana jelly."

My mother smiled and said, "Did you get a chance to eat yours?"

"No," I said. This had been a bitter blow.

"Never mind," said my mother. "I'll make you one. Did you like Jason?"

I said, "Oh, yes," though privately I had thought him rather dull.

My mother said, "You mustn't take any notice of General Pellew. He's rather eccentric."

I did not know what eccentric meant, but not wanting to talk about General Pellew, I did not ask her. Next day I tried to look it up in the dictionary, but could not find it.

* * * * *

I never went to the Pellews' house again—at least not to that one. Nor, for some years after, did I meet the general. But Mrs. Pellew and Jason sometimes used to come to tea, and these visits were always quite pleasant and uneventful. I did not care for Mrs. Pellew, and disliked the fact that whenever Jason and I returned from playing in the garden and she had been talking alone with my mother, she used to look as though she had been crying, and my mother always seemed serious and depressed.

On the other hand, Jason improved on acquaintance. In our garden, where there were plenty of things to do, he was not at all dull; and though he was younger than I and smaller, he picked up games very quickly. Indeed, at some of them, particularly the one where you throw a ball on to the sloping roof of the barn and the other person had to catch it, he was soon as good or better than I, being very quick and neat on his feet, while I was rather clumsy.

But I think the main reason why I found him pleasant company was that he flattered me. Most of my friends boasted all the time, and would always insist that something they

44

had was better or bigger than what I had. But Jason had a sort of polite and modest submissiveness in such matters. It was pleasant to be with somebody with whom one was allowed to do all the boasting; and who, even when he could climb a tree rather better than one could oneself, always asked for advice and instruction. Apart from games, he also used to ask me a lot of questions about flowers, of which he was very fond. Hardly knowing a rose from a peony myself, I still used to answer with great firmness, and he never questioned what I told him; even if, as sometimes happened, I told him that the same flower was a hollyhock one week and a dahlia the next.

The other thing that I noticed about Jason during this period was the way in which he lied to his mother. Not that I did not lie to mine when necessary; but it seldom *was* necessary, because there were few things that my mother minded my doing. My lying to her was therefore an occasional and amateurish affair, usually involving a very red face and a lot of shifting of the feet. Jason, on the other hand, never seemed to want his mother to know what we had been doing, even when to me it seemed entirely innocent. If we had been climbing trees for example, and his mother asked what we had been doing, he would reply calmly and innocently that we had been looking at the tomatoes; and on several occasions when, with full permission, I had let him pick plums or strawberries, he never admitted to his mother that he had done so.

I did not hold this tendency against him. I merely thought it was odd. On one occasion I also found it embarrassing. We had been playing cricket, and I hit harder than usual, so that the ball went over the hedge and landed on the glass of a garden frame, cracking it. It was not a very bad crack and I did not take it very seriously. I should probably simply have said nothing about it. But Jason seemed very worried, and at once suggested that we should stop playing and

45

go inside. As soon as we rejoined our mothers he said casually, "A cat broke one of the frames."

"Really?" said Mrs. Pellew.

"Yes," said Jason. "I saw it. It was a black cat with white paws, and it came running along the hedge and jumped right on the frame and cracked the glass. You come and see."

My mother glanced quickly at me, and I realized that I had gone bright scarlet, not so much with guilt as with surprise and embarrassment. She smiled at Jason, who was gazing at her with wide, innocent eyes, and said, "Oh, we won't bother now, Jason. It's tea-time. The cat didn't cut itself, did it?"

Jason said, "Oh no. It just jumped on and cracked the glass. That's all. And then ran off into the shrubbery. I think it was the cat from next door."

My mother said, "I expect it was. Never mind. It doesn't matter."

I remember being angry and resentful about this incident, because there was no way in which I could put it right with my mother. I was perfectly willing to tell her I had broken the frame, since she would not have been angry. But if I did so, I should be making it clear that Jason had told lies, which was unthinkable. I was uncomfortable about it for several days, until when we were out in the garden together, my mother said, "Show me what the cat did to the frame." I hesitated and went very red and my mother added quickly, "Or that *something* did." I showed her in silence and she said, "Oh well, that's not too bad, is it?" and kissed me, and after that I knew it was all right.

* * * * *

Not long after this the Pellews left the district, and I neither saw nor heard anything of Jason for nearly five years. It was the longest gap in the whole of our acquaintance. I was fifteen by that time, had been at Amblehurst for two

46

years, and was in the Lower Fifth. One evening in the Summer Term, when at the nets, I received a summons to the headmaster. I had spoken to him perhaps three times since I came to the school, and my reaction was the simple one of wondering which of my sins, coming to light, could possibly be bad enough for the headmaster to be brought into the matter. He was standing on the lawn outside his house, talking to a stocky little man with grey hair, and a small boy. I did not recognize either of them at first. The headmaster said, "Oh—here's Payne," and the stocky man said, "Don't know me, do you?" Then I saw the popping brown eyes and the colourless lashes and said, "Yes, I do, General Pellew."

I shook hands with him and with Jason, who grinned at me cheerfully. That was the main way in which he had altered. The large grey eyes, the pouting mouth and the general cherubicness were the same. So, underneath a preparatory school cap, was a mop of yellow hair. He had grown a good deal, of course, though he was still small. But whereas five years ago he had hardly ever smiled, now he had a charming, rather shy grin which was never absent for very long, and indeed has seldom been absent since. The general seemed to have aged a good deal. He was fatter, and his hair now had no trace of red. My first impression was that he had also mellowed, for he told me quite politely and kindly that Jason was coming to Amblehurst next term, and that the headmaster had given permission for me to go out to dine with them.

After my last experience of a meal with the general, I was not very keen to go, but I could not very well refuse, and anyhow, I was glad to see Jason.

My first reminder that I was with General Pellew came as soon as the expedition started. The general opened the back door of the car and said, "Get in." Jason and I climbed in, and we drove off with the general alone in the front of the car like a chauffeur. I thought perhaps he had done this so that we could talk, but when I said something to Jason he did not reply, but merely nodded warningly at his father's back. Puzzled, I repeated what I had said. The general thereupon shouted over his shoulder, "Now then, quiet, you boys. I don't want a lot of chatter while I'm driving."

After that we sat in silence. The general drove very slowly. I don't think he ever exceeded twenty miles an hour. He constantly sounded his horn, not only as a warning but as a rebuke to other drivers, practically all of whom he seemed to think were driving with criminal recklessness. Sometimes he leaned out and waved them towards the side of the road; and on a couple of occasions he let out great roars of, "What the hell d'you think you're doing?" I decided that he had not really mellowed much, and that his previous politeness had been due to the presence of the headmaster.

After we had driven a few miles he shouted back, "Is there anywhere you know where we can get an eatable meal?"

The normal place to be taken by parents was the Star and Garter at Linton. I suggested it tentatively. The general said, "What's the good of telling me that now? It's in the opposite direction. Why couldn't you speak up and say where you wanted to go in the first place?"

I could not help noticing that, whereas when I had known him last this sort of thing had reduced Jason to silent terror, it now seemed rather to amuse him. Several times he grinned and winked at me, and made ferocious faces at his father's back when the general was shaking his fist at some passing car.

General Pellew's method of selecting somewhere to dine was characteristic. After driving a certain distance he began to pull up at every place which looked as though it might serve meals. We would then alight and enter. The general would then say, "Have you got any decent food?" The reply naturally being, "Yes." He would then demand the menu,

look at it, give a snort of disgust and walk out in silence, with
Jason and myself trailing after him. He did this four times
before he found a place which passed this preliminary
examination. It was a large, rather pretentious main road
hotel. As soon as the general had looked at the menu and
given a rather grudging nod he turned away, saying, "Wait
here," over his shoulder, and disappeared into the bar. Jason
and I sat down at a table and smiled at one another rather
shyly.

I said, "What house are you coming to?"

"Mr. Gladstone's."

"That's my house."

"I know. The head said so."

I said, "He's never called 'the head' at Amblehurst. Either
'the headmaster' or 'the gaffer'."

"Thank you," said Jason with his old polite submissiveness.

I was not really sure what I felt about Jason coming to
Gladstone's. I liked him well enough, but I did not particularly want the job of a wet-nurse to a new kid of thirteen.

I said, "Of course you realize that we shan't see much of
each other. I shall probably be in the Upper Fifth next term.
Know what form they'll start you in?"

"The Upper Fourth, I think."

"Not at thirteen, my dear man."

Jason said, "I thought that was what he said, but I'm sure
you're right."

The general came out of the bar and said, "Jason—have
you ordered your friend a lemonade or anything? What sort
of manners do you think that is? You're like a yokel, boy."
He then went back into the bar.

Jason said, "Would you like a lemonade?"

I said, "No thanks."

"I think you'd better have one," he said sombrely. "Otherwise there will be trouble. You needn't drink it." He sud-

denly grinned the wide, rather rueful, rather shy grin, and I realized that it had nothing much to do with how he was feeling, but was just a knack that he had acquired.

We were quite a long way from Amblehurst, and it was sheer bad luck that Bryce should be there. He was the first person I saw as we went into the dining-room. He was with a handsome grey-haired man. They were distinctly alike, and I think the man must have been his father or his uncle. I smiled at him rather shyly and Bryce nodded with his cool smile. As we sat down I said in a low voice to Jason, "That's Bryce. He'll be head of the house next term. Awfully decent chap." I was not really on "decent chap" terms with Bryce, and did not really like him. The general said loudly, "Don't mumble. What's his name? Price?" He turned round, stared at Bryce for a moment or two and then turned back with a grunt. I was sitting facing Bryce. I saw his eyebrows go up rather superciliously and he said something to the man, who glanced at us quickly. The general said, "Well now— I suppose you're hungry. Let's see what we can have." He picked up the menu and fumbled in his pocket. "Dammit. I haven't got my glasses. . . ." He held the menu away from him at arm's length and then suddenly tossed it across to Jason saying, "Can't read it. Read it out." Jason picked it up and hesitated. It was a rather large menu, entirely in French. The general said very loudly, "Go on, go on, you can read, can't you?"

Jason had gone very red. He started to mumble something. The general said, "Can't hear a word." Jason said more loudly, "Potage Parmonteer." The general shouted, "Parmontee—ay. Parmontee—ay. Good God, boy. . . ." Mercifully there were only about a dozen people in the room, but by now they were thoroughly interested. My face was burning hot, and I stared down at the tablecloth.

"Consomme Mad—Madriline," said Jason wretchedly. The general leant across and snatched the menu out of his

hand and thrust it towards me saying, "Here—give it to him."
For one awful moment I stared at the card in terror, and
then a voice said quietly, "Good evening, sir. Now what
would you like to begin with. A little soup, or hors
d'œuvres . . . ?" The head waiter had realized that this
was a matter that required his personal attention. I looked
at Jason. He was still very red and there were tears in his
eyes, but as they met mine his mouth slowly quivered into
the shy, practised smile.

I have little recollection of the rest of the meal, but I am
fairly sure nothing catastrophic happened. Indeed, I fancy
that under the influence of half a bottle of wine and a steak
the general quietened down and became almost genial.
His geniality was a rather terrifying affair, since it took the
form of pressing one to eat great quantities of things that
one did not like. But at least it did not involve public
humiliation. When we were half-way through, Bryce and
the grey-haired man left, and after that it did not matter
so much. Bryce gave me the cool smile and nod once more,
and I saw his dark eyes go to the general and Jason with
interest.

It was nearly nine o'clock when we started the drive back
to Amblehurst. As before, Jason and I sat together in the
back seat. It was getting dark now, and the general drove
more slowly than ever. In fact, when he met another car,
he usually stopped altogether until it had passed, shouting,
"Dim your bloody lights, you lunatic."

In between these encounters, however, he talked, or rather
shouted over his shoulder on the subject of Jason and
Amblehurst.

"Now, in sending you to this place, Jason, I'm making a
sacrifice. I can't really afford it, as you'd realize if you knew
the sort of pension a grateful country gives you for forty
years' service. I'm depriving myself to give you a chance.
You see you take it."

The general paused to swear at a passing lorry.

"You've got to work hard and play hard. Perhaps they can smarten you up a bit. Be a good thing if they can. I've no use for shirkers and failures. You've got Payne here to show you the ropes. And keep yourself *clean*. You know what I mean, don't you, Payne?"

I said, "Yes, sir." Nobody who had heard my headmaster preach could have failed to know what he meant—up to a point.

"It's not my fault that you've been spoilt and made a fool of," shouted the general. "But you'll find all that's over now. You've got to grow up and be a man. Stand on your own feet without your mother and me to fuss over you."

This went on throughout the half-hour's drive back to the school. Once or twice I glanced at Jason. It was dark, and I could only see the glimmer of his face. He was sitting quite still, hunched up in the corner of the car. Throughout the journey he neither moved nor spoke. I doubt if he heard most of what the general said.

When we reached the school gates the general stopped the car.

I said, "Well, thank you very much, sir . . ." and moved to get out. The general held up his hand and said, "Wait a minute."

I paused, and we sat in silence for a while. I was rather worried, because my pass was only till half-past nine, and the car clock said nine twenty-five. The general suddenly turned in his seat, held out a hand and said, "Well—good night, Payne—and remember it's coming." I thought he was referring to Jason and said, "Yes, sir."

"It's absolutely certain," said the general quietly. "There are plenty of people who thought the last war was it. But it's all there before their eyes if they liked to use them. It won't be in my lifetime, but it'll be in yours and Jason's." He was still holding my hand and staring at me. Now he pressed my hand hard and said very gravely, "Make yourself worthy of it, my boy, as we tried to be in our time. Good night."

I got out thankfully and said, "Good night, Jason." He said "Good night" in a low voice. I think he was nearly asleep. They drove away with Jason still sitting huddled in the back of the car. I ran up the drive and got in just as the half-hour was chiming from the chapel.

*   *   *   *   *

That must have been in July or August, 1929. I never saw General Pellew again. But during the summer holidays I went one afternoon to play tennis with some neighbours, and when I returned my mother had disappeared. My father told me rather evasively that she had gone to Mrs. Pellew, who was ill. She was away for a week, and it was not till several days after she returned that my father told me what had happened.

It appears that the general's conduct had been gradually becoming more and more eccentric and violent for some years, and that on several occasions he had attacked his wife, without doing her much actual physical harm. On this occasion, however, he threw something at her and cut her forehead, making it necessary to call a doctor. The doctor discovered what had happened (Mrs. Pellew had never told anybody but my mother about the previous incidents) and foolishly told the general that if he could not control himself he was in danger of being certified. The general then flew into a rage, shouting that the doctor was trying to seduce his wife, and rushed out of the room saying that he would shoot the pair of them. The doctor and Mrs. Pellew ran out of the house and drove away in the doctor's car. As they did so the general fired at the car from an upstairs window with a service revolver, luckily without doing any damage.

The police were called, and a sergeant and a constable

arrived. Both, of course, were unarmed. As they walked up the drive the general appeared from the shrubbery carrying a Remington repeating rifle and challenged them. The sergeant, with great courage, tried to rush him, and was at once shot through the upper arm. Luckily both he and the constable had the presence of mind to dive into the shrubbery and escape. The general fired a couple of shots after them, one of which hit and killed a horse in a nearby field.

The police now faced the very awkward job of tackling a well-armed lunatic in a house and garden which afforded him plenty of cover, and there was a lull while armed reinforcements were gathered. It was during this lull that Jason returned from some expedition. Not far from the house he met the milkman, and was given a lift up the drive on the milkman's cart. Finding the house empty (it had long been impossible for the Pellews to keep any servants) Jason went to look for his mother in the garden. While he was doing so the general appeared with his rifle. The milkman said, "Getting after the rooks, general?" and he said, "That's right." They stood and chatted quite normally for a few moments, and then the general told Jason to take a pint of milk and the milkman drove away quite unsuspecting. As soon as he had gone, however, the general started to talk wildly to Jason. He seems to have thought that there had been a German invasion promoted by the doctor (whose name was Schwartz). He told Jason to go down the drive and hide in the bushes, and to whistle when anybody approached. Jason realized that his father was mad, but he had enough wit and self-control to go off down the drive as he was told. As soon as he was out of sight he started to run towards the village, and was picked up, exhausted and sobbing hysterically, by the police as they moved towards the house.

In fact, no one else was hurt in the short siege that

followed, except the general himself, and only one shot was fired. They worked towards him skilfully through the shrubbery, and then as the general had his rifle at his shoulder, a police inspector fired a shot which broke his wrist and left him helpless. They then took him off to an asylum.

Naturally, Mrs. Pellew was completely shattered by these events, and she was in a nursing home afterwards for some months.

It was not easy to see what to do about Jason, and I knew it was proposed at one time that he should come to stay with us. I never knew quite why he didn't. Instead he went to his godmother, Lady Peasmore, and it was from there that, about a month later, he came to Amblehurst. I remember being rather relieved when I heard he was not coming to stay. I liked him well enough, and I was duly and properly sorry for him about General Pellew. But he was just an awkward amount younger than I, and I did not want to be on too intimate terms with somebody who would soon be a new kid at Amblehurst. I was finding the place difficult enough without encumbrances of that sort.

★ 2 ★

"GIVEN A FIRST-CLASS EDUCATION . . ."

THE BEGINNING of the Christmas term was an exciting time
when one was fifteen. The great men of the previous year
were gone, and in their places were people whom one could
remember when they were not very impressive. One was not
yet somebody, but one was certainly no longer Nobody. The
Upper Fifth, to which I had duly got my remove, was the
School Certificate form, and membership of it carried the
right to a share of a two-man study, as well as other valuable
privileges like the right to come in at the front door, to wear
one's scarf with the tails at the back, and to have one's own
supplies of sugar at mealtimes.

In the excitement of all this, I completely forgot about
Jason, and was only reminded of him when Leslie Jackson
pointed out with howls of laughter that according to the list
on the house board there was a new kid named Plover-Dyer.
The name above was Pellew, J. I said, "My oath, I'd
forgotten. I knew that one at home. I suppose I ought to dig
him up."

Jackson said, "All the new babes will be along in the Little
Room. Let's go and cast an eye. I want to see Plover-Dyer."

The Little Room was the dormitory where new boys were
always placed. There were half a dozen of them sitting on
their beds, or rather feebly unpacking their trunks. They
were waiting to be sent for by the house matron.

Jackson and I strolled in with hands in pockets and looked
them over critically. Jason was not there. We agreed, loudly,
that they looked a pretty mangy lot. Jackson, who was a wag,

said politely, "Which of you young gentlemen is Mr. Plover-Dyer?"

A rather fat boy with glasses said, "I am," quite calmly.

Jackson said, "Do you dye plovers?"

"No," said the fat boy. One felt that he had been asked this question before.

"What colour do you dye them?" said Jackson.

"I don't dye them."

"You lie, Plover-Dyer," said Jackson, "or you die, Plover-Liar." He burst into a roar of laughter. A small dark boy sitting on the next bed giggled. Jackson said, "Ah—here's a man with a sense of humour. What's your name?"

"Tambourne."

Jackson turned to me and said, "What extraordinary names they all seem to have."

Jason came in and said, "She wants Parker." Then he saw me and smiled shyly and said, "Oh—hallo." I said, "Hallo, Pellew." I wanted to make it quite clear that we were not on Christian-name terms. I had been rather afraid that Jason might rush up to me and act as though we were intimate friends, which would have been embarrassing. But I need not have worried. He was properly shy and respectful, and just answered my questions briefly. Yes, he was quite all right. Yes, he had been to Matron. No, he had not yet seen Mr. Gladstone. I said to Jackson, "This is Pellew. We knew one another at home." Jackson said, "Welcome, young man," and held out his hand with a flourish. Jason took it and said, "Thank you," quietly. Jackson said, "You are fortunate to have as protector my friend Payne, the biggest stinker in the house."

I suddenly remembered about Jason's father and hesitated as to whether I should say something sympathetic. But I could hardly do so in front of Jackson, so I did not mention it—and indeed, continued not to mention it, as far as I remember, for the next twenty years. But Jackson's ragging of Plover-Dyer had reminded me of something, so while he was cross-examining another new boy I took Jason aside and said, "By the way, I shouldn't tell people your name's Jason. It's rather a rum name to have, and you may get ragged about it."

"No, I won't. Thank you," he said gravely, in his best gratefully-submissive way.

I said, "Well, I expect I shall see you about," and then Jackson and I went away. As we went downstairs, Jackson said, "Well, the infant you knew at home is certainly the pick of a very *very* mangy lot."

*   *   *   *   *

Even had I wished to see much of Jason, at Amblehurst, it would have been difficult. Dr. Evans, the headmaster in my time, was, amongst other things, a fine scholar, an excellent administrator, a good man of business, a strict disciplinarian, and the worst judge of character I ever met. He had two bees in his bonnet—litter and impurity of heart. Most of his sermons in chapel were about one or the other, and he seemed to feel that they were of precisely equal importance. Because of his feelings about litter, the rather beautiful grounds of the school were dotted with horrible wire rubbish bins at intervals of about twenty yards. Impurity of heart was dealt with by a series of rules about those with whom one might and might not associate. One might not, for example, go for a walk with a boy from another house; one might not associate with a boy more than one year younger or older than oneself, or one in another form.

This made one's choice of friends rather limited. Indeed it was rumoured that there had once been an infant phenomenon in Gladstone's who reached the Lower Sixth at the age of fourteen, and was thus automatically prohibited from having anything to do with anybody.

As usual, when there is too much complicated law, nobody

took the rules in this matter quite literally. But it meant that the greater part of one's time was spent with the half dozen people who were both in one's house and one's form. It landed me, for example, sharing a study with Jackson, and hence with a lifelong dislike of puns. It also meant that I saw practically nothing of Jason except on public occasions.

Judging from these, however, he seemed to have made an excellent start. He was placed in the Upper Fourth, which was high for his age, and in the fortnightly lists he was usually somewhere in the middle of it. Although he had never played rugger before, he picked the game up very rapidly, and with his quickness, neatness on his feet, and complete lack of physical fear, soon had the makings of a good scrum-half. This was not as important in Gladstone's as it would have been elsewhere. We were not a good games house, since our housemaster regarded all games as an oafish waste of time. But even in Gladstone's a good footballer was a sound asset. The most important thing for Jason, however, was that people liked the shy grin and the slightly deferential manner and the mop of yellow hair. He was neither cheeky, nor very shy, nor a weed. If the tragic business of General Pellew had made any difference to him, no one would ever have suspected it. Toward the end of the term Bryce, who was now head of the house, came into my study where Jackson and I were working and said, "Payne—that kid Pellew—didn't I see you out with him once last term? Out at Parkstone?"

I said, "Yes, Bryce."

"You knew him at home?"

"Yes, Bryce."

"Who was the chap with you with the loud voice?"

I flushed and said, "His father."

"Seemed a curious bird."

"Yes."

"The kid himself seems very bright. What's his name apart from Pellew?"

I hesitated and said, "Jason."

Bryce's eyebrows went up. "Jason?" he said. "Good God!" and went out. When the door had closed Jackson looked across at me and spread out his hands with a sigh. "I thought so," he said. "I *thought* it wouldn't be long."

It wasn't long. In fact it began that evening. Rather oddly, considering the usual policy of segregation, preparation in Gladstone's was a jumble. The first part of it lasted, in the winter terms, from six till seven and took place in two rooms with a house prefect in charge of each. The second half lasted from 7.45 to 8.45. Members of the sixth form spent both halves in their studies; but for some obscure reason people in the Upper Fifth only went to their studies after supper for the second hour, spending the first in a room with people from the Upper Fourth and Lower Fifth. I was therefore positively in the same room with Jason.

The house prefects did prep. duty by rota, and on this occasion Bryce was in charge of our room, sitting at the big desk on the rostrum. I was working hard (we were very hard driven at Amblehurst) when I heard Bryce's cool, rather supercilious voice say, "Well, Jason of the Golden Fleece, exactly what are *you* doing?"

I don't think anybody else knew what he meant. Jason went very pink and said, "Nothing, Bryce."

Bryce smiled at him and said, "Well, *don't* do nothing. Do some work."

Jason smiled back shyly and lowered his head to his book. Bryce continued to look at him with the same smile for a moment, and then returned to his own work. Jackson kicked me sharply on the ankle.

That was all for the moment. By itself, it would have been quite enough to tell most of us the way the wind was blowing. We were not given six sermons a term on purity of heart for nothing, and we knew Bryce. But twenty minutes later he put the matter beyond all doubt. It was the tradition that juniors might, if they wished, ask the prefect on duty for help over knotty points in their work, and for this purpose prefects usually strolled down the length of the room a couple of times during the hour. In due course Bryce walked slowly down the length of the room. I don't think anyone asked him a question. Most juniors were too much afraid of him. But on his way back he paused beside Jason and asked him something. He spoke quietly, and I was too far away to hear what he said, but it was obviously something to do with Jason's work. Jason hesitated, and then pointed to his book. Bryce picked it up and started to read. After a few moments, still reading, he sat down on the empty seat at the end of the row beside Jason, and after a pause began to explain something in a low voice. I think he was translating. I saw Jason's face turned towards him with the big grey eyes very intent and solemn. Then Bryce said something and he broke into the broad grin. Bryce went on sitting there, smiling and talking in an undertone, for quite five minutes. Then he got up and went back to the rostrum. Jackson kicked me again.

When we went back to our study after supper, Jackson said, "It might perhaps be a good thing to tell your little friend from home a few things about Bicycle" (Bryce's nickname). He thought for a moment and then added, "I doubt if he knows the facts of Bryce," and laughed very heartily.

It was almost the end of the Christmas term, and when I went home a week later I told my parents that Jason seemed to be settling down very well. But I could not say it with the complete conviction that I should have felt a fortnight earlier. One had seen all this happen before.

*　　*　　*　　*　　*

And of course in the next two terms one saw it again. The smiles, the Christian name, the gentle hair-pulling, the public teasing, the half-victimisation, half-favouritism, the general singling out for attention, the encouragement to be cheeky and precocious—the whole process of "taking up" and being taken up. By half-way through the Easter Term there was not a soul in the house who did not know that Bryce and Jason were what we called "a sad case." This was all twenty-five years ago, and I cannot remember very clearly what I felt about it. I know I was very religious at the time, and felt extremely strongly about purity of heart. But I don't think it was Jason's morals that I was worried about. I am not at all sure that I saw any very close connection between "taking up" and "sad cases" and purity of heart. I saw them as a social rather than a moral issue (in which I may well have been nearer the mark than my headmaster), and what was worrying me was the effect on Jason's position in the house. People don't like the King's favourite, even if he does play for his House Colts and has a pleasant smile.

Moreover, one of the things that had pleased people about Jason had been his air of slight shyness and modesty, and after a term of friendship with Bryce these were rather tarnished. To do him credit, he never became as impossible as some small boys I have known in similar circumstances; and with me particularly, he remained polite and almost deferential. But the smile that had been shy now had something slightly mocking and superior about it, as though I, and all the rest of the world, must be humoured, but need not, of course, be taken seriously.

It would have been odd if Jason had not been slightly swollen-headed at this time. Practically the whole discipline of the house was left to the house prefects, and they were a poorish lot, who were dominated by Bryce. Whatever Jason did within wide limits, he must have known that no one would touch him, where other people would have been pounced on at once. Being fourteen he naturally enjoyed the situation, and experimented with it to see just how far he could go—walking calmly into prep. ten minutes late, getting off games when he wanted to do something else, ignoring the silence bell in the dormitory, openly consuming illegal tuck, and so on. These things did nobody else any harm, but they did him a good deal, by provoking furious jealousy. Characteristically, Bryce allowed him, and almost encouraged him, to be casual and cheeky with other prefects, but never allowed the same attitude towards himself; and on the one occasion that Jason was cheeky to him in public, the result was a brisk visit to Bryce's study and a hearty tanning. This gave considerable satisfaction to one and all at the time. But it made no difference, for if afterwards Jason was more careful with Bryce himself, he seemed even less careful than before with everybody else.

It was in the Summer Term that he first ran into trouble with Gladstone. Gladstone was a strange, bitter person of about fifty. He was a big, bulky man, completely bald, and it was believed that the house matron polished his head every day with Ronuk. He had been a schoolmaster all his life, but gave the impression that he strongly disliked boys and everything connected with them. He openly despised games; he taught grudgingly and as though it bored him; and he took as little part in the life of the house and the school as he possibly could. For the greater part of the time he left the running of the house to his prefects, most of whom he nevertheless seemed to despise and distrust. Occasionally he would descend and make an enormous fuss about some small matter. Then he would disappear again into his queer, angry lack of interest.

It so happened that early in the Summer Term of Jason's first year at Amblehurst, Gladstone made one of his descents. The subject was the condition of changing-rooms after games. Perhaps the headmaster had been talking to him about litter. Certainly, the changing-rooms were usually an unholy mess, as people tended to hang about until the bell went for tea or prep., and then dash away leaving games clothes and towels all over the place. This, Mr. Gladstone told the house, must cease. In future duty prefects would visit the changing-rooms, after games, and there would be dire penalties for anybody whose belongings were found lying about.

Now normally, having made this announcement, Gladstone would have left the whole matter to the prefects; and Jason, at that time, would certainly not have hurried himself or been more tidy on account of any prefect but Bryce. But it so happened that Gladstone himself went into the changing-room a couple of days later and found that whereas the place was far tidier than usual, a few incorrigibles had left articles about, and amongst them Jason.

This would not have mattered if he had behaved sensibly. But when Gladstone produced the articles in public, and began to award detention to their owners, Jason took it into his head to deny that he had left his things about. His towel, he said, he knew he had hung up because he remembered that one end of it had fallen into a footbath and was very wet. The other items, shoes and a cricket shirt, he had lost at the beginning of the term and had neither worn nor seen since.

Just why Jason should have gone to the trouble of spinning this improbable yarn to avoid an hour's detention I could not see. I was vividly reminded of the garden frame and the imaginary cat.

It was quite obvious that Gladstone, who seldom believed anybody even when they were telling the truth, did not believe him.

"So after you hung your towel up, Pellew," he said with his bitter smile, "someone came and took it down and threw it on the floor?"

"I don't know, sir," said Jason with worried innocence. "But I'm sure I hung it up."

"And having stolen your shirt and shoes, somebody—perhaps the same mysterious person—wore them or left them

64

about—or just left them about to get you into trouble?"

"I don't think anyone would do that, sir," said Jason correctly.

"No," said Gladstone. "But I can imagine some people lying to avoid punishment."

There was a general titter.

"It's not really very amusing," said Gladstone. He picked up Jason's belongings and tossed them toward him. "Among gentlemen," he said contemptuously, "one has to assume that people are telling the truth unless one can prove that they are lying. Here are your things, Pellew."

He turned and walked out. I saw Jason's face as he picked up the things. For a moment his lip quivered. Then he pursed the pouting red mouth in a curious way, and broke into that odd smile—the smile that nowadays had something in it of triumph and contempt.

Jackson said quietly, "Knowing our esteemed housemaster, that won't have done Mrs. Bicycle any good at all."

It did not do him any good with the House either. The general code of the place laid down that whereas one need not rush to "own up" to one's sins, one must admit them when directly challenged. The criminal, once found, must be prepared to admit that it was a "fair cop." To escape detention by simple bare-faced lying was to gain an unfair advantage by altering the rules of the game. Previously, whilst plenty of people had been jealous of Jason and irritated at the way he was allowed to get away with things, they had had little else against him. Now they could happily despise him as well.

It may have been a vague sense that he had made a fool of himself that drove Jason to his next exploit—if it was his. One night all the chamber pots in the West dormitory were found to contain small quantities of carbide. This is one of the oldest schoolboy jokes in existence, and it did not even come off very well. But there was a filthy smell of acetylene and, of course, a first-class row, in which Gladstone summoned the whole House and demanded that the joker should come forward.

Public opinion, as I have said, never required this, and Gladstone must have known that it was most unlikely that anybody would own up. But his next move was the old cheating schoolmaster's trick of announcing that unless somebody did so, the whole house would go to detention every afternoon for a week.

Now I don't know to this day whether Jason had put the carbide in the pots. I never heard any evidence to suggest that he had. But the House got it firmly into its head that he was responsible. When challenged he denied it, but as people pointed out to one another, Jason was known to be a liar. Feeling ran very high about the matter, and there were those who favoured getting hold of Jason and applying third degree methods. But there was Bryce to consider, and the idea came to nothing. Bryce himself, who hated and despised Gladstone, then made matters worse by remarking publicly and contemptuously that he rather hoped nobody *would* own up, as he disliked blackmail. The House immediately took this as proof positive that Jason was the culprit and that Bryce knew it. In the event, nobody confessed, the House went to detention and there the matter ended. But it left one more social black mark against Jason.

It was shortly after this that I decided to speak to Jason, I don't know why, but whereas in his first successful term I had felt no responsibility towards him at all, now that he was becoming more and more unpopular I was very worried about it. It was not a job that I liked, for nowadays, whenever I said anything to him, I had an uncomfortable feeling that he was laughing at me. Moreover, it was not easy to decide exactly what I wanted to say. I think I remember asking for God's guidance in the matter. I certainly reminded myself that I was sixteen and that Jason was only a kid.

The interview took place in my study one evening when I had managed to get rid of Jackson. I called Jason in, sat down at my desk and said firmly, "Jason, I want to talk to you. You're making a fool of yourself."

I think I had been afraid that he would just smile the rather superior smile. But instead he made it all much easier for me by continuing to stand there, like one confronting authority, with the large grey eyes very solemn, and saying, "Am I? I'm sorry," very humbly.

I said, "Of course you are," and hesitated.

After a moment Jason said, "How, Payne?"

That was the awkward question, since it wasn't easy to define. I said, "Well, all this business with Bryce. People don't like it."

"I haven't done anything with Bryce," he said rather sullenly.

"I dare say. But you know you're his favourite."

"But I couldn't help it. I haven't done anything. What could I do?"

This again was not easy to answer. I said, "What you've got to realize is that next term Bryce will be gone. And then where will you be?"

That went home. I don't think it can ever have occurred to him before. He stood there staring at me in silence while the full horror of the prospect came to him. I said, "You've put yourself in wrong with Gladstone and everybody else by telling lies. . . ."

Jason said, "But I did hang it up. I remember because. . . ."

"I don't only mean over that."

"It wasn't me that did the carbide. Honestly it wasn't."

I said, "You've got yourself a thoroughly bad name, Jason."

I don't suggest that God was really doing much guiding in this interview. I had suffered a good deal from Jason's polite mockery in the last two terms, and I think I was enjoying having him there with his lips quivering and tears in his eyes.

67

"What you've got to do," I said firmly, "is to pull yourself together."

He said, "Yes," almost in a whisper.

"And stop swanking."

"Otherwise you'll put everybody against you."

"Yes."

There was a long pause, while I tried to think of some other helpful piece of advice. I was still trying when he said, "Thank you very much, Payne," gave a sort of little bow and went out. I remember thinking that the interview had gone rather well and that I might now hope for some improvement in Jason. But that evening as I passed the open door of Bryce's study, I caught a glimpse of Bryce holding Jason by the hair and trying to force a bun into his mouth. Jason was squealing happily. I passed on rather pensively.

*   *   *   *   *

That summer I got my School Certificate and when we returned to school I was moved into the Lower Sixth, and was Somebody at last. For being in the Sixth meant almost automatically being a house prefect, particularly if, as I was, one was in the running for one's school football colours. Jackson was a prefect too. We were not perhaps a very impressive collection that year. There was certainly nobody with the calm, adult superciliousness of Bryce. His successor as Head of the House was a rather stupid, rather loutish person named Farthing, who had taken so long over getting into a University that he had outstayed all his contemporaries and was now by far the senior prefect. I think Gladstone despised him nearly as much as he had disliked Bryce. Gladstone always disliked anybody as soon as he had appointed them to a position of authority. "Under the dashing leadership of Farthing," he said acidly, when he spoke to the prefects on the first day of term, "I don't doubt that the House will be run in accordance with its best traditions. At least, *this* year,

I hope for some measure of loyalty from those who have the honour to be prefects. And for goodness' sake see that these new boys get their hair cut properly. There's one who looks like a sheep-dog."

After he had left us Farthing said, "I suppose we'd better give out something at prep. about the hair-cutting. By the way, you new chaps—don't stand any nonsense from anybody if you're taking prep. If you tan a couple of people the first night, you won't have any trouble after. There are quite a few who can do with it. Young Arter and that swanky little tick Pellew for example."

With this guidance from my housemaster and Head of House, I began my career in authority.

I saw Jason that morning but only to say, "Hallo." I thought he had changed surprisingly in the eight weeks of the holidays. He had grown, and his face was spotty, which it had never been before. He was now rising fifteen, and in the Lower Fifth. It may have been the spots, but there was something untidy and awkward in his appearance, where previously he had always been unusually neat. Gladstone must have thought so too, for on the second day of term, at House breakfast, he suddenly called down the table, "Pellew —get your hair cut at once. You look like a tramp." Telling people to get their hair cut was his main contribution to the life of the House for some days.

After the excellent advice that I had given him at the end of the summer term, I had hoped that Jason might turn over a new leaf. He may even have intended to do so. But in the first few days of the term it was quite obvious that the House had no intention of letting him forget what was written on the old one. Farthing's "that swanky little tick Pellew" seemed to express the general feeling.

The pathetic part of it was that Jason, who in the past had often seemed unusually tactful, simply did not seem to realise that he was heading for trouble—or if he did realise it, could do nothing about it. With Bryce gone, he could only have avoided a thoroughly nasty time by singing very small for a couple of terms. But instead he carried on with the same casual, rather mocking attitude towards authority, and the same process of slacking and wangling as before. He took no notice of Gladstone's order to get his hair cut, and as a result was told sharply and in public that it was time he learned to do as he was told, and given an afternoon's detention.

In the first fortnight of the term he was twice tanned for cheek by Farthing and Giles, who both had scores to pay off from the days of Bryce. Even Jackson, who had always rather liked him and was a good-tempered soul, said to me one evening, "I fear that if matters continue as they are now going, I shall be reluctantly compelled to smack the bottom of your little friend from home, Henry. It simply must be brought home to the Widow Bicycle that Bicycle is no longer amongst those present."

I said, "What's he been up to now?"

"I was standing by the front door, and he just walked straight in past me with his hands in his pockets. I said, 'Hey, Pellew—hasn't anybody ever told you to use the side door?' He looked at me with his eyebrows raised and said, 'I was in a hurry,' and with that he strolled on, still with hands in pockets. I said pretty sharply, 'Go out and go round to the side door.' He just grinned at me cheekily and said, 'Certainly, Jackson,' and off he went. Still with hands in pockets."

It went on like that all the term. In fact the only direction in which Jason did any good at all was at football, where he was given a game for the School Colts and did very well. Otherwise, the term was one long series of near scrapes and general disapproval. Just before Christmas I had one more go at him, telling him that he was riding for a fall. But I found him a very different person to deal with from the small boy of the term before. Then he had been humble and grateful. Now he was alternatively sullen and sarcastic. He said, "Well, what am I supposed to do? If people have a down on me, there's nothing I can do about it."

"But why get across people like Farthing and. . . ."

"Oh, Farthing?" said Jason contemptuously. "You surely don't want me to suck up to people like that?"

"It's not a question of sucking up."

"Farthing doesn't like me because Bryce did and he was jealous of Bryce. If he likes to jump on me because of that I can't stop him. I don't even care."

"But why go out of your way to cheek Jackson, who's always been very decent to you?"

He said, "Jackson? I never have cheeked him. Never in my life."

"He says you did."

Jason said, "It seems to me that I can't speak to anybody in this place without being told I've cheeked them. I suppose I ought to kneel down when I speak to prefects."

After that I gave it up. I knew there was trouble coming, but I couldn't see what more I could do.

It came towards the end of the Lent term, and ironically it was a row with Gladstone about football, which was the only thing that Jason was doing decently, and a thing about which Gladstone didn't care a rap.

The inter-house cup matches were in full swing, and Jason was the scrum-half of Gladstone's Second Fifteen. He would probably have been captain of it if he had been less unpopular. He was certainly the best footballer in the side. Although everybody was playing football four afternoons a week, it was the custom for House sides to go into solemn "training," which meant no tuck, and a run of half an hour before breakfast.

One morning when the members of the Second Fifteen were supposed to be on their run, Gladstone, for some extraordinary reason, was wandering about the grounds at seven-thirty a.m. What he was doing about at that time nobody ever knew. Anyhow he came on Jason, who should have been sweating round the countryside, sitting comfortably in a gardener's shed reading a book and eating a large piece of coco-nut ice. He had started off with the others, dropped out unnoticed after a few hundred yards, and was now waiting to join the tail of the run when they returned. Of course, with his usual inability to admit a fair cop, he proceeded to make things worse by starting some taradiddle about having twisted his ankle.

Now had it been almost anybody else in the House, Gladstone might quite well have done nothing about it at all. He was always very contemptuous about the whole business of training, and always went as near as he could to washing his hands of the whole business. But he had obviously been waiting for a long time to catch Jason out, and this was too good a chance to miss. He came into the prefects' common room just after morning school when we were all there, and after congratulating Farthing, with heavy sarcasm, on the enthusiasm for games which he was inspiring in the House, told us about Jason and the gardener's shed. "Far be it from me," he said, "to interfere with your arrangements for 'training.' But it seems to me that if people are instructed to go for a run and not to eat sweets, something had better be done to ensure that they do as they are told. Particularly people like Pellew, who is a conceited little slacker and a thorough-paced liar into the bargain. In fact, Farthing, if you were to come to me and say that in the opinion of the prefects, what that boy needs is a House beating, I should probably agree with you." With that he went away.

Farthing said, "Well, that's clear enough anyhow." He looked round at the five of us and said, "Anybody disagree?"

I said, "Disagree with what?"

"That Pellew shall be given a House beating, of course."

Giles said, "Well, I'll put up my hand for that. In fact I'll put up both hands."

Now, twenty-five years ago people at Amblehurst were caned for almost anything, and sometimes for almost nothing, and nobody took it very seriously. But a House beating was another matter. Apart from the fact that it meant getting two strokes from each prefect, which added up to double the usual maximum dose, it carried with it a stigma which an ordinary caning did not. It was the ultimate mark of social disapproval, meaning that one had not only fallen foul of authority but of society in general. In the whole time that I had been at the place there had only been one House beating, and that had been for a gross case of bullying which ended with a small boy getting his arm broken.

I said, "But you can't give him a House beating for that."

"Why not?" said Farthing.

"Well . . . it's not the right sort of thing. After all, it's only ordinary slacking."

"Ordinary slacking?" said Farthing loftily. "I can't think of anything much worse than not training for your House." He was a particularly incompetent games player and knew it, and was therefore very zealous with slackers.

Giles said, "Anyhow, we can't do anything else after what Gladders said. He told us to beat him."

"Only if we thought so."

"We do think so. At least all the rest of us do, don't we, Ashes?"

Ashley said, "He's been asking for it for months."

I was the junior prefect present, with the exception of Jackson. I muttered something about letting Gladstone do his own dirty work. Ramage said, "Not on your life. This is a games matter."

Farthing said, "Jacko?"

Jackson hesitated and looked at me. "The trouble is," he

said doubtfully, "that the lad has never recovered from the influence of the late lamented Bicycle."

"Hear, hear," said Giles. "Well, it's time he did."

"It's a bit difficult for Henry," said Jackson, trying to help. "You see he knows the lad at home."

"What's that got to do with it?" said Farthing loudly. "He can't let a thing like that interfere with his duty. I know young Pryde at home if it comes to that, and I tanned him only last week."

"Pryde's Purge," said Jackson.

Nobody else laughed. Farthing said, "Well, come on, Henry. Do you agree or not?"

I looked at his fat, stupid, pasty face and thought of Gladstone with his polished bald head and the thin bitter lips. Giles said in a loud undertone, "Perhaps he wants to take over from Bicycle."

I said, "You can do what you like. I shan't have any part in it."

That startled them. Farthing said, "Oh no, you don't get out of it like that. You're a prefect."

"What about it?"

"Well, you won't be one long if I go and tell Gladstone that you won't beat Pellew because he's a pal of yours."

I said, "You can go and tell him what you like. I shan't have anything to do with it and I shan't come."

"You damn' well will."

Jackson said, "I think Henry is pleading a conscientious objection. Let us respect Henry's conscience, which is a very notable conscience. After all there are five of us, and the lad isn't a very big lad."

Farthing hesitated and said stupidly, "But then he'll only get ten."

I turned my back on them and went out. I remember that as I walked along the corridor my main feeling was one of blind fury with Jason for having put me in wrong with everybody. Far from not beating him, at that moment I could have murdered him. But not to please Gladstone and Farthing.

I gathered later that at first Farthing wanted to make an issue of my un-co-operativeness, with Gladstone. But Jackson pointed out that the decision to give anyone a House beating was supposed to be unanimous, and that if Gladstone was told about me, he might refuse the necessary housemaster's permission. So in the end Farthing simply went to Gladstone and said the prefects wanted to beat Pellew, and Gladstone of course agreed happily. I saw Jason at house tea, and there was no doubt that he had been told what was coming. He was very pale, and the spots showed up on his face in an unwholesome way. He was not talking to anybody, and kept his eyes on his plate for most of the time. Once he glanced up and caught my eye, but only for a second. Then he looked down again sullenly. It occurred to me that he would think I was one of the executioners, and I suddenly found myself desperately wanting to tell him that I was not—that I was on his side—or at least not on theirs. But I could not think how to get a moment to speak to him without everybody seeing, nor what to say if I did. With the exception of Jackson, the rest of the prefects ignored me at tea, talking and laughing amongst themselves rather more loudly than usual and, I thought, rather nervously. Jackson said quietly, "If you want to avoid the execution, Henry, it is after prayers this evening. The condemned man doesn't seem to be eating a very hearty tea, poor little bastard."

After prayers that evening I went to Matron to have a cut on my shin dressed. I then went and sat in my study. I was still sharing with Jackson, though strictly speaking we were now entitled to a study each. After a while Jackson came in and said, "Well, Henry. . . ."

I said, "Hallo," and went on reading.

75

Jackson sat down at his desk and there was a long pause. I knew he was itching to tell me what had happened, but I would be darned if I would ask him.

After a while he said, "Well, you didn't miss anything, dear boy. It was neither very funny nor very edifying."

"I didn't think it would be."

He sighed and said, "I trust it has done good to somebody. But I rather doubt it."

"I expect Farthing had a nice time."

"Well, up to a point, perhaps. In your absence he and Giles, as the seniors present, decided that they would give him three each to make up the round dozen."

"How did he take it?"

"Well, rather oddly. They brought the child in, and Farthing said all the things that you would expect Farthing to say, about the crime of slacking and the need for keenness in the interests of the house. As you know, Farthing is one of the most notable cart-horses in the place, and scarcely the man to talk like that to an excellent footballer. I think he felt rather uncomfortable, because he suddenly roared, 'Take that smile off your face.' I had not seen the lad smile. After all, he hadn't much to smile about. He said, 'I didn't smile.' Farthing said, 'You're a liar. You did. You always are a liar. You lie about everything. Now we're going to show you what the House thinks of lying little slackers. Bend over that chair.' The lad started towards the chair and then suddenly stopped and said, 'Have you permission from Gladstone to do this?' Farthing went purple and shouted, 'What the hell's that got to do with you?' He said, 'I just wanted to know,' very quietly. Farthing hesitated and then looked rather a fool and said, 'Yes, we have. Now, get on with it.'"

"As the junior present, Henry, I was to play the part of First Murderer. So I took the cane and gave him two flips which can't greatly have inconvenienced him. I had slightly over-estimated the strength of my stomach, and wasn't enjoying myself. The others then lammed into him good and proper, but he never moved nor made a sound, until we had all given him two. Then he got up.

"Farthing said, 'Get down. Two more yet.'

"The lad had tears in his eyes, which was not surprising. But this time he certainly did smile. He said, 'Oh no, two from each.'

"Farthing said, 'Do as I tell you, you little funk.'

"The lad said, 'Go to hell,' and burst into tears.

"Well, of course that was too much for them, and Giles and Ashley grabbed him. He struggled like a little fiend and I saw him catch Ashley a lovely hack on the ankle. But they got him half across the chair again and then to my great satisfaction Farthing lashed out at him like a madman with the cane and hit Giles across the back of the hand. Giles let out a yell and let go of the lad, and before anybody could do anything he had dodged past them and out of the door. Farthing was for going after him, but there was a general feeling that enough had been done for . . . well, shall we say for *honour*, Henry. So there the matter rests. Giles's hand is a lovely sight."

Jackson sighed again and tapped on his desk with his fingers.

I said, "I think I shall resign. I can't work with a—a lot like that."

Jackson said, "I don't see that that would help anybody much, Henry. It would be more to the point, perhaps, if you went and saw the lad Pellew and uttered words of cheer. I can't very well."

It was about half-past nine by now and silence bell was nearly due. I went up to Middle House dormitory. Everybody else was undressing or in bed, but there was no sign of Jason. I said, "Where's Pellew?" There was a moment's silence and then everybody told me at once. "He's with Mr. Gladstone, Payne." "Mr. Gladstone came and fetched him, Payne. A minute ago, Payne." "He said he was to come to the head-master, Payne."

I suddenly realized that the whole room was staring at me with a sort of awe-struck curiosity. I went back and said furiously to Jackson, "What on earth are they doing to the poor little devil now?" I even thought for a moment that perhaps Farthing had complained to Gladstone about Jason's resistance, and that they had hauled him off to the head on some ridiculous excuse. But Jason did not reappear that night, or the next morning, and after morning school Gladstone told the prefects curtly that General Pellew was dead and that Jason had gone home. He told us without comment, and seemed slightly embarrassed. After he had gone there was an awkward silence and then Farthing said, "Well, we weren't to know, were we?" and the matter was left at that.

It was only a week till the end of term. Jason did not come back after his father's funeral, and any "words of cheer" from me remained unspoken. But in that week an odd thing happened. Of course Farthing and Giles had been careful to spread the news that Jason was to be given a House beating, and when he disappeared afterwards there were the wildest rumours. One was that he had run away; another that he had been taken to hospital as the result of his injuries. A third and more imaginative one (founded on the fact that he had been sent for by the headmaster) was that he had drawn a revolver and kept the prefects at bay, and had subsequently been expelled. But when the comparatively dull truth was known, there was an immediate and violent swing of public opinion to Jason's side, and very strong feeling against the prefects and Gladstone. People who had thoroughly disliked Jason, and had been delighted he was to be given a House beating, now came out as his strongest champions. To beat a chap when his father had just died was felt to be the limit of

78

barbarity. The fact that nobody *knew* his father had died was somehow no excuse. Indeed it was whispered that Gladstone had received the telegram some hours earlier and had deliberately withheld it until the beating was over. Farthing was hissed instead of being clapped when he entered at the traditional end-of-term supper, and there were even some faint and cautious hisses for Gladstone.

Since nobody knew that I had not taken part in the beating of Jason, I shared the general unpopularity of the House authorities, which amused Jackson enormously. "John Hampden Payne," as he put it, "is now lumped together with Strafford Farthing." But it was not really very funny and I was glad when the term was over.

My mother could tell me that the general had died quite suddenly of a heart attack. There was no likelihood that he would ever have left the asylum and my mother felt that it was a "happy release."

* * * * *

It may have been his father's death, or his encounter with Farthing and his friends, but the Jason who came back from the Easter holidays with a black band round his arm was a very different person from the Jason of the term before. The casual cheekiness, the slightly supercilious manner that he had picked up from Bryce, and the occasional adolescent sullenness, were all gone; and in their place was something that reminded me, at least, of an older edition of the Jason I had known seven years ago—quiet, courteous, almost submissive, but with a serious silent watchfulness. The grin was rarer now, and it was shy again, instead of being faintly superior. We were back, in fact, to the stage where the peas in anybody else's garden would, of course, be larger than those in Jason's.

There is no doubt that from the immediate social point of view it was a change for the better. Farthing was soon pointing out that, clearly, all Jason had needed was a good hiding, and that the House beating had been the best thing that could have happened to him. It had changed him, in Farthing's view and that of plenty of other people, from a conceited little slacker into a decent little fellow.

It might have been possible for Jason to settle down as a decent little fellow for the rest of his time at Amblehurst, but for one thing. The House still felt that it owed him an apology. After all, he had been beaten the day his father died. If, therefore, he was now prepared to be a decent little fellow, public opinion was prepared to come rather more than half-way to meet him. He had been handled roughly for his small peculiarities, and had now submitted. He must now be mildly indulged. He had been beaten and now he must be patted. He was too quiet nowadays for the coveted post of buffoon and court jester, so the House decided that the proper role for Jason was that of amiable eccentric.

Gladstone himself launched the idea. He was still feeling strongly about people's hair, and one day at lunch, speaking to Farthing, and at the rest of the House, he said, "Apart from Pellew, who is a law unto himself, and to be regarded more as a flowering shrub than as a member of the House, I deplore shagginess." This was accompanied by the nearest thing to a quizzical smile that Gladstone's thin lips could manage. There was a general laugh and Jason blushed and grinned the shy grin. This struck the keynote, and from then on it was easy.

"Pellew, who shares my scepticism about your training, preferring to feed mind and body in the workshed, but who seems, by his own peculiar methods to play football reasonably well. . . ." "Pellew, who, if rumour is to be believed, once carried his enthusiasm for clinical experiment into the dormitories. . . ." They even contrived to do it about his notorious lying. "Our ingenious Jason, whose luxuriant imagination is never satisfied with mere dull facts. . . ."

80

In the five previous terms that he had been at Amblehurst I had never heard anybody but Bryce call him Jason. After that summer term he was never called anything else in the House, and seldom outside it.

Of course he accepted the part. I think that at that time he would have accepted anything—up to a point. After all, it did not involve doing anything much. Once one was accepted as an amiable eccentric, it was not necessary to do anything very odd, any more than it was necessary for the Court Jester to say anything very funny. For some while Jason did no more than to grin shyly while everybody pointed out what a lovable odd fellow he was; and it was only in his third year that he began, in a mild way, to live up to the reputation he had so carefully been given.

It began to show first, oddly enough, in his football. Before he had been a good, rather orthodox scrum-half. Now he became a moody, incalculable one, with days of individual brilliance and others of dullness. He was sixteen now, and playing for the House. He nearly lost us the semi-final of the House cup by simply kicking for touch every time he had the ball in his hands, and won us the final, for the first time in twenty years, by scoring two wonderful solo tries. He never did play for the school, and after I left I believe he became so variable that he only just held his place in the House fifteen.

Being in the Upper Fifth he had a study, and here again he was faithfully the amiable eccentric. Soon after he took the room over he bought a lot of paint and painted the walls in a brilliantly coloured abstract design. On these walls he pinned a number of Edwardian coloured picture postcards. One was not, of course, supposed to paint one's study walls, but, significantly, nobody ever objected. Nor did they later when he imported a Siamese kitten; or when he acquired a passion for gardening and used to go and work for hours with

81

Blake, the House gardener; or when in the end of term examinations he turned in a paper in which he had spent three hours on a single question and ignored the other four which were supposed to be attempted.

These mild oddities, of course, were nothing to the ones with which he was credited. Even before I left, most juniors believed that Jason regularly smoked opium in his study and went duck shooting at night with a revolver. Clearly, it was the same revolver with which he had held off Farthing and Giles. But somehow the attitude towards it was different. For the House was proud of Jason now. As, indeed, it had cause to be.

But though it was fond of him, as an institution, it naturally never knew quite what to make of him. To find him odd and incalculable was part of the game, and despite his general indulgent kind of popularity, he had no close friend. He shared his study with a plump, smiling Chinese, known for school purposes as Ling, and rumour said that though always on good terms, they often did not speak to one another for days together.

My last two terms at school were happy and busy ones for me, and I saw little of Jason, except in public. In fact our last talk before I left took place entirely by accident, at least as far as I was concerned. I had gone out for a walk one Sunday evening alone. I am fairly sure that I was taking a romantic farewell of the place and telling myself that in a week now All That would be behind me and All That stretching ahead. It was a lovely evening. I was eighteen and I was very properly, if rather vaguely, recalling the lines of Robert Nichols:

> Day like a tragic actor plays his role
> To the last whispered word and falls gold-clad.

I think I was even repeating them aloud, when a voice said, "Hallo," and I saw Jason sitting on a bank a few yards away.

Slightly embarrassed, I said, "Oh, hallo, Jason," and went and sat down beside him.

We did not speak for a while, but sat staring at the sweep of the Weald below us. Most of the corn was cut and the stubble was a brilliant gold in the evening sun.

Jason went on looking at it in silence, chewing a straw. Silence where most people would have made some casual remark was now one of his best-known peculiarities.

I said, "Well—this is about the last time I shall see all this."

"Nice for you," said Jason briefly.

"I don't know. In a way, of course. But I've enjoyed this term. Haven't you?"

"Oh, yes," said Jason politely.

There was another long silence. This time I was determined that he should break it. After what seemed like several minutes he said suddenly, "Thank you for standing up for me over the beating business."

I said, "How do you know I did?"

"Jacko told me. It was good for me, of course, but you weren't to know it would be."

"You really think it was?"

"Oh, very good for me," said Jason gravely. "If I ever have children I shall beat them like that all the time."

I looked at him sharply, but he was staring down at the Weald, with very serious grey eyes.

He said, "Everybody's liked me so much better since. Haven't you noticed?"

"Yes, but. . . ."

"Well, that's what I mean."

I said, "Is it all right now, Jason? I mean, you are having a decent time and so on?"

"Yes, thank you," he said in the formal polite way, as though I had asked him if a headache was better.

"You'll find it's better every term now. After all, you'll probably be in the Sixth next term."

"You think so?"

"Of course."

Jason shook his head. "I don't think I shall like that."

"Why not?"

"I don't want to have to take prep.," he said vaguely. "Anyhow, I probably shan't be here."

"Why not?"

He hesitated and said, "I may be going to South America. As a tea planter. A man I know asked me to."

I said, "I may be wrong, Jason, but I don't think they grow tea in South America."

"This man said they did," said Jason.

For the first time he turned and looked at me with the wide-open frank grey eyes. This was a sure sign that our ingenious Jason's luxuriant imagination was at work.

I said, "Why don't you come to Cambridge?"

"If I was clever like you I would."

"You know perfectly well you're cleverer than I am. Not that that's saying much."

"Oh, no," said Jason gently. "I'm not clever at all."

I could go for several terms neither having much to do with Jason nor even much wanting to. But whenever I was alone with him for more than a few minutes I always had a strange feeling of frustration, and a desire to get on to less formal terms—to get beyond that odd polite barrier.

I said, "Look, Jason—I've never done much for you here, and now I'm going. I know you'll be all right now, so I don't mind. But you do realise that—that I *want* it to be all right and—and so on . . . ? After all," I added lamely, "we've known one another a long time."

Jason said, "Yes, we have, haven't we?" He gave me a quick glance and added, "I always think old friends are best."

"Oh, for God's sake, why can't you ever say something you mean?" I said irritably.

"But I do mean it," said Jason solemnly. "Old friends *are* best. So are old enemies," he added gently.

I said, "Have you any old enemies?"

Jason considered, "Most of them have gone now," he said rather reluctantly.

"You mean people like Farthing?"

"Not particularly Farthing. Except that he was a fool and I don't like fools. I think all fools are enemies. Anyhow he was ill-bred."

After a pause he said, "I'm sorry you're going. But quite probably I shall be leaving myself. I think I shall go into the Army."

"You can't for a while, can you?"

"I can go as a Young Soldier. It's practically arranged."

I said, "Instead of tea-planting in South America or as well?"

Jason grinned. "As well," he said promptly. "I shall grow tea and then come back and set up a N.A.A.F.I. canteen with it. I like growing things. Have you seen that marrow I grew in the garden?"

"The one with your initials on? Yes. It's a whacker."

"It's very easy really. I only planted the seed and then stuck the plant on the heap. It was a fluke that it came so big."

He sat for a few moments in silence and then got up and said, "Well, I must be going. And thank you for being so decent about the beating business."

I said, "Well, in case I don't have a chance to say it again before I go, good-bye, Jason, and good luck."

I held out my hand and he took it with a sort of little bow and said, "Good-bye. And the same to you."

It was time for me to be getting back too, and I could have walked back with him. But I knew somehow that he did not want that, so I sat for a few minutes watching him as he went down the long grass hill toward the road. After a while he took off his cap and flicked it by the peak so that it spun ahead of him. Then he walked on with his yellow head bare, picked the cap up, and flicked it again, and so on until he turned on to the road and disappeared. A week later I left Amblehurst. I went by one of the earlier trains and quite a lot of people came to see me off; but Jason was not amongst them. I don't think he or I had ever really decided whether we were friends or whether we had merely known one another as children. Certainly we never wrote to one another after I left. But I learned from others that in the following year he continued the role of amiable eccentric. He was made a house prefect, but it was not altogether a success, since he was in the habit of putting the names of all in his prep. room into a hat, drawing one, and doing all the prep. of the person whose name was drawn. It was also rumoured that he had become a Buddhist.

This sort of thing went on for a year. Then came the news that Jason had left Amblehurst. "He told me," my informant wrote, "that he is going to the place for foreigners at Perugia. But he told Billy that he is going to the Slade School. You know Jason's yarns."

After that there was silence; and as my mother had lost touch with Mrs. Pellew, it seemed quite likely that I had seen the last of Jason.

*   *   *   *   *

I usually say that I enjoyed my time at Cambridge enormously, but when I really come to think about it, I don't think I did. Nowadays, the place is full of serious young men with scholarships who have done their National Service, and find themselves, at the age of 21 or 22, trying hard to make up for the lost time and to equip themselves for some sort of job. Nobody who is not a worker is likely to survive very long. But in the early thirties some people could happily take three years over a very ordinary Ordinary Degree. Undergraduates, as a whole, were younger, and freshmen were not

ex-parachute troops but ex-Sixth Formers; and there was
plenty of time.

Yet, for the scientists, of whom I was one, the place was
already a technical college, with far too much work to be
done in far too little time; with lectures all the morning and
laboratory work all the afternoon and reading all the evening. And so I spent three years learning an immense amount
of very dull stuff, not one-tenth of which I have ever used, or
even thought of, since; and missing, in consequence, much of
what might have made the place worth while.

I had, therefore, very little social life, and cannot
remember how it was that, early in my third year, I came to
be at Simon Grieves's party. Simon was the college aesthete,
and I remember that on this occasion he was wearing plus-
fours made of pale blue velvet. He greeted me in his high
swooping voice as "Henry—darling . . . !" though we only
knew one another slightly; and said that if I would hold The
Tempter he would get me a drink. With that he held out to
me a large grass snake.

I said rather hastily that I could quite well get myself a
drink and went to do so, and it was then that I noticed Jason.
He was standing in front of the fire, holding a mug of beer
and talking volubly in Italian to a serious-looking dark man
in glasses who occasionally said, "Si." Physically Jason had
changed very little since I said goodbye to him on the hillside
at Amblehurst over two years before. He had grown a little,
but he was still very small, and the dark man, who was tall,
was bending to catch what he said. The mop of yellow hair
and cherub's face were unchanged. But they were now set off
by a brilliant red bow-tie, and a green velvet smoking-jacket.
The general effect, frankly, was to make him look rather a
little bounder. I said, "Hallo, Jason." He turned and stared at
me for a second as though he did not quite recognize me.
Then he smiled the slightly crooked shy smile and said,
"Why, hallo, Henry." There was something odd about this,

87

and as we shook hands I realized that this was the first time for many years that Jason had called me by my Christian name. But the little bow and the habit of looking down at the hands as they shook one another was familiar enough.

I said, "What are you doing here?"

Jason said, "Oh, I'm up now. At St. Mark's."

"You might have called on me."

"I did, but you were out," said Jason, looking at me with very wide eyes.

"What are you reading?"

"Modern languages," said Jason with a grin.

"Did you go to Perugia?"

"Oh, yes. That's why I'm doing modern languages. If you speak Italian and practically everybody else doing Italian doesn't, you don't really have to do much." He suddenly broke off and said, "Oh, *no*, Simon—don't put The Tempter in there. He won't like it." He dived across the room and snatched the snake away from Grieves, who had been about to put it on the coal box. Jason said, "I'll have him," and allowed the thing to coil lazily round his wrist.

Jason came back and said, "Where were we?"

I said, "I'm not going to talk to you while you've got that damned thing. I can't bear snakes."

"Oh, all right," said Jason, "I'll find somewhere comfortable for him."

He wandered away, without, as far as I could see, trying to get rid of the snake, and a few moments later I saw him in earnest conversation with somebody else.

A voice beside me said, "You know Jason Pellew?"

I looked round and saw a very tall, very thin man with a stoop so great that it was almost a deformity. He had a pale, thin, unwholesome-looking face with thick steel-rimmed spectacles that magnified his eyes. He was smiling at me and showing a lot of very bad teeth. He said, "My name's Laidlaw. Of Mark's. You know our Jason?"

I said, "Yes. We were at school together."

"Oh yes," said Laidlaw significantly. "At Amblehurst. I've heard something of that." He looked across the room at Jason with the loving smile. Jason was talking to Grieves and trying to persuade The Tempter to go up his sleeve. Laidlaw said, "What an attractive fellow he is. I'm devoted to him."

"Yes. He is attractive."

"He has a sort of childish wisdom and—and *goodness*."

I said, "How long have you known him?"

"Oh, only since he came up. We got into conversation on the first evening of term, and since then we've seen a lot of each other." Laidlaw smiled modestly. "As a third year man, I've been trying to show him the ropes. I suppose you didn't know the father?"

"Whose father?"

"Jason's. The missionary?"

I said, "Surely his father was a retired general?"

"Oh no," said Laidlaw. "His father was a missionary who lost his life somewhere in the South Seas. It's a tragic story. Jason never says so in so many words, but reading between the lines I gather that he was actually murdered and—and well—devoured."

"But Jason *did* tell you that he was a missionary?"

"Yes. Why?"

I said, "I didn't know that."

"No," said Laidlaw with quiet satisfaction. "I'm not surprised. Jason doesn't talk intimately with many people." He hesitated and then said in a low voice, "As a friend of his —or at least an old acquaintance—you can be discreet?"

I said, "I hope so."

"You know, perhaps, that he has been in Perugia?"

"Yes. Studying languages."

Laidlaw smiled. "Exactly. Studying languages. . . ." He lowered his voice still further, "And, incidentally, preparing a report on Fascism for the British Government."

I looked at him sharply. Laidlaw thought I was surprised, and smiled with pleasure. I said, "He's rather young for that sort of thing, isn't he?"

"Exactly," said Laidlaw. "There's the genius of the thing. Who would suspect him, looking like that?" He looked across the room again with the loving smile and then glanced at his watch and said, "I think perhaps I ought to take him away soon."

"Did you bring him?"

"No, as a matter of fact he asked me to come along, Grieves struck up an acquaintance with him somehow." Laidlaw hesitated, "I hope he's not a friend of yours, but between ourselves I don't care much for Grieves and his set. Certainly not for Jason."

I said, "Well, don't take him away until I've had a chance to ask him in one evening."

"No, no," said Laidlaw. "We'll fix that." He put his hand on my arm, which was a most unpleasant sensation, and piloted me across the room.

He said, "I don't know your name . . . ?"

"Payne."

"Ah. And college?"

"Luke's."

Jason was standing a little apart, passing the snake from one hand to another with a sort of pouring motion. His face was sullen and abstracted.

Laidlaw said, "Jason—here is Payne of St. Luke's who wants to make an appointment with you, and after that we must go."

"Oh no," said Jason. "Not yet, Arthur. I want another beer." He said it exactly like a small child who has been told that it is time for bed.

"No, no more beer now," said Laidlaw quietly. "Give the snake back to Grieves and make your arrangement and we'll go along."

Jason went slowly and reluctantly up to Grieves, who was talking loudly to a group of people, and placed the snake carefully in the jacket pocket of the blue velvet suit. Grieves said, "Oh, thank you, darling," and went on with what he was saying. When Jason came back to us I said, "How about coming in one night for a chat?"

He said, "That would be very nice, Henry."

"Sunday night?"

"Yes. Thank you."

"I'm in college. Staircase B in Old Court."

"Thank you."

"After hall?"

"Thank you."

Each of the "thank you's" had a little bow.

Jason suddenly turned away, picked up somebody else's beer and took a sip of it. Then he put the mug down, put out his tongue at Laidlaw, and went quietly to the door. Laidlaw smiled indulgently and said, "Good night, Payne. I'm glad to have met you."

When they had gone, Grieves came up to me and said, "Darling, who was that *extreme* person with little Jason Pellew?"

"Heaven knows. His name's Laidlaw."

"Well, he's a most extreme person." Grieves giggled. "He's a naughty little boy, that Pellew. But so sweet. Don't you think so?"

"I rather like him."

"Oh, Henry, don't be so po-faced. He's adorable. He says he knew you at school."

"He did."

Grieves sighed. "How I envy you," he said. "Nothing as gorgeous as that ever happened to *me* at school."

* * * * *

I was rather surprised when Jason turned up on Sunday

91

night. From the way he had treated my invitation I had not thought he would. Perhaps Laidlaw remembered and made him come. Anyhow, Jason not only came, but brought Laidlaw too.

I found this very irritating. I had not invited Laidlaw, and did not want him. Heaven knows, it was difficult enough to get anything out of Jason when one had him alone, and with Laidlaw fussing over him it was quite impossible.

However, there was nothing to be done about it, I made them some coffee rather ungraciously, and we talked generalities. I asked Jason whether he was playing football and he said, no—he might row later. I was in a bad temper and said, "As a cox?" and then wished I hadn't because he looked hurt. Even before I had left school he had begun to be sensitive about being small. He asked me about reading science and listened gravely while I complained about it, but we were not much helped by Laidlaw, who would keep cutting in and explaining what it was really like to read science, and correcting me on details. He himself, I gathered, was reading economics. After a while Laidlaw informed me that Jason was doing a translation of Bembo. He then waited hopefully for me to ask who Bembo was. I was childish enough to say, "What, Lucrezia's friend?"

"The Italian Renaissance poet," said Laidlaw, not to be denied.

"Is he worth translating anyway?"

"No," said Jason promptly.

"It's a remarkable piece of work," said Laidlaw, "really remarkable. Jason's so—so *inside* it. Of course he has the language quite perfectly, so. . . ."

I said, "You speak Italian?"

"Not actually," said Laidlaw.

"Then how on earth do you know whether he has it perfectly or not?" I said rudely.

"I told him," said Jason with a grin. "True too, as it

happens. The real *inglese-italianato-é-diavolo-incarnato*. That's me. How are your father and mother?"

"They're very well, thanks. How's your mother?"

"Jason's mother is dead," said Laidlaw in a tone of quiet rebuke. "She died last year."

After that I gave it up and concentrated on getting rid of them. It was not only that whenever I asked Jason a question Laidlaw answered, but that I had no idea whether what he told me so promptly was true or the wildest nonsense. For all I knew Mrs. Pellew's death might be on a par with General Pellew having been eaten by cannibals. They were not difficult to shift. Laidlaw was clearly anxious to go, and I was rather hurt to find Jason apparently equally keen to do so. They only stayed about twenty minutes. But on the way to the door Jason said in my ear, "Only be five minutes," and winked.

Sure enough, shortly after, he came back alone. He dropped into a chair with a sigh of relief and said, "Sorry, Henry. All clear now. But Arthur did so want to come, and I hadn't the heart not to let him."

I said, "What have you done with him?"

"Taken him back to college, said good night and gone to my room, and then slipped out again."

"But what *is* all this, Jason? Why do you always have him hanging around?"

"I don't know," said Jason vaguely. "He likes it. And he's been very kind to me in his way."

"I dare say. But that's no reason for trailing him around and telling him your father was eaten by cannibals."

Jason grinned rather guiltily. "Well, he would keep asking me about my people and I felt I had to—to do something *nice* for him. He has a very dull life, you know," he added solemnly. "They're very poor and live in Oldham, and Arthur's working his guts out so that he can get a good job and keep them all."

93

"And you thought the cannibal story would make it nicer for him?"

"That's right. You see he's a romantic really."

"Is your mother dead in fact?"

"Oh yes. She died last year."

I said, "I'm sorry about that, Jason."

He stared down at the floor and said rather sombrely, "Oh, I don't know. It's probably just as well. She hadn't had much fun for a long time." There was a long pause.

I said, "Where do you live now?"

"Where I was before, with my godmother, Lady Peasmore. She's my trustee. Have you got any beer?"

He stayed for a couple of hours, and seemed, for once, glad to talk. He was certainly more relaxed and less watchful than I had ever known him. I gathered that he had inherited a small amount of money from his mother. "Just enough," as he put it, "to keep body and soul apart." But it was in trust. He would have no capital till his godmother died.

I said, "And then what are you going to do?"

"I shall buy a boat," said Jason as though that dealt with the future.

"Are you enjoying Cambridge?"

"Very much, thank you," he said in the old formal way. "Except that it's a bit childish."

"Childish after Perugia?"

"Oh no. Not after Perugia. That was terribly childish. After Amblehurst."

"After *Amblehurst*?"

"Yes," said Jason rather vaguely. "Everything mattered so much there, and you have to be careful. But here everybody seems to do as they like. There's no discipline."

"Don't you like that?"

"Not much. I don't think I shall stay here long."

It was getting late. I said, "You'll have to be going soon or you'll be locked out."

"Oh, that's all right," said Jason. "It's dead easy climbing into Mark's. That's why I went there. That and the gardens."

"You still garden?"

"Rather. When I get my money I shall buy a market garden and grow branded vegetables. Nobody ever sells branded vegetables. You know—Pellew's Super Onions. I think there'd be money in it."

He sat for a while in silence, presumably thinking about Pellew's Super Onions. He was still wearing the scarlet bow-tie. But now his shirt was dark blue. I said, "Is Simon Grieves a friend of yours?"

"Oh no," said Jason simply. "I've got a girl. Simon's furious about it. You must meet her in the vac."

"What's her name?"

"Leah. She's a Jewess. I think that's very important, don't you?"

"Why, Jason?"

"Well, with all these things that are happening in Germany. Are you Jewish?"

"No."

"I mean never at all—any of your ancestors?"

"No. Not any of them as far as I know."

He nodded and said, "I just wondered. Have you got nice gardens in Luke's?"

About half-past twelve I turned him out. As he was going he said, "I hope you'll come and see my rooms one day. That is if you've got time."

I said, "I should like to. When?"

"I don't know yet. I shall have to let you know," he said rather coldly, and I realized that he had not meant the invitation seriously.

I said, "Did you bring a gown?" "No, I think the business about gowns is nonsense. Good night." He went out and then put his head round the door and said, "You wouldn't like to come and see my rooms now? It's dead easy to climb into Mark's."

"No," I said. "Not now. Too late. Good night, Jason."

The invitation to visit him never came, and for the rest of the term I saw little of Jason. We met on a couple of occasions in the street, and once I saw him coming out of Luke's with Simon Grieves. They were both wearing yellow turtle-necked pullovers and Jason looked rather like a stable boy. I was carrying an exercise book, and as we met Grieves hooted, "And here's dear old Henry, with his collected works. . . ." Apart from these chance encounters, the only news I had of him was from Jackson, who was reading medicine and whom I saw quite often. Jackson said, "You seem to have put the wind up the lad Pellew."

"How?"

"Well, I met him in the Unicorn the other night and he told me that you had taken him to your rooms and lectured him for two hours about homosexuality."

"That's pure Jason. I don't think the subject was ever mentioned."

"I thought so, from the way he said it. Though from the people the lad goes about with it mightn't be a bad idea if somebody *did* drop him a word. That Grieves character is an open sewer, and if Nobby Jones isn't sent down before the end of the year the authorities will be run in for keeping a disorderly house."

I said, "Did he tell you he thought Cambridge was childish?"

"Oh yes. Too many restrictions."

"I don't think he really likes me at all, you know."

"I think," said Jackson, who was attending a course in Abnormal Psychology, "that you are something of a father figure to the lad. Hence the business about homosexuality. He *wanted* you to lecture him about it."

I said, "Well, at present he's got a perfectly good grand-mother figure in one Laidlaw. Have you met him?"

"The cadaverous bloke in glasses? Yes," Jackson frowned. "I shall have to look Laidlaw up," he said thoughtfully. "I'm not quite sure where he fits in. Did Jason ever have a nannie?"

"Not since I've known him."

"I think you'll find he did," said Jackson with quiet confidence. "At some point. Otherwise Laidlaw simply doesn't make sense."

Just before the end of the term Jason gave considerable pleasure to the University by a mild return to his old role of amiable eccentric. A reader in modern languages whose lectures he attended was troubled with asthma, and always delivered his lectures standing at an open window, which made him difficult to hear. One rainy day Jason, instead of sitting in the lecture room went and took up a place in the Don's garden outside the open window, sitting on a shooting-stick in oilskins, and with a raised umbrella. The lecturer, who was a feeble little man, tried to get him to come in, but he refused, saying that this was the only place from which he could really hear. In the end he was allowed to stay there, and sat on solemnly, occasionally putting down the umbrella to make a note, until the hour was almost over, when he closed the umbrella, folded up the shooting-stick, and wandered away. He was reported to his tutor, but nothing ever came of it, and the general verdict was that Jason had brought off a pleasant and successful personal rag.

A few months later, however, he was involved in something that was neither pleasant nor successful. Apart from the Boat Club Dinners after the Lent Races, which were usually pretty hearty affairs, the end of the Lent term was the traditional time for all the College Societies to hold their annual dinners. Indeed, a good many of them existed simply to provide an excuse for a club tie and an annual "blind." In St. Luke's we had the Cato Club, which consisted of a dozen people who were supposed to be of some distinction, each of whom brought a guest from an outside college, also of some distinction. I had been surprised when I was elected, as though I played football and tennis for the college, most of the members were people who lived a far more social life than I.

The kitchens at St. Luke's were the best in the University, and I remember that the dinner that year was extremely good. I had taken as my guest the Secretary of the Union, and it was a very cheerful evening, with everybody eating and drinking too much, and making the kind of speeches that undergraduates sometimes do better than anybody else in the world. We broke up just before ten, so that people could get out of college and into other colleges if they wished; and though most of us had had plenty to drink, the whole thing was comparatively quiet and orderly. I had gone to the gates to see my guest off, and was going back to my rooms when I heard a lot of shouting and loud argument going on in Great Court. I did not take much notice—one did not take notice of a few yells after a Lent Dinner. But suddenly there was a loud scream and somebody began to yell, "My God, you've hurt him—you've hurt him!" I dived through the arch into Great Court and saw, in the dim light, a group which looked rather like a dramatic late Victorian painting. Lying on the ground was Jason Pellew. He had a nasty scrape above one eye, which was bleeding a lot, and he seemed to be unconscious. Supporting his head was Laidlaw, as white as a sheet, and screaming up at four people in tails who were looking rather scared and sheepish. Simon Grieves, slightly apart, was being quietly sick in a flower border. Laidlaw was still yelling, "You've hurt him," at the top of his voice. One of the people in tails said, "I didn't touch him." As I came up Jason opened his eyes and said, "What on earth's happened. Where's Simon?"

Before I could do anything the porter had arrived from the lodge, and half a dozen other people had come out of their rooms. We got Jason on to his feet and into Grieve's rooms and sent for a doctor. Three of the four people from the dinner had quietly disappeared. The fourth kept telling us that Jason had "been pushed and just stumbled."

It took about half an hour to sort the thing out. By the time the doctor arrived Jason was quite all right, though a bit shaken, and the graze on his head had stopped bleeding. He was escorted home by Laidlaw, though Laidlaw was so pale and trembling so violently that it was not actually certain who was escorting whom. The fourth man in tails had disappeared, and Grieves was gently sponging marks off his fancy waistcoat and shrilling about "the poor brave darling," and "those murderous thugs."

It appears that the four people from the Cato dinner had met Grieves, Jason and Laidlaw in the Court. They were hearty games-playing types who had been properly brought up to dislike æsthetes, intellectuals, and all such, and they were distinctly drunk. Grieves and Jason were wearing fancy brocade waistcoats and the four decided that these waistcoats were a challenge, if not an insult. They therefore stopped Grieves and Jason and demanded that the waistcoats should be worn inside out. Grieves ("I'm a *complete* cowardy-custard, you see") was quite willing to wear his waistcoat inside out to keep the peace. But Jason had refused, and when hands were laid on him, he had biffed one of the men from the dinner smartly in his white waistcoat. Accounts after that varied. But the end of it was that Jason was knocked down, and in falling struck his head on the stone edging of the lawn.

That was all there was to it. There was a mild inquiry, I think somebody was gated, and Jason had a black eye for a week. But the main result, rather unfairly, was to identify him more closely with Grieves and his friends. The general impression was that four upstanding games players had very reasonably tried to put a couple of pansies in the fountain, during which one of the pansies had been slightly damaged; and for a long time after "You've hurt him, you've *hurt* him" was one of the most popular College cries. "And that," as Grieves complained, "after he had fought like a little *tiger* with those *hulks*."

*   *   *   *   *

I cannot remember with certainty how I came to visit Jason at home, but it was certainly in that Easter vacation that I first went to the house in Cheyne Walk and met Lady Peasmore. I gathered that she was the widow of a colonial governor, and an old friend of Jason's mother.

The house was red-brick Queen Anne and rather beautiful but it was crowded with all sorts of things that the late Sir Phillip Peasmore, a man of peculiarly catholic taste, had collected. Apart from several shrunken human heads, they included sets of chessmen, glass paper-weights, early examples of fountain pens, Chinese back-scratchers and a complete range of shell cases from the ammunition used in the First World War. These objects were dotted about the house in glass show-cases, carefully labelled, so that the effect was that of a remarkably dull museum. Jason told me that whereas Lady Peasmore had never cared very much for her husband while he was alive, she had never allowed any of his possessions to be moved since the day of his death. At the time of his fatal seizure he had been playing "The Blue Danube" on the pianola, and the half-played roll still remained in position. "Between ourselves," said Jason, "I don't think Myra really left things as they were out of respect to the old boy, but because she was too darned lazy to move them. She's the laziest woman I know. Though quite a pet."

Jason's own rooms were at the top of the house. He had his own sitting-room, bedroom and bathroom, and I noticed that apart from the absence of show-cases, they seemed to be furnished in exactly the same style as the rest of the house— comfortably but dully. Apart from a large number of Italian books, there was nothing to connect them with Jason.

But they were pleasant enough, facing on to the Embankment and the river, and we sat there for an hour or so, drinking sherry and chatting. Jason said, "What I've really asked you round for isn't so much to meet Myra, who's rather a bore, poor old thing, but to meet Leah."

I said, "Is she coming to dinner?"

"Oh lord, no. It's not like that. But Myra will go off after dinner and then we can slip out and see Leah. She's only just down in the Fulham Road." He paused and smiled to himself. "She's an odd girl. You know she's Jewish, of course?"

"Yes. You told me."

Jason said, "I think that's very important. After all one's got to be on one side or the other."

He finished his sherry and said, "I think perhaps we'd better go down and meet Myra."

This is nearly twenty years ago, and Lady Peasmore cannot very well have been much over sixty. But at the time I thought she was much older. She was white-haired and very stout, with a red, rather coarsely-handsome face. She moved very slowly with the aid of a stick, and I think Jason told me she was supposed to have valvular heart disease.

She greeted me politely, but unsmilingly. She seldom smiled, and spoke in a rather sharp commanding way that reminded me of some ancient nannie. She immediately ordered Jason to give me a glass of sherry, and took one herself. I noticed that Jason did not give himself any sherry and said casually, "Aren't you having any?"

Lady Peasmore said, "Jason doesn't drink. Personally, I like a glass of wine. But I suppose it's wise in a young man."

She said it without enthusiasm, and I could not resist a quick glance at Jason.

But he was looking at his godmother with the solemn grey eyes. He said, "Henry's got his finals next term."

"Oh yes," said Lady Peasmore without interest. She turned her head towards me, but without taking her eyes off Jason, and said, "How is Jason getting on, Mr. Payne? I'm always told the most wonderful stories, but of course you can't believe a word he says."

This was a little tricky. I smiled at Jason and said, "Oh, I think he's getting on very well. As a matter of fact we haven't seen very much of one another. We've both been too busy."

Lady Peasmore turned and looked at me for a moment with her rather cold blue eyes. "Oh well," she said with a slight shrug, "if there was anything, I don't suppose you'd tell me. But I must say that the only Cambridge friend of Jason's that I've met, apart from yourself, seemed to me a ghastly creature."

I looked at Jason and said, "Simon?"

He grinned and said, "No, Arthur. Arthur Laidlaw."

I said, "I rather agree with you, Lady Peasmore."

"Poor old Arthur," said Jason. "He's rather a pet really. And he's been very good to me."

"Ghastly," said Lady Peasmore. "Quite ghastly. The mere recollection of his face. . . ." she shuddered slightly. "Let's have dinner," she added briskly, as a maid appeared. "I'm hungry."

It was a large dinner, and it took a long time. Lady Peasmore ate soup, a sole, two helpings of duck and vegetables, a piece of fruit flan, and some cheese. She ate them slowly and with great enjoyment, talking meanwhile about greyhound racing, about which she appeared to know a great deal, and about which neither Jason nor I knew anything. She and I drank some excellent claret, and Jason drank

Pellegrino. "I lived on this stuff in Italy," he remarked solemnly. "But it's very difficult to get in England." This seemed to remind him of something and he suddenly said rather bitterly, "It doesn't matter if you have an efficient bully at the head of a nation that's slightly crazy. But it matters a hell of a lot if you get a crazy man at the head of a nation of efficient bullies." This was an odd thing for Jason to say, and I felt at once that he was quoting somebody.

Lady Peasmore looked up from her second duck leg and said, "What are you talking about, Jason?" in her sharp way.

"Hitler," said Jason briefly.

"Then don't," said Lady Peasmore. "Not at my dinner table. I don't want to hear anything about it."

"You realize . . . ?"

"My dear, I don't realize anything. I repeat—I don't want to hear anything about it. The world is full enough of horrible things without having them brought up at meals."

Jason was staring at her with a strange, intense way, and for a moment his lips opened as though he was going to say something. Then he pursed up his mouth and twisted it into a smile and said, "All right, darling. Would you like some more claret?"

About nine o'clock Jason and a maid helped Lady Peasmore away to her bedroom, taking with her the Greyhound Editions of the evening papers. After a few minutes Jason came back and said, "She's rather an old pet, isn't she? Let's go upstairs."

We went up to his room and Jason produced a bottle of brandy and two glasses. I said, "Not for me, thank you." He nodded silently and poured himself out a brandy. I said, "Why do you let her think you don't drink?"

"Oh, she likes it better like that," said Jason casually.

"But does she? I shouldn't have thought she cared a damn about your having a glass of sherry. She practically said so."

Jason stared moodily at the carpet. "She may *say* so," he said bitterly, "but it would be a different story if I did. She's frightfully suspicious really. She's always accusing me of things. The other day she accused me of playing the pianola."

"Had you?"

"Oh yes. I play it quite a lot when she's in bed. There are some cracking good rolls. But I always keep the soft pedal on so that she can't hear it in her room. And of course I always put 'The Blue Danube' back to where it was when Phillip fell off the stool, so she can't possibly prove it. She was just guessing."

I said, "Look, Jason—I'm not Laidlaw. Do you *really* do that?"

"Of course I do," said Jason with a sudden grin. "Honestly. I'll bet you would if you lived here." He reflected, "At first it was only that I *had* to hear where Phillip had got to in 'The Blue Danube' when he pegged out. So I just played the rest of the roll and then put it back as it was. But then I realized that I could play other things, and *then* put it back. So I do." He glanced at his watch. "I should think Myra will be pretty well settled by now. Let's go and see Leah."

Leah lived in a tall, dirty yellow brick house in a turning off the Fulham Road. As we went up the steps Jason said, "This is rather a grim place. They've only got two rooms and she has her mother. But I want you to meet her."

We went up several flights of linoleum-covered stairs. The place was full of chocolate-coloured paint and a smell of gas. The last flight of stairs was not covered at all. Jason knocked at the door at the top. There were footsteps and a voice said, "Who's that?"

"Jason."

The voice said, "Oh," and there was a rattle as the chain was undone. Leah opened the door, glanced swiftly at me, and then said, "Hallo. Come in," and led the way inside.

The room was hardly furnished at all, except for two basket chairs, two kitchen chairs and an unstained whitewood table. An old woman dressed in shabby black got up from one of the basket chairs. Leah said something to her in a language that I did not recognise, and she smiled at us and went out. Jason said, "This is Henry Payne, Leah Garland."

Leah nodded briefly and said, "How d'you do?" and turned and said something to Jason in Italian. I think she was asking who I was.

She was a rather tall, slim girl, wearing a high-necked green sweater and an old pair of men's grey flannel trousers, which were much too big for her and were belted in at the waist. Her hair was short, black and straight and looked rather greasy, and her skin was olive. She had rather fine dark eyes and a finely hooked nose. The general effect was Italian rather than Jewish. I guessed her age at about twenty. Jason had answered her in Italian and she seemed satisfied and nodded, without looking at me. She pointed to the table and said, "I've got some stencils. It isn't really very much quicker but it makes a much better job."

There was a sheet of white cardboard on the table. On it was stencilled in big black letters, "Fascism Means. . ." and then in red "Wa. . . ." Leah said, "The trouble is that I've only got one set and all the letters are the same size. You really want several sizes. 'War' ought to be much bigger."

Jason picked up the stencils and said, "We could cut some out of cardboard."

"It's not as easy as that. If you do, the ink runs at the edges."

Jason said, "Anyhow I think it would be better if you had it more square and had 'War' underneath."

"Yes," said Leah reflectively.

"Underneath. And bigger."

They thought about it for a moment. Jason turned to me and said, "What d'you think?"

I was slightly taken aback. I said, "Well, it rather depends how it's going to be used. Is it to—to be stuck up somewhere? Sort of poster?"

"No—this is for carrying. You know—on a stick or slung on your back."

"Then I should think the square shape would be best. The long shape will flap."

Leah said, "Yes. I'm afraid you're right. Damn." She turned to Jason. "Have you got any money?"

"How much?"

"Oh, about five bob. Only I haven't got any and I shall have to get some more cardboard. I've promised to do a dozen by Sunday."

Jason took out his wallet and gave her ten shillings. He said, "Look—I'll do some at home if you like. Then you can stop now and talk to us."

"Would you really?"

"Yes, of course. Do you want them all the same?"

"No. Four of these, four 'Down with Mosley,' and four 'Stop Hitler Now.'"

"I'll do 'Stop Hitler Now,'" said Jason. "'Now' bigger, like 'War'?"

"That's it."

"All right. Now come and talk to Henry."

Leah came and sat down, rather reluctantly I thought. Previously she had hardly looked at me. Now she stared at me with the dark, rather unfriendly eyes for a moment in silence.

She said, "This is all very funny, isn't it?"

I smiled and said, "It is rather."

"I thought you'd think so," she said bitterly. "People like you always do."

"I don't think Fascism is funny. But ordering four 'Down with Mosley' and four 'Stop Hitler Now' is. At least, to me."

106

"Of course it is," said Jason solemnly. "Damned funny. You can see it is, Leah."

"I'm afraid my sense of humour's stopped working on this subject," she said coldly. She stared at me again and said, "You don't think Fascism's funny. But equally, of course, you don't think it's serious?"

"I think it's serious in Italy and even more so in Germany. But I don't think it's serious here, or likely to be."

"It can't happen here," said Leah with a bitter smile.

"And if it were," I said, rather irritated by the smile, "I shouldn't think it would do much good just to carry placards about saying 'Down with Mosley.'"

Leah said, "Then what *would* you do about it?"

I did not know the immediate answer to that. I said, "I say, I don't think Fascism will get anywhere in this country."

Leah smiled and turned to Jason. "He ought to come down with us one Sunday."

I said, "Come where?"

"To the East End. You'd know then whether there was anything to fight or not."

"You mean you go to Fascist meetings?"

"Yes. We go and we break up their meetings—or try to. If there are enough of them we may get broken up ourselves. But at least we don't let them talk that poison in peace." Leah's dark eyes were flashing.

I hesitated and said, "I'm not sure that I agree with. . . ."

"With interfering with free speech?" she said at once. "I thought you wouldn't." She closed her eyes and dropped back wearily in the basket chair. "God help us all," she said quietly.

"You go on these expeditions, too?" I said to Jason.

He nodded. "I've been on a few. When I'm in London."

"And you really think it does any good?"

"Of course. You ought to see them—the B.U.F. people. They're really awful."

107

"I daresay. But. . . ."

Leah sat up and said, "Listen . . ." and then paused and closed her eyes again. There was a moment's silence. Then she said quietly, "It's like this. The Fascists go down there every Sunday, and a good many weekdays as well. They choose the places where they know there are a lot of Jewish people. They get up and they preach hatred of the Jews, and all the crazy Hitler stuff about their being responsible for everything. If a Jewish person passes he's insulted, and if he says a word in protest he's manhandled. Or she, if it's a woman. Of the people listening, ninety per cent don't agree with what's being said. But they're not organized and the Fascists are. People aren't going to risk being knocked about. So they keep quiet and let the Fascists talk."

I said, "But if they don't agree. . . ."

"Wait a minute. By the time this has happened week after week and the people see that nobody stands up to the Fascists, they begin to think that nobody can—that it's all hopeless. And since everybody likes to be on the winning side they begin to wonder whether the safest thing isn't to start wearing a black shirt themselves. See?"

Jason said, "It's a bluff, you see, Henry. Of course Fascism always is. After all, Mussolini's march on Rome. . . ."

"It's a bluff," said Leah curtly. "But it's a bluff that's got to be called everywhere, every time it's tried. *Every time. Everywhere.*"

I said, "But these East End shows. Can't the police do anything? I mean if people are being manhandled and . . . ?"

"The police?" said Leah. She smiled at Jason and said, "He must certainly come with us. By the way, I had to run for it last night."

"Where?" said Jason.

"On the embankment. Not far from your house. I was doing a wall with Joe, and two bobbies got up to within

108

about thirty yards of us before we spotted them. I shouldn't have had a chance if they'd come for me. That's one of the bloody things about being a woman. You can't run fast enough. But for some reason they both went after Joe, and he had rubber shoes on and they never got near him. But we lost the brush, which is a nuisance."

Jason grinned and said, "Never mind. You can pinch another." He turned to me and said, "Leah works in Woolworths. It's extraordinarily useful, because she can pinch a lot of the things one wants for this work, like brushes and paint and drawing-pins and rolls of paper and so on."

"Yes," said Leah rather sombrely. "I don't know what we should do without Woolworths. I wonder if Mosley has shares in it? I hope so." She suddenly smiled at Jason and, putting out a hand, rumpled the yellow hair. She said, "You wouldn't like to kiss me I suppose. You haven't kissed this evening."

"Yes, I should," said Jason simply. He got up and went and knelt by the low basket chair and began to kiss her gently and rather tentatively. But she wriggled her long, slim body round toward him and put both her arms round his neck and kissed him passionately.

I was not very old or very used to this sort of thing, and it embarrassed me. Besides, there was something unpleasant about seeing Jason, with his baby cherub face and his mop of hair, being kissed like that by that dark, passionate girl. It was the wrong way round somehow. When they paused for breath I got up and said, "I must go. Don't let me disturb you."

"Oh, don't go," said Leah calmly. "There's some coffee coming." She still had her arms round Jason's neck.

I said, "I really must."

She hesitated and then said, "All right. As you like." She smiled at me suddenly and said, "Are you coming on

Sunday?" and then, as I hesitated, added, "I think perhaps you hadn't better. It's rather tough sometimes."

I don't think I really wanted to go with them. But she lay there with Jason kneeling beside her, and her arms still round his neck, staring at me with her dark eyes and the faintly mocking smile, and somehow the thing was not avoidable.

I said, "I should like to."

Jason was delighted. He said, "That's fine. It's great fun. I'll let you know where to meet us."

I was staying in Battersea, and on the way home I went along the embankment. Near Battersea bridge someone had painted on the wall in large letters, "Fascism Mea. . . ." An effort had been made to scrub or scrape it off, but it was still clearly visible. I remembered that Joe had been wearing rubber shoes and had got away. But they had lost the brush.

*　　*　　*　　*　　*

We met at Charing Cross on Sunday. I had gathered from Jason that we were going to Bethnal Green. Leah was still wearing the green sweater and the old grey trousers, and somehow in the open air she looked a good deal more aggressively trampish than she had done at home. Women in trousers were a good deal rarer then than they are now. Jason was wearing a reasonably respectable tweed jacket and flannels, but with an open-necked cricket shirt and no tie. He might have been somebody's rather good-looking errand boy. I remembered the scarlet bow-tie and green velvet smoking jacket, and wondered what Simon Grieves would have made of him.

On the way down in the train Leah explained the procedure. She said, "You needn't do anything unless you want to. In fact you'd better not, because you don't know the ropes. There'll be other people of ours there, of course, and the main thing is to scatter through the crowd. If you bunch up they can get you all with one rush."

I said, "What are you going to do exactly?"

"Anything that will break it up. The best way is to make them lose their tempers and start a fight. You see most of the crowd loathes them really, only they're afraid to start anything. If it gets really tough and there are too many of them, or if the police start in, just bolt. Don't wait for anybody else—look after yourself. If we get separated, get back to my place and wait for us."

Jason said, "About the police, Henry—remember that once they really get started they don't know who you are and don't care, so get out of the way." He grinned and added, "They're quite different from the ones on point duty."

As we approached Bethnal Green we fell silent. I had a slight sinking feeling in my stomach and I could see Leah's hands clenching and unclenching nervously. Jason was sitting staring straight in front of him with a smile of pleased anticipation, like a small boy on his way to a football match.

As we got out of the train Leah said quietly, "There's Joe and Lewis." I saw two young men in blue serge suits. Both wore open-necked shirts like Jason's, and one had a spotted silk wrap round his neck. I noticed that he was wearing black plimsolls and decided that that was Joe. He was small and dark and active-looking. I remember thinking that plimsolls might be all right if you were going to run, but that they might be a handicap in a fight. Lewis was a big, bulky man with a broken nose. He looked like a boxer, and I hoped he was. They saw us, and Joe acknowledged Leah with a quick wink. That was all.

A lot of people off the train seemed to be making for the meeting-place. It was not far from the station, in a side road which was a blind alley for traffic, but which had a footway out at its far end between iron posts into an alley.

111

As we approached the turning, about every second person in the main road seemed to be a policeman, and there were half a dozen standing about at the corner.

In the side road itself was a crowd of about a couple of hundred. From a rostrum in the middle of the street a smallish man of about forty, with thinning sandy hair, was speaking in a strained, hoarse bawl. He was wearing a black shirt and tie, no jacket, and very beautifully creased black trousers. He was not a very impressive figure.

Round the rostrum, however, and facing the audience, were about twenty young men in black shirts and breeches, who must have been a hand-picked bodyguard—big chested, hefty people, several of them really strikingly handsome. They were staring out at the crowd with what seemed to me a sort of impassive contempt, and somehow one would never have been surprised if they had started to give a physical training display and form themselves into pyramids or what not. Leah said quietly, "There won't be much today. This is only the second eleven. Look after yourself." With that she wriggled her way into the crowd. I looked round for Jason but he had vanished, and I was left alone, feeling rather nervous and rather a fool, being not at all sure why I had come. I decided to keep fairly near the opening to the main road.

The sandy-haired man on the rostrum was going on in his monotonous hoarse bawl, occasionally waving an arm or pointing a finger. He was shouting, "We know them. We can name twenty-thirty. And you can see them any night you like, spending money like water—the ivy that is rotting the oak tree of this land. . . ."

I did not know who "they" were. Presumably Jews, though which particular twenty or thirty was not clear. I looked at the crowd, and noticed how very small most of them were compared with the bodyguard. The men on either side of me barely came up to my shoulder. A few here and there were wearing black shirts, some of whom I should certainly have taken for Jews. I was wondering vaguely if there *were* Jewish Fascists, and if so exactly how it worked, when a woman's voice—I am fairly sure it was Leah's—shouted, "Fascism means War!"

Everything had been very quiet up till then, and I felt a kind of tremor go through the crowd. The man on the rostrum took no notice, but just went on bawling. Then the same voice yelled, "Down with Mosley!" and other voices began to shout and boo and catcall from various parts of the crowd. The sandy-haired man stopped suddenly in the middle of a sentence and there was silence for a moment. He smiled round in a tight-lipped way and said, "Now, I don't want any trouble. . . ."

There was an immediate booing from the crowd at this—it seemed to me from most of them. The little man on my right, who had been listening in silence, contributed a yell of "Bastards!" I glanced behind me and saw one of the policemen on the corner quietly raising his helmet from his head and resettling it more comfortably. The sandy-haired man shouted, ". . . But if you want it, you can *certainly* have it."

All the bodyguard were smiling now. I think they must have been trained to smile at that point. The noise lessened for a moment, and I heard what was unmistakably Jason shout, "You bullying nit-wits." Somehow that, shouted in Jason's rather clipped University voice, was extremely funny. There was a roar of laughter in which the sandy-haired man and the bodyguard joined. The speaker waved a hand and shouted, "Be silent, Ethel," and went back at once into his hoarse roaring denunciation of somebody or something. But the crowd had found its voice by now and it shouted him down. Somewhere a group of people were shouting, "Fascism means War, Fascism means War," in a steady chant. The little man beside me was shouting

"Bastards! Bastards!" as quickly as he could draw breath. The sandy-haired man went on bawling inaudibly for a few moments and then he whipped round like lightning, dropped his hands and pointed quickly to three places in the crowd, and half a dozen of the bodyguard went flying into the people towards each of the places he had indicated, like a well-drilled rugger pack going for the line.

Immediately there was chaos. Judging from the shouting the crowd was almost solidly against the Blackshirts, and there were enough of them to have torn the bodyguard to pieces. But shouting was one thing and fighting quite another, and anyhow they were, of course, completely unorganized. I saw one of the bodyguards stumble as somebody tripped him, and I had a fleeting vision of Joe swinging a bottle by the neck. But the only object of most of the crowd was to get away. The little man beside me let out a final shrill yell of "Bastards!" and was off like a shot, treading painfully on my foot as he went. The only person who beat him to the end of the street was the big man, Lewis, whom Leah had pointed out to us, and who got away to a remarkable start. Perhaps he was not a boxer after all.

I hesitated for a moment (though I must confess it was only for a moment) to see whether there was anything to be done for Jason and Leah. But I could not see them, and the main stream of the crowd was between me and the nearest group of the bodyguard. There was a lot of screaming and shouting and people were being pushed and jostled, but I don't think there was much actual fighting, and the only real violence I saw was when one of the Blackshirts landed a tremendous kick on the behind of a lanky boy who was trying to get away, and sent him stumbling forward, nearly falling on his face. Then a man barged into me and sent me staggering and I suddenly realized how nasty it would be if one were knocked down among the feet, and made for the end of the street as fast as I could.

It was not a big crowd, and it could have dissolved in a few seconds but for the police. They had now gathered at the corner where the meeting-place led into the main road and had left only about ten feet in the middle of the street through which the people had to go. As I ran through this gap a policeman with a red, angry face pushed me hard in the back and shouted, "Get off!" As I was already getting off as fast as I could, this made me very angry. There were still people running hard fifty yards up the main road. But as no one seemed to be chasing me I preserved what dignity I could by slowing down to a walk.

There was no sign of Jason or Leah at the station, so I went back to Leah's place as directed. By then it was nearly one o'clock. The old woman let me in, and I tried to explain that I had been told to come and wait for Leah. I don't think she understood English, but she let me in, bowing and smiling at me shyly, and then disappeared. I went and sat in Leah's room and smoked a cigarette. I was surprised to find how much my hands were shaking.

I waited about half an hour, and was just thinking that something must have happened to Jason and Leah when they arrived together and quite undamaged. Leah said, "I'm sorry that was so dull. It's usually a good deal livelier than that."

I said, "It was lively enough for me. Did anyone get hurt?"

"Joe cracked one of them a good one and cut his head open, and an old chap got kicked down and trodden on. I think his leg was broken. But that was about all that I saw."

Jason said, "They nearly had me at one point, but some people got shoved between us."

"Yes. It's your hair. You ought to dye it or wear a hat, otherwise they can always spot you."

I said, "Why did the police line up across the entrance like that when people were trying to get away?"

"To give the Fascists a chance, of course," said Leah indifferently. "I was surprised they didn't start knocking people down. They usually do when a crowd starts to run."

"It's not as much fun when they haven't got the loud-speaker," said Jason discontentedly. He turned to me, "Usually they have a microphone and a loud-speaker and you can't shout them down so easily. And then when things start you can bust it up."

I said, "It didn't strike me that the crowd was very willing to stand up to them."

"It never is," said Leah calmly. "Anyhow, that's not the idea, unless it's a big show and we're properly organized. The main thing is to break it up."

Jason said, "Let's go to the Bear and have a sandwich. I'm hungry."

While we were eating our sandwiches and drinking a glass of beer Leah smiled at me and said, "Well—did you enjoy it?" She was sitting on a high stool with her long legs stretched out in the old flannel trousers, and for the first time I thought she looked handsome and attractive.

I said, "It was very interesting but. . . ."

"Go on."

"Well—a bit childish. Rather like shouting 'yah!' and running away."

"Well, that's about all it is," she said frankly. She put out a hand and gently pulled Jason's hair. "But *he* likes it. Don't you, Sonny Boy?"

Jason said, "I like it better when they have the loud-speaker."

Leah turned to me and said, "Well, anyhow, thank you for coming," and to my surprise held out her face with her lips pouted to be kissed. There were quite a lot of people in the bar, and I was embarrassed. But there was nothing to be done but to kiss her, so I did so rather grudgingly, and as I did she flicked her tongue out so that it just brushed my lips. She laughed and said, "That's right. I didn't really think you'd come, but I'm glad you did." The smile disappeared suddenly and she added, "God knows we need everybody we can get."

I said, "I didn't *do* anything you know. I didn't even shout."

Leah had turned away and was drawing patterns with some beer that had been slopped on the bar. "It doesn't matter," she said quietly. "You'll have plenty of chance to do things later. We all shall."

*   *   *   *   *

I went home the next day and saw no more of Jason until term began. After that, I saw, if anything, rather more of him than I wanted. My Tripos was at the end of the term, and I was desperately busy. But whereas before I had been rather hurt by Jason's neglect of me, he now seemed to have decided that we were close friends, and tended to drop in at all sorts of times. What made it worse was that he usually brought either Laidlaw or Simon Grieves, neither of whom I wanted.

On the first occasion, when Laidlaw was there, I asked Jason how Leah was. He said, "Oh, she's all right," and changed the subject. Later, on one of the few occasions that we were alone, he said, "By the way, I'd rather you didn't mention Leah or—or any of that in front of Arthur, if you don't mind."

I said, "Why not?"

"Well—he doesn't like it."

"You mean he doesn't like Leah or doesn't like your anti-Fascists stuff?"

"Oh, he doesn't know about that," said Jason rather

117

hastily. "And he hasn't actually met Leah. He just doesn't like the idea. Nor does Simon."

"I can well believe that."

"I never talk about any of it in front of them. After all it's nothing to do with them." He smiled slightly. "Anyhow Simon's all for Mussolini, because he made that law about not letting Italian pictures and things go out of the country."

I said, "Well, Jason, the easiest way to make sure that I don't say the wrong thing to either Simon or Laidlaw is not to bring them here. I think Grieves is a stinker and that Laidlaw's a bore, and I can't think why you go around with either of them."

He looked hurt and said, "Oh well, of course I won't bring them if you don't *like* it," and went away. Two days later he turned up with Grieves, who squeaked and whooped away for an hour about Ezra Pound. In the end I practically had to throw them out. This sort of thing was made even worse by the fact that on these occasions Jason took his cue completely from them. With Grieves he did not exactly squeak and whoop, but he wore whatever happened to be the æsthetic uniform of the moment, quoted Leopardi and D'Annunzio, and writhed with horror or ecstasy at the slightest provocation. With Laidlaw he was alternately kittenish and solemn —the naughty child with a heart of gold. I decided that on the whole I preferred Jason looking like an errand boy, or even kissing Leah. By the middle of term I was sick of these visits, and used to keep my oak sported in the evenings.

The weather that term was superb—too good for anybody who had a lot of work to do. Jackson and I were both reading physiology, and one hot afternoon we took a punt up the Cam, moored it in a quiet spot under some overhanging willows, and asked one another questions. I had the book and was looking for a question when Jackson suddenly said, "Ah—look what's coming." A punt was coming slowly down the river, propelled in a very leisurely way by Jason. He was wearing nothing but bathing trunks, and his whole body was dark brown, which made his yellow hair seem yellower than ever. I had never fully realized before how extremely well made and muscular he was, despite his small size. Simon Grieves was lying in the punt, holding an open sunshade of bright blue. He was fully dressed in a cream tropical suit. His eyes were closed.

They were going to pass within a few yards of us, but we were hidden by the trees. I was just going to shout, "Hallo," when Grieves called languidly, "Darling, what *shall* we do this evening? I should like to do something *nice*. A treat."

Jason shoved in the pole and called back. "We'll go and see Henry."

Grieves let out a wail of disappointment and said, "Oh, *no*, not Henry, darling, Henry's such a *bore*. I want some *fun*."

Jason turned with the dripping pole in his hands. He was only about ten yards away and I could see his grin. He said, "But it's so *funny*, Simon. 'Oh, hallo, Jason—hallo, Grieves. Well, I must do some work.' "

Jackson kicked my foot. It was really a very good imitation of my voice.

Jason said, "Let's see if we can stay an hour without his actually *telling* us to go." As they floated away out of earshot Grieves was wailing, "Oh, darling, I don't want to. It's so dull. I can't think *why*. . . ."

After a moment I said, "I didn't know Jason was as good a mimic as that." I could feel that my face was red.

Jackson said thoughtfully, "You know I've long regretted those two whacks."

"Which two whacks?"

"The ones I gave him when he was beaten. If the occasion were to arise now, I should really lay on—and with great satisfaction."

119

I said, "I don't think he means any harm. He's a bit all-things-to-all-men. He always has been."

Jackson said, "And to all pansies?"

*   *   *   *   *

Although Jason visited me a good deal, I had never been in his rooms. After his vague invitation at our first meeting in Cambridge, he had never suggested it, and I gathered that he had now moved out of college for some reason.

There was nothing very odd in this. I had other friends—particularly people who lived a long way out—to whom I never went and who never came to me. But towards the end of term, not long after I had seen him on the river, I found a note asking me if I would lunch with him.

Had it not been for the river incident, I doubt if I should have gone. The Tripos was only a week away, and I was refusing all invitations by then. But I think I wanted to prove to myself that I was not hurt—that I did not mind if Jason laughed at me to Grieves.

Jason's lodgings were rather a long way out along the Maddingly Road. He had a pleasant sitting-room on the ground floor of a medium-sized house, looking out into its garden. But the thing that immediately struck me was that the main decoration of the room was almost an exact repro-duction of his study at Amblehurst. I couldn't remember if the abstract design was the same abstract design. But it was the same sort of thing, painted in the same bright colours, and the Edwardian photographs were pinned about as before. There were, of course, a number of new items of the sort that æsthetic undergraduates usually collect, and I was amused to see among them one of Sir Phillip Peasmore's shrunken human heads from Cheyne Walk.

Apparently nobody else had been invited to luncheon, which was a relief. I had expected Laidlaw, or Grieves, or possibly even both. While his landlady laid the table we went out into the garden. Jason said, "Come and see my lettuces," and showed me a neat row of young ones.

I said, "You're allowed to garden here?"

"Oh, yes. That's why I moved out of college. I don't like it if there isn't anywhere to grow things. I had some awfully good radishes but we've eaten them all. The trouble is that these lettuces won't be ready until after we've gone down. But it's nice to have them."

I said, "Are you staying up for May Week?"

"I don't know. Probably not. I haven't got anybody to bring."

"How about Leah?"

Jason looked at me in a startled way. "Leah? Well—no. I mean it wouldn't be her sort of thing. Anyhow she wouldn't have a dress. She's awfully poor, you know."

I don't know why, but I said, "You could always get her one."

Jason stopped short and looked at me for a moment in silence. Then he said slowly, "You mean—buy her a dress? Yes. I suppose so. I hadn't thought of that."

It was understood that one could invite people to luncheon without bothering to give them a serious meal. But Jason by that time had a reputation to keep up, and though we simply ate bread and cheese and celery, the bread was from a crisp fresh French loaf, the cheese was a ripe Camembert and they were accompanied by one of the lovely hocks of the late twenties that were already expensive, but which some colleges were still selling to undergraduates at about five shillings a bottle.

As we sat down I looked around the room and said, "This seems familiar."

Jason said, "Oh, yes," and blushed, and I felt that he was slightly embarrassed.

He was very silent while we were eating—more silent than

121

I had known him for a long time. I thought he seemed depressed and was wondering why, when he suddenly said. "Is there going to be a war?" Then I understood.

I doubt if any man who did not grow up in the late twenties and thirties can fully understand how the prospect of war overshadowed those of us who did. I don't think we were more cowardly or more selfish than other generations. But we had read and heard a great deal about the war of 1914-18, and of the times when the average expectation of life of a subaltern was a fortnight, before he was trodden into the mud to rot. We could not see how men had endured some of these things, and did not believe we could endure them. I don't think the possibility that there might be war, but that we might survive it, ever entered our heads. We were the young men, and to us it was axiomatic that in another war the young men would die, if they were not blinded or maimed. And so during those years, but particularly from when Hitler came to power in 1933 onward, my contemporaries asked one another frequently, and themselves almost daily, if there was going to be a war; and when they asked that, they were asking whether and for how long they were to be allowed to live, like a man questioning his doctor after an X-ray examination.

I had been working so hard that for some time I had not even lifted my head to glance at this eternal cloud. But even I had seen the news that Addis Ababa had fallen and that the Italian-Abyssinian war was virtually over.

I said, "I should think there's less likelihood of a war now than there was a few months ago. For what that's worth."

Jason said, "Leah thinks there will be soon."

"I should think she's all for it," I said rather bitterly. "She's the fighting type." At that time one was always angry with people who prophesied war. They seemed, in some vague way, to bring it nearer.

"I wish one knew," said Jason unhappily.

"Why, particularly?"

"Because if there is a war, of course one will be in it and it's hardly worth doing anything else, is it?"

"I think the only thing to do is just to go on the assumption that there won't be. Then, if there isn't, you'll be all right, and if there is—well, there is."

After we had lunched we went and sat out in the garden. I said, "You've heard from Leah?"

"Oh, yes. I often do." Jason hesitated, "This is confidential, because she doesn't want anybody to know, but she's joined the Communist Party."

I said, "I thought she was a Communist anyhow."

"Yes. But now she's actually joined. They've wanted her to for a long time—Joe and people—but she never would, though she worked for them. But now she has."

I said, "Are you going to join?"

Jason pulled a leaf of lavender and rolled it in his fingers. "I don't know," he said slowly. "I like Joe, but I don't like some of the others. They're so—so *cliquey*. And they will keep talking about Russia, which never seems to me to be much to do with it."

"To do with what?"

"Us. I mean, it's quite a different country. But still, if I've got to be on a side, of course I'm on theirs rather than the Fascists'." He threw the leaf away, "Anyhow, I don't think I shall stay here. I'm tired of just messing around with people like Simon and going to parties and so on."

I couldn't resist saying, "You don't by any chance find Simon a bore?"

He looked at me very seriously with the big grey eyes. "Yes, I do," he said, "I think he's a crashing bore."

"Is there anybody you think isn't a bore?" I said quietly.

"I don't know," said Jason. "I can't think of anybody. Except you of course. I suppose it's having nothing to do."

123

"How about the translation of Bembo?"

Jason grinned, "Oh, that was only Arthur."

"But he said he'd read some of it?"

"Oh, I used to talk a lot of rubbish to him in Italian saying his feet smelt or something like that and say it was Bembo, and then translate it for him. You know:

'Lady, that little hand which now plucks at the lute strings, makes music on the strings of my heart.'

That sort of thing. It's awfully easy to do."

I said, "Jason, why do you play these games with poor old Laidlaw? It's rather unkind."

"What d'you mean 'unkind'?" he said in surprise. "He loves it. Otherwise . . ." he sighed. "Otherwise what the hell would be the point? If I did get a dress for Leah, what would it cost? About?"

* * * * *

I had not been to a May Week Ball in my first two years, but Jackson and I had decided to go this year, as a sort of celebration if we thought we had done well, or to drown our sorrows, if we thought we had made a mess of things. I had no obviously suitable lady to take, and it was therefore arranged that I should partner Jackson's sister, and that he should bring his cousin.

As a party, it was not a success. I had never met Miss Jackson before. She turned out to be a rather fat, dark girl of eighteen, who seemed to be in a state of frozen terror when she arrived, and remained so throughout. I did my best, but in the three days that they were in Cambridge I don't think she ever volunteered a remark to me, or answered one of mine in more than three words. Jackson said she was shy about being fat. Rather irritatingly, the cousin was an uncommonly smart, pretty girl with plenty of assurance, and she and Jackson were obviously old sparring partners. The wretched

Miss Jackson and I therefore trailed miserably around in punts, at Fenners, and eventually to the ball, as a sort of dual gooseberry to their entirely happy May Week affair.

The St. Luke's Ball was held in Old Court, which was floored and roofed in for the occasion. People who had rooms round the Court had been asked to "place them at the disposal" of the Ball Committee, and I believe most of those who were not coming to the Ball themselves actually did so. The rest of us, of course, simply kept our rooms and used them as sitting-out space for our own parties. I remember thinking bitterly that if Miss Jackson had been a seduceable type, or if I had wished to seduce her, there could hardly have been a better opportunity. As it was, we kept on the ballroom floor as much as possible to give Jackson and the cousin, who were being rather embarrassing, a free run.

We had arranged (before I met Miss Jackson) to do the proper May Ball thing, which in those days was to dance right through the night, appear in the photograph taken in the morning light, and then drive out to Clayhithe for breakfast. Seen coldly at a range of twenty years, it strikes me as a barbarous idea, even if one had been with Jackson's cousin. With his sister it was unbearable, and by about two o'clock the one thing in the world I wanted to do was to drop the poor girl in the Cam, preferably with a large stone attached to her, and go to bed. Jackson and the cousin had disappeared some time ago, and there was nothing for us to do but dance, which we both did rather badly, or sit in miserable and sleepy silence.

Then a minor miracle happened. Somebody who knew Jackson and his family at home asked her to dance; and since by then each dance was going on for anything up to half an hour, I had a while to myself, for the first time for seven hours.

I was just reflecting on the extreme ugliness of cheap

coloured lights on the fourteenth-century walls of Old Court, when I saw Jason and Leah among the dancers. She was about a couple of inches taller than he was and they looked rather comic. Jason saw me at almost the same moment, and immediately let out a loud whoop and dragged Leah off the floor towards me.

I said, "Hallo there. Hallo, Leah," and she said, "Hallo," quietly and rather shyly.

Jason said, "We're gate-crashing. Jolly good show—for Luke's. (In the early hours of the morning, to gate-crash other college's balls was standard practice.) Jason's hair was even more untidy than usual, and his white tie was drooping. Like most small men, he looked odd and short-legged in tails. He was obviously very happily tight. He took Leah by the hand and said, "Look at her. Doesn't she look beautiful?"

I said, "She certainly does," but privately I didn't think so. She was wearing a cream satin dress with a sort of halter round her neck and her shoulders bare, and it made her olive skin look rather yellow. Even so, she was a handsome girl.

Jason said, "D'you know, it was Henry who told me to get you that dress. It was entirely Henry's idea."

Leah said, "I know. You told me." She curtsied to me and said, "Thank you, sir, for my nice dress." It struck me that she was a long way behind Jason from the drinks point of view.

Jason said, "Who are you with, Henry? Where is she? Come on, wheel her on. I've never seen a girl of Henry's."

I said, "I'm with Jacko's sister. She's dancing."

"And left you all alone? Never mind, we'll stay with you, won't we, darling?" He peered round, "Where's Simon? He's got some drinks in his room. Come on, let's go and find Simon."

"Never mind Simon. I've got some drinks too. Come and have those."

"But I promised Simon I would. He wants to see Leah. . . ."

Jason hesitated. "I tell you what—you stay here—and I'll go and find Simon and then we'll go up and drink his drinks. Don't you move, mind." He shook a finger at us and went off, walking straight, but rather carefully.

Leah said, "Am I going to like Simon?"

"I doubt it. I don't."

"I doubt it too from what I've been told. So don't let's go to him."

I said, "Would you like to dance?"

"I dance like a cow. Is there anywhere we could sit down? My feet ache."

I hesitated and said, "We could go to my rooms if you think Jason will find us."

"Oh, my dear, I shouldn't worry about that. He'll find us eventually. He may not come back for ages. He keeps forgetting he's got me."

As we walked round the edge of the floor she looked down at herself and said, "God, I look terrible."

"Don't be silly. You look very handsome."

"But, you see, he went and bought it by himself—as a surprise. By the mercy of God it wasn't hopelessly wrong for size, and by sitting up all night for the last three, I've made it wearable. But of course I look awful in this colour. A sort of muddy yellow."

We went to my rooms. Leah sat down on the sofa with a sigh and said, "Do you mind if I take these darned shoes off?" She kicked them off and curled her feet up under her. I noticed that she didn't seem to worry about her dress, whereas Miss Jackson had taken about five minutes to arrange herself every time she sat down.

Leah looked round and said, "Nice room."

"This is one of the oldest bits of the college."

"And how old's that?"

"Fourteenth century," I said. This was rather like Miss Jackson, and I realized suddenly that I desperately didn't want it to be like Miss Jackson. I said, "Have a drink?" and picked up a bottle of champagne.

"I don't think I will," said Leah. "I don't really like it. This is the first thing of this kind I've ever been to," she added simply. "I mean champagne and tail coats and so on."

"Are you enjoying it?"

Leah said, "It's very interesting. And rather sad in a way."

I remembered what Jason had told me. I smiled and said, "I suppose now you're a Communist you're against champagne and white ties. Bloated capitalists and all that?"

Leah frowned slightly and said, "So he told you? That's one of the difficulties about Sonny Boy. He can't keep that pretty little mouth shut." She shook her head. "No, I was only thinking that it was sad because—well, because it's out of place. Rather like what's-her-name's ball before Waterloo."

I said, "You think there's going to be a war tomorrow morning?" I tried to say it lightly.

"Not tomorrow morning. But before most of these nice silly children are much older. At least—I hope so."

"You hope so?" I said with something like hatred.

"Well, don't you? If the Fascist boys have got away with it in Abyssinia, you can bet it won't be very long before they try it somewhere else; and then somewhere else; and so on. Presumably we have to make a stand somewhere. Or do we?"

"We might have to if. . . ."

"Then the sooner the better, before they've got it all set up."

I said, "Don't you think we'd better go and find Jason? He's rather tight."

"Let him alone," she said wearily. "He's quite happy, and that's not a thing that happens to him often." She shook her head and said irritably, "I can't understand most of you people. You just stick your heads in the sand and keep them there."

Somehow, after seven solid hours of Miss Jackson, this was

too much. I jumped up and said, "Well, good God—I work my head off for months and then I come to this bloody thing hoping it may be some fun, and Jason buys you a dress and then you have to sit there saying we shall all be dead in a few months and. . . ." I felt I could have burst into tears.

Leah sat and looked at me for a moment with the dark eyes wide open in surprise. Then she laughed and jumped up too and said, "Oh, poor Henry. What a darned shame." Before I realized what was happening she put her arms round my neck and said, "You're quite right, my dear. I'm so sorry."

I tried for a moment to push her away, but she clung to me and said, "No—kiss me and say I'm forgiven," so I did the only other thing possible which was to kiss her hard and angrily, as though I was hitting her, until she was panting for breath. She tore herself away at last and I thought for a moment that she was going to be angry. But she threw herself down on the sofa and smiled up at me with her eyes bright, and held out her hand. And then the band stopped for the first time for a long while, and I suddenly remembered Miss Jackson and Jason and quite a lot of other things.

I said, "Look—I think I ought to go and find my partner."

Leah said, "Damn your partner. Come here."

"No—really, Leah. Anyhow, how about Jason?"

"What about him?"

"Well," I said righteously, "after all. . . ."

Leah said quietly, "I think you're all mad. All quite mad." She bent down and put on her shoes. Then she got up with a smile and said, "Dear Henry. Now let's go and find people."

As we went outside the band started again. Jason was sitting beside the drummer, tapping rhythmically on two empty champagne bottles with a large door key. Miss Jackson was still dancing with her acquaintance, and what is more, I distinctly saw her say something to him.

I don't think anybody had left the floor in the short pause. I felt a sudden wave of empty disappointment, and for a

moment it was on the tip of my tongue to ask Leah to come
back to my room and to go on, as it were, where we had left
off. But somehow it was not possible, and anyhow at that
moment Jason started to hit the big drum with one of the
champagne bottles and the drummer stopped playing to
restrain him. Leah said, "I think perhaps I'd better take
Sonny Boy away now. Goodbye, Henry, and thank you very
much."

I said, "Oh, don't go."

She smiled with gentle mocking and said, "Yes, really,
Henry, I must go and find my partner."

"I'll take you over."

Jason was tired of the champagne bottles and quite willing
to go. In fact he looked very tired altogether, like a child who
is having difficulty in keeping its eyes open. He said,
"Goodbye, Henry. Jolly good ball—for Luke's," and started
for the door, walking rather less straight now, and even more
carefully.

I said, "Goodbye, Leah. I shall now go and get ready for
tomorrow."

"What's happening tomorrow?" she said vaguely.

"I thought you said it was the battle of Waterloo." It felt
like rather a witty parting thrust at the time, but then I had
drunk a good deal of champagne.

Soon after they had gone the band stopped again and this
time Miss Jackson was returned to me. She seemed to regret
this as much as I did. Some hours later the photograph was
taken. I have a copy of it still. I am glaring at the camera with
a face like a thundercloud. Miss Jackson has moved slightly.
Jackson and the cousin are beaming happily, and Jackson has
obviously put on a fresh shirt and tie.

*   *   *   *   *

About a week later I left Cambridge, and a fortnight or so
later heard that I had got a First. My father was delighted,

The Companion

"A blessed companion is a book"—JERROLD

NEWS OF THE COMPANION BOOK CLUB *for APRIL 1957*

How they cheered the...
ONE-MAN 'KON-TIKI!'

WILLIAM WILLIS was over 60—yet he sailed ALONE, farther, faster than the six-man crew of the "Kon-Tiki."

Next month brings you his own thrilling story: THE EPIC VOYAGE OF THE *SEVEN LITTLE SISTERS.*

SIR JOHN HUNT
EVENING STANDARD

" One of the outstanding human performances of modern times."

NANCY SPAIN
DAILY EXPRESS

" Astonishing, inspiring story, full of mysticism and romance."

PETER QUENNELL
DAILY MAIL

" An uncommonly exciting adventure story."

JOHN BRAGG
DAILY HERALD

" The most fantastic sea voyage of the century."

NORMAN COLLINS

" Truly terrifying account of solo heroism."

AND NEWS OF **HAMMOND INNES** INSIDE ▶

THE EPIC VOYAGE OF T

William Willis—aged 61

The Man who dared!

With the sailor's traditional companions of a cat and a parrot, William Willis, at 61, set out to do what few men would have attempted even at the age of 20 or 30. He wanted to test himself against every peril of the Pacific, to find danger and excitement. " I guess I'm just a primitive," he said recently, in an interview with Kenneth Allsop of the *Evening Standard.* " Gold prospecting, lumberjacking, ranching, sailing—that's what I've always done."

He wanted adventure. He certainly found it on the voyage he made alone on a seven-log raft, 6,700 miles across the Pacific. He looks like a Red Indian; lean, creosote-coloured, talking with the guttural tone inherited from the days when—as a lad of 15—he sailed as deck boy on a squarerigged sailing ship from Hamburg, where he was born, to the United States.

When he first conceived the idea of his Pacific crossing, his wife, Teddy, said " No ! " It took him two years to change that " no " to " yes." But in just one month's time you'll be revelling in the excitement of his story—an epic adventure without parallel in any age !

"*It was written at* . . . *dawn lights and u*

says WILLIAM WILLIS

IT WAS a night I will always remember. . had fought clear of the haze that shroude the west coast of South America and w almost 1,000 miles out of Callao. T sky was full of stars and my raft, t *Seven Little Sisters,* was rolling a pitching through a moderate sea. Eve once in a while a big wave smash roaring into the ends of the logs, buryi them in foam that broke up in whi swift streamers rushing forward a sometimes squirting up through the de of split bamboos.

I was alone in space steering through t darkness, for I carried no lights in ord not to be blinded. Hour after hour I s there watching my mastheads gro among the stars.

Far behind me, like a nightmare, lay t long months of preparation—months flying low over the jungle in tiny plan or crawling through swamps searching for logs; and then the labour of getting them out of

SOUT

JOURNEY'S END

SAMOA

Some of the exciting photographs from the

HAMMOND INNES is back!

And without doubt this is his **greatest** story!

ONE of the most successful novelists of the day returns to our lists next October. Hammond Innes, whose fast-paced adventure story set in the Canadian Rockies, *Campbell's Kingdom*, thrilled members a year or two ago, comes back in a blaze of glory with THE MARY DEARE. It's a book that's already made a fortune in dollars for Britain. M-G-M paid recently £28,000 for the film rights. *The Saturday Evening Post*—most prized of all rewards open to the novelist, because it pays the world's highest prices and is the most selective and critical—has chosen it for a serial. The American Dollar Book Club wants it, too . . . you can judge for yourself, then, that **THE MARY DEARE** is a novel of some moment.

A BRILLIANT MYSTERY

It's a brilliant mystery that starts with *an empty ship* ploughing full steam ahead through the stormy night. It tells of Taggart, the captain who died of drink, of Higgins, the brutal first mate who terrorized the crew and of Gideon Patch, who found himself facing a Court of Inquiry when *The Mary Deare* was wrecked. It was natural that in his loneliness and desperation he should turn to Janet Taggart, the captain's lovely daughter. That she should hate him was inevitable and part of his personal tragedy.

These are the makings, then, of one of the finest mystery stories we have come across in years; THE MARY DEARE, next October's selection.

" *I thought you were a man,*" she sobbed, " *but you're not. You're a—a monster!*" *A gripping scene at the Court of Inquiry into the wreck of* The Mary Deare.

15,000,000 in five years!

Fifteen million books in five years is a tremendous achievement! The Companion Book Club has swiftly swept far into the lead for one simple reason—it's the biggest because it's the best. Its selections, taken over the whole programme, are " tops " and the Club truly lives up to its slogan " A good book *every* month." Members have shown their appreciation by writing to us and, best of all, by telling their friends how they, too, can enjoy these good books at the very low Club price. Top-line books and enthusiastic recommendations have been the foundation for our success. On the eve of our Anniversary issue, may we say to you " Thank you for your continued support." Here are a few extracts from recent letters.

I would like to say how thrilled I have been with your excellent choice of books in the past; noting the future editions I know I shall enjoy them equally as much: also your " first-class " speedy and efficient service ! Without a doubt this is the finest Book Club of today.
M.E.M., LIDDYMORE, SOMERSET
A very kind comment.—Ed.

I would also like to add how much we, the family, have enjoyed your selections. We have now twenty-seven Companion books and have enjoyed every one of them. I am sincerely hoping that the excellent selections will continue.
(MRS.) V.C.S., NEW BARNET
We're doing our very best to see that they do.—Ed.

I must add my congratulations for the wonderful photographs throughout HIGH ADVENTURE. Marvellous . . . this book . . . is among the treasured and outstanding books in my collection.
W.M., LEEDS

The standard of books is really excellent, especially this month's choice HIGH ADVENTURE, which to my mind is one of the most treasured volumes to be placed on my bookshelf.
J.A.S., SUTTON

I will never regret the day I became a member.
G.C.S., MWADUI, TANGANYIKA

I am very grateful to you in your choice of books that I enjoy reading very much.
(MISS) S.G., LINLITHGOW

My wife and I sincerely hope that your future selections will *not* include editions dealing with Everest climbers. . . . it's a boring subject at the best of times !
R.J.T., NEWCASTLE WEST, EIRE

May I thank the staff concerned for the excellent service I receive as a " Companion Book Club " member, and congratulate you on the choice and standard of the books.
(MRS.) R.P., KIDDERMINSTER

Introduce a friend!

15,000,000 books and five years' continuous success have made Club Membership a social asset. " Have you read this month's book ? " What a grand start that's been to thousands of conversations. That's why it's a good idea to let friends know about the Club's activities. We've done our part by providing an unequalled programme of good reading—will you do yours by showing them page 5—and the Priority Enrolment Form below which, makes a friend into a fellow member without delay ?

and characteristically announced that as I had worked so hard at physiology he would now give me fifty pounds to go to Paris and study anatomy for a fortnight. Accordingly, in July I went to Paris with Jackson, who was also celebrating, having dealt faithfully with his examination for 2nd M.B. That was how it came about that we learnt of the outbreak of the Spanish Civil War when sitting outside the Select in Champs Élysées.

I don't think the news made much impression on us. After all, as Jackson remarked, it was purely a private quarrel between the Spaniards themselves and quite unlikely to involve anybody else. It was late when we returned to our hotel that night and raining slightly; but as we paid off our taxi about twenty people passed, shuffling along in a ragged column. They were chanting monotonously, *"Sau-vez L'Espagne. Sau-vez L'Espagne."* Jackson, whose French was even worse than mine said, "What's all that?"

I told him.

He said, "What are we supposed to save it from?"

"I suppose they're Popular Front people."

Jackson said, "My God, some of these people do like to fish in troubled waters, don't they? Two a.m. and raining, and they have to be putting an oar in other people's affairs."

It had long been decided that if I got a First, I should spend a fourth year at Cambridge doing Part II in physiology, so I was able to enjoy the Long Vacation with a sense that everything was arranged. It had always been one of the odd things about my relationship with Jason that it existed, so to speak, in bursts. I was therefore not at all surprised when, for the first few weeks of the term, I saw practically nothing of him. Being in my fourth year, I had moved out of college to the other side of Parker's Piece; and since he was still in the rooms on the Maddingly Road, we were some distance apart.

It was, I think, about half-way through the term when I returned from the Physiology School and found Laidlaw waiting for me in my rooms. Since I thought Laidlaw was a boring ass, and he heartily disliked me, this was unusual. I put down my books and said, "Why, hallo, Laidlaw." I noticed that he looked even paler than usual.

He said, stiffly, "I am sorry to intrude on you, Payne, but there is an urgent matter in which I need your help."

I said, "What about—Jason?"

Laidlaw said, "Yes. . . ." He hesitated for a moment and his Adam's apple moved up and down. He said, "This girl. Do you know her?"

"You mean Leah? Yes. I've met her once or twice."

"She's a Communist, isn't she?"

"Probably. She's certainly very Left Wing."

Laidlaw drew in a long breath and said, "Then that's probably the explanation."

"Explanation of what?"

Laidlaw sighed again. "Ever since the beginning of the term," he said wearily, "Jason's been very strange, and talking very wildly."

"He often does."

"Mainly about political matters."

"Yes. That'll be Leah all right."

"Well, two days ago he suddenly told me that he was proposing to leave Cambridge at once and go to Spain." Laidlaw swallowed convulsively. "To support the Spanish Government in the war."

The thought that immediately came to me was that if Jason could have seen Laidlaw's agonized face at that moment, he would not have thought the joke a very good one.

I smiled and said, "Oh. Well, I wouldn't take that too seriously, Laidlaw."

"Seriously? Do you realize . . . ?"

"I realize that Jason's pulling your leg."

"I assure you he isn't."

"And I assure you he is."

Laidlaw shrugged. "Well, I was there, Payne, and you were not. And I've never seen him more serious in my life."

I said, "Look, Laidlaw—I know you're fond of Jason, but you really mustn't swallow these wild yarns of his so easily. I know of half a dozen instances where he's told you some complete nonsense and you've believed him. It's just a game of his. He's done it ever since he was a kid."

It was not, perhaps, very tactfully put, and I could see that I had hurt him. Laidlaw said stiffly, "Jason is a friend of mine, Payne. I don't care for the suggestion that he lies to me."

"Well, he does. Like a trooper. He doesn't mean any harm, but he likes seeing you rise to things."

Laidlaw hesitated and then said, "Even if that were true, which I don't believe for a moment, it would have nothing to do with this. I tell you he's completely serious." He heaved the sigh again. "I've reasoned with him. I've pointed out that the rights and wrongs in the matter are not at all clear, and that even if they were, war can never be an answer to any-thing. I have told him that if he really feels strongly about World Peace, the only possible step is the one I have taken myself—to pledge myself never in any circumstances to take part in any war."

I said, "You're a pacifist?"

"Of course. A little while ago, when we had been discussing these things, I thought I had convinced Jason. We had even arranged to go to Peace Pledge Union meetings together. And then suddenly he comes out with this ghastly proposal. What is more, he won't even discuss it rationally. All he will say is that he 'doesn't like the jackboot boys,' and because of *that*. . . ." Laidlaw's voice rose slightly. "On thinking no more adult than *that*, he proposes to go and risk his life in a war in which his own country isn't even concerned. I said to him, 'If England had been attacked, it would be different. For myself, I should still refuse to take any part, but I can see that there might be another point of view. But this *seeking out* of war is pure lunacy.' " Laidlaw shook his head. "I am sure it must be the girl. It's the only possible explanation."

I said, "I still think you're taking Jason much too seriously, you know. He's only trying to scare you."

"On that we must agree to differ," said Laidlaw with dignity. "But why I came to see you was to ask whether, since you appear to have some influence with him, you would reason with him. I have never been sure how far you were really his friend, and some of the things you have just said about him made me even less sure. But presumably even you wouldn't wish. . . ."

I said, "Laidlaw, stop being such a pompous ass."

He got up. His face was very white and he was trembling slightly. He said, "I am sorry to have intruded on you, Payne," and started towards the door.

I said, "I'll speak to Jason if it'll put your mind at rest. But I assure you you're having your leg pulled."

He said, "You must do as you please," and went out. A few moments later I watched from my window as he went off across Parker's Piece with his extraordinary dragging, stooping shamble.

When he had gone, I was sorry that I had snapped at him. It was always a lot easier to be sorry for Laidlaw when he had gone than when one was talking to him. But knowing how bitterly jealous he was of any sign of friendship between Jason and myself, I realized that it must have been a great effort for him to have asked for my help, and that he must be genuinely worried. I resolved to see Jason and speak sharply to him about it. I fancy I decided to drop a note in at St. Mark's inviting him to lunch at the week-end.

I never wrote that note, because in the meantime Jason sent

me one. It came two days after Laidlaw's visit, and was accompanied by a brown paper parcel. It ran:

DEAR HENRY:
   There seems to be rather a big meeting of the jackboots going on in Spain, and I have decided to go and shout "Yah" at it (and then, of course, run like hell!). Anyhow, I have never been to Spain and would like to. I am sorry to go off like this without seeing you, but I was afraid you might not approve and I don't want to be disapproved of any more for the moment. I have told old Arthur to have anything I have left in my rooms, but I would like you to have this as a sort of keepsake. You don't have to feed it or polish it, but it looks better if dusted occasionally. Tra la la, and thank you for having been so decent that time. Yrs. JASON P.

I opened the parcel. It contained the shrunken human head from Cheyne Walk. I did not want it about, but it was an awkward thing to throw away, so I shoved it in a cupboard that I never used, and only remembered it again long after I left Cambridge. For all I know it may be in the cupboard still.

★ 3 ★

"THE HONOUR TO HOLD HIS MAJESTY'S COMMISSION . . ."

It must have been in November or early December, 1936, that Jason went to Spain, and in trying to recall the next eighteen months or so, I am once again astonished at the way I seem to have been able to keep my head down and my eye off the ball. I cannot believe that, by that time, I had any real doubt that a major war was coming. But I seem to have been able at once to accept this, and to find every possible excuse, national and personal, for doing nothing about it.

I got my first in Part II, I got a job as a demonstrator and stayed on at Cambridge, and while Hitler bullied Benes and Schusnigg, and Franco, with German and Italian help, was grinding the life out of the Loyalists in Spain, I was moving, with the utmost concentration, towards becoming a don.

During this time—that is to say between the end of 1936 and the middle of 1938—I never heard from Jason, and only once heard of him.

It must have been in the autumn of 1937, because I remember that Franco had just captured Gijon and the Spanish Government had moved from Valencia to Barcelona. The writing on the wall was clear enough now, and for once I had been thinking about Jason, which was a thing I seldom did. I had occasion to go to London, and one evening, going into the Café Royal, I saw Leah. She had changed so much that at first I did not recognize her. She was dressed in a very smart black frock, and her hair was longer and looked as though she had taken to washing it. She was with a rather good-looking young man of about my own age, in a Guards' tie, and when I noticed them first they were laughing heartily about something, and seemed extremely happy.

They were right across the other side of the big room, but before I could sit down Leah saw me and waved a greeting. I waved back, but did not go over. I had, as I say, been thinking about Jason, and somehow seeing Leah in those circumstances came as a shock. For no reason at all I had always assumed that she was in Spain, too—not roaring with laughter with Guards officers in the Café Royal. I was not, perhaps, quite the person to feel indignant about it, but I remember that it made me distinctly angry on Jason's behalf.

I sat for a while feeling angry and then Leah and the guardsman rose and went to the door, exchanged a word or two and parted. He went out and Leah came over to me and said, "Well, Henry—how nice to see you."

There was nothing to do but to offer her a drink, which she accepted.

I said, "So you're not in Spain?"

"No," said Leah, looking slightly surprised. "I never have been. Why?"

"I thought you were probably there fighting for the Cause. Is Jason?"

"Oh yes. I don't know exactly where, because I haven't heard from him for a bit. But my guess is that he'll be in Barcelona now."

"Is he well?"

"Yes. He's all right now. He did have rather a bad go of pleurisy but it's cleared up. I gather that he's being bombed rather a lot, but that otherwise he's fine."

"Is he in the International Brigade?"

"Oh lord, no. He's organizing hospitals."

She said all this very calmly—almost uninterestedly.

It irritated me still more. I said, "You're looking very smart."

"Thank you, Henry."

"And keeping very respectable company."

"What d'you mean?" she said, looking puzzled.

"Your Guardee friend. I shouldn't have thought that was much in your line."

"I don't think I have a line," she said rather coldly. "I just happen to like Ronnie Soames because he's a nice person. Do you mind?"

I said, "And where do you propose to send him?"

"Send him?"

"Yes. Surely there's somewhere where *he* ought to go and fight for the Cause?"

She looked at me for a moment and then said quietly, "Henry, are you trying to be unpleasant?"

"Yes."

"Why?"

I said, "Because I don't think it's very fair to pack Jason off to Spain if you're going to sit around in London drinking with Guardees. If you were so keen on people going to Spain, why didn't you go yourself?"

Leah said, "Oh God . . . !" and closed her eyes for a moment. Then she opened them again and said, "You think I sent Jason to Spain?"

"Well, didn't you?"

"There are times when you're not only a fool but a rather nasty one. Of course I didn't."

"In fact it was entirely his own idea and your influence had nothing to do with it? I just don't believe it. I know Jason and he. . . ."

She said, "You know nothing about Jason at all, never have and never will."

"I see," I said sarcastically.

"Over going to Spain, it *was* his own idea. I doubt if I

138

could have stopped him if I'd wanted to. I didn't want to, and if it was my influence that made him want to go, I'm darned proud of it. So now you know."

"You think it's a good thing for him to go and be 'bombed rather a lot'?"

She closed her eyes again for a moment and then said slowly, "I think it was a good thing that he should go."

I said, "I thought you were fond of Jason. I should have realized that to you people individuals don't matter."

It was a filthy thing to say, and I regretted it the moment it was out. She stared at me for a moment and then looked away across the room and I saw that her eyes were full of tears. "That's right," she said in a low voice, "that's right, Henry. Individuals don't matter. Thank you for reminding me of it." She blinked and turned back to me with a bright smile. "And how's science?"

"Science is all right."

"It seems an awfully long time since that night when I tried to seduce you at the May Ball."

"Did you try to seduce me?"

"You know I did. You were very shocked because you had thought I was fond of Jason. Never mind, you repelled me like a gentleman and a true friend." She was staring at me with the big dark eyes very bright, and that cold, brilliant smile.

"Look, Leah," I said, rather unhappily, "don't let's. . . ."

"Oh God!" she said suddenly, "I can't do with any more of this." She grabbed quickly for her bag and gloves, and rose. As I got up she held out her hand and smiled and said, "Goodbye, Henry. I don't think you really understand much about women, but after all, why the hell should you?"

I said, "Look—I'm sorry if—if I hurt your feelings. But you see I like Jason and. . . ."

She said, "I know you do. So do I. Isn't he a lucky little so-and-so? Goodbye, my dear."

*   *   *   *   *

In the middle of the following March, Hitler annexed Austria, and my father, who liked to make a book in these things, offered me three to one in half-crowns that there would be war before the end of the year. "Classically speaking, Henry, it should happen in September—after the harvest and before the winter sets in. But perhaps armies don't mind about the winter nowadays." He also asked me quietly what I proposed to do about it, which was most unlike him. He had a passion for minding his own business.

Since the beginning of 1938, even I had been forced to think hard about this—indeed, I had not thought much about anything else; and the answer was both clear and rather grim. I was twenty-three and completely fit; and if I had a strong objection to war, it was not exactly a conscientious one. In fact, if there was a war, I was precisely the sort of person who would have to fight in it. I disliked the sea and knew nothing about aeroplanes. I said, "I think the only thing to do will be to join the Army."

"The Army," said my father thoughtfully, as though there were several hundred possibilities. "Yes. I think probably that will be the safest place."

"The safest?"

"Oh yes. You see, the one thing that's absolutely certain is that we and France won't do the sort of thing that was done last time. We simply haven't got enough men. If you're in the Army, you will be a valuable property to be looked after and protected. The thing to avoid being is a *civilian*, which will be very dangerous indeed."

Even then, however, I did not follow the example of a number of my friends and join the Territorial Army, with a view to "getting in on the ground floor." I just went doggedly on measuring the electric potentials of muscle fibres and waited to be summoned to the slaughter-house, with all the dullness of a bullock, and none of its courage.

And so it went on all through the summer—a summer when one never failed to listen to the news on the radio, and grew to dread the sound of the newsboys calling a special edition. So it went on into September, with the German pressure on Czechoslovakia reaching its climax; and so it was still going on when one day I was walking down Oxford Street and saw Jason buying pears from a barrow. He said, "Oh, hallo, Henry," and then turned to the barrow boy and said, "I'll have another pound. In a separate bag." Then to me, "We can go and sit in the Park and eat these. They're rather good. Comice."

We went into Hyde Park and sat down. It appeared that Jason had been out of Spain for some months, but that in the interval he had been working among the refugees on the French frontier, and had only reached England a few days before. He was neither very clear nor very communicative about the whole Spanish business. To this day I do not know, in any detail, exactly what he did in Spain or why he eventually left. His work, as Leah had told me, had been something to do with hospitals, and had not involved actual fighting. Then, early in 1938, he had come back to England for some purpose, and had been told not to return because, by then, Franco's advance had closed the way to his headquarters. That was his story, and he was very emphatic that it was only on the orders of the London Committee that he did not return, but went to work with the refugees instead. It sounded probable enough.

About the war itself he would say practically nothing—except that both sides were a crazy lot, that the Quakers were doing a wonderful job, and that he was quite sure that Franco must win now. He gave me an odd impression of having lost interest in the whole business—as though he had closed a book, and neither remembered clearly, nor wished to remember, what he had been reading.

I was surprised at how little he had changed in appearance. He had filled out a little (he was now twenty-one, and I had not seen him since he was nineteen). But he was still as cherubic as ever. Whatever illness or hardship he had been through seemed to have left no mark on him at all, and as he sat there eating pears with the juice dripping off his chin on to his tie, he might still have been at school. There was something very frustrating about the distant uncommunicativeness and absence of change, and I was conscious of an irritable desire to catch hold of him and shake *something* out of him, no matter much what.

And then, quite suddenly, I saw the point. We were sitting just inside the Park, and a newsboy started to call a special editon, somewhere at Marble Arch. Jason whipped round, and then, without a word, jumped up and went quickly off to buy a paper. I saw him hurry across the road, take the paper and look at it for a moment or two. Then his shoulders seemed to drop, and he folded it up and walked slowly back to me. I knew from that gesture that Jason was frightened. In the excitement of meeting him I had forgotten for a moment what was hanging over us. But he had not. As he came slowly back I said, "Well?"

"Nothing much," said Jason bitterly. "Roosevelt's appealed to Hitler. There isn't anybody much now who hasn't."

There was a long silence. I said, "It looks as though we're for it all right."

"Yes. And the devil of it is that people here don't know what they're taking on."

I said, "I think they do, Jason. There's not a lot of joy and singing as far as I can see."

"Oh no." He shifted irritably in his chair. "Oh no, they don't want war. But if they knew what I know they'd want it even less."

"You mean about bombing? We've been told plenty about that."

"No. Not about bombing. I don't care for it myself, but you get used to it. About the French." He looked at me with eyes that were full of fear. He said, "They're strong, those Fascist bastards. Damned strong. They've got all the stuff, and they know what they want. And the French haven't got the stuff and don't want anything except to be left alone. The jackboots will go through the French like a knife through butter. And then where are we?" He shook his head. "Do you remember when we used to go and cock a snoot at Fascist meetings?"

"I remember going once."

"Well, what used to happen? There were never all that number of them, but they were organized and we weren't, and they knew what they wanted. I've seen a crowd of five hundred run like hares from a dozen of them. The only reason why we've kept them working as long as this in Spain is because the Spaniards know what they want, too—or at least some of them do. But we don't know what we want, and nor do the French. We're just being sane, and no sane man's got a chance with them. You see, Henry, what people don't realize is that they're crazy, and that gives them an advantage. I found that in Spain. I wasn't very crazy and therefore I wasn't much good. If there's a war they'll knock us down like ninepins until they come to the Russians. And I'm not sure that even the Russians are mad enough nowadays to be much good."

This was altogether too like what I had been thinking myself to be comfortable. But he said it with such misery and looked so young that I wanted to be comforting. I said, "Well, never mind, Jason. We're all in this together, for what that's worth."

"All in it together?" he said with a frown. "Of course we're not. That's the whole point. You see it doesn't matter what happens to *me*. Obviously if the jackboots win, life would be impossible for Leah, so it's her war—and mine. That's why I told you it was important that she was a Jewess. And that's why I went to Spain, so that there would be no doubt what side I was on. But it's people like you and my godmother I'm worried about."

I said, "I don't know that you need bracket me with old ladies of seventy, Jason."

"No. What I mean is that neither of you is *interested* in it, and I don't see why you should be dragged in, just because people like Leah and me don't like the jackboots."

"But I don't like them either."

He looked at me for a moment and then broke into a broad grin of relief. "You really don't?"

"Of course not. And I know they've got to be stopped, whatever it costs."

Jason said, "Ah well, if you feel like that, of course, it's different. It ought even be rather fun—though as a matter of fact it wasn't as much fun in Spain as I thought it might be. Are you going to stay in London?"

"Yes. I've got a silly feeling that if I go away something will happen behind my back."

"Well, then, look here, why not come and stay at Cheyne Walk? I'm shipping my godmother off to the country tomorrow morning and I shall be there alone." He gave me the peculiar direct, wide-eyed stare. "We might ask Leah in occasionally. She's alone, too."

*　　*　　*　　*　　*

Early next morning I went with Jason to Paddington to see Lady Peasmore off. By seven o'clock the place was swarming with people who were bent on getting out of London before the bombing began. Lady Peasmore was in a bad temper, and obviously felt that the whole crisis was some trick of Jason's. She had apparently refused to discuss it for weeks, and Jason was sure that it was only the cancellation of greyhound racing which had eventually persuaded her to go. Whenever she was angry, she became more and more immobile, and on this occasion it took two porters, as well as Jason and myself, to get her into the train, which was crowded anyhow. As it drew out she was still issuing instructions to Jason in her sharp, Scots-nannie voice, about covering up furniture with dust sheets. He stood and waved after the train, though she could not possibly have seen him. Then he turned to me with a sigh of relief and said, "Now I don't care what happens. The one thing I couldn't cope with would be Myra in an air-raid being sure it was all my fault." He looked round at the crowds as we walked down the platform. "My God, there is an exodus. It might be a bank holiday."

I said, "Not if you look at their faces."

"Oh, I don't know. People at stations always look miserable. Now let's go and get gas-masks."

It was about half-past seven and the bus in which we came away from Paddington had only a dozen people in it—all working men and women going to their jobs. I remember vividly how completely silent they were and that for a while we drove with no other sound than an occasional monosyllable as people bought their tickets and the clang of the conductor's bell. Then somewhere near the Edgware Road we came on an odd sight. A large Lyons' delivery van had overturned and was lying on its side. On it were the words, "Lyons Swiss Rolls." I turned to Jason and said fatuously, "Lyons Swiss Rolls seem to have done so."

Jason roared with laughter. He always liked that sort of joke. The laugh sounded very odd in that silence, and I can see now the surprised, almost indignant faces of the people opposite as they looked at him. Jason pointed to the van and said, "Lyons Swiss Rolls, eh?" to the world in general. There was a moment's pause. Then the conductor gave a tiny chuckle and said, "Looks like it"; and gradually an effortful smile spread over several faces. Somebody said, "Wonder how they managed that now"—and thereafter, though it was still rather quiet and people spoke only in low voices, they were not completely silent.

We went and stood in a queue and drew our gas masks, and to have them was oddly comforting. The woman immediately in front of me kept on repeating, "Two of the Mickey Mouse ones, one's for my sister's kid." She started to say it long before it was her turn.

After that we went and walked in the Park. A group of young men were digging trenches and laughing a great deal. One of them, in a club tie, called out to us half jokingly and half aggressively to come and help. Jason said, "As a matter of fact, if you're going to be bombed, a trench is by far the best place." But we did not go and help. I don't know why, because the chief horror of that day was that there was nothing whatever to do, and mighty little to say; and since we had begun it unusually early, it seemed to go on for ever. I remember looking at my watch, hoping that it was nearly time to lunch, and finding that it was ten forty-five.

In the afternoon we went and collected my suitcase from my hotel and went to Cheyne Walk. While I was unpacking, Jason came in looking carefully surprised, and said that the married couple who acted as cook and houseman had disappeared, taking all their possessions. He said, "I had an idea they were going to skip it when I took Myra away this morning. They were in a bright blue funk. What an excellent thing. Now we can have Leah to stay." I am morally certain, from the way he said it, that he had told them to go. Jason said, "Let's have a drink and play the pianola. I've never heard it played properly. I had to keep it very soft because of Myra." He went over to the thing and fiddled for a moment, and suddenly it started, loudly and distinctly out of tune, in the middle of "The Blue

Danube." Jason said, "Remind me to put it back in the right place. Though if there's going to be a war I suppose it doesn't really matter for a bit."

About an hour later Leah arrived with a couple of suit-cases, and obviously by appointment. She was surprised to see me and not, I thought, very pleased. But she was entirely friendly and seemed to have forgotten our last meeting. I said, "Well, Leah—when does the war start?"

"Oh, I don't think it'll start for a long time yet," she said with a bright smile.

"You really don't think so?" I said, mildly comforted. It was the first even slightly optimistic comment on the situation that I had heard for days.

"No," said Leah, smiling so much that she showed a lot of very white teeth. "After all, we haven't given Hitler Australia yet. Or Buckingham Palace. There's plenty of time."

"God, you can't bear to wait for it, can you?" I said bitterly. "Well, I hope you like it when you get it."

Leah said, "If you're going to call me a warmonger, Henry, don't bother. You've done that before. As for liking it, I don't suppose I shall. But I hope I shall like it better than this. Personally I feel that there are some things worse than being dead. Now, let's talk about something else. Where's your godmother staying, Jason?"

But the trouble was that there wasn't anything else to talk about. One either talked about that or was silent. Soon we had no more to say; and since we could not sit any longer in that silent house, we went out and wandered aimlessly and restlessly in the strange quiet of London—a quiet full of all the usual familiar noises, but in which, somehow, one could have heard the faintest whisper. It was through that strange, noisy hush that half an hour later we heard the voices of the paper-sellers shouting the news of the Munich Conference.

It is so easy now to make bitter fun of the reaction to that news—of the House of Commons throwing its Order Papers into the air, and cheering off the obstinate, dictatorial old dove of peace with his aeroplane and his umbrella and his delusions—of the people who danced in the street for joy because now there was not going to be a war. A few days later, when the terms of the agreement were known, there were plenty of people who saw the wryness of the joke. But if there were people whose first reaction to the news of the conference was not profound relief, I did not see them. All I know is that suddenly the town was alive again, and people were laughing, perhaps a trifle hysterically, and talking, perhaps rather more loudly and quickly than usual. I remember beaming round and saying to the world at large, "I couldn't *really* believe that the world was mad enough to let it happen. Not in this year of grace." Yet a quarter of an hour before, I had had no difficulty in believing it.

Perhaps this is what one might have expected of me, and of most of the other people who had been mortally scared for their own skins. But Leah thought there were worse things than to be dead, yet her first reaction was to throw her arms round Jason's neck and kiss him. As soon as she let go, Jason held out his hand to me. His face was flushed and beaming, and there was a smudge of lipstick beside his mouth where Leah had kissed him. As we shook hands he said, "I'm so glad, Henry—I really am so glad. . . ." He said it in a tone of congratulation, rather as one might congratulate a close friend on his engagement or promotion. Then he turned and shook hands with a small bespectacled man in a green porkpie hat and said, "I'm really frightfully glad." The little man beamed and shouted, "And the same to you and many of 'em," and started to run down the street shouting something. There were a lot of people now running and shouting and laughing. Jason said, "Come on, this calls for a drink," and we went in somewhere and Jason ordered drinks, and then found he had no money to pay for them, and I found I had very little money either, and in the end we had to borrow half-a-crown from Leah, which made us all laugh very much.

After that there is a gap. I have an idea that we walked back to Cheyne Walk through Hyde Park, but I cannot remember anything of what was happening there—nor indeed anything else till we were back at the house listening to the news. It told us nothing that we did not know already, and while we were listening to it I happened to glance at Leah, who had been rather silent for some time. She was staring distractedly out of the window with the big dark eyes very sombre. She caught my eyes on her and immediately smiled brightly. I smiled back, but I had seen that sombre look, and I was immediately conscious of a furious, childish anger.

Jason said, "I don't think we shall get anything more tonight." He switched off and said, "Let's have another drink and play the pianola."

Leah said, "I don't think I will. I've got rather a head."

I said roughly, "Is that why you're looking like a dying duck in a thunderstorm?"

She smiled with an effort and said, "Am I? I'm sorry. I'm a bit tired. Too much excitement."

"Poor old thing," Jason said. He rooted among the pianola rolls. "What shall it be, Henry?"

I said, "What you like. I don't care." It was spoilt and over for me now."

"Sonata Appassionata," said Jason, "played by Paderewski. Lovely loud noise."

He started to put it into the machine. I was looking at Leah. She caught my eye again, and this time neither of us smiled. As I continued to stare at her she lowered her eyes.

Jason hesitated, looking from one of us to the other, and

then turned back and started the pianola. At the first notes Leah burst into tears and went quickly out. Jason stood looking after her, but said nothing.

"Disappointed because she hasn't got her nice war," I said viciously.

He looked at me with anxious eyes and said, "Well, it . . . it's different for her, you see, Henry."

I shrugged but said nothing and there was a long pause. Jason said, "I'd better go and see to her," and went out, leaving me alone with Beethoven and Paderewski and a number of notes which were badly out of tune. The roll seemed to go on for hours, but it came to an end at last and there was a blessed silence. I sat on for half an hour or so, but Jason did not come back, so I went slowly and miserably to bed.

The following morning I rose early and packed my things. It was only eight o'clock when I came down, but Jason was pottering about in his dressing-gown, looking very tousled and childish. I told him I thought I ought to get back to Cambridge and he accepted this without comment.

I said, "Leah's all right?"

"Oh yes," said Jason. "She's still asleep."

I said, "Good. Well, say goodbye to her for me. Cheerio, Jason, and many thanks for putting me up."

He said, "Goodbye, Henry, and thank you," and gave a little bow and looked down at my hand as we shook hands, as he had always done. He came to the door to see me off, and the last I saw of him was standing there looking after me with a very untidy mop of yellow hair, clutching a striped towelling dressing-gown round him, looking very small and rather deserted.

*　　*　　*　　*　　*

I have said that many people, as soon as they knew the terms of the Munich Agreement, saw the wryness of the joke. For my part I think I saw it that evening at Cheyne Walk when I looked at Leah's face; and that was why I was so angry with her. My father, having lost money because there was no war in September, 1938, was soon offering substantial odds that there would be one in September, 1939.

Personally, I think I took this, or something like it, completely for granted; and if I went on with my normal work it was no longer because I would not see, but because one had to do something to fill in the time of waiting.

Moreover, work and war, which I had always regarded as mutually exclusive, now began to seem considerably less so. I happened one day to talk to Pearson, whom I had been assisting at Cambridge. He was a big, quiet, solid person of about forty-five, who had been a sort of professional survivor in the 1914-18 war and had emerged from it with the D.S.O., the M.C. and a slightly stiff arm. I happened to say one day that the chief fear of people like myself was not so much the likelihood of being killed as of panicking under battle conditions. Pearson sucked at his pipe and said briefly, "Oh, you'll be all right."

I said, "I wonder."

"Yes. Because you'd get interested in it. No time to be frightened if you're interested." He hesitated as though he was going to add something and then didn't.

I said, "D'you think perhaps the thing to do would be to join up now, and at least learn what it's all about?"

"No," he said slowly. "I'd rather you didn't. Not for a bit anyhow. I may need you."

"What for? Of course, I know this stuff is important, but. . . ."

"It isn't this stuff I'm thinking about. It's just that there are some things under discussion. Can't tell you about it. But anyhow, don't just go and join up without asking me."

On 1st September, 1939, I was lunching with my father and mother, and trying to explain to my father something of the work that Pearson and I were doing. In the middle of the meal the telephone rang and my father answered it. We heard him say, "Yes. Oh yes. Well, well. Yes. Thanks for letting me know." He then came back, smiled brightly at each of us in turn and said, "Phillipson says the war's started."

My mother gave a slight groan. I said, "How d'you mean— started?"

"Hitler's invaded Poland."

"Oh," said my mother with relief. "It's not a war with *us*?" She did not deal in international affairs, regarding them as outside her sphere.

"Not at the moment," said my father, cocking an eye at me. "But it soon will be. At least, I don't imagine we can let this one go, can we, Henry?"

I said, "I don't see how we can."

My mother groaned again and said, "Oh *dear*, dear, dear."

"Never mind, darling," said my father. "It's merciful that it didn't happen yesterday. We're in September now and I stand to win fifteen shillings. If the thing had started in August I should have been heavily down." He turned to me and said, "If the heart is made of muscle is it possible to do exercises and *develop* the muscle, like those beefy chaps in the advertisements?"

Two hours later Pearson rang up and asked if I could meet him in London the next day.

It was dark by the time I reached London. The black-out had begun and it was raining heavily. There was a time later when one moved about in the black-out with complete ease, but this was complete chaos. There was a surprising number of people blundering about in the darkness, falling over things and swearing. Buses seemed to be groping their way at a walking pace, and it was a great relief to get down to the normality of the tube. Everyone seemed to take it for granted that there would be heavy air-raids at any moment —almost certainly with gas bombs. Nevertheless, there was none of that universal hushed, frozen fear that had been there at the time of Munich; and I could not help feeling that a lot of people like myself had talked to the equivalent of Pearson and found some wall to put their backs against.

I saw Pearson next day at his club. He said, "Well, here it is, Henry. Now I can tell you what for some damned silly reason I wasn't allowed to tell you before. Obviously there's going to be a lot of physiological work to do for the Army. The R.A.M.C. aren't set up for it, they'll have their hands full picking up the dead, and anyhow they mustn't be mixed up in anything to do with offensive war because of the Geneva Convention. Apart from which, being doctors, they don't know a damn' thing about physiology." (Pearson had a lifelong contempt for doctors.)

"So the obvious thing to do is to use people like you and me." Pearson paused and lit his pipe, a foul old thing with a broken stem bound together with copper wire. "Well, after a lot of argy-bargy, that's been agreed, and the War Office has told me to get cracking with a physiological research unit —*not*, thank God, under the Army Medical people. Incidentally, lord knows who we *are* going to be under but that can be fixed later."

I said, "What sort of thing are we going to do?"

"Well, our terms of reference are 'to study the special physiological problems arising under Service conditions,' and as being alive at all is a physiological problem, it leaves us a pretty wide field. I can tell you about thirty things now that we might start on. Do you know what percentage of his own body weight the average infantryman is carrying when he's fully equipped?"

"No."

"Well, if you did, you'd see one job for us."

I said, "This sounds as though it might be great fun, A.P."

Pearson held up his hand. "Wait a minute. This is the tricky bit. The Army want the best people it can get to do this job. But, on the other hand, two of you are under thirty, and there's a school of thought that thinks everybody under thirty ought to be in uniform. It's a damned silly point of view, but you can see what they feel."

"Yes," I said unhappily.

"So I've said, 'All right—then give us all commissions and that gets you out of that.' They chewed that over for a bit and eventually they've agreed. *But,* they've said, we can't have chaps holding commissions who can't form fours or put a Sam Browne on right. So anybody you want will have to go and learn to be a soldier first."

He paused, "Well—are you on?"

I laughed and said, "You bet I am."

"Good. Well, I've arranged for you to have a medical tomorrow."

London might not be as frightened as it had been before Munich, but on 2nd September, 1939, it was not a very cheerful place to spend an evening alone, and at about six o'clock I rang up Cheyne Walk. I had not seen or heard anything of Jason since Munich, and had no idea whether he would be there or not. But somehow he seemed the obvious person to contact now.

Jason answered the telephone himself, sounding very cheerful.

I said, "How about dining with me?"

"Well, as a matter of fact, Henry, I'm off later this evening."

"Off where?"

"To join my regiment."

"I didn't know you had a regiment."

"Oh yes. A nice one."

"What time are you going?"

"Not till ten. But I've said I'd go to a thing first with old Jerry Dollar. I tell you what—why not come along?"

"What sort of thing is it?"

"Oh, just a sort of farewell party. I don't know the people who're giving it. Jerry's taking me."

"Well, if you don't know who's party it is, I don't think I can very well come, can I?"

"Oh, nonsense," said Jason. "That's the sort of thing it is. Come along there right away."

Except in Jason's room everything in the house was covered with dust sheets, which made it more museum-like than ever. Jason was in Service dress, with one pip and the badge of a county regiment. The tunic suited him, since without exactly making him look bigger it showed that what little of him there was was solid and well-proportioned. Even so, he looked very small beside Jerry, who was a huge young man with a broad grin, a red face, and the biggest and dampest hands I ever shook. He was also in uniform, and I gathered that they were platoon commanders in the same company.

They seemed excited and extremely happy.

I said, "How long have you been in, Jason?"

"Oh, nearly a year. I joined up the day after you left. It's been quite fun, though bits of it really aren't my sort of thing."

Jerry grinned and said, "Jason can't read a map without turning it upside down."

"Yes. You see I always like to look *down* on things. You know, as if I was at the North Pole. But I'm all right if they let me do it my own way."

I said, "Your hair's more orderly, but I don't think much of your buttons."

"Well, I like them this nice gold colour, Henry—I don't like them nearly white, like Jerry's. So when I'm on leave and there's nobody to curse me, I just do them every few days."

I said, "Well, I hope to be cleaning mine in a few days."

"You're joining up?" said Jason quietly and, I thought, rather anxiously.

"Yes—in a rather bogus sort of way." I told him about the Pearson proposition.

Jason nodded and said, "Oh—now *that* seems to me to make sense. It would be damn' silly if you joined an outfit like ours."

"Why?"

"Well, it's all right for chaps like Jerry and me who can't do anything else, but you've got brains."

I said, "Still classing me with your godmother, eh? How is she?"

"Fine. Down in Dorset."

"And how's Leah?"

"Oh, Leah's having a wonderful time driving an ambulance. She's at it now. If you like to come and see me off tonight she'll be at the station." Jason glanced at his watch. "How about this party?"

I did not really want to go to a party. I would rather have stayed and talked, or gone quietly out to dinner. But Jerry assured us that it would be "a cheerful binge, not to be missed. Kathy's parties always are."

I said, "Who is Kathy?"

"Well, her name's Grayson and she's got a lot of money and she's married to a rather dim bloke, but I don't think she lets that interfere with anything much. I don't really know her very well, but I've been there a couple of times with a chap I know."

"Well, it seems to me that if I go, I shall be the friend of a friend of a friend of somebody she knows."

"Oh, that's all right. That's the sort of thing it is."

That, indeed was exactly the sort of thing it was. We went

to a big house in Eaton Square at about seven. The door was opened by a white-jacketed manservant who took our coats. A second showed us upstairs and announced us as "Lieutenant Collar, Lieutenant Pellew and Mr. Main." The room was very big, very lush and very hot, and there must have been a couple of hundred people in it drinking champagne and making a noise like a football crowd. A lot of the men were in uniform, and I noticed that there hardly seemed to be a soul over thirty.

A big woman in a remarkable frock which seemed to be made entirely of gold scales came forward and seized Jerry by the hand and said, "Why, Bill, my dear . . . !" and kissed him.

He grinned and said, "Not Bill. Jerry."

"Of course. How are you, darling?"

"I'm very well, thank you, Kathy. This is Henry Payne . . ." She took my hand and held it for a moment while she gazed closely into my eyes, and then smiled with an upward flicker of her eyebrows and said, "Hallo."

". . . and Jason Pellew." She took Jason's hand and said, "Jason Pellew. . . ." and stared as she had stared at me. Jason flushed, and dropped his eyes to their hands and gave his queer, almost Oriental little bow. Kathy turned to Jerry and said, "Well, isn't he absolutely *sweet*! Well, come on, my dears—get yourselves a glass of wine. Everybody's got to be terribly jolly tonight because this may be the last party for a long time. If we're all going to be killed we may as well die happy." She swept away to greet someone else.

Jerry grinned and said, "What a girl. Let's go and get a drink."

As we sipped our drinks I had a chance to look at Mrs. Grayson more carefully. I guessed her age as about thirty—perhaps a little older. Her figure was magnificent in a slightly full-blown way, and she had very beautiful shining dark red hair. Apart from that she was not really good-looking, her eyes being too small and a rather indefinite brown, and her

157

features too heavy. But in the glittering gold frock she certainly looked impressive, and I noticed that she was wearing big yellow diamond stud ear-rings and a yellow solitaire diamond ring the size of a sixpence.

I said, "Where does she get her money? Or is it her husband's?"

"Oh lord, no," said Jerry. "I don't think he's got a cent. It's Kathy's money, and what's more she wears the trousers. I think her father was a big shipowner or something. That's her husband over there."

We looked and saw a pale, rather fat young man in a dinner jacket who was staring glassily before him and swaying slightly on his feet as though moved by a gentle breeze. Jason said, "He looks somewhat tight."

"He always is. At least he always has been when I've been here. Well—here's to us, chaps."

The whole of one end of the big room was taken up by a bar and a huge table of superb cold food, and after a while Kathy came and insisted that we should eat. She stood with us for a few minutes and while Jason and Jerry were getting their food she said, "You know it's awful, all these nice boys going off. I suppose you'll be going too, won't you? Or have you got a nice reserved job?"

I said, "I shall be in the Army in a few days," and was thankful to be able to say it. I had an idea, from her tone, that Kathy might easily be a white-feather-hander.

"That little one—is his name really Jason?"

"Yes."

"I think he's quite adorable. So—so *miniature,* and yet so pretty."

"He's fairly tough really. He was in the Spanish war."

"Really? *That* baby?"

"He's twenty-two."

"I should have thought he was about sixteen." She put a hand on his arm as he came back with a plate of chicken and said, "Come on, Jason. Come and sit down over here and talk to me while you eat."

As they went off Jerry chuckled and said, "Jason seems to have clicked. It's annoying how they fall for him, isn't it?"

I said, "Do they? I haven't seen him in action much in that direction."

"Oh, my dear man, it's terrific. And sometimes maddening. He just does nothing and looks shy and they come for him with bared teeth. Particularly *big* women." He shook his head. "I wouldn't really mind a slice of Kathy myself, would you?"

I said, "I like her dress."

A group in the opposite corner of the room began to sing "Mademoiselle from Armentières," led by a gunner subaltern who was very drunk indeed. Jerry hummed the tune and said, "I suppose this is rather like that ball before Waterloo. You know—whooping it up and then going off."

"Yes," I said rather doubtfully. I couldn't really imagine Wellington singing "Mademoiselle from Armentières," and anyhow I was trying to remember where I had last talked to somebody about the Duchess of Richmond's Ball.

By about 8.30 I had had quite enough of it. Everything was getting very noisy without really being very funny. People were still singing, but since they had divided into half a dozen groups who were all singing different things, it sounded like turning-out time in a pub. Jerry had joined one of the singing groups and was bawling away, with his cheek resting on a girl's hair and his arm round her waist. Jason had disappeared completely. The drunk gunner suddenly roared, "Ladies and gentlemen—the King!" and raised his glass. About half the guests stopped singing and drank the toast with a sort of owlish seriousness. The rest went wailing on. The gunner was very angry and started to weave his way across the floor towards them. For a moment it looked as though there was going to be a row, but somebody took the

159

gunner's arm and turned him round, and he went weaving back again to his own group.

Just as I was deciding to go away, Jason reappeared, looking very sulky. He said, "This is a frightful bore. What's the time?"

"Twenty to nine."

"Then how about going? The train isn't till ten, but we've got to get our stuff, and anyhow I'd like a few minutes with Leah."

I said, "Fine. If you hadn't turned up I was going anyhow."

Jason said, "I don't like that woman. She's bloody rude and bloody ill-bred. I wish I hadn't come to her bloody party. Where's Jerry?"

We had some difficulty with Jerry, who was enjoying himself and did not want to come away. I suggested leaving him and letting him meet us at the station, but Jason would not hear of it. He clearly felt responsible for Jerry, and in the end led him out, like a destroyer fussing round its battleship. I said, "Ought we to say goodbye to our hostess?"

Jason said, "I've said all I want to to her."

We went back to Cheyne Walk and picked up their luggage. It had stopped raining but it was very dark and there were no cabs. Jerry went to sleep in the Underground, and was never altogether with us throughout.

On the way to King's Cross Jason said, "It would be damned funny if there wasn't a war after all. Leah thinks there may quite well be another sell-out. In which case all these people will look uncommonly silly."

"Oh, I don't know. I expect Kathy would just throw another party to celebrate peace."

"I'll bet she would," said Jason viciously. He seemed to be in a very bad temper.

It was twenty to ten before we reached King's Cross. The place was swarming with people, mostly in uniform. Jason had arranged to meet Leah in the Refreshment Room, but we could not get near it, and anyhow it seemed to have sold out of everything except very weak tea. Eventually we ran into Leah quite by chance in the crowd, looking very tall and slim in her uniform. She greeted me with apparent pleasure. I said, "Well, I think you've got it this time, Leah," and she laughed and said, "I'm keeping my fingers crossed."

There was only about a quarter of an hour to go by then, and it wasn't easy to think of anything much to say. Jason was very silent, and Jerry still seemed half asleep. Leah asked us where we had dined, and Jason said at once, "Oh, at Scott's. There was a lovely old major there, with a napkin tucked under his chin, eating prawns by the bucketful. You know—those *big* prawns. He must have eaten at least twelve dozen." After that he relapsed into silence. Leah told us a story about her ambulance. It appeared that a man had tripped over a sandbag in the black-out and had banged his head on something, knocking himself out for the moment. He was not badly hurt, but the First Aid people had pounced on him, and as one of them was bending over him his tin hat fell off and landed on the man's face, breaking his nose. They then put him on a stretcher, but in lifting it they dropped one end, breaking the man's collar bone; so that eventually he was borne away a complete ruin. Leah and I laughed a good deal about this and even Jerry woke up enough to realize that somebody had made a joke and laughed too. Jason just smiled rather painfully and went on staring straight in front of him.

It was a relief when it was time for them to get on the train. Jason kissed Leah briefly and said, "Goodbye, darling. Look after yourself."

Leah said, "You smell. What have you been up to?"

Jason shook hands with me in his formal way, and said, "Goodbye, Henry," and then added in a low voice, "keep an eye on Leah if you get a chance. I've got a feeling that this is going to be the most dangerous place to be, and she's so darned reckless. Cheer-ho."

As the train pulled out there was a lot of handkerchief waving and last moment hugging. Leah said, "I suppose this was what it was like when people went off in the last war. I've often wondered. Damn, I'm going to cry. No, I'm not. Let's get out of this mob, for God's sake."

We went back to Charing Cross and managed to get a cup of coffee at the big Lyons at the bottom of the Strand. Almost as soon as we were seated Leah said, "Where did you *really* go this evening? Not that it matters."

I said, "To Scott's. Jason told you."

"All right," she said wearily. Then her eyes filled with tears and she said, "He's going to be killed, you know. I've always known he would be if—if it happened. I may and you won't. But he will, poor little man."

"Oh, half a minute," I said uncomfortably. "We aren't even at war yet."

Leah's lips were trembling. She smiled and said, "No. I forgot. There's always Mr. Chamberlain." After a moment she stared at me with anger in the dark eyes and said, "That was a lie—the thing you said about my having made him go to Spain. I never did—or would have. And I didn't make him do this."

I said, "I accept that, Leah. I never really thought. . . ."

"I couldn't have anyhow. I couldn't make him do things. You see, he doesn't love me at all, really."

"I think you're wrong there."

She shook her head miserably but could not say anything. The tears had welled over now and she dabbed at her eyes with a rather dirty handkerchief. I said, "Have mine."

Leah blew her nose and said, "He doesn't, you know. He—he loves majors in Scott's that—that use scent. But he doesn't love me. He—he won't let me get anywhere near him."

"He won't let anyone come very near him, you know."

162

"But why not, Henry? Why *not*? He's the loneliest person I know, and yet he won't let me help. I wouldn't have asked for anything or—or been a nuisance. Honest, I wouldn't. But he doesn't trust me, and he lies to me and. . . ."

My head was aching from Kathy's champagne and I was feeling very tired and empty. I said, "I don't really understand myself, but I'm pretty sure it's a long story."

Leah took a deep breath and said briskly, "Well, anyhow, I don't see why I should come and weep on you about it. Let's have some more coffee and tell me about this job of yours."

*　　*　　*　　*　　*

The next day I had my medical and Mr. Chamberlain told the nation that we were at war. I did not hear his speech but I heard the sirens adding their appropriately forlorn comment as it ended; and outside the building in which I was being examined, a very small air-raid warden in a tin hat rode by on a bicycle, blowing a whistle. He blew so vigorously that he lost control of the bicycle and rode into the kerb and went hopping along on one leg for a few yards. And with that collection of silver trumpets singing to the battle, the war began.

*　　*　　*　　*　　*

When I set out to tell this story, I realized that I was dealing with a rather elusive character; but at least I was sure that if anybody knew Jason Pellew, I did.

Yet the more I think about it, the more I realize—that the amount of time we spent together in nearly thirty years was really very small; Jason was an all-or-nothing friend—he either turned up every day or disappeared for a year. In the whole of our acquaintance I do not think I ever received a letter from him through the post. But, on the other hand, I don't remember ever writing him one. For some reason which

I have never understood we never made much effort to keep our friendship alive, in the way that, say, Jackson and I did.

It was, in fact, from Jackson that I had my only news of Jason for the next seven or eight months after we parted at King's Cross; and that was merely a line in a letter to say that Jason's battalion was in Northern France, "energetically respecting Belgian neutrality," as Jackson put it. Jackson himself had just qualified, and "having hastily mumbled the Hippocratic oath," had joined the R.A.M.C. I received this letter while I was at Luddenham Camp, in Wiltshire, receiving the four months' training which the War Office had insisted was necessary before I could join Pearson.

I have never known what the authorities had told them to do with Jeff Hays and myself, but certainly nobody ever took the business of turning us into soldiers very seriously. Everyone was far too busy, and in any case instructors were very scarce.

We were therefore left, more or less, to work out a "course" for ourselves, with the complete run of the place and its equipment, unhindered by regimental duties, parades or sergeant instructors, and able to spend all our time on things which we found either amusing, or thought might be useful later. The result was that we learnt more in four months than we should have done otherwise in two years, and did nobody any harm; except for one occasion when we inadvertently fired away the depot's complete supply of Thomson Sub-Machine gun ammunition in a single morning; and another when we lost ourselves and a utility van in the middle of Salisbury Plain at two in the morning, when attempting some rather fancy night navigation.

We therefore enjoyed ourselves very much, and by contrast, the unit, when we got to it early in 1940, was a disappointment. The authorities, having accepted Pearson's scheme, had made him a full colonel, given him a requisitioned house in Highgate and a small quantity of whitewood furniture, and quietly forgotten about him. When Jeff and I arrived it was still not clear to whom, if anybody, we belonged; and Pearson himself had spent most of his time since September writing memoranda asking for another typewriter. Nobody was very glad to see us, as it meant that we had to have something to sit on, and there were already eight physiologists and only seven chairs. Altogether my chief recollection of the first few months of 1940 is of sitting on a box in my Army overcoat in a freezingly cold room, drinking tea, wondering what to do, and how on earth to set about doing it. Even the invasion of Norway in April, and the departure and withdrawal of the British Expeditionary Force, never seemed to produce a job for us, and it was not until May that Pearson came in one morning and said, "I think the balloon's gone up at last. They're coming through Belgium again."

Pearson at once began to pester the War Office to allow Jeff and me to go to France. But in a fortnight's time it was becoming distressingly clear that France was no place for research people carrying Douglas bags and sphygmomanometers. I remember that when the news of the fall of Amiens came, Pearson sat staring at the newspaper for a long while in silence and then said quietly, "They never got so far as that last time." That night Jeff Hays said solemnly, "I don't think we shall have to go and *look* for the war after all, Henry. If we just stay where we are, it will come to us."

It was either on the last day of May or the first of June that Pearson came in and said, "Looks a wee bit better. Apparently the Jerry planes can't get at us because of the weather, and if it holds like this we may get quite a lot of people out from Dunkirk. I've got permission for us to go down to the ports and see if we can pick up anything useful. You two take Folkestone. Get cracking."

There was a moment's pause and then Jeff said mildly, "Er —what *sort* of thing, A.P.?"

Pearson said, "Well, my God, with a bit of luck you'll see a sizeable chunk of an army that's fought a rearguard action for three weeks, and been living in holes on the beaches for several days. If you can't find anything of physiological interest in *that* . . . !"

He then went away looking irritated, and there were the terms of reference of my first real war assignment.

Pearson always felt that if one could only *go* somewhere, the rest was easy.

Of course it was a hopeless wild-goose chase. Jeff and I decided solemnly that the most useful thing to do would be to try to get hold of a sample of men and test them for fatigue by measuring the power of their hand grip with a special gadget designed for the purpose which we had brought from Cambridge. This was not as silly as it sounds, in the sense that it was a perfectly normal experiment which we had both done before under laboratory conditions, and which we actually did use later in the war with troops straight out of battle. What *was* silly was to think we could do it without prior organization, and under those conditions.

We spent most of a day wandering round the crowded chaos of the harbour area at Folkestone, trying to find somebody to ask permission to try people's grips. Towards the evening we had succeeded in putting the proposition to a rather elderly lieutenant-colonel who at least had an improvised office in a shed down at the docks, and seemed to be in charge of something. He had not been to bed, I fancy, for several days, but he listened to us until we came to the bit about measuring hand grip, and then rising, laid a hand on Jeff's arm and one on mine and said very quietly and carefully, "My dear fellows, take a look round you. Lots of troops, eh? Bit jammed together, eh? Now if the weather happened to clear and Jerry could get into the air, he'd be over here in very, very short order with as nice a target as

166

the beaches themselves. So we've got to *move* people. See? Not keep them about here frigging around being tested for things."

We said we quite understood. He nodded as though he was glad that his point was taken and said, "Then, if you want to measure people's hand grip, go away and shake hands with one another, and don't bother *me*. Goodbye."

As we came out, Jeff said, "You know, Henry, I think perhaps the best thing will be just to *observe*, as it were."

Many newspapers reporting the return of troops from Dunkirk announced that there was no depression and that the troops were in the highest spirits. In a sense this was true, since everybody was certainly uncommonly glad to be out of it, and happily surprised to be in England, and not dead or in a German prison camp. But my chief impression was of an almost universal bewilderment. The Army was like a boxer who has taken a terrific punch to the jaw, has staggered to his feet at the count of nine, and is still trying to remember where he is and why.

There were whole groups of men who seemed utterly finished—dazed, exhausted, dirty and with no equipment whatever. There were others who seemed at first glance to be in better shape, but who could not stop talking, and kept up a perpetual nervous chatter about nothing in particular. There were the French, sullen, silent and angry. And there were groups who still had all or most of their equipment, still fell in and marched smartly and proudly, and even looked as though they had shaved.

I watched one of these coming away from the dock area. It was led by a big dark captain with a thick ash walking stick, and consisted of about a hundred men of one of the oldest regiments of the line. The leading files were all fully equipped and might almost have been on parade. Then farther back in the column one began to see an odd man with no steel helmet or bayonet or without a pack; and finally, in the rear perhaps a dozen without rifles, helmets or any other equipment. But all were marching smartly, the men in the rear, without equipment, swinging their arms with a sort of self-conscious swagger which was oddly moving. They halted close to me and fell out. I went up to the dark captain and said, "Hallo, Bryce."

He turned and stared at me for a moment, and I saw that his eyes were very bloodshot. Then he smiled the old, slightly supercilious smile and said, "Why, hallo, Payne. I didn't know you were in the Army. *Now* I begin to see a possible cause for this slight débacle."

I said, "No, it wasn't me, Bicycle. I wasn't there and I'm not really a soldier at all."

"Well, you didn't miss anything," he said wearily. "This is what used to be my company."

"Casualties as heavy as that?"

"Pretty heavy. But a hell of a lot of people just got mislaid. By the way, you'll be sorry to hear that a friend of yours has gone—little Jason Pellew. You remember little Jason?"

I tried to say, "Yes," but nothing happened. After a moment I said, "Is he dead?"

"I don't know. Either dead or a prisoner, I imagine. I hope he's got away with it. He was a rum little cuss, but I always rather liked him." Bryce stifled a yawn and said, "Sorry. You know the odd thing is that I'm not really tired, but I *am* uncommonly sleepy."

I said, "Do you know what happened to Jason?"

"Well, up to a point. Apparently he's been out ever since the war began and so have I, and most of the time we were quite close together. But we didn't run into each other until this last show was in full swing. His battalion and mine were over on the left, and when the Belgians packed up a few days ago, we were left gently waving in the air. There was a hell of a mess on the roads, what with refugees, and odd bits of the Belgian Army which weren't sure if they were going or coming, and Jerry occasionally helping things along from the air. I should avoid being dive-bombed, by the way, if I were you. Very unpleasant. Anyhow the whole thing rapidly turned into a complete mess, with units getting very mixed up. One kept mislaying one's own people, particularly at night; and at the same time other odd characters who had *been* mislaid by their own units kept turning up and tagging along. There was one time when apart from my own men I had chaps from five other battalions with me—including an R.C. padre and a despatch rider from another *division,* who'd lost his bike somehow."

I said, "But Jason. . . ."

"Well, that's what I was going to tell you. It was very foggy one morning, which kept the bombers off but made everything else even trickier, and Jason just turned up out of the fog with about a dozen chaps and a corporal. His platoon had been left behind to do something or other, and then there'd been a lot of bombing and a big road block, and they'd just never been able to get through to their battalion again. I must say he had his chaps in hand extremely well. I wouldn't have thought the little man had it in him."

"Well, they joined up with my mixed bag, and we kept together for a few hours, by which time the fog had cleared. I didn't get a chance to say much to Jason, but he seemed very cheerful, though a bit over-excited. Then some time in the afternoon we had the bloody thing that's been happening all the time in the last few days. We heard firing quite close at hand on our right, and slightly *in front* of us. In fact, Jerry'd run a bit faster than we had, and was overlapping us. I suppose by that time we were about a hundred and thirty strong. My chaps and Jason's still had their rifles, but practically none of the strays had anything. We had four Brens, and apart from that not a sausage—not even a mortar. As what was over on the right was most probably German armour, it seemed to me that the thing to do was to keep going in the general direction of the Atlantic and to go a bit faster. Then the firing started again. It can't have been more than a mile away, but there was a thick belt of wood between it and us and I thought we might just get away with it. And then Jason, who'd been walking with me, suddenly said, "Oh, my God, I'm sick of this. I hate walks. Give me that." He turned round and grabbed one of the Brens from two of his chaps who were carrying it, yelled, "Keep going with Captain Bryce, Corporal. I'm going to have a go," and went haring off towards the wood. I yelled at him to come back, but he took no notice and we saw him disappear into the wood.

"I think there must have been trouble even nearer than we thought, because only a minute after he got into the wood we heard the Bren open up. You could tell it, because previously there hadn't been any Bren fire. We heard several bursts, and then all the firing stopped, and that was that."

Bryce paused and poked moodily at the ground with his stick. He said, "I don't think there was anything we could have done. I can see exactly how he felt. I've felt like it myself a good many times in the last week. But I thought I must try to get what was left of the company back. When we got back to the beach-head I managed to find his battalion and hand over his chaps. But of course he'd never shown up. It's a great pity. I was fond of him, crazy little coot as he was."

*　　*　　*　　*　　*

I went back to London the following day. I knew I must tell Leah, but I had no idea where she was living, and the only address I had, even vaguely, was her ambulance station. In the end I managed to get a message through asking her to ring me. She rang at about seven. All the way back to London I had been trying to think what to say to her, but when the time came I could do no better than, "Leah, I'm afraid I've got some bad news for you."

"What, Henry?"

"You—you haven't heard about Jason?"

"Yes. I heard this afternoon," she said calmly. "Rotten luck, isn't it?"

I said, "I'm most frightfully sorry, my dear."

"Well, I suppose it might be worse. It was damned silly though."

She said it with an almost complete lack of emotion, and I remember thinking that if I had not known about Leah's real feelings for Jason, I should have thought she was being callous. I said quietly, "I should think he's almost certainly a prisoner, you know."

"A prisoner?" said Leah in a puzzled way. "Why should he be?"

"Why not? I mean they don't know exactly what happened to him, do they?"

"Yes, of course. It was an ammunition box or something."

I said, "Leah—what exactly are you talkng about? What have they told you?"

"Well, what are *you* talking about, Henry? All I know is that he got to Dover all right, and then some oaf dropped this box on his foot and broke a bone in it, and he's had to be sent to hospital."

I did not say anything for a moment. Then I said, "Leah—are you sure of this—about getting to Dover and . . ."

"Oh yes. He made Jerry ring up to tell me. Why? What's your version?"

I said, "I don't think I've got one, thank God."

He turned up three days later, walking with a stick and with his right foot in a big bandage with a soft shoe over it. He had had his hair cut very short in France, and the effort was to make him look less cherubic and slightly foxy. But other-

171

wise he seemed very well and extremely happy. Leah and I met him at Charing Cross, and we all went back to some rooms that she had near Victoria.

I said, "How the hell did you get back to Dover?"

Jason looked at me a trifle warily and said, "Well, I walked as far as Dunkirk. Everybody had to. The buses weren't running. Then I took a boat."

"Yes, but what happened after you left Bryce?"

Jason said, "Oh, Bicycle? Yes, I saw him."

"I know you did, I talked to him at Folkestone, and according to him. . . ."

Jason's eyes had flickered for a moment to Leah and back again. "By the time I left Bicycle," he said quickly, "we were practically there anyhow. You know this is a complete nonsense about my foot. They say it'll take nearly a month."

Leah said, "Who is this Bicycle character and what did he tell you, Henry?"

"Darling," said Jason patiently, "it's all quite simple. Bicycle is a chap we knew at school. I saw him on the way back to the coast and then left him because I knew a quicker way than he did. What is this stuff you're doing, Henry?"

Leah was on duty that evening. After she had gone I said, "I take it you didn't want to tell me what happened to you in front of Leah?"

Jason looked confused, as he always did if you tackled him about spinning yarns, and said, "Well, she fusses."

"What did happen, Jason? Apparently the last Bryce saw of you was haring off to take on the whole German Army with a Bren. He was certain you must have been either killed or taken prisoner, and as a matter of fact I damned nearly broke the sad news to Leah, only Jerry had found her first."

Jason reflected. "Let's see, what did happen after that . . . ? Well, I went into a wood and there were some Jerries about a hundred yards away working through the trees at right

172

angles to me, so that I was enfilading them. The trouble was that the trees were rather close together and I couldn't get a proper pop at them. But I got behind a good big tree and fired two or three bursts, which shook them rather, coming from their flank like that. Anyhow, they all disappeared like rabbits, and then after a few moments they opened up at where they presumably thought I was, which wasn't far from where I *really* was. I nipped along to another tree and had a pop at where I thought *they* were. I don't suppose any of us hit anything useful, because the trees made it so tricky. But it was rather fun for a while, until I suddenly realized that I hadn't remembered to bring any spare magazines at all. So there really wasn't much to be done. I waited until there was a slight lull and then left the Bren, which was damned heavy, and started to fade quietly away in the general direction in which I'd come. But by that time they'd worked round to that side, so what I faded quietly into was about a dozen of them, and that was that."

"They took you?"

"Well, yes. You see, there were a lot of them, Henry, and I hadn't got anything to fight with except a forty-five, and I couldn't hit an elephant at six yards with a forty-five anyhow, so it seemed time to pack it in. Incidentally, I don't know to this day what people of ours they'd been firing at, if any. Perhaps they were shooting rabbits. Anyhow, I think it had been worth while having a go at them because from the way they were moving when I saw them first I think they would soon have been on top of Bicycle and his little lot, which would have been a pity.

"As it was they put me in charge of a large cove with a completely square head, who started to take me somewhere— presumably back to some sort of gathering place for prisoners, except that it seemed to me to be in the wrong direction.

"Well, I didn't care for this square-headed man at all, and though he'd got a tommy-gun, I remembered how difficult it was to hit anything among the trees. So I waited until we were well away from his pals and then gave him soft words and a cigarette, and while he was lighting it I did a rapid bunk in and out among the trees."

I had a sudden vision of a small, muddy figure with yellow hair and a peculiar snipe-like run. I said, "Real scrum-half stuff, eh?"

"Yes. It was really absurdly easy. In fact, he never got in anything like a sensible shot at me at all, and after my own efforts with the Bren I can see why. Anyhow, I soon lost him.

"After that, of course, there wasn't much to it. I'd turned round so many times that I wasn't sure which way to head, and I hadn't a compass. I didn't want to go tramping off and then find myself back in Brussels or something. So I lay low until it was dark and got a bearing by the stars, and then went on back to Dunkirk. It was only about twenty miles by then anyhow."

"Bryce says he went to look for you in the perimeter and that you weren't with your battalion."

"I doubt he did, you know. I don't think Bicycle is the type who goes and looks for anybody much. Between ourselves, Henry, I don't really *like* Bicycle. Though I must say he was very nice to me when I was young. Anyhow, that may have been before I got back. It took some time because Jerry was all round by then and one kept nearly walking into him. That part of it was rather fun in a way. I say, what do you think will happen now? Hadn't we better listen to the P.M.?"

*   *   *   *   *

". . . if necessary, for years. If necessary, alone. . . ."

As the first of the great speeches ended, Jason snapped off the radio and said, "Well, that's all right. Now I shan't marry Leah for a bit."

I said, "Why? Were you going to?"

"Oh yes. If we'd been going to have peace or have Germans

174

over here or anything. You see it would have been very tricky for her, being Jewish."

"Would it have been less tricky if she was married to you?"

"Well, perhaps not. I just thought it would be the right thing. I say, I was afraid we might be going to pack up, weren't you? Which would have been a nuisance."

"Yes." It had not seemed a nuisance at all a few hours ago. In fact it had seemed about the only thing possible. But after Churchill's speech it was clearly unthinkable.

I said, "What I don't quite see is what we're going to *do*. We may be able to keep them out of England. But I don't see how we're going to get *at* them to win."

"The R.A.F. and the Navy," said Jason vaguely.

"I suppose so. But it'll take a hell of a long time. And they've got an Air Force too."

"They certainly have," said Jason feelingly. "Still, I suppose it'll all work out."

"I suppose so."

At about this time the Prime Minister was circulating to the Chiefs of the Services an inquiry as to how they thought we should now proceed to win the war. He would not have got much help if he had asked Jason and me. But at least he would have had our support for the underlying idea.

Jason looked round the small attic room and said, "You know I think I must move Leah into Cheyne Walk. It's going to be tough now, and this place could easily fall down even if nothing hit it. Where are you living?"

"In digs in Hampstead with Jeff Hays."

"Well, you wouldn't like to go to Cheyne Walk, too, would you, and keep Leah company? I can't be there myself, of course, but you'd be very welcome."

* * * * *

The Cheyne Walkers, or, as they were sometimes known, Jim Pitt's Underground Artillery, were a curious organization. There were a few permanent residents—Leah, Jeff, myself and a fat girl named Rose who had a red face and spectacles, worked in the Ministry of Supply, and unlike the rest of us, occasionally dusted things and cooked. She was not a very bright girl, and did not add much to the company. But she was useful, and except on one occasion I never saw her show any emotion whatever about the raids. That was when a bomb fell rather near, raised her several inches from the floor on which she was sitting, and put her back again. On that occasion she blushed and looked indignant and embarrassed as though someone had made an improper gesture towards her.

Apart from these four, there was a considerable floating population, including Jason himself and Jerry when on leave, Pearson on a couple of occasions, a rather sulky and frightened girl friend of Leah's, and almost anybody whom any of us happened to know who wanted a bed for the night.

I don't know why we stayed there. It was not a particularly safe place, being, as Jeff was always pointing out, in the perfect position for a boss-shot at Battersea Power Station. It had a basement, but the basement was full of hot water-pipes and gas-pipes and could have been a death trap. We never went to it. I think the point was that the house gave us some sort of anchor, and some sort of regular company, which were two things that were very necessary during the heaviest of the bombing.

Leah was usually out at night, of course, driving her ambulance; and Jason was stationed somewhere on the East Coast, and only turned up occasionally. I cannot remember why they were both there one night in, I think, October 1940. Jason was having a bath when the sirens started. He put his head round the door and shouted, "There we go. Start up, Rose." Rose went over to the pianola and started "The Blue Danube," which was our normal defensive measure. The gunfire started almost at once, but it seemed to be a long way away down the river. Rose was knitting.

Leah said, "I'll bet you Fergy will be on the telephone for me within ten minutes. I'm practically defending this town single-handed."

Jeff said, "It doesn't sound like it." The firing was very heavy.

I was always very frightened in the early blitz—more so, I think, than most people. Later on in the war, when I had more to do, I minded much less, and in the end took an almost proprietary interest in the flying bombs and rockets. But the ordinary piloted raids of '40 and early '41 really scared me. Everybody knew this and just took no notice. One grew, at that time, to accept people as they were.

Jason came out looking very pink, with his hair plastered down with water. He listened for a while, and the firing was definitely coming closer.

Jeff said, "Coming up the river apparently."

Just at that moment our nearest battery opened up from somewhere in Battersea.

I said, "*Have* come up the river from the sound of it."

The guns from this place always made the house shake slightly. Rose looked up, stared expressionlessly through her spectacles straight in front of her for a moment, and then went on knitting. Jeff said, "I don't think that means anything. That chap always has a pop if there's a Jerry within twenty miles."

There was an almighty crash that shook us a lot.

I said, "That sounded like Waterloo Station."

"Everything always sounds like Waterloo Station," said Leah. "The last time we thought so, the thing was in Lewisham." She said it very calmly, but her face had gone the curious yellow colour which meant that she wasn't liking it much.

Jason said, "I think we'd better take up action stations. I'm always scared about glass. I can't think why these windows haven't gone by now. Rose—action station." Action stations meant sitting on the floor away from the windows.

It was an uncommonly heavy raid even by the standards of that October, and it seemed to be uncomfortably overhead; though, of course, things always sounded a good deal more overhead than they were. But after about ten minutes it quietened down a little.

Leah said, "You know, I think I ought to get across to the station and see what goes on."

Jason said, "I never knew such a girl for not missing anything. What's the sense of going out in this, if you're off duty?"

"Well, Fergy will almost certainly be trying to ring me. Anyhow, you can tell by the row that it'll be all hands to the pump tonight. And I'm no good at just sitting." She got up.

Jason looked at her for a moment and then grinned and said, "All right. I'll see you to the Underground."

"What for?"

"I'd like the walk."

"So would I," said Jeff. "Let's all go and look for incendiaries."

Jason glanced at me and said quickly, "Someone's got to stay with Rose."

Rose looked up and said, "Oh no. I shall be quite all right. You go and enjoy yourselves. Your tin hat's in the kitchen, Henry."

I swallowed and said, "All right. Let's go."

It was better outside. There was still a lot of firing, but in the open air you could feel and see that it was a good way away now. There was a huge orange glow in the sky down east, which looked as though it might be the docks, and a sizeable fire across the river behind Waterloo. The factories on the south bank stood out in solid black against it. Leah said, "That one looks uncommonly like us." Her station was not far from the Elephant.

Jason said, "I can't think why they never seem to pop one on the War Office. I suppose they're just letting well alone."

We made that joke in practically every raid.

We were making for Sloane Square, which was the nearest Underground, and just as we were passing the Royal Hospital Jason suddenly leapt about two feet sideways and said, "What the hell's that?"

There was a faint scrabbling noise in the darkness. Jeff said, "Probably a cat," and shone his torch in the direction of the sound for a moment.

It was a cat—or the remains of one. You often saw stray cats about at that time, but this was the worst I had ever seen—just a tabby skin and a lot of bones. It stared at the light for a moment. It only seemed to have one eye left. Then it started to scramble away amongst a lot of rubble. Its back legs didn't seem to be working, but it moved surprisingly fast. Jason said, "Oh God . . . !" and started to go after it.

"Oh, come on," said Leah irritably, "You can't go messing about after that now." Jeff switched the torch off and we started to walk on.

Jason stood still and said, "But we can't leave it here."

"What the hell else can we do with it? Come on."

Jason said, "Hand me that torch, Jeff."

A gun opened up not far away. I said, "I think we'd better get on, Jason. It sounds as though the fun's beginning again."

Jason said nothing, but took the torch from Jeff and started to scramble up the rubble heap. The light picked up the cat at the top of the heap for a moment and then it disappeared again over the top with its queer, rapid, maimed scramble. Jason stumbled and said, "Hell!" and went on after it.

There was a lot of noise all round now, and amongst it you could hear a plane flying unusually low. I think he was coming up the river and only just above cloud level.

Leah said, "Jason, *will* you stop shining that bloody torch and come *on*!"

Jason was on top of the pile. He said, "But it ought to be put out of its. . . ."

I heard that curious crescendo whistle and yelled, "Look out!" and hit the ground partly on top of Leah, with my chin in the middle of her back. I am not sure that I actually heard anything, but there was a curious sensation of something being torn open, and the ground seemed to heave so that I was thrown off Leah. There seemed to be complete silence for several seconds and then the windows fell out of a house about thirty yards away and tinkled into the street. As I raised my head Jeff said, "Everybody all right?" very slowly and with his drawl much exaggerated.

I said, "That was near enough," and started to get up. My legs were very shaky. Leah was just getting up, too. As she got to her knees she suddenly let out a terrific yell of "Jason!" It was a scream—not a frightened scream, but an angry one. Jason's voice said, "Coming!" and there was a slithering noise as he came down the rubble heap. Jeff was saying, "I don't think it was all that near but it was a big one," when there was a sharp crack as Leah slapped Jason hard across the face and said, "You bloody little fool! You bloody, *bloody* little fool!"

Jeff said, "Hey—steady, children."

Leah said, "Going mucking off like that after a maimed cat. We might all have been killed, and it would have served you right, you fool, you silly little fool . . . !"

Even in the darkness I could see that she was shaking all over. Jason said, "Sorry, darling," very gently, and put a hand on her arm, but she shook him off and shouted, "Don't touch me—I don't want anything to do with you. You're not

180

fit to be about, you silly little runt." With that she set off towards Sloane Square.

I went after her and said, "Leah—where are you going?"

"To drive an ambulance. At least that's a useful thing to do and not like going messing about after cats."

"But you can't go like this, my dear. You're all shaken up and. . . ."

She said, "I'm not in the least shaken up. For God's sake go away, all of you, and let me alone."

She set off again. Jason said quietly, "Let her go, Henry."

I said, "But she's in no state. . . ."

"Well, damn it all, she's my girl, isn't she?" he said with sudden fury. For a moment I thought he was going to hit me.

There was a silence and then Jeff said, "What I think we all need is a drink."

Jason said, "Hadn't we better go and see what that hit? There might be something we could do."

"All right. But I think it was probably just the other side of the river."

We walked down in the general direction of the explosion, but Jeff must have been right, because there was nothing new on our side. It must have been at least half a mile away. That was always happening. You were always feeling that one had landed almost on your big toe, and then finding that it wasn't even in the same postal district. We went back to Cheyne Walk. The windows were still all right, and when we asked Rose if the bomb had shaken her she said it had a bit, but not as much as the week before. Altogether there didn't seem to be much to have been lying in a heap in the street about, which was rather irritating. We were all very jumpy, and Jeff and Jason nearly had a row about where it could have landed. Then we had a drink, and that helped a lot.

181

Later on Jeff said, "By the way, what happened to the cat, after all that?"

Jason said, "I shot it."

"Shot it? When?"

"Just before the bomb fell."

"But what with?"

"My revolver. It had to be put out of its misery. Its back legs were paralysed." Jason was looking at him with wide sad eyes.

Jeff, who did not know Jason very well, looked baffled and said, "But you haven't got your revolver, Jason."

"No, but I had then. I took it off when I came in. It's in the kitchen."

I caught Jeff's eye and shook my head at him and he said nothing. Jason said, "I'll go and get it and show you." He went and fetched the revolver, took it out of its holster, and said, "There you are." It looked as though it had not been fired for months, and probably hadn't. Jason looked at it thoughtfully for some seconds, and then put it back in the holster and said, "Let's play the pianola."

There was another raid in the early hours of the morning, after we had gone to bed. But it was not as heavy as the first, and nothing came very near us. Leah came in at about seven, very tired, and said that the first one had been very bad, and that there had been a ghastly mess from a direct hit on a pub just off the Old Kent Road. Nobody said anything more about the cat business, and about nine we all went off to our jobs. As we were on the way to Highgate, Jeff said, "Why on earth did Jason say he shot that cat? He can't possibly have done."

I said, "Of course not."

"Then why say so?"

"He does that sort of thing at times."

182

"But why, Henry? I don't see the point."

I said, "Nor do I entirely. Usually it's when he thinks something would be pleasant, or pleasanter, for all concerned, so he says it's happened. He thinks it would be better if the cat had been shot, so he says he shot it."

"Does he really *believe* he shot it?"

"Oh no. I don't think so. I doubt if he even thinks *you* believe it."

Jeff shook his head and said, "I don't get it."

* * * * *

Until Dunkirk, Pearson had never been able to get anyone to give us work to do. From the end of 1940 right to the end of the war the problem was not to find the work but to find enough people to do even a part of it. One of the first things we tackled was Pearson's old problem about the amount that the infantryman had to carry; and for several months in 1941 Jeff and I plodded and doubled about Salisbury Plain in full infantry equipment, breathing into Douglas bags. It was hard work, but quite amusing, and in the end we produced a report which said in effect that if you gave the infantryman too much to carry, he rapidly became tired. But it also said a few other more original and practical things, and some of its suggestions were adopted.

We were still working on this in the summer of 1941. I had gone down to spend a few hours with my parents in Hampshire, as I often did. Jeff was with me, and we were sitting in the garden in deck-chairs, as a change from working in full equipment, when my father came out looking very smug and said, "Hitler's invaded Russia. He always invades somewhere when you're here."

I said, "Has he, by God!"

"Yes." My father frowned, and shook his head. "You know, to a historian, the man's almost embarrassing. After all—to conquer most of Europe—to come and sit on the

183

coast looking at England—to find you can't get at it, and then go off and invade Russia . . . ! He can't possibly have a sense of humour to run as true to Napoleonic form as that. Or perhaps that's the whole point. He wants to show that he can do it all, too. I expect he'll be putting one of his relatives on the throne of Spain next."

Jeff said, "Well, it's extremely comforting, sir. After all, there's so *much* of Russia and so *many* Russians. . . ."

"Moreover," said my father, "I don't doubt that people will now talk knowingly about General Janvier and General Fevrier. But how much that's worth I don't know. Does winter make any difference nowadays?"

"It makes a hell of a lot of difference if you're marching," I said feelingly.

"But people don't march now, do they? They motor and fly. I fear that General Janvier and General Fevrier are now old-fashioned Blimps. But still, I'm glad Hitler's done it. It will give people who like saying things like that a chance to say history repeats itself."

I saw Jason for a few moments about a fortnight later. He said, "I say, this is an awfully good thing about Russia, isn't it?"

"Well, yes. As it puts about another two hundred divisions on our side, I should say it is."

"Yes. And, of course, it puts everything right again for Leah, you see."

"Why?"

"Well, she had a terrible time over the Russo-German pact, and the carving up of Poland, and the Russians invading Finland and so on, because being a Communist she had to explain it all, and she didn't really believe the explanation. When we heard about the Russo-German pact she cried, and really she's hardly been the same girl since. But now, of course, it's all fine, with Russia on our side,

184

and she's almost getting out the old paint pot and brush."

I said, "I don't quite see what she's going to put on the walls now. It can hardly be just 'Down with Hitler.'"

"Oh, I don't mean literally. But she's back to form, if you see what I mean. By the way, did I tell you about poor old Arthur?"

"Arthur who?"

"Arthur Laidlaw. You know Arthur's a pacifist?"

"Yes."

"Well, he was in some ministry or other—I think it was the Ministry of Health. Anyhow it was a perfectly good and necessary job, but not directly to do with the war. Of course he was too young to be reserved, so they called him up for a medical. Well, poor old Arthur's got a funny spine and a weak heart and flat feet and God knows what, and there wasn't a chance that any of the Services would take him. But being Arthur he wouldn't just go and take the medical and be turned down. He insisted on going before a Conscientious Objectors' tribunal.

"Well, old Arthur was in full flood telling the tribunal about his conscience when the chairman, who was rather a tough old boy, suddenly stared at him and said, 'Wait a minute. Have you got a spinal curvature?' Arthur said, 'Yes. I also have a weak heart and flat feet.' The chairman said, 'Well then, what d'you want to come here wasting our time for?' Arthur said, 'I do not feel that the issue is one of physical disability but of conscience, sir.' The old boy grunted and said, 'Well, with that lot you can have any sort of conscience you like,' and with that they sent him back to his job. Poor old Arthur was furious about it. I think he hoped they'd send him to jail or something."

I said, "Do you see much of him?"

"Oh no," said Jason hastily. "I never see him. You see, Leah doesn't like him."

"Then how do you know about this?"

"Oh—well—somebody who was there told me."

That was somewhere in the summer of '41, and it was the last I saw of Jason for a long time, because a week later I went down into the West Country and started what I suppose was one of the most useful jobs I did in the war, on tanks. It was straightforward enough. Being a member of a tank crew is fine as long as you are driving along a road with the lid up, looking out of the turret and whistling at the girls. But when you are travelling over rough country with the lid down, it begins to be a tough job. If you are driving, you can see the bumps coming, but if you are in the turret you can't, and you get thrown about and bruised quite a lot. What is more, if you do it again the next day, you hit the same bruises on the same bit of tank again, which after a few days can be very unpleasant. To crown it all, when this work started, you only had to have your guns firing for a few minutes, and everybody began to be poisoned by the fumes. My terms of reference were to find out what would be likely to happen to tank crews under battle conditions, and after about a week going at it really hard, the answer seemed to be that they would mostly be in hospital with concussion or broken bones or multiple bruising or carbon monoxide poisoning, without the enemy having to do anything about it.

I can't say I vastly enjoyed this job. It was too uncomfortable and exhausting; and to this day when I think of hell I always imagine it as being rather like eternally travelling fast in the turrets of a tank, over rough country on a very hot day with all the guns going. But at least one felt that the job was worth doing, and at the start I went at it with such enthusiasm that after a couple of months I was rather a wreck, and had to be pulled out for a rest. After that we got three more people on the job, and could share the work out a bit.

This went on until some time at the beginning of '42. Then one day Pearson sent for me and said, "I think you've had enough of tanks for a bit."

I said, "There's still a hell of a lot to do."

"I know. But Freddie can carry on now. Would you like to go and jump out of aeroplanes?"

"No. I can't bear heights. Why?"

"Well, the parachute people are getting going and there's obviously a lot for us to do. But it's no good unless the people who do it are prepared to jump themselves. Nobody's going to take any notice if we just stay on the ground and theorize. I thought you might like it." Pearson sounded disappointed.

I said firmly, "I don't think I should like it at all."

"Jeff's there and *he* says it's rather fun."

"He would."

"I don't want to *press* you into it, Henry. It's a job for a volunteer. But the difficulty is that most of our people are a bit old for the job and liable to break themselves. Anyhow, think it over."

I went away and thought it over, and the more I thought about it the less I liked it. I dislike even looking over the parapet of a high building let alone jumping out of an aeroplane. On the other hand, it was difficult to see how I could get out of it. I was the youngest and fittest person we had.

But even then the fantastic luck that I had all through the war still held. Two days later I went to Pearson and said, "About this parachute job. I suppose I had better do it. I don't see who else there is."

Pearson said, "Fine, Henry. Thank you. But I'm afraid I've got to disappoint you in one way." He paused and grinned at me. "They aren't at all keen for you to jump."

Since for the last forty-eight hours I had been seeing myself falling like a stone from 10,000 feet with a parachute that wouldn't open, it was a moment before I could take this in.

I said, "But I thought we agreed that it was no good going if we didn't jump?"

"That's what I thought. But it seems that all sort of people —senior officers and so on—have been going up there and chucking themselves out of aeroplanes to encourage the boys and show how brave they are. And since they hadn't been trained for the job, of course a lot of them have been breaking ankles and generally messing themselves up. The people up there are very short of aeroplane time and every-thing else, and they're very fed up with these stray characters. So they've made a rule that nobody is to jump who hasn't absolutely got to; and that in any case people have to do six weeks' training first. They say that Jeff's jumping is quite enough for us, and that what they want is somebody to come and get on with some of the stuff which can be done on the ground."

"Is there anything to be done on the ground?"

"Well, my dear man, when these chaps have jumped, their job's only begun. They've got to fight afterwards, haven't they?"

That is how I became a chairborne assistant to airborne forces, and became quite an expert in the physiology of the thing, without ever jumping off anything higher than a ten-foot wall.

One of the first people I met on the job was Jackson, who had been with the outfit since it started and had made as many jumps as anybody there. He was now acting as a sort of half-qualified psychiatrist instead of as an ordinary doctor, dealing with what he described as "the mental problems arising from people insisting on being so damned brave."

"And really, Henry," he told me, on our first evening together, "really, these are the only *important* problems there are in the job. I don't deny that you physiological people can do a lot that's useful. Jeff's done some fine work on landing postures and how not to break your leg and so on. But the main problem is what to do about ingrowing heroism."

"You mean people being reckless."

"Not exactly. You see, in the purely statistical sense, jumping out of a plane with a parachute isn't so wildly dangerous, for a trained man. Landing's always rather an uncomfortable business, and can be a very uncomfortable one if you're swinging. But the chance of actually being *killed* because your chute doesn't open or something is very small indeed. On the other hand it does *feel* uncommonly dangerous, and most of the people who volunteered in the early days did so to show somebody, usually themselves, how brave they were.

"Now, the really excessively brave chaps aren't usually the calmest of most stable citizens, and an outfit consisting almost entirely of them isn't likely to be very calm or stable either. So there used to be a mildly hysterical note about the whole outfit, with a lot of people cracking up, and refusing orders to jump and so on. And since a trained man who refuses to jump has to be court-martialled, it all became a bit alarming to the top brass. So nowadays we pipe down on the knight-in-shining-armour suicide-squad aspect of the job, and try and get people to see that this is just another way of getting troops to the right place, and that what matters isn't jumping out of a plane, but what you do after you've hit the ground."

I stayed at Hanwick for six months and did quite a lot of useful stuff, mainly on clothing and equipment. But I never really enjoyed it. It was Jeff's job rather than mine, and somehow, though everybody was very nice to me, I never really felt part of the outfit.

In the time I was there, only one man was killed by a

parachute failure and the effect was most extraordinary. Nobody talked about it, but you could *feel* the tension like a silent scream. That afternoon Jackson went out and did four jumps in succession. Afterwards he came into the mess where there were a lot of people, limping slightly and cursing, and said loudly, "Of all the bloody uncomfortable jobs ever invented, this is the bloodiest. I've twisted my ankle and I've got a bruise the size of a saucer on my blasted hip." It was beautifully done.

A week later I was moved to Rushton, the preliminary training place, to work on the ground training exercises for jumpers, and it was there somewhile in the summer of '42 that I saw the name of Captain J. R. Pellew among a list of new arrivals. Jason arrived two days later, and his opening words were, "Oh, hallo, Henry. I say, there's been a hell of a row about the pianola."

He looked fit and cheerful. I had not seen him for months, but, characteristically, he had very little news. Leah, it appeared, was well but bored. Lady Peasmore had returned unexpectedly to Cheyne Walk and had found the usual odd menagerie in possession, including a large negro sailor whom Jason had picked up somewhere and given a bed for the night. She had taken the whole matter very calmly, until she had found that the pianola was not at the right place in "The Blue Danube." She had then flown into a violent temper and accused Jason of having played it. "And nothing I can say will convince her that I haven't, Henry. I explained that the bombing must have jerked it on or something, but she won't have it. She's a suspicious old woman. So now we're not on speaking terms—or at least, not very."

I said, "Why did you join this racket?"

"Well, there didn't seem to be very much to do, and I got rather fed-up, and I thought it might be fun. Is it?"

I said, "I don't know. I don't jump. But Jeff Hays likes it."

"I think I probably shall, you know. Anyhow I had to do something. It was all getting too boring."

"Does Leah approve?"

"Well . . . she doesn't actually know yet. You know how she fusses. But I'm pretty sure she will in a way, because, after all, it is getting *on* with it, Henry—with the war I mean. And Leah's been being awfully bitter."

"What about?"

"About *not* getting on with it. I mean she's furious about our not having invaded Europe to help Russia. She's even gone out and painted things about it on walls like she used to. So I don't see that she can really make much fuss if I do this."

I saw what had happened. It was the thing that had happened so often before—about Fascism—about Spain— about joining the Army; and it made me angry every time. I said, "I wish to God Leah would stop painting things on walls and use her brains. She must know that we're all doing our damn'dest to help Russia."

Jason said, "Yes. But you see, Henry, it's different for her."

I saw him every day for the next six weeks. There was no jumping at Rushton—only the preliminary ground training exercises. But I had seen a good many people go through the course by then, and if it is possible to be a born parachutist, then, physically speaking, Jason was one. He was neat, compact and very strong for his size, with that rare sense of balance and physical trainability which he had since childhood; and as far as one could see his attitude to the job was just right—neither over-heroic nor over-nervous.

In other ways, however, I was less happy about him. He was all right with me, but with other people, in the mess and elsewhere, he seemed to have gone back a step—almost to the days of the "amicable eccentric." As Jackson had said, volunteers as parachutists were a mixed bunch, and we always had a fair number of people at Rushton who seemed to feel that having joined Airborne meant being almost childishly tough and rowdy. As soon as he arrived, Jason joined up with a wild Irishman named O'Hallorhan, a Glasgow Scot named Lumsden, and a curious, rather loutish West Countryman named Roberts, who were the star toughs of the moment. They were always about together. The other three were all big men and Jason hardly came up to their shoulders. But they hadn't a brain among them, and they accepted him as a sort of mixture of ringleader and pet.

I went into a pub one night just before closing time, and the four of them were there. The three toughs were sitting on stools at the bar with two girls, one of whom was rather pretty. Jason was playing at a pin-table machine in the corner. He played slowly and with great care, and seemed to be taking no notice of the others.

It was a big room and rather full, and none of them saw me. The three at the bar were making a lot of noise and seemed slightly, but not very, drunk. They were doing no particular harm, except that they turned rather aggressively and rudely when anybody wanted to get to the bar to get a drink. But there was that slight general air of discomfort about the place that one can always feel in a bar when somebody is making too much noise and generally being obtrusive.

After a while Jason stopped playing and sat for a moment looking at the backs of the others and their girls. His face was peculiarly blank and expressionless. Then he placed a coin in the machine and started to play again.

I went over to him and said, "What-ho."

Jason looked up and said, "Oh—hallo. Have a drink."

I said, "I don't think I will, thanks. I've got to get back to camp. You coming back?"

"Not for a bit," he nodded towards the bar, "I'm with the boys."

192

"You don't seem to be very much with them."

"No. But I must see them back. Anyhow, I want to see what will happen."

"I should have thought what will happen is pretty obvious."

"Yes. But it's a question of who'll get Clare. You see nobody wants the other. They all three want Clare." He looked at me for a moment in silence and then added almost defiantly, "I'll bet I can tell you what will happen. I know the boys by now."

"Well—what will?"

"It's really awfully interesting," he said dully. "The girls always go for Pat first—I mean he's the one who picks them up in the first place and so on. But after a bit—I mean after half an hour or so, they get tired of him and go on to Lumsden or even sometimes Robby. You look now." He jerked his head towards the bar. The pretty girl was sitting between O'Hallorhan and Lumsden, and now she was giving her entire attention to the Scotsman.

Jason said, "It's awfully interesting, isn't it?"

I said, "Not as interesting as all that. At least not to me." I got up.

Jason said quickly, "Don't go. Have a drink."

"No, thanks."

"Well then, have a go at this thing. I've just scored six thousand seven hundred."

He put a penny into the machine and shot the balls into position.

"There you are. Have a try. I'll bet you can't beat six thousand seven hundred." He said it anxiously—almost entreatingly, and I realized suddenly that it mattered a great deal that I should not go.

I said, "Oh, for God's sake, Jason, you don't want to sit around watching those toughs squabbling about which of them shall have a girl. Come on back to camp."

He hesitated for a long moment and then said sullenly, "There's nothing to do back at camp."

"There's nothing to do here."

"I can't leave the boys."

"Oh, damn the boys. They wouldn't even notice you'd gone."

"No. I came out with them so I can't leave them."

"Well, what do you want to do? Sit around until they get drunk and start fighting? Where's the fun in that?"

Lumsden, the Scot, suddenly turned round and shouted, "Jason! Where are you, you little runt?" He saw us sitting together and laughed in a silly way and said, "Oh—pardon." He turned back to the others and said something and they all roared with laughter. One of the girls looked at us over her shoulder for a moment, and then turned back and put her arm round Lumsden.

Jason said doggedly, "There's nothing to do back at camp." He stared at me in silence for a moment, and his mouth was twitching so that for a moment I thought he was going to cry.

I said, "Oh, come on—cheer up," rather uncomfortably.

He said, "There's nothing to do. There never has been anything to do. Not at Cambridge. Or before that. Or in Spain. Or in France, except for a few days. I'm twenty-five and there still isn't anything to do. I can't even have Leah."

A good many people felt like that in 1942, and there was never any real answer. I said, "Well, in a fortnight's time you'll be going to Hanwick and then you'll be able to jump out of aeroplanes and enjoy yourself."

Jason hesitated and then grinned the shy grin and said, "Yes. There's that. You know, I think I might rather like it. I wish you were coming."

"Jeff and Jacko are both there. I've told them you're coming."

There was a short silence and then Jason suddenly got

up and gave a little bow and said politely, "Excuse me,
Henry—I think perhaps I ought to go and talk to the
boys. . . ."

I said, "That's all right. I'm going anyhow." I knew I
had failed him somehow, but I couldn't see how or what
to do about it. As I left the bar I saw the girl who had her
arm round Lumsden put her other arm round him. Standing
at the bar, his head was only level with hers as she sat on the
high stool.

About three weeks later I received a letter from Jackson.
Jacko was a great letter writer. He wrote, "The lad Pellew
arrived as per your advices and yesterday cast himself down
from a pinnacle of the Temple—to wit a Wellington—for
the first time, arriving safely on earth without incident,
accident or mishap. His claims to have enjoyed the experience
and his eagerness to repeat it as often as possible are,
perhaps, a little over-emphatic, but, as you know, that is
normal with a certain sort of new boy. I am allowed now
to go up with some of the young entry when they make
their first jumps, and I saw J. Pellew go through the hole
for the first time, which he did not only without hesitation,
but with almost suspicious alacrity. Frankly, I could not
help being glad that we work with static line, and don't
leave people to pull the opening string themselves, as I had
a suspicion that J. Pellew might not have bothered to do so.
This suspicion was confirmed later by conversation and
observation in the mess, since beneath a cloak of bonhomous
eccentricity, the lad seems to be carrying about a death-wish
the size of an elephant. However, I gather there is a girl in
the case, so it may be that the death-wish is not a death-wish
but a frustrated life-wish—in other words that the lad just
wants his woman, as don't we all. There is nothing like
modern psychology for arriving slowly and polysyllabically
at the obvious.

You, by the way, seem to be something of a father-figure in J. Pellew's life—and a slightly repressive one. Have you, in fact, Dutch-uncled him much? Or just your usual amount? Anyhow, I will continue observations and report later."

* * * * *

It was amazing to see, as the war went on, how the Army accumulated experts. They started to build up immediately after Dunkirk and went on until, by the end, we had experts on very nearly anything you could think of, and on one or two things that you probably never *would* have thought of.

It was not really difficult to become an expert. All you had to do was to be in at the beginning of something that the Army had not tried before or studied, and therefore knew nothing about. Thereafter, in six months' time, you might not be an expert, but you were the nearest thing to one available.

This was the process by which I became an expert in training parachutists. As I have said, I never made a jump in my life. But by 1943 I was one of the most knowledgeable pavilion parachute critics in the business, and saw nothing funny in lecturing parachute instructors on how to do their job. Nobody else seemed to see anything funny in it either. Perhaps there wasn't anything.

I was therefore surprised, and even slightly hurt, when early in 1943 Pearson sent for me and told me that I was to be moved to a new job. The main tide of the war had turned by then. In the autumn there had been the German disaster at Stalingrad, followed shortly by the invasion of North Africa. It was as clear as daylight that sooner or later there would be an Anglo-American invasion of Europe, and that airborne forces would be vitally important. We were desperately busy with training, and it was difficult to see what I could do which would be of greater value.

I said something like this. Pearson just nodded and said, "Well, we'll see. You know Colonel Fry who was in here the other day?"

"Little dark man?"

"Yes. Well, he wants you."

"What for?"

Pearson hesitated and said, "He runs an outfit called the Parachute Testing Station."

I said, "I didn't know there was such a place."

"Well, in a way there isn't, Henry. It's all rather complicated."

"I don't get it."

"No. Well, I think I'd rather Fry told you about it himself. He's coming in this afternoon."

Colonel Fry was a small man with wiry black hair, a yellow skin and very dark eyes. He did not look English. Pearson simply introduced me to him and then went away and left us together. Fry then started to cross-examine me about what I had been doing. He had a curious, abrupt, rather unfriendly manner, and my first impression was that I was not at all sure that I wanted to work for him. He obviously knew quite a lot about parachute work, without by any means knowing it all.

After a while he said, "You take six weeks training people on the ground before you let them do a drop. Could that be shortened?"

I said, "It might—if we had more instructors and more equipment."

"And could the training in dropping be shortened?"

"Once again—it might, if we had more plane time and so on."

He nodded, "Well, supposing you had everything you want—one instructor to each man, and all the equipment and plane time you want . . . ?"

"It would be much quicker then, of course."

He nodded again and sat in silence for a while. Then he said, "Well, I've got a job for you. I run the Parachute Testing Station, which isn't a place for testing parachutes."

Light began to dawn at last. I said, "It's a cover for something else?"

"Yes. It's called Parachute Testing because people are bound to see drops going on, and the name offers them a reason why. In fact we do two things. We train certain people in parachute work; and then later on we drop them where they've got to be dropped."

"Agents?"

"That sort of thing. There are a lot of places in Europe that we can get people into in other ways. But sometimes they have to be dropped. We do that."

Fry paused and frowned. "They're a mixed bag. Normally they've never done any parachute work before. But when we want them we usually want them quickly. We can't afford to mess about for a couple of months. That's where you come in." He paused and then said abruptly, almost rudely, "Well—d'you want the job?"

"It sounds very interesting."

"All right then. I've fixed it with Colonel Pearson, and I've had you screened. You'll have to see my security people and be sworn, and listen to a lecture about not telling friendly strangers in trains all about it. All of which is quite useless. People either talk or they don't."

I said, "I don't think I do."

He looked at me for a moment with the rather mournful dark eyes. "No," he said, almost contemptuously, "if you did, you wouldn't be here. Anyhow, the best way on this job is to know as little as possible. Then you can't give much away."

After he had gone Pearson sent for me and said, "Well— I gather you're going?"

I said, "Nobody seemed to be offering me much choice."

Pearson lit his pipe and said, "What exactly are you going to *do*, Henry?"

I was just going to tell him when I saw his eyes flicker up for a moment from the bowl of his pipe. I said, "I really don't know, A.P. He was very vague. Presumably test parachutes." My cloak-and-dagger period had begun.

The Parachute Testing Station was a curious place. Its headquarters were a very large fake-Elizabethan country house. We used some of it for ground training. I never knew, and still don't know what went on in some other parts of the place, though I know there was a department that spent its whole time faking identity papers and ration cards for every part of Europe, and a wardrobe department that dressed people for the jobs they were going to do. The aerodrome was about two miles away and might have been a normal, rather small R.A.F. station. Colonel Fry's principle that if you knew nothing you couldn't give anything away, permeated the whole place, and nobody ever talked about work in the mess—or indeed at any other time unless it was absolutely necessary. It was an uncommonly lonely and unfriendly place, and until I went there I had never realized how dependent men are on being able to talk shop.

My job was comparatively simple. We never had more than half a dozen trainees at a time, and to deal with them I had three ground instructors, and two drop instructors over at the aerodrome. The trainees themselves were a very mixed bunch. They always arrived in the charge of an officer, who lived with them in one of the lodges in the grounds and never, as far as I could see, let them out of his sight. There were Englishmen, Frenchmen, Poles, Italians and even occasionally Germans, or people who sounded like Germans. They seemed to come from every social class, and they were all shapes, sizes and ages. We had one Frenchman who must have been well over fifty, but surprisingly enough he never broke himself. One or two spoke practically no English, which made things difficult. They seemed to be under the most rigid discipline, and on the whole they were easy to train. In the whole time that I was there, I only remember one refusal to jump and then the man concerned — an Englishman — disappeared immediately after, and I never saw him again. Almost without exception, when on the job they were grave, quiet and unsmiling; though I believe that in their own mess they occasionally let go to some purpose. We were not encouraged to have anything to do with them outside working hours.

Usually they stayed with us for about a fortnight doing as intensive a course as possible. I don't know what else they were taught during this period, but I know they did do other things in the evenings. Then, after the fortnight, or sometimes a little longer, they would go, and another batch would arrive.

For my first few months at the place that was all I did and all I saw. The people came, we trained them, they went away, and more came. Then one day Colonel Fry called me into his office. He seldom dined in the mess, and was away a good deal, so that I had seen very little of him since my appointment.

Fry said, "Do you remember Dupont?"

"The young Frenchman who was here about a month ago, sir?"

"Yes. Well, he's going tonight. Care to come and see your pupil off?"

"I should like it very much."

"All right. I'll pick you up at the mess at ten."

That was all. I have no idea why he suggested it.

Punctually at ten he picked me up and we drove out to the aerodrome. It was a perfect night and the moon was rising. The colonel looked up at the sky and said, "Nice weather." Otherwise we did not speak. I desperately wanted to ask him where Dupont was going and what he was going to do, but one did not ask Colonel Fry questions. I remembered Dupont well. He was a big, handsome, cheerful young Frenchman who had once made a joke during instruction, which was almost unheard of.

The lights were not on, of course, but we could see the outline of a Wellington on the runway in the moonlight, and as we got out of the car she started to warm up with a rumble and a roar. There were a group of half a dozen people standing some distance from the plane, with a subdued light shining on a table with a map on it. I recognized Dupont by his height. He was wearing a heavy belted overcoat and I remember thinking, "Surely he isn't going to drop in that?"

The others were all talking together and nobody seemed to be taking any notice of him. He was standing a little apart from them, staring at the plane and chewing gum. I could not see his expression in the dim light.

Fry went up to the other group, and exchanged a curt word with them, and then went over to Dupont, who greeted him with a bow and a charming smile. They shook hands and Fry said something and Dupont bowed again. Then Fry beckoned me and said, "Here's Captain Payne come to see you off."

For a moment I don't think Dupont recognized me. Then he said, "Ah . . . !" and beamed and took my hand in both his.

I said, "The very best of luck, Dupont."

He laughed and said, "Yes, I know all, eh?" and put his feet and knees together in a caricature of what we had taught him. His English had never been very good. One of the people from the other group came up and said, "All set, sir."

Dupont spread out his hands and said, "O.K." He shook hands again with Fry and me and bowed but said nothing. Then he walked briskly away towards the Wellington with his hands in his pockets. A few moments later the lights came on, and she taxied away into the distance. Fry immediately said, "Well, that's that," and made for the car, so that we did not even see her take off. But we heard the noise, and as we drove out of the aerodrome she went roaring overhead on a southerly course. Fry took a deep breath and said, "Good. Very good."

I said, "He's a good chap."

"Yes," said Fry without enthusiasm. "He's too young, of course, but you have to take what you can get."

Even then I did not ask any questions, so I never knew why Dupont was too young, nor why I was taken to see him off, nor indeed what happened to him.

*   *   *   *   *

One of the difficulties about life at the Parachute Testing Station was that one was very much cut off from the rest of the world. For some reason, we were not allowed to receive personal letters there, which struck me as a peculiarly silly piece of "security," since literally thousands of people must have known that the place existed, even if they did not know what it did. Worse, Fry was very grudging about leave. I think he felt that every time one of us went away from the place, there was a risk that we should end up trotting it all out in the arms of a blonde enemy agent. I had been at the place nearly four months and was sick of the sight of it and completely stale, before he allowed me to go to London to collect letters, see Pearson, and find out if my parents were alive or dead.

There were a lot of letters for me, most of which, by not

being answered, had answered themselves. The only surprising one was from Lady Peasmore, asking me to ring her at Cheyne Walk and go to dinner.

I had not seen Lady Peasmore since Jason and I sent her off from Paddington at the time of Munich, nearly five years before. She had then looked about eighty. She now looked a reasonable seventy, and moved about a great deal more easily. Her voice and manner were more like those of an elderly nannie than ever.

I don't know how she had done it, at a time when servants were practically unobtainable and food very difficult, but the house was practically back to normal. The dust sheets had gone, and the show-cases were in their places, carefully polished. I took a surreptitious look at the pianola, but there was no roll in it. I assume that she had accepted that the memorial to Sir Phillip's last moments had gone for ever. Apart from that, we might have been back in 1938. The meal itself was enormous, and certainly quite illegal. I reckoned that in the course of it Lady Peasmore ate at least two people's rations for a week. I asked her tentatively if she found food difficult and she replied briefly, "You get what you pay for the world over. You can't alter human nature." Jason told me long after that at least two people went to jail in seeking to provide Lady Peasmore with what she paid for.

I don't think she had ever liked me, and she certainly made no pretence of having asked me to dinner for the pleasure of my company, or of any interest in what I was doing. The whole idea was to pump me about Jason. "I have asked you here, Mr. Payne" (she did not notice my three pips, or preferred to disregard them), "I have asked you here because I wish to hear about my godson. There's something going on and I should be glad if you would tell me what it is." This was rather awkward, since I had no idea if she knew that Jason had joined Airborne Forces.

I said, "I'm afraid I shan't be much help to you, Lady Peasmore. I haven't seen Jason or heard from him for months."

"Well, I have," she said grimly. "I saw him a fortnight ago, and there's no possible doubt that something is going on. Jason may think that he can pull wool over my eyes, but he can't. I always know." She drank some claret, leaving a rim of grease where her lips had touched the glass. "The trouble with Jason," she said sharply, "is that he tells so many lies that even when he does tell the truth one doesn't believe him."

"What did he say he was doing?"

"This ridiculous flying nonsense."

"You mean parachute work?"

"Yes. Jumping out of aeroplanes and so forth."

"Well, he probably is. He certainly was when I saw him last."

"Why did you allow him to do anything as silly, Mr. Payne?"

"I had no means of stopping him, Lady Peasmore. It was his own affair."

She stared at me for a moment with her cold blue eyes and then gave a little grunt of contempt. "Well, *I* should certainly have put a stop to it if I had known in time. But of course I was lied to, as usual." She finished her claret and poured herself another glass before I could offer to do so. "But in any case, Mr. Payne, there's more behind this than I have been told. You say you don't know what it is?"

"No."

She stared at me for a moment in silence, as though making up her mind whether to believe me or not. "Then I should be glad if you will find out," she said coldly.

I said, "I can try, of course. But I'm very busy, and I'm not in touch with Jason. . . ."

"He will be in London tomorrow. You can take him out. I will, of course, repay whatever it costs you."

I started to say, "I doubt very much if there is anything . . ." but she waved her fork at me and said, "I don't mind what you 'doubt,' Mr. Payne. I am *quite certain*. And I may say that if there is any more of this hanky-panky, I shall have to get him out of the Army altogether."

She said it almost as a threat. I smiled and said, "I don't think you could do that, Lady Peasmore. Not as things are at present."

"Why not?" she said calmly. "There are hundreds of thousands of young men who aren't in the Army. I see them every day."

"Only because they are doing necessary jobs."

"Well, Jason is necessary here. It's quite wrong for a woman of my age to be living in this house with nobody but those two old creatures."

She turned and hacked herself off a very large piece of cheese with angry energy. "In any case," she said with finality, "Jason is my heir. Or *may* be. It might be worth while to remind him of the fact, if you profess to be his friend."

There was clearly nothing to be done with it. I said, "Lady Peasmore—I'll willingly take Jason out. I should like to anyhow. But I doubt very much if he is doing anything you don't know about; if he is he probably wouldn't tell *me*. There are a lot of things people don't talk about in a war."

"I suppose you'll soon be saying that 'there's a war on,' like the tradesmen," she said viciously.

"Well, there *is*, you know."

"I am quite aware of it, Mr. Payne," she said with dignity. "Nobody has better cause to know it than I." There was a short pause, and I saw to my horror that her eyes had filled with tears. "Bundled about," she said with quiet bitterness. "Sent here—sent there. My house turned into a shambles. No servants except useless old creatures. A struggle to get enough to eat. I don't think an old woman alone needs your reminder, Mr. Payne."

"I'm sorry," I said humbly. There seemed nothing else to say.

"Well, well," said Lady Peasmore gallantly. "Don't let's be morbid. We all have our difficulties. Now I expect you would like a glass of port?"

She was right about Jason, of course. I had expected that she would be. I should not have ranked Lady Peasmore as a very sensitive or percipient person, but anybody who had known Jason for some time did not need to be very sensitive or percipient to know when "something was going on." For a man who spent so much time and trouble trying to mislead people he was about as bad at it as anyone I have ever known. He had only three tricks—the wide-eyed, almost painfully honest gaze; the curious tone, with too much inflexion, like that of a rather bad amateur actor speaking lines in a bad play; and extremely good manners in small things. If Jason was telling you the truth he would cheerfully charge through doors ahead of you. If he was lying he always stood aside to let you go first. All these symptoms were there in a marked degree, and when we met he bowed over my hand as though I was an ambassador.

It was never any use to rush him. If I had asked him point blank what he was up to I should probably have been told that he was going as Military Attaché to Moscow, complete with circumstantial detail; I just took him out to dinner in Soho and waited.

It was not easy to wait very long over dinner in 1943. There wasn't enough of the dinner. By half-past nine it was becoming necessary to probe slightly. My private bet had been that he had married Leah. But there was no sign of a reaction here. Leah was well. She had more or less forgiven him for joining Airborne Forces, though there had been a

206

hell of a row at the time. She was still very bitter about our failure to invade Europe; thought that the invasion of North Africa was a deliberate evasion of the issue, was sure that the Western Powers wanted to see Russia conquered, and had had a miscarriage. Jason told me all this without even having to open his eyes any wider than usual. He also told me, with equal ease, about Airborne Training and a new type of parachute; about what a good fellow Jackson was; about the reasons why his old regiment had not been sent to Africa, and about a girl he had met in Manchester who was more beautiful than the dawn, but inaccessible. Altogether it was all very normal and uncommonly dull.

I then took him to a small club of which I was not a member, where he approved of the cigarette girl, drank nothing but tonic water, asked me about my work, accepted my standard cover story without comment or apparent interest, and then told me after the war he proposed to start a new form of market garden growing nothing but lettuce. He appeared to know a great deal about lettuce, and this took until nearly midnight. He then bought some cigarettes so as to be able to exchange gallantries with the cigarette girl and said, "By the way, do you happen to know a bloke named Colonel Clare-Hanson?"

It was a disconcerting question to be asked when I had spent about four and a half hours trying to get something out of Jason, for I did indeed know Colonel Clare-Hanson, but not, as it were, publicly. He was one of our three main contacts with London, and visited us about once a fortnight. For the life of me I could not avoid too long a pause, and then said vaguely, "Clare-Hanson? What does he do?"

"I don't know," said Jason. "I think he's something to do with the Foreign Office. Italy." I took a quick look round but there were not a dozen people in the place and the nearest were twenty feet away.

I said, "Clare-Hanson . . . I seem to have heard the name somewhere but . . . why? Do you know him?"

"Slightly," said Jason. He finished his tonic water. "As a matter of fact, he's offered me a job."

I saw it all then. I said, "Really? Doing what?"

"As second-in-command of a battery of Jim Pitt's Underground Artillery," said Jason promptly. "It's a new development and very hush-hush. The guns fire out of the breech instead of out of the muzzle, so you leave them about, the enemy captures them, tries to fire them at you, and gets blown up, causing roars of laughter. The recoil of the gun then causes it to run back into your lines."

I said, "What lines?"

"Well—if you *have* lines. Are you an enemy agent, Henry?"

"Yes."

"Then I think I'd better tell you about this, because it will gain you credit in your agency, which would be nice, and in any case I want your advice." Jason considered for a long time and then said, "This is tricky. What between the parts I don't know and the parts I can't very well tell you about. . . . Anyhow, about a couple of months ago I met an old boy who was a pal of my family years ago. He's immensely old and very retired of course. He took me out to dinner and asked me what I was doing. I told him, and happened to say I was a bit bored with everything."

"You're still bored?"

"Yes. Rather. Well, anyhow, this old thing can't really be as retired as he looks because a week later he produced this Clare-Hanson character. We dined together and talked about this and that, and he asked me to stick down the things I could do, if any. Well, as you know, Henry, apart from being a nifty gardener, about all I can do is to speak French and Italian pretty well. So I said so. There was then an interval, and I rather forgot about the whole thing." Jason hesitated.

"But I then saw Clare-Hanson again, and it appears that he has a vacancy in his business for somebody who can speak Italian."

"Coaching people at the Berlitz School of Languages?" I said to help him out.

"Exactly," said Jason gratefully. "Well, this is where I want your advice. This particular school of languages is some distance away, and the question is, what shall I tell Leah?"

I said, "Look here, Jason—is your Italian good enough for this?"

"For what?"

"For—for what Clare-Hanson wants?"

"I speak Italian about as well as an Englishman can."

"But is that good enough?"

"I think I could get by, Henry. In—in the particular bit of the school we're talking about anyhow."

"You realize that you *look* about as un-Italian as any man living?"

"That can be coped with, I understand." There was a long pause.

I said, "I don't really like it, Jason. Not if I've got the idea right."

"Well, you hardly could, Henry, from what I've told you."

"Oh God, it's clear enough," I said impatiently. "Anyhow, I know Clare-Hanson and his outfit."

Jason looked startled and, I thought, rather annoyed. "Ah well, then, we know where we are," he said rather huffily. "Anyhow, what do I do about Leah? I can't very well tell her."

"Of course not. You mustn't even give her a hint." I suddenly realized that I felt this very strongly, and that Leah must not be trusted an inch.

I said, "They'll give you a cover-story anyhow."

"Will they?"

"Of course. If you go away there's got to be some explanation of where you are and what you're doing. Otherwise the whole thing stinks."

"And you think I just tell her that?"

"You tell everybody that if you have to tell them anything." I hesitated and then said, "And for God's sake, Jason, *don't* start embroidering it, or you may land in an awful mess." It was striking me rather forcibly that if Clare-Hanson had known Jason as well as I did, he might have been a little uneasy about providing him with a cover-story, in case Jason thought up another that he liked better, probably with cannibals in it.

I said, "Any idea when you go?"

Jason stared me straight in the eye and said, "Oh no. We haven't got as far as that yet."

I reflected that as they hadn't to teach him to jump, it would probably be within the next three weeks. They never liked keeping people about.

I said, "Just one thing, Jason—I'd keep away from Cheyne Walk. Your godmother's already noticed that you're up to something."

Jason looked startled, "How could she? I haven't said a word."

I said, "No. Well, go on not saying one, and keep away."

*　　*　　*　　*　　*

I rang up Lady Peasmore next day and told her that I had had a long talk with Jason and was sure her fears were groundless though Jason appeared to have met a girl in Manchester whom he rather liked. Lady Peasmore contrived to convey cold disbelief and deep distrust of both of us in about six words over a telephone wire, and that was that.

I then went back to the Parachute Testing Station and thought it over. I can't say I liked it. Presumably, from what he had said and from what I knew of the form, they were going to drop Jason in Italy. Even if he was right, and his

Italian was good enough to get him by, he seemed to be about the last person to choose for such a job. A blind man in a dark room could always spot if Jason was trying to conceal something, and my own feeling was that he wouldn't get away with it for twenty-four hours.

On the other hand, it was difficult to see quite what I could do. I couldn't very well go to Clare-Hanson or Fry and say, "I understand that a friend of mine is joining you and I don't think he's suitable," without getting the very awkward question, "How do you know, anyhow?" And to do Jason justice, though he had told me more than he should, I should not have known exactly what he was going to do if I had not been in the racket myself.

In the end I hit on what seemed at the time an idea of subtle brilliance. I went to see Fry and said, "I don't know if what I am going to say is permissible, sir, but when I was in London the other day I met an old friend of mine named Jason Pellew."

"Yes," said Fry—and try as I might, I couldn't decide whether he had ever heard the name before.

"Well, Pellew is in Airborne Forces, sir, and fully trained in parachute work. He's also more or less tri-lingual— English-French-Italian."

"Yes?"

I said, "It did just occur to me that he might be useful to you. He's a tough little man with a lot of guts."

Fry did not say anything. He just went on sitting there staring at me with the very dark brown eyes. I said rather uncomfortably, "I hope you don't mind my mentioning it, sir. . . ."

"Not at all," said Fry. "Did you sound him?"

I am pretty sure that if the answer had been "Yes," I should have been court-martialled. I said, "Oh no. But it just occurred to me. . . ."

Fry said, "Pellew. All right. Thank you," and made a note.

Three days later he called me in and said, "You mentioned a Captain Pellew, Payne."

"Yes, sir."

"That's in hand."

"You're going to see him, sir?"

"It's in hand."

I took a deep breath and passed on to part two of the plan, "I think I should say, sir, that I can't be *sure* that you'll find him suitable. He has the qualifications that I told you about, but of course, I'm not certain that he could do the job—temperamentally speaking, I mean."

"Why not?" said Fry curtly.

"He's a rather strange person."

"If he wasn't he wouldn't want a job like this. Does he talk?"

"Not as far as I know."

"Drink?"

"No."

"Then what?"

Now that I had a chance to say it, it was very difficult to get into words. I said, "I just have doubts about—about his ability to carry off a thing of this kind single-handed. I'm not sure how good his languages are nowadays and. . . ."

"That's not our business. The experts can answer that. What else?"

I said, "He's—he's rather young—rather immature. He always has been. I have a nasty feeling that he might think the whole thing as a game and. . . ."

Fry nodded slowly in silence. After a while he said curtly, "That's my impression. What about it?"

"Is that sort of person suitable, sir?"

"No. But one may have to use them. This man's a friend of yours?"

"Yes, sir."

"Well, he's volunteered and been accepted. The people

who've accepted him know what they're doing. You can take it that he won't be allowed to do any harm. Except possibly to himself, and I'm afraid we can't worry about that."

"But surely, sir, if he doesn't get away with it . . . ?"

"Then he doesn't. What about it?"

Fry was staring out of the window. After a while he said. "Nobody goes off from here who hasn't got a reasonable chance—as chances go in this sort of job. There's too much trouble involved to waste time on things that are hopeless from the word go. But as long as there *is* a reasonable chance —a reasonable business risk—we've got to go ahead. Otherwise we should never send anybody anywhere." He went on staring moodily out of the window. Then he turned the dark eyes to me and said coldly, "D'you want to see Pellew before he goes?"

"I should very much like to, sir."

"Well, that's all right. You can come and see him off. Probably Friday."

"He's going from here?"

"He's been here two days," said Fry wearily. "At the Lodge. He doesn't appear to know that you're here, they tell me."

"Of course he doesn't."

"Well, I don't want him disturbed, Payne, so keep away and then just come and see him off. That clear?"

The Lodge was about a couple of hundred yards away in the grounds. One could see the lights of it from my bedroom. That night there seemed to be some sort of party and when I leant out of my window I could hear somebody playing a piano accordion, and some rather discordant singing. I thought once or twice that I recognized Jason's voice, but it may have been imagination.

*   *   *   *   *

Fry drove me out to the aerodrome in silence, as he had

213

done before. Looking back, I think he probably disliked this dispatching business more than I gave him credit for at the time. We did not go straight out on to the aerodrome but to a hut beside it. Fry said, "I've given you a bit longer this time."

The hut was the usual sort of Nissen affair. At one end of it a conference was going on over a map, as before. I glanced at the map as I passed the table, but it was on a big scale and there was no coast-line in it, so it did not tell me anything. Fry just jerked his head towards the other side of the hut and then joined the group round the map. I remember that a man in captain's uniform stood aside for him; I thought a trifle too deferentially.

I had somehow expected that Jason would be by himself—rather notably by himself, as Dupont had been. But he wasn't. He was sitting at the end of the room with two men. They were both talking at once in Italian with great animation, and Jason was sitting between them with his eyes shut, occasionally saying a word. He seemed to be smiling, but whether at what they were saying or at something else, I did not know.

His appearance was a shock to me. I don't know quite what I had expected—that they would have dyed his hair, or darkened his skin, or given him a barrel-organ and a monkey or what. But in fact they seemed to have done nothing to him whatever. He was wearing no hat, a British warm, and, of all things, a woollen scarf in our house colours. One of the men who was talking to him looked exactly like everybody's idea of an Italian, and beside him Jason, with his yellow mop of hair and his pink and white skin and those ridiculous clothes looked less like a typical Englishman than a typical English public schoolboy.

I went over and waited for a pause in the flood of Italian, but as none seemed likely, and as Jason still had his eyes shut, I said, "Hallo, Jason." He opened his eyes and stared at me for a moment. Then he said, "Oh, hallo, Henry," and at once looked away as though embarrassed. He made no move to get up, shake hands, or greet me in any way. Jason never greeted me very effusively and it is possible that they had told him I was coming. But even so, there was something odd about that immediate look away, and I thought his eyes seemed glassy, and as though he had difficulty in focusing them. It flashed through my mind that he might be drunk or drugged, but that seemed unlikely.

I stood there for a moment rather uncomfortably. The other two had stopped talking and were waiting politely. Jason was still not looking at me. Then suddenly he looked from one of them to the other and waved his hands impatiently and said something in Italian. I think he was saying that he wanted to talk to me. Anyhow, they smiled and got up at once and bowed to me and went away. I sat down and said, "Well, how's everything?"

Jason looked at me for a moment with the glassy eyes. Then he closed them again and the smile came back that I had noticed before. He said slowly and rather carefully, "Everything's fine. By tomorrow I shall be in a civilized country with some sun, while you poor bastards will still be here."

I had a curious impression that it was a formula—something that he had said many times before. I said, "I thought I'd better come and see you off."

"Yes," he said without interest. He opened his eyes and looked towards the two Italians who had crossed to the side of the hut. He said, "God, how those boys talk! There's nothing like Italians for talking about absolutely nothing."

"Are they coming with you?"

Jason hesitated and then said, "Well—not exactly *with* me. It's a sort of all-stations-to-London-Bridge affair."

He closed his eyes again and sat smiling quietly to himself in silence. I did not want to press him, but I saw the people

215

at the other end looking at their watches. I said, "Anything you want done?"

"No, thank you," he said politely, as though I had offered him a cigarette.

I said, "Look, Jason—just one thing. What did you tell Leah in the end—in case I see her?"

He said, "Oh, yes. Well, you might look her up and—and keep an eye on her, you know—like you've done before."

"Yes, but what have you told her? What's your cover-story?"

Jason wrinkled his forehead as though trying hard to remember something. "The general idea," he said slowly, "is that I've gone to North Africa to help with Airborne Training. She'll get various letters from me there."

"Fine. As long as I know."

He suddenly sat up and said very tensely, "Yes, Henry. But I've got pins-and-needles."

I laughed and said, "Well, that doesn't matter much either, does it?"

Jason said, "You don't know. Nor does anybody else. . . ."

There was a moment's pause and then he said in a low voice, "It's in my right leg. When I get pins-and-needles it means that ten minutes after my right leg just won't work. I can't even stand on it without falling down. I've had it before."

He said it in a way that startled me. The glassiness had gone out of his eyes and he was looking at me with a sort of terrified entreaty.

I said, "You've had it before?"

"Yes—two or three times."

"Well then, you must tell Fry or—or somebody. It's no good going off on a thing like this with a game leg."

He shook his head impatiently and said, "No—that's not the point. It's only a question of getting into the ruddy plane.

216

After that it's all right. It's sitting about. It gets stiff or something."

He looked down at his leg as though it was something frightening which belonged to another person. I could see that the muscles of the thigh were twitching violently.

He said, "Last time it happened I made them bunk me up into the plane, and of course it was all right. I knew it would be. But some of these people are such bastards. . . . Look here, will you come over to the plane, and then if it plays up, you can give me a bunk up when nobody's looking."

I said, "Of course I will. Anyhow it'll be all right because we're going now." The R.A.F. officer who was always in charge of these things was waving to us from the other end of the hut, and everybody was getting up and moving toward the door. We were at the end farthest from the door and that meant that they all had their backs to us. Jason gave an odd little grunt and got up, and then to my horror his right leg seemed to give way under him and I only just grabbed him in time to prevent him falling sideways over a chair.

He said, "Blast! . . . half a mo'," and stood leaning on my arm with his eyes shut.

I said, "Look—this is no good, Jason. . . ."

He opened his eyes and said very calmly, "Well, well, well. Collapse of small party. Lead on, will you, Henry—rather slowly. I think I see about this."

The others had gone out. I led him towards the door. He was leaning heavily on my arm, dragging his right leg as though it was made of lead. Suddenly he let go my arm and said, "I can make this work if I want to. But I have to tell it to make each step, which is odd. You watch." He moved towards the door swinging his leg though with a curious, stiff movement as though it was artificial.

I followed him through the door. It seemed very dark for a moment after the lights of the hut. I could just see the rest of the party as a dark patch in the darkness, twenty yards ahead. Jason said, "I'll bet I could make it dance if only I could concentrate on it. It's concentration that you need." It was difficult to tell in the darkness, but he seemed to be walking more normally.

There were engines running, but they seemed a long way away. The group ahead had paused beside some cars. We joined them. I found myself beside Fry. He said, "The plane's right out on the runway, Payne, so they're driving out to her. I don't think we'll bother."

I said, "I should very much like to go out, sir, if it's possible."

"Well, it isn't possible," he said curtly. He held out his hand to Jason and said, "Goodbye, Pellew, and good luck."

Jason said, "Thank you, sir," and gave his little bow over the hand.

Somebody said, "Captain Pellew . . ." and held the door of a car open.

Jason said, "Tomorrow morning I shall be in a civilized country with some civilized sun and you poor bastards will still be here," and got into the car with no trace of difficulty. He did not shake hands with me.

The window of the car was open and I said, "Well, good luck, Jason," into the darkness inside.

His voice said, "Thank you very much, Henry," very formally and politely, and then the cars moved slowly away towards the sound of the engines. She must have been a long way out, because this time we were back at the station before she went roaring overhead.

Fry pulled up at the door of the mess and said, "D'you want a drink?" as though he hoped I didn't.

I wanted a drink very much, but I did not want it with Fry at that moment. I said, "I don't think so, sir, thank you," and he nodded and drove away without a word.

*   *   *   *   *

It was all very well for Jason to tell me to "look Leah up," but I had no idea where she was living now, and in any case I was stuck down at the Station under Fry's beloved system of preventive detention. All I could do for the moment was to write to her Ambulance Station in the hope that she would still be there, and ask her to give a telephone number to Pearson's outfit, so that I could ring her when I was next in London.

In fact, it was three weeks after Jason had left before I went to Town again, and found an envelope containing a slip of paper which simply said, "Leah Garland. TRE 0020." There was no message.

I judged from this that Leah was cross. I was not surprised, but it didn't make the prospect of seeing her any more inviting. I had only those half-dozen words from Jason to tell me what his cover-story had been, and no idea whether he had told her that I knew anything about it or not. I half wished that I had never written to her and left her to get in touch with me if she wanted me.

However, there was nothing to be done about it now, so I rang her up and invited her to dinner. She was polite without being enthusiastic, but she accepted at once for the same evening. Neither of us mentioned Jason on the telephone.

I then sat down and tried to work out exactly what I was going to say to her. Clearly the thing to do was to let her tell *me* as much as possible of what Jason had told *her*. If she did not know that I knew anything about it, I could accept the whole thing as news. If she did, then I must just fit in with his story.

We had arranged to meet at 7.30 but it was not till 8.15, when I was beginning to think that there had been a muddle, that Leah turned up. She was not in uniform and she looked slimmer and longer than ever, and, I thought, unusually handsome. Leah was a person whom one never remembered as being particularly good-looking, but who often was when one saw her.

My heart sank as we greeted one another. She was entirely polite, and even smiled at me. But it was the wrong sort of smile, and as I was ordering her a sherry I caught her looking at me with the curious hard, slit-eyed expression that always meant trouble. I remember thinking with some irritation that "Keeping an eye on Leah" had always meant going and getting the rough edge of her tongue when Jason had gone off somewhere.

I said, "You got my letter, then? I wasn't sure if you'd still be there."

"I'm not," said Leah briefly. "It was forwarded."

"Been moved to another station?"

"Yes."

We sipped our sherry in silence for some time. Then Leah said, "What did you want to see me about?"

This was a trifle awkward. I hesitated and said, "Oh—just to see how everything was."

Leah smiled the wrong smile again and said, "That was very kind of you, Henry."

I realized that she was going to make it as difficult as possible so I took the plunge and said, "And about Jason of course."

"Yes?" she said. "And what about Jason?"

I said, "Let's order first. I hate people coming and waving the menu when I'm talking."

I have no idea what we ordered, but ordering gave me time to work out my next bit.

I said, "I heard about his new job, but only very briefly."

"You saw him before he went?" she said politely.

"Yes. For about five minutes. I gathered that he was off to North Africa on some Airborne Training job, but that was about all. I thought you might know more details."

Leah said, "Oh yes. I know all about it. I've even had a

letter from him. I've brought it along in case you'd like to see it. It doesn't say much, but then Jason's letters never do."

She fumbled in her bag, produced the letter and tossed it across to me with an odd, jerky gesture.

I took it out of the envelope, inwardly thanking God for the efficiency of the organization. It was an excellent letter for the purpose, saying practically nothing, referring vaguely to people she would never have heard of, indicating that he was well and rather enjoying himself but that it was "damned hot," and ending with a lot of affection.

I put the letter back in the envelope and said, "Well, he seems to be all right, anyhow."

Leah said, "He was all right when he wrote that."

"How long ago did you get it?"

"About ten days ago."

She suddenly put out a hand as I offered her the letter and waved it away. "No—please—you keep it. I don't want it."

I said, "But why, Leah? It's your letter."

Leah said in a low voice, "When did you see him last?"

"Just before he went."

"As he was getting into the aeroplane?"

"Well no. But the same day. Why?"

She laid down her knife and fork and placed them carefully together and said, "You silly bloody fool."

"Why am I a fool?"

"You silly fool. You silly *bloody* fool."

My mind went back to the night of the bomb and the cat. I said sharply, "Steady now, Leah."

She said, "You've always professed to know Jason *so* well and to understand him *so* beautifully, and yet you think he could keep that from me!"

"But he didn't keep it from you, my dear girl. He told you he was going."

"Yes, my dear fool, he did. And he told me where."

I glanced round instinctively. Leah laughed bitterly and said, "It's all right. Don't worry. Nobody can hear, and if they did I expect most of them have heard it several times before."

I said, "I don't know what you're saying, Leah."

"I can't think where any of your brains can have been," she said. "Surely you know by now that the little man never kept his pretty mouth shut in his life?"

"I still don't know what you're saying."

"I've told you. I know where he went. D'you want me to tell you, or draw a map on the tablecloth or something?"

I tried to tell myself that she was bluffing, but I knew she wasn't. It was all too terrifyingly in character.

Leah said dully, "What you didn't realize when you got him into this. . . ."

"I didn't get him into anything."

"All right. Have it your own way. I can't prove you did. But anyhow, what nobody seems to have realized is that when he went into this he was doing it just for bravado. That's why he always does these things. Just like a kid. 'I could climb that tree.' 'I could jump that stream. . . .' And then of course when people take him up on it he gets scared—more scared than anybody I know. More scared even than you. You made enough fuss about a few bombs. God knows. But you weren't as frightened as he was—not really."

I said, "I doubt if that's true. But anyhow. . . ."

"You can doubt what you like. But I know. You see I happen to sleep with him—when I get the chance. It doesn't seem to have occurred to you that he loves me. Oh, yes. You mightn't think so but he does—quite a bit. As far as the poor little bastard can love anybody, which isn't much."

"I know he loves you."

"Yes, and you hate me for it, and always have. Hence this."

I said, "Leah, that sort of stuff doesn't help at all. It's quite untrue."

"Oh, shut up," she said wearily. "You bore me. Let's see —where was I . . . ? Oh, yes. Well, they did their best, these people of yours. From the moment he knew anything they tried to keep him away from me. But they must have slipped up once—just once—because he came to see me and we had five hours together—just five hours. Between the hours of midnight and five in the morning. It was the first time for months." She shrugged, "And of course that was that."

"You got something out of him?"

Leah smiled the bad smile. "I didn't have to get anything out of him, my dear man. I knew there was something wrong of course. But I didn't have to do anything."

She paused and lit a cigarette, and shook her head reflectively. "I don't suppose you've ever seen Jason when he was really frightened?"

"I think I have."

"I wonder. Well, he makes quite a job of it. Trembling, and crying. And clinging to you. I've had it before and it's quite simple to deal with. Maybe any woman could do it for him. I daresay she could. Anyhow he happened to have me that time, so I coped. And then when he'd stopped trembling and crying and all the stuff, out it came."

I said, "I think you probably know far more about it than I do. I never knew any details."

"I tell you, I don't care in the least what you know or don't know."

"What did you do?"

"What d'you think?"

"I should have guessed that you'd try to stop him. "

"Wonderful. Well, I did stop him."

"You mean you tried to?"

Leah gave a short laugh. "I not only tried. I succeeded. You see I abandoned my maidenly modesty and reserve and told him I loved him, which was true; and that I couldn't live without him, which wasn't. And I made him swear that he

223

wouldn't do it—that he wouldn't go—that he'd get out of it. We'd done a lot of swearing that night, because of course he'd made me swear that I'd never tell anybody on earth that he'd told me. Anyhow, he swore by God's truth he wouldn't do it. So I stopped him, didn't I?" Leah paused.

I said, "Well?"

"Well, then I went to sleep," she said drearily. "I shall never know how or why. It's not a thing I often do nowadays. But I'd been up all the previous night, and this had all been a bit tiring, and *he* went to sleep—or pretended to. Anyhow I went to sleep. I suppose that was about three o'clock. I woke up just before five and . . ." she shrugged.

"He'd gone, of course?"

"Why of course?"

I said, "I beg your pardon. I don't sleep with Jason, so of course I shouldn't know." I merely put it on record without comment that I said that, and said it viciously.

Leah smiled and said, "No. You don't sleep with Jason and don't love him, and therefore you would think he'd do that. That's the trouble you see. He's always had to deal with people like you. Anyhow, he'd gone. And apart from that nice letter I showed you, that's the last I saw of him—or ever shall. I wonder who wrote it, Henry? It's a very good forgery."

I said, "He wrote it himself, of course. Before he went. You'll get others."

"Oh yes. Odd that I never thought of that. Quite simple too. It's all quite simple really. Just dirty, that's all." She shrugged again and began to collect her bag and gloves.

I said, "Leah, there are some things I want you to know. . . ."

"Yes."

"Firstly, I never did get Jason into this. In fact, I tried to keep him out. Do you believe me?"

She smiled and said, "Why not, if you say so? It doesn't matter anyhow."

"Secondly, he didn't go out of bravado. He *was* scared sick, and there were plenty of times when he could have got out of it. But he didn't because he thought he ought to go."

"I thought you were going to say I sent him."

"In a way you did. The reason why he thought he ought to go was you."

She looked at me for a moment in silence. Then she put down her bag carefully and said, "Go on, Henry. This is fascinating."

"It's true. That was the reason why he's done everything in this war—and before it. It was *your* war. That was the only thing he was interested in—or ever has been."

"So it was for my sake that he took this on, and then swore he wouldn't, and then sneaked out of bed while I was asleep and—and left me?"

I said, "Yes."

She looked at me for a long moment in silence and then said slowly, "I never knew a man who wouldn't let you down. I never knew a man who wasn't a coward and a liar. I never knew one who didn't want to bully half the time and cry on your bosom the other half. And I never knew one who didn't end up by telling you that he'd done it all for your sake. Thank you for telling me that. It ties up with all my previous experience. And it lets me out."

She picked up her bag and gloves and rose. I got up too and said, "What do you mean by 'Let's you out,' Leah?"

"I mean that I can now fight my own wars without having to worry about little liars and cowards—or big ones."

I said, "What does that mean—apart from just being rude?"

"You say it's my war. You always thought so and always told him so. If you'd had your way you would have sold Poland the way you sold Spain and the Czechs and the way you're selling Russia. My war. . . . All right—I accept that. It is my war and I'll fight it." She turned away and said over her shoulder, "Goodbye, Henry. And be careful you don't get your feet wet."

I watched her walk out of the place, very tall and slim, with that curious loose, almost mannish stride. "The trouble about being a girl is that you can't *run* fast enough." That was the trouble. It always had been.

I sat down again and ordered myself a cup of coffee, and found myself wondering whether I ought to do anything about her from a security angle. She almost certainly knew far too much to be comfortable. But it was difficult to see quite what to do.

*   *   *   *   *

The whole of one wall of the study was covered by a huge map of Europe, embellished with a large number of coloured pins and little flags. My father lay on the sofa and stared at it critically. His breathing was so heavy and effortful that the sound of it filled the room.

My father said, "To invade Italy via Sicily is rather like starting to seduce a woman by tweaking her toes."

My mother pursed her lips and shook her head at him. I said, "A possible approach."

"Yes," said my father. "But liable to be a long job. Surely we could have started at the knee?" He paused to get his breath. "Anyhow, as I remember it, you can't get *about* in Sicily. Etna's always in the way. And getting from one end of Italy to another's hard enough, even if nobody's trying to stop you except the railways." He shook his head. "No—for me the shortest way to the Continent remains Dover-Calais."

It was difficult, because he wanted to talk, but it tired him because of his breathing. To give him time I got up and looked more closely at the map. The largest flag was in Hampshire and approximated to the position of the house. On it was neatly printed, "Supreme Hindquarters and Nervous Centre."

I said, "I don't quite get this. What are all these British flags in Portugal? We're not there."

"That isn't you. That's Wellington."

"What's he got to do with it?"

"Don't be silly," said my father irritably. "This isn't one of your 'situation' maps—at least, not just the *present* situation. On the right, for example, you'll see Marlborough's march to the Danube."

"You mean it's some sort of historical map?"

"Well, frankly, Henry, it got like that because I had a lot of rather pleasant pins and nothing to do. It's too dull just reading the newspapers and altering one pin. But I think something might come out of it. All the major European campaigns of history on a single map. I've never seen it done before."

"Nor have I."

"An overall view," said my father. "That's what we need." He closed his eyes and breathed heavily for a while in silence. Then he frowned and said, "I wish you wouldn't *chase* things so, Henry."

"Chase things?"

"Yes. 'Why this? Why that?' To an intelligent man the value of a map like that is obvious. But not easy to explain."

"I'm sorry. It's a lovely map."

My father's eyes were still closed. My mother was staring at him with the curious watchful, almost wary expression that she usually wore nowadays. Her fingers still knitted rapidly.

My father said, "What you don't realize is that my job is quite different from yours. You only have to fight this war and win it. But I've got to think of the future. What will matter is that between 1700 and 1950 repeated efforts by the Rhineland peoples to establish mastery over Europe broke down on Anglo-Saxon and Slav resistance. I use Anglo-Saxon in the widest sense."

My mother said, "I think you'd better have a rest now, darling, and Henry and I will come in later for tea."

"No," said my father. "I want to hear about his parachutes. How are your parachutes?"

"My parachutes are fine."

"How's Jeff?"

"Very well."

"Is that little chap we used to know still with you? Had a mad father?"

"Jason Pellew? Oh, he's all right as far as I know. I haven't seen him for months. I think he may be in this Sicilian show."

"Well then, put a flag in for him, Henry. And one for yourself. The whole point about this map is that it must be comprehensive."

He lay and watched me while I solemnly wrote "Henry" on a flag and planted it somewhere in the mass round London. I wrote "Jason Pellew" on another, hesitated and put it in North Africa. I said, "That's where I actually heard of him last."

My father said sleepily, "Good. Now we're up to date," and closed his eyes.

My mother nodded to me and we went quietly out.

He died three weeks later. I went down for the funeral and after it I went into his study and looked at the map. He had kept it up to date. The Russian, German, Italian, American and British flags were all in their right places, with the Russians back on the Dneiper, and the American flag in Naples, and British and American flags just south of Cassino. There were also now some Swedish flags going right across Russia into Turkey which must, I think, have been Charles XII. My flag was still in position but Jason's had been moved into Umbria, and "Jason Pellew" had been crossed out and "Hannibal" substituted.

*   *   *   *   *

My father's death took place towards the end of 1943, and by then the pressure of work was rising every week as the great invasion build-up went on.

By the early days of 1944 I was a major with a department of about a dozen people, divided into two sections. I think we did some good work, but there was one part of it about which I was becoming increasingly unhappy. We trained people, we sent them out into the blue, and never saw them again, so that we never had a chance to hear how what we had taught them worked out in the field, or to alter our methods in the light of experience.

I explained this to Fry, and asked him repeatedly if we could have on the staff somebody with actual experience of being dropped in our peculiar circumstances, as opposed to ordinary parachute instructors. He could never get me anybody.

In the end I went to him and pointed out that the methods we were teaching might easily be hopelessly out of date, or even plain murder, and that unless I could get some check on them, I did not feel that I could carry on. Characteristically, he tried bullying, tried being sarcastic, and in the end reluctantly agreed that something must be done. I could not have an experienced person on the staff. That was out of the question. But I should be allowed to meet certain people who had come back, and get any tips from them that I could.

It was while I was in London on this job that I received a message one day to go to see Commander Lewis at the Admiralty. Nobody told me why. Nobody ever did tell me why anything, and I think I assumed that Commander Lewis either was, or had, another person from foreign parts for me to interview. The Admiralty, for this purpose, was a rather seedy house in Bloomsbury with a faded notice on the railings outside prohibiting parking, hawkers, circulars, street criers and a number of other things. Its lower windows were covered in whitewash, like a greenhouse in hot weather. It did not look like the Admiralty, but it did look exactly like the sort of place in which curious organizations tended to have their hideouts. (To this day, I occasionally see houses which I am convinced belong to some intelligence service. There is a certain air about them which is unmistakable to the experienced eye.)

I rang the bell and the door was opened by a small man in overalls who was carrying a pot of white paint. I don't know whether he was a piece of camouflage, or whether he was just a painter, but certainly the whole ground floor smelt strongly of paint. I asked for Commander Lewis and he jerked a thumb and said, "First floor up." He said it almost with contempt, as though he thought little of Commander Lewis, or me, or the whole outfit.

Commander Lewis was a big, rather heavy man with grey hair, a big hooked nose and eyes that were rather too small for the rest of him. I can best describe him by saying that it came as a shock to me to realize, some hours after I had left his office, that he had not been wearing naval uniform. We shook hands and he checked my identity, smiling and saying something about "the usual nonsense." Then he gave me a cigarette, sat back, thought for a moment, nodded to himself as though he had received and understood some message and said, "Well, now, Major Payne ... does the name Linsky mean anything to you?"

It didn't.

He nodded again as though he was rather pleased with this and said, "Garland, then?"

I was thinking entirely of people we had trained and I nearly said "No." Then I remembered and said, "I know a girl named Leah Garland."

"Yes. You didn't know that her real name was Linsky?"

"No."

"Not a relative of yours, by any chance?"

230

"No."

"But a close friend?"

I said, "Yes . . . up to a point. She's more the friend of a friend of mine."

The Commander hesitated and then said, "Do you mind if I ask you a personal question. . . . Was she ever—your—your lady, so to speak?"

"No. As I say, she was somebody else's lady. A friend of mine."

"Do you mind telling me his name?"

I thought that I knew what was coming, and it flashed through my mind that I had always known Leah was not to be trusted.

I smiled and said, "I think that's his story, not mine."

"Any relatives that you know of?"

"I believe she had a mother."

"No," said the Commander. "The mother died in 1940. Nobody else?"

"Not as far as I know. I didn't really know her very well."

The Commander sat in silence for a moment, received his message from his peculiar internal telephone exchange, nodded and said, "Well, I'm sorry to have to tell you, Major Payne, that Miss Linsky—Miss Garland—is dead."

I think it was because I had been expecting something quite different, but I sat and stared at him for what seemed a long time without being able to think of anything to say. The Commander's face was full of careful gravity. One felt that he had removed his hat.

After a while I said, "How?" rather stupidly.

He hesitated and said, "That's the difficulty. I can't give you any details."

"But what did she die of?"

"She was shot," said the Commander briefly.

"Murdered or . . . ?"

"In a sense. But she killed a couple of men in the process

so I suppose one could hardly call it ordinary murder . . ."

I said, "What was she doing? I mean—was this on a job or . . . ?"

"She was working for us. And if it's any consolation to you, doing very fine work too."

"In England?"

"That, I'm afraid, I can't tell you. I'm sorry." He opened a drawer in his desk and said, "You may wonder why I've passed this on to you, if she wasn't really a very close friend. But the fact is that she doesn't appear to have had any relatives, and she gave you as a—as a sort of next-of-kin. You know—in the usual way." He paused. "I gather that you're rather surprised that she should have done so?"

I said, "No. I can see why she might do that."

Lewis said, "Well, there it is. She did." He hesitated for a moment and then, getting up, handed me an envelope and went out.

It was a long O.H.M.S. envelope with "Captain Henry Payne, General List," typed on it. There was no address. I opened it. Inside was a single sheet closely written on both sides in a curious half-script hand. I don't think I had ever seen Leah's writing before, except on walls and cardboard notices.

There was no address or date at the top of the letter. It said:

DEAR HENRY:
I hope you will forgive me for implying that you are my nearest and dearest. The fact is that you are the only person whom I can be pretty sure will be alive and kicking if this ever has to be used. I have great faith in your ability to survive. I did not really want to write a letter like this at all, but the Navy, which is a sentimental organization, seemed to think I should, and I don't want to hurt their feelings. Anyhow it's all rather difficult because here I am writing a letter that almost certainly won't ever need to be read by you, and certainly *will* be read by the security boys. Luckily I haven't got anything to say that matters, except that Jews don't always

232

expect other people to fight their wars for them, as you seem to think. I know you always hated me, and were jealous, and thought I was at the bottom of everything, but you were quite wrong. I've never done anybody any harm, and there was no need to be so beastly that time at Cambridge, because I wasn't doing dirt. You always thought I was doing dirt, whatever I did. But it doesn't matter because I don't think any of us have had much of a chance, and I suppose that includes you.

I think I know what is going to happen, but I don't mind, because I have always known it would.

The only thing that does worry me rather is what we should do if none of it *did* happen to us and we had to start all over again.

The last words were pale and scratchy as though written with a fountain pen that was running out of ink. The rest was in pencil.

I don't think there is any likelihood that the little man will turn up again, but just in case he does, you must tell him whatever you think best. After all, you've always known what was good for him better than I have. But personally, I should just keep my mouth shut if I were you and know nothing. He never was much of a one for the truth, particularly if there was anything difficult about it.

I am sorry to give you this trouble.

Yours sincerely,

LEAH GARLAND

I read this twice and then folded the letter up and put it back in the envelope and sat and thought about it. After a while Lewis came back, still with that expression that people wear at the funerals of distant relatives.

I said, "Look—I know this is difficult, but surely you can tell me a bit more about it without risking anything? After all, I'm fairly used to keeping my mouth shut."

He said, "Yes. I've talked to my master and he seems to think it's all right. . . ."

He sat down, took his instructions from within, nodded

and said, "Well, you ask me what you want to know and I'll tell you, if I think I can."

"How long ago did this happen?"

"We don't know exactly. Within the last three weeks."

"How long had she been with you?"

"About six months."

"You say she was shot?"

"So we understand."

"And that she got two people in the fight?"

"Yes." The Commander wriggled slightly uncomfortably. "I should perhaps say that I wouldn't like to swear to any of that part of it. Frankly, our source of information tends to dress things like that up a bit, and it doesn't sound too probable to me. On previous form it would have been more likely if somebody had just stuck a knife in her quietly."

"But you're sure she's dead?"

"Oh yes. No doubt about that at all, I'm afraid."

I said, "I assume she was in Europe—I mean enemy territory. After all, these things don't happen much in England."

Lewis hesitated and said, "Yes. She was in Europe."

"Did you drop her?"

"Drop her?"

"Yes. By parachute."

Lewis smiled broadly and said, "Good heavens, no. We don't do romantic things like that. She went in the ordinary way—by sea."

I wondered just how one "went in the ordinary way by sea" to enemy territory, but I knew he wouldn't tell me and it didn't matter. I said, "I don't suppose you can tell me what she was doing, but there's one thing that puzzles me. I didn't know she had good enough languages for—for that sort of job."

The Commander shrugged his shoulders. "It depends what the job is, doesn't it? In fact she was like a lot of people with

·—with that sort of background. She spoke a bit of most things—none of it perfectly. But it so happens that where she was working there were a lot of foreigners, and people coming and going who spoke different languages, so that she could get by as belonging to any race they *didn't* belong to, if you follow me."

I said, "I take it you mean that she was at a port and working among sailors."

"I'm afraid I can't give you any more details," he said curtly.

I said, "I quite understand. Thank you for telling me so much."

"You realize of course that—that this comes under your security oath? Otherwise I couldn't have told you."

"Yes."

The Commander gave his quick little nod, sat for a moment in silence and then got up rather abruptly. "Well, she was a fine girl and did a fine job. God rest her. I was afraid you'd turn out to be her husband or something."

As we shook hands I said, "There's nothing more I can do?"

"I don't think so. I don't think she had any property or anything. At least, she said she hadn't."

"No. I don't think she had anything like that."

"You've got her letter?"

"Yes."

"Well, I understand that it's all right, so you can keep it. Goodbye."

I don't know why, but I have always seen it as Antwerp. It might of course have been Marseilles or any of a dozen other places. But to me it has always been Antwerp.

*   *   *   *   *

I was due to go back to the Parachute Testing Station at the end of the following week. Before I left, Clare-Hanson sent for me. He looked more worn-out than any man I have ever seen. He was a small, thin, wiry man, and at the best of times he had a white, deeply lined, hollow-cheeked face. But now it seemed almost transparent, as though somebody had just put a thin layer of some plastic over the bones. He greeted me with a bright smile and a handshake and said, "Well—have you got what you wanted?" as though it was the one thing in the world that he really minded about.

I said, "I think so, sir. I still feel that we're liable to get out of touch with the field, down there. But this has certainly helped."

Clare-Hanson made an odd face, and I realized that he was yawning without opening his mouth. He said, "Colonel Fry says you've been asking for somebody with field experience on your staff?"

"That's the real answer of course."

"I dare say. But we all want those, and there aren't many of them."

"I quite see that."

"All the same, I see your point. . . ." He considered, "Would it be any use if you had somebody temporarily? Just between jobs?"

"Yes, sir. Very much so."

"How long would you have to have him for?"

"Anything for a week upwards would help. The trouble with just interviewing people up here is that I can't show them what we're doing now. Anybody with practical experience who saw the course going on might be able to spot things that were wrong at once."

Clare-Hanson nodded and said, "Well, I think we might be able to fix that. In fact it might be quite useful to have somewhere where a man could hang up his hat and keep himself occupied for a few weeks. . . . The only thing is that I might have to snatch him away at five minutes' notice."

"Of course."

"All right, Payne—I'll try and do that. You can take him at any time?"

"Yes, sir. If Colonel Fry agrees, of course."

"Of course. Only I've got a man coming back in a couple of days' time who we might spare for a bit." He wrinkled his brow. "Wait a minute, though—I'm not sure that he went through your course? Pellew?"

I said, "Jason Pellew?"

"That's right. Was he one of yours?"

After a moment I said, "No. He didn't go through the course. But I know him very well."

"Well, d'you think he'd be any good to you? He's certainly had field experience, but if he didn't do the course in the first place . . . ?"

I said, "I should like to have him."

The man I was to have interviewed that day could not be produced, so I went and sat in the Park and thought about it. From the moment I had read Leah's letter I had known that this might happen one day, but I had managed to put it out of my mind, as something to be considered quietly later. But now that it was right on top of me, I realized that there were altogether too many possibilities—all of them unsatisfactory. I could forget the interview with Lewis, and Leah's letter and know nothing—nothing beyond that day when I had seen her walk out of the restaurant, or even before that. That, after all, was what Leah herself wanted—or said she wanted. I could know something—that she was dead—but without details, or with a minimum of them. Or I could put together what I knew, and what I guessed, and forget promises and security oaths and everything else, and show him the letter and have done with it all. I remember thinking that it was rather like knowing that a person had cancer, and deciding whether to tell him or not. I knew that if it had been me, I would rather have known. But I was not Jason, and I had

237

never known the truth about him and Leah and didn't know it now.

I sat there for a long time, and then it began to rain, and I started to walk slowly back across the Park, still thinking about it and still getting nowhere. At one moment I decided that the best thing was to do as Leah had suggested—to say and know nothing; and I took her letter out of my pocket meaning to tear it up. But I glanced through it again and realized that to tear it up was irrelevant, for I could never have shown it to him. Whatever she had felt about him, it wasn't that.

That evening I rang up Fry and told him that I was being lent an officer and would like to stay in Town and meet him and bring him down with me. He consented with all the enthusiasm of a spinster letting her slavey out for the day.

*   *   *   *   *

I knew Jason was coming sometime on Monday. He arrived when I was out of the office and when I went in he was talking very fast to a rather pretty girl who was somebody's P.A.

His face was dark brown, and he had grown a rather ludicrous small beard, which for some reason had come almost black, so that the tan and the beard made his hair yellower and his eyes bigger than ever. He was in battle dress, with a major's crown on his shoulder, and the ribbon of the Military Cross. My first thought was that he looked a great deal fitter and much happier than when I had seen him last. He said, "Oh—hallo, Henry . . ." and then turned to the P.A. and said, "That's an awfully good show. I do hope it goes well. And thank you very much." He then shook hands with her, bowed, and opened the door for her, and said, "Goodbye, and thank you again," and seemed to turn back with regret. All this was very much as I had expected. What I had not expected was that as he shut the door behind him he would whip round and shake my hand hard, without looking at it and without bowing over it, and say, "Henry— by God, it's good to see you!" He had never greeted me like that before, and I don't think he ever did so again.

I said, "Well, Jason, how are you?" and he said, "I'm well, Henry. Terrifically well," and gave a curious hop backwards so that he was sitting on my desk, and sat there and swung his legs and chuckled, a sort of burbling chuckle which seemed to be of sheer delight.

I said, "I like the beard. Was it part of your cover?"

"Oh lord, no. I only started it a fortnight ago when I knew I was coming back. Not bad for a fortnight, is it?"

"It's a rather rum colour."

"Well, yes, perhaps it is. I shall probably shave it off now. I really only grew it to annoy a colonel."

I nodded towards the ribbon of the M.C. and said, "I didn't know they'd given you that. Congratulations."

"I think it rather suits me, don't you? What's this about my coming to you? Did you fix it?"

"No. I asked for somebody and they offered me you."

"Good God, how frightfully funny!"

He leaned back and swung his legs still harder and laughed heartily.

I looked at him sitting there and swinging his legs and laughing, looking happier than I had ever seen him, and I knew that whatever had to be done, it could not be done for the moment.

I said, "I explained that I knew all about you, but they didn't realize that that was a protest, and went ahead and fixed it."

"But what do I have to do?"

"Tell us what's wrong with our training. The dropping part."

"How can I, Henry? I haven't touched a parachute in anger for months. But anyhow, it might be fun."

I said, "If you'll get off my desk and sit in a chair, I can sit down. How were foreign parts?"

"Foreign parts were fine. Bit dodgy at times, but only when there were Germans about. The poor old Wops. I do adore them. I was always having the greatest difficulty in remembering which side I was on."

"That must have been a bit difficult?"

"Well, as a matter of fact, you know, it helped rather a lot, in a queer way. Incidentally, I now speak perfect Genovese, which is quite something for an Englishman. I say, how much am I supposed to tell you?"

"I don't know. We'll ask somebody."

Jason said, "It's a very queer place this. I had two hours with a chap this morning and he asked me a lot of questions and went into the back end of everything, absolutely the back end. And then I happened to mention a—a certain gadget and he held up his hand and said, 'You mustn't talk about that,' and I said, 'Well, surely I can talk to *you* about it, because the damn' thing doesn't work anyway—or not much.' But he said, 'No. It hasn't been cleared to me yet, so we'll keep off it.' Very odd."

I said, "When did you get in, then?"

"We landed at six o'clock this morning. Damned cold it was. I haven't seen a soul yet—I mean not anybody outside the racket—nor even had time to ring anybody up."

I looked at my watch and said quickly, "Well, I suppose it isn't really lunch time but I think we might go out, in the circumstances."

Jason said, "I want a large English gin, Henry. Gin is a foul, barbaric drink and I loathe it. But I want a large one today. Just to remind me how foul it is."

He kept off it for a surprisingly long time. We were half-way through the meal before he said, "Look—what are you doing tonight?"

"I don't know."

"Then why don't we beat up the girl Leah and all go out to dinner? Because if you and I are pushing off to this place of yours soon . . . ?"

I said, "I'm not sure how to get hold of her."

"We can ring her ambulance place."

"She's left there."

"Then where is she?"

I said, "I don't know, Jason."

He looked surprised and said, "Well, you're a fine chap. I told you to keep an eye on her. Haven't you got her number or anything?"

"I've got a telephone number but it's no good ringing that. She's left there."

Jason looked hurt and said, "Well, damn it, Henry, it's a bit thick to come back like this and find that people have mislaid your girl. How the hell am I going to let her know I'm home?"

I remember that I looked at his plate and saw that he had eaten practically all his food, and that for some reason I was glad about that.

I said, "It's no good trying to find Leah because she's gone. . . . She's dead."

A waiter was rattling cutlery close by, and he can't have heard what I said, because he said, "D'you think the ambulance place would know?"

I said, "I tell you she's dead."

He heard this time, and stopped and stared at me blankly for a long moment and then said, "Dead . . . ? You mean Leah is?"

"Yes. I'm terribly sorry, Jason."

He went on staring at me and then gave a curious, incredulous half-smile and said, "But — what of, Henry——?"

"She went abroad to do a job and—and it went wrong."

241

"Abroad? Not for *this* bloody outfit?"

"No. For the Navy."

"But what the hell had *she* got to do with the Navy?"

I told him most of what Lewis had told me. I didn't mention the letter. There was no point in it, because he would have wanted to see it, and it wouldn't have helped him. He sat there and listened, never taking his eyes off me. His lips were trembling and they had gone a queer pale colour, and as he sat there it seemed that he grew smaller and smaller—as though the whole man was shrivelling up inside his clothes.

When I came to the end he went on staring, as though he was waiting for more, and then he looked slowly away. After a while he said quietly, "I see."

I said, "I didn't know whether to tell you or—or what. . . ."

"Well, of course. . . ." He was silent for a moment and then sat up and said, "I must go and see this chap," and looked quickly round as though he thought Lewis was somewhere in sight.

I said, "I don't think there's any point in it, Jason."

"Why not?"

"He won't tell you any more than he told me. Probably not as much."

Jason said furiously, "But, God damn it, she was my girl, wasn't she?" His eyes had suddenly filled with tears.

"Yes, but they don't know that. You see she just gave them my name because she didn't know where you were."

"But of course I must see him. He'll tell me all right. My God, he will, if I have to get it out of him with a gun!"

"I honestly don't think he knows any more, Jason—or not any more that matters."

"Matters?" he said bitterly. "It all matters. I want to know. . . ." He stared at me for a moment, with the pale lips twitching violently. "Don't you see that it probably didn't happen like that at all? They probably picked her up and. . . ." He stopped suddenly and shut his eyes for a moment. Then he opened them again and said viciously, "And anyhow what the hell did they think they were doing to let her? She'd no languages—not even decent French."

I said, "I asked Lewis about that and he said. . . ."

"*Monsieur l'agent de Gestapo,*" said Jason suddenly. "*Avezvous la plume de ma tante?*"

He suddenly started to laugh, "That's what she'll have gone round saying. It was just about her form. *Monsieur l'agent de Gestapo. . . .*" He went on laughing more and more violently, until he was leaning back in his seat with the tears pouring down his cheeks and gasping, "*Monsieur l'agent de Gestapo. . . .*"

He was laughing so much that several people turned their heads to look, some disapprovingly, some with rather wry smiles. I think they thought he was drunk.

I said gently, "Steady on, Jason."

He took no notice and went on laughing, but gradually more quietly, so that eventually he was quite silent. I sent for the bill, and while I paid it he sat and stared at the table-cloth. Then he looked up and said, "Well, now—when do we start?"

"Start what?"

"This job of yours?"

"We go down tomorrow."

"Fine. Then I'd better just pop along to Cheyne Walk and see the old girl. I suppose *she* isn't dead?"

"Not as far as I know."

"She wouldn't be. Still, I suppose I'd better go and see her." He saw my face and said, "It's all right. You can come too if you like. In fact I think you'd better. Or shall we go to the flicks? More fun."

He had slammed the door on it, and I could hear the turning of the key. To me, at least, that door was only opened again on one occasion.

*　　　*　　　*　　　*　　　*

I took him down to the Station the following day. I think he was glad to go. He was rather quiet, but otherwise seemed normal. He had shaved his beard off, and though I had only ever seen him with a beard for a few hours, he looked oddly naked without it.

Fry greeted him unusually cordially—far more cordially than he ever greeted me—and annoyed me a good deal by having a long session with him at which I suppose they discussed matters too important for my ears. Personally I never asked Jason about his work, partly as a matter of principle and partly perhaps as one of pride. He did in fact tell me things from time to time, when he wanted to illustrate a point about training. But apart from that we did not discuss his field work in detail, and he had a slightly irritating habit of assuming that I knew more about it than I did. It was a habit of Jason's not to tell you things and then to assume that you knew all about them.

From the working point of view his visit was reasonably successful for a while. There was not a great deal that he could tell us about training that we did not know already; but there were some useful small points, and for the first fortnight or so he seemed interested and worked hard. He was also very quiet and modest and in no sense the expert laying down the law. If there was anything that he thought was wrong, he always took care not to mention it in front of the trainees or the staff, but asked me about it rather diffidently in private. He certainly got on very well with everybody.

Outside working hours, I was less happy about him. As I have said, the Station was a quite foolishly and unnecessarily unsociable place, and we were alone together a good deal. On these occasions Jason was either very silent, or else he would talk continuously about absolutely nothing, like a man who cannot bear silence and must say something to break it.

In particular, I had great difficulty in getting him to go to bed at any reasonable time. He liked to sit on in the Mess smoking-room for as long as anybody would let him, and then to come to my room and stay till three or four in the morning. And this was so whether he was in his silent mood or his talkative one. He never mentioned anything of importance. It was all on the lines of "I say, Henry, do you remember Gladstone's dog? It was a rum beast that. The gardener used to say it was a cross between a doormat and a scraper. You know I really don't think I like spaniels much. Very pretty but rather dumb. I think if one were going to have a dog, an Alsatian would be the only thing. . . ."

On other occasions he would do long, rambling fantasies about the future—particularly about his new type of market garden. All this would go on till 3 a.m.

I was working very hard, and could not keep late hours in comfort. Often I remember dropping off to sleep and waking up again to find Jason still talking or else just sitting there in silence. But whenever I insisted that he should go to bed, or at least that I was going to do so, I had a feeling that I was doing something almost brutal; and I know that even when he did go to bed he seldom slept. After a while I got the doctor to give him some sleeping tablets, and they improved matters a little, but not much. I noticed with relief that he hardly drank at all, and would spend a whole long evening over half a pint of beer.

After the first fortnight, however, I began to notice other things. He rapidly lost interest in the work. Sometimes he did not turn up at all when I was expecting him; and when he did he sat and watched or listened in moody silence, and had nothing to say afterwards. He also became rather unsociable, even by the Station standards, and on a couple of occasions was quite unnecessarily rude to people who made some innocent casual remark to him.

I was worried, but found it difficult to know what to do for him. I could probably have arranged for him to go. He was no longer doing much to help anyhow. But though I knew he was unhappy at the Station I could at least keep an eye on him, which I felt that he needed. I remember wondering, in one of my more brilliant moments of insight, whether he would be happier back in the field with more to do, more excitement and more action; and whether to try to arrange it.

I soon knew the answer to that one at least. One day when he had been with me about three weeks, Jason came into my office, sat down and said with a bright smile, "Henry, much as it grieves me, I shall soon have to leave you."

"Why?"

"Well, Clare-Hanson was down last night and it seems that he can no longer manage without the services of the boy wonder. So there we are." He sat back and smiled at me very brightly indeed.

I said, "He always told me he probably couldn't spare you for long. You're going off again?"

"Yes."

"Foreign parts?"

"That's it. Cook's are fixing it now."

"Can you tell me anything about it?"

"John the Baptistry."

"Why John the Baptist?"

"Behold I send my messenger before my face to prepare my way before me."

"I see. France?"

"You needn't think I'm going to give you a lot of stuff to tap out to Berlin on your little wireless set, Henry."

I said, "All right. Sorry."

He was still sitting back in his chair beaming at me, but I

happened to glance down at his hand on the arm of the chair and saw that his fist was clenched so tightly that the knuckles showed white.

I said, "How d'you feel about it?"

"I feel fine about it, Henry. It's just what I need. It'll be very good for me."

My mind went back to a hillside many years ago. "It was very good for me."

I said, "I was wondering about that the other day. This is a bloody dull place, and must certainly seem so to you, after the other."

"Not at all," said Jason politely. "I've enjoyed myself very much. I only wish I could have done more to help."

"You've done a cracking job. Any idea when you're going?"

"In about a week's time I expect."

I started to say, "Well, I hope . . ." and then glanced at him and stopped. He was looking at me, no longer smiling, but with a face contorted as though in acute pain, and as I watched he leant slowly forward, put his arms on the desk, sunk his head on them and began to sob—big shivering sobs which shook his whole body.

I was not as surprised as I might have been, because of the over-bright smile and the clenched fist and all that had been happening in the last few weeks. But even so, I did not know quite how to handle it. I got up and went round the desk and gave him a pat on the shoulder and said, "Hey—steady there." He shook his head, but he could not speak and I decided that it was better to leave him for a bit, and moved away slightly and stood there in silence for what seemed a very long time while he went on shaking and choking. Then he raised his head and stared at me for a moment and said, "I can't. Not now. I *can't*."

I said quietly, "You mean you can't—go off again?"

He said, "No. I *can't*. I'm finished. I can't do it **again**," **and** covered his face again and shook violently. After a while he took his hands away and said almost calmly, "It's the dropping. I could do the rest but I can't do that again. Not now. It's the dropping." I said nothing, and that seemed to frighten him because he looked at me with fear and said, "I can't and I won't. They can't make me. It's . . . you have to volunteer." He was trembling violently and his voice was almost shrill.

"Now look, Jason," I said gently, "I'm quite sure nobody's going to try to make you do anything you feel you can't, so. . . ."

He started to sob again and said, "It's the dropping. I could do the rest. I swung in once. You never heard about that. I swung in when there was a wind and broke my collar-bone and knocked myself out. I couldn't jump again, Henry. Don't let them make me. Don't *let* them."

I don't know how long it went on like this, but it seemed a very long time. I knew from the look and sound of him that it wasn't just a temporary thing—that something had really broken—and I desperately wanted to get him up to his room. We were in the offices, and to get to his room meant going right through the place, and for a long time he could not stop crying and shaking. But at last he seemed to quieten down, and sat for a long time in silence with his head on his arms. After a while I said, "Jason . . . ?"

He said, "Yes?" without looking up.

"I want to get you back to your room and to bed. Think you can make it?"

He said, "Yes. Yes, of course," and got up and started for the door without even looking at me. As it happened we got there without meeting anybody.

I said, "Get into bed," and he undressed and did so without a word. He seemed dazed or half-asleep now, but all the same I got one of his sleeping tablets and gave it to him and said, "Now go to sleep and don't worry. I'll arrange things."

248

He mumbled something and shut his eyes. In a little while he seemed to be asleep and I went away.

I had a lot of work to do up at the aerodrome, so all I could do was to go to Harton, the Station doctor, and ask him to keep an eye on Jason while I was away. As usual in that place, everything was made much more complicated because I couldn't tell him all the facts—about Clare-Hanson and Jason going off again and so on. All I could say was that he seemed to be having some sort of nerve-storm. Harton was a sharp-tongued, rather cynical old boy who drank too much; but he was a good doctor on the whole, and quite used to being asked to cope with people without being told what had really happened to them.

When I returned from the aerodrome Harton was sitting in my office reading *Tit-Bits*. He said, "I've seen your boy."

"What d'you think of him?"

Harton said, "Well, in the old days before everybody knew everything about psychology, it would probably have been called a sizeable nervous breakdown—whatever that meant. Nowadays they call it an acute anxiety state—whatever *that* means."

"Is he all right at the moment?"

"Yes. I've got him doped up and he's quite quiet now. But he's a sick boy all right."

"What had we better do with him?"

"He's only attached here, isn't he?"

"Yes."

"I'm never allowed to ask questions here. They don't even like me to ask people if they've got a pain. But is he a member of the main outfit?"

"Yes."

"Then we'd better try and get him to Fordington."

"I don't know about Fordington."

"It's a sort of rest place for people in the outfit who . . . well, who need a rest place. Have you told the Colonel about it?"

"Not yet."

"Well, you'd better. And tell him I think it's a Fordington job."

I said, "How long do you think it'll be before he's fit again?"

"If I knew what it was all about I might be able to tell you. As it is, I can't. But some weeks anyhow."

I went and told Fry, whose first comment was, "Oh God—one of those."

I said, "I thought perhaps Colonel Clare-Hanson should be warned, sir, because he did tell me, when Pellew came, that he might want him back quickly."

Fry said, "Yes," looked at me to see if Jason had talked, saw he had and gave a grunt of dissatisfaction.

"Harton thinks it may be some weeks before he's fit again."

"How does Harton come into it?"

"He's seen him and given him some dope."

"Well, I don't know that I want him to be seen by Harton —certainly not if he's in that state. Why didn't you see me before bringing Harton in?"

I said rather stiffly, "I'm sorry, sir. But you were not here, and the man was obviously ill, so I felt that the doctor should see him."

Fry shrugged his shoulders and said brusquely, "What's the matter with him anyway? I mean what's caused this? Seemed all right two days ago."

"He's had a fairly tough time, sir, and a girl he was very fond of died recently. I think he's over-strained."

"Well, it's a damned nuisance," said Fry moodily. "You'd better send Harton to see me, if he's brought in on it."

That was all. Yet until then I could have sworn that he particularly liked Jason.

The outfit could be very slow and clumsy at times, but it could move fast enough when it liked. I sent Harton to see the Colonel and went up to Jason's room. He was asleep. I went away without disturbing him and came back two hours later. The room was empty. I asked Harton if Jason had been taken to Fordington, but he merely shrugged his shoulders and said, "It's out of my hands, old boy. You'd better ask the Colonel."

Fry came into the Mess for once that night and seemed in a slightly more friendly mood than usual. I plucked up the courage to say, "About Pellew, sir. . . ."

Fry said, "He's being taken care of."

"Would it be possible for me to go to see him? I should very much like to."

"No," said Fry irritably. "There's too much to do for people to go pottering about sick visiting. I'll keep you in touch if there's anything you need to know."

* * * * *

It must have been in March, 1944, that Jason broke down, and Fry was certainly right—there was plenty to do. In fact, there was an amount to do that could not possibly be done by the staff I had, and night after night I used to fall into bed completely exhausted. Apart from our normal trainees we now had a number of Americans coming to us, less to be trained than to exchange notes. They were a fine lot on the whole, and very keen to learn, and despite their lack of experience I often felt privately that they knew at least as much about the job technically as we did, though some of them had the oddest ideas about Europe and European conditions.

During this time I never had a day off, and never even saw

my mother, though I knew that she was not well and desperately lonely. So it is not very surprising that though I occasionally thought of Jason and wondered vaguely what had happened to him, I neither worried about him nor tried to do anything about him as much as I should otherwise have done. It was some time in May, when things were obviously coming to the boil, that I was driving up to the aerodrome with Fry in the usual silence when he suddenly said, "Oh— your friend Pellew. No go, that."

I said, "He's still ill?"

"I don't know if he's ill, but they think he's no more good to us. Finished."

"Why, sir?"

Fry shrugged his shoulders in silence.

I said, "Could you tell me what will happen to him now?"

"Well, I think they've hung on to him till now because of course when he broke up he was fairly hot—I mean knew quite a lot. They couldn't have had him in circulation. But I think he's cooled off enough now to be returned to store."

"What store, sir?"

"Regimental duty, I suppose. That's where he came from."

I said, "But he came from Airborne, sir. Will he be any use to them if he's cracked up? I thought it was the dropping part of it that got him down."

"That's Airborne's business. He's their body. They must cope with him."

I said, "It wouldn't be possible to give him a medical board and—and get him out altogether . . . ?"

"Don't be silly," said Fry irritably. "We can't possibly mess about with that sort of thing. We borrowed a body from Airborne and now we're returning it, that's all. The rest is up to them."

After a pause I said, "Could you tell me where he is?"

"I think he's at home, wherever that may be. Anyhow he's left Fordington on a fortnight's termination leave, and he's no longer anything to do with us."

"There's no objection to my seeing him?"

"Why should there be? I tell you he's been sworn out and he's nothing to do with us now." Fry frowned. "But don't waste a lot of time on it, Payne. There's plenty to do, you know."

A week later I was in London for a meeting, and as soon as it was over I went straight to Cheyne Walk. Jason was back in his old rooms at the top of the house. Although it was about six o'clock he was in pyjamas and a dressing-gown and unshaved. He looked thin and decidedly ill, and he greeted me sullenly and with a kind of underlying anger. Almost at once he said, "You know what's happened?"

"I gather you're out of the racket?"

"Oh yes, they've got all they could out of me so now all they want is to forget me."

I said, "Then what happens now?"

Jason laughed bitterly. "That's the joke. They think they can just send me back to Airborne. They've got another bloody think coming." He hesitated and then said in a completely different tone, "I couldn't *do* it, Henry. I've told them."

I said, "Well, obviously they *can* send you back to Airborne—in fact in theory I don't think you've ever left it. But I don't suppose. . . ."

"I shan't argue," said Jason sullenly. "I shall just tell them to go to hell, and let them do what they like."

"What do you mean by 'tell them to go to hell'?"

"If Airborne send for me I shan't go. And if they get me there I shall refuse to go in a plane. And if they carry me into one I shall refuse to jump." His eyes suddenly filled with tears. "I'm *damned* if I will! I'm *damned* if I will! I can't. I'm not fit. I. . . ."

I said gently, "I quite see how you feel, Jason, but I don't think perhaps that's the best way to do it."

"I don't care what way I do it," he said furiously. "Go on, you *tell* me the way to do it. You ought to know. You've always managed to keep yourself in a soft job. I suppose if I'd done the same everybody'd think I was a grand chap by now. But because I went and tried to do something . . . they smash me up . . . now want to treat me. . . ." He was shaking violently and half-sobbing.

I said, "Look, Jason—don't worry—I'm sure this can be fixed."

"I don't want it fixed," he said with sudden dignity. "I want them to know that I realize that I was quite wrong ever to take part in war. I saw Arthur the other day. . . ."

"What Arthur?"

"Arthur Laidlaw. I talked to him about it and he quite agreed that the only thing to do was to refuse to have anything to do with it, like he did and—and let them do what they like. To suffer for one's principles if necessary."

I said, "But, Jason, be sensible. Laidlaw was a pacifist."

"So am I."

"But he said so and got himself out of it from the beginning, whereas you're an officer. If you suddenly decide you're a pacifist now, nobody will believe you, and there'll be an awful mess."

"I must put up with that," said Jason doggedly. "It's my own fault for not sticking to my principles in the first place. If I have to suffer for it now, it'll be good for me."

I said, "Have you got a doctor? I mean here? Your own doctor?"

"No. I've had enough of doctors. They don't do anything for you. Anyhow, it's quite clear. It's all happened because I didn't stick to my principles. People are being killed and tortured . . . all because none of us have the guts to say we won't do it."

"Is your godmother here?"

"No. She's away."

"Who's looking after you?"

"Old Ella. Anyhow, I don't want looking after. I shall simply stay here till they send for me and then tell them to go to hell."

I stayed another half an hour but I could see that it was no good. In the end I told him that I would drop in again the next day, and went away and thought it over. I had been in the Army for four years, but I knew practically nothing about how these things worked, and badly needed somebody who knew the ropes. It was no use appealing to Fry or any of our outfit. Obviously they had washed their hands of him. To do them justice, this was one of the things one was warned about when one joined them—that if one got into any sort of mess they could do nothing about it. On the other hand, unless something was done, it seemed on the cards that Jason would simply refuse to obey orders and land himself with a court-martial and heaven knows what. And then the thought of a court-martial reminded me of something in a letter from Jackson. "I hear that Bicycle has given up soldiering and is now a considerable nob in the Judge Advocate General's Department. I would much dislike being court-martialled by Bicycle."

I only had about a couple of hours to spare the following morning, and it took me over half an hour on the telephone to track Bryce down. When I did get on to him, he was decidedly cool. I said, "I want to see you."

"Well, I'm afraid I'm rather busy, Henry. Is it important?"

"It's about Jason Pellew."

"Pellew? I thought he was dead."

"Well, he isn't, and I need your advice about him."

"Oh . . . well, would Wednesday do?"

"No. It must be right away. It's urgent." There was a

long pause and then he said rather grudgingly, "Oh, all right. But it'll have to be brief, Henry."

Bryce was wearing the red tabs of a full colonel, and looking remarkably handsome and well-groomed. He sat and listened, with that curious air of intelligent concentration while I told him as much of the story as I could.

When I had finished he just nodded and said, "Yes, I see," and then thought for a while. Then he said, "Well, I'm glad the little fellow's alive, but it does look a bit tricky. Of course the organization which we've agreed shall be nameless won't do a thing for him?"

"I don't think so."

"That's normal." Bryce reflected. "Well, clearly he can't get away with this nonsense of refusing to obey orders and saying he's a pacifist and so on. Otherwise he'll just get hurt, and the sooner someone tells him so the better."

"I have told him so."

"This pacifist character—Laidlaw. We can easily fix *him*, of course. It's an offence to encourage people to disobey orders."

I said, "I don't think pacifism has got anything to do with it, really. I think he's just scared sick and using that as an excuse."

"Yes, but *how* sick is he scared?" Bryce frowned. "You see, Henry, the Army's attitude toward these matters nowadays is one glorious muddle. It's perfectly prepared, in theory at least, to shoot you for straightforward cowardice —and that goes even if you've previously won the V.C. But if you can wrap the cowardice up and call it something complicated and medical, you become a sick man, and the Army is very sorry for you and hands you over to the tender care of the psychiatrists. Just how sick *is* our little Jason?"

"Well, what he says makes no sense. He's liable to burst into tears and shake. He doesn't sleep. He. . . ."

Bryce held up a hand. "Enough. Henry—there's no doubt that the answer to your problem is the trick-cyclist technique."

"Well, obviously. But how do I get him to one before he gets into trouble? The people in our outfit know he's not fit, of course. That's why they've chucked him out. But for some reason they can't or won't just say so to the Airborne people."

"No." Bryce was silent for a moment. "What you do, Henry, is this," he said slowly. "Firstly, you get a doctor to see him at once. A nice modern doctor—preferably a psychiatrist—anyhow somebody who takes the trick-cyclist very seriously. You get him to write a letter to whom it may concern saying that Jason is very ill indeed. You then persuade Jason that he must go back to Airborne in accordance with any orders he gets. He *must* do that, because until he does he doesn't quite belong to anybody, and nobody can do anything for him. On arrival he presents the letter to the M.O. of his unit. The M.O.—if he happens to be the right M.O. for the purpose—then calls in the trick-cyclists; and after that you can be sure that if they can possibly find anything wrong with the lad they will. Their general attitude seems to be that practically everybody in the Army is half crazy and ought to be discharged."

I said, "I wonder if Jackson could help. He was the psychiatrist on Airborne training at one time."

"The Jackson who was at school with us? Rather a little ass?"

"He's not a little ass now."

"No? Well, he's exactly the sort of bloke whom I should have expected to be a psychiatrist. Anyhow, I'm sure he'll give you all the help you need." Bryce rose with a smile, "And now, Henry, you must forgive me, but I really have got a lot to do. Give the little chap my love."

I went back to Cheyne Walk that evening. Jason was lying on the bed, still in pyjamas and dressing-gown, and still unshaved. He looked as though he hadn't moved since I left him the previous night. But I could tell at once that something had happened, and when I saw the envelope lying on the side table I guessed what it was.

I said, "Have you got your posting yet?"

He stared at me in the old open-eyed way and said, "No. No, I haven't heard anything."

I don't think for a moment that he expected me to believe him. I picked up the envelope and took out the letter, while he lay and watched me, blinking and twitching. It ordered him to report to Rushton in three days' time for a refresher course.

I said, "Thank God. I never thought of that. What a bit of luck."

"Isn't it?" said Jason bitterly. "Isn't it?" He turned over with his face towards the wall and said, "I shan't go. They can go to hell."

"But don't you remember? Jackson's there."

"What about it?"

"Well, he's the psychiatrist there. You'll be able to tell him about it, and he'll look after you."

There was a long pause and then he said, "I shan't go."

"But you *must* go. Once you're there, people can help you, whereas if you don't, there'll just be a nasty mess."

He said, "I'm not going to have anything more to do with it. They can do what they like. I don't believe in war. Arthur says. . . ."

"To hell with Arthur!"

"To hell with them. If we'd all said we wouldn't have anything to do with it like he did. . . ."

"Well—what?"

There was a pause and then he said in a low voice, "Then

258

it wouldn't have happened," and turned his head towards the wall again.

I glanced at my watch. It was seven o'clock. My train was at eight-thirty. I said sharply, "Jason—sit up and listen to me."

There was a long pause and then he slowly sat up and stared at me sullenly.

I said, "Are you going to obey that order?"

"No."

"Right—then I'm through with you. I've done my best to help you, but I can't if you won't help yourself. In an hour's time I've got to go back to my job. Now, if you'll promise me that you'll obey that posting, I'll write to Jacko tonight and make sure that he meets you and looks after you, and probably everything can be fixed. But if you won't, then I shall simply go and leave you to manage how you like."

He looked at me with something like hatred and said, "I shan't go." But I knew from the moment he sat up that I had won.

I said quietly, "You'd better go and shave and put your uniform on, Jason."

He hesitated for a moment and then got up and walked slowly towards the door. On the way he paused and idly turned over a book which was lying on the table. I think the pause was just a rather pathetic gesture of independence. Then he went out. I sat and waited for about half an hour. Then he came back, shaved and in Service dress uniform. There was no M.C. ribbon on it but it had the Parachute flash on the sleeve. As he came in he said casually, "God— these buttons need cleaning."

"They certainly do."

"Personally I like them better when they've this goldy colour. Can I come to the station with you?"

"Yes, of course."

"Then I'd better clean them. . . ."

He went and got his cleaning tackle and sat in his shirt sleeves cleaning his buttons. As he was doing so he pointed to the parachute badge and said, "D'you think I'd better take it off if I'm not going to do it any more?"

I said, "I shouldn't bother now."

"Only I'm *not* going to, Henry. You do realize that?"

"You'd better talk to Jacko about it."

"Yes. He's a good chap. You won't forget to write to him?"

"No. Of course not."

He looked at me in silence for a moment and then said, "I don't think I'll come to the station after all. There's no point in it. Then I can do these tomorrow." He put down the cleaning things and hung the tunic on a chair and said, "I don't want to hurry you, but oughtn't you to be thinking about your train, Henry?"

* * * * *

I never had any serious doubt, after that, that Jason would obey the posting order. It was always possible, of course, that he would go to see Laidlaw and be told to "stick to his principles." But since I had never known Jason take the slightest notice of Laidlaw's views unless they happened to be convenient, the risk was not great.

I wrote to Jackson that night in the train, and a week later collected the following letter:

> We duly received your consignment, to wit, 1 (one) Pellew, returned for repair and general overhaul, and agree that the same is at present not in working condition. It can certainly be repaired up to a point, and this will be put in hand. Whether it can be made fully Serviceable again is quite another pair of trousers. We would point out that the condition of the consignment is far worse than when it left our hands, and we feel that it must have been subject to abnormal usage of a type not covered by our guarantee.
>
> The only slight snag, Henry, is that like all the rest of us, I am liable at almost any moment to be translated to another

see—or even into another language. If this *should* happen, I shall try to ensure that he is left in good hands—perhaps, if that were conceivable, even better ones than mine.

The lad is very fond of you, but still says you bully him. Perhaps it would have been better if you had taken part in that jolly school auto-da-fe after all? Or perhaps not. That, as I remarked before, is the joy of modern psychology. You never know. Anyhow, leave it to me, in the assurance that if the lad *can* get into an even bigger tangle, there is nobody better qualified to help him do it than

Yours ever,

JACKO.

A fortnight later there was a brief note.

In haste—I am leaving this place to go and do a bit of honest doctoring—if there is such a thing. I am not too happy about little J.P. though I think he's improved slightly. He is in good hands, and if you want to write to him he is at Limehurst Hospital (PC), Limehurst, Nr. Birmingham.

Yr. obed. svt.

L. G. JACKSON (Major).

Since then there has been silence from Jacko. For, on June 6th, 1944, the pot that we had all been heating for so many months finally boiled over in the Normandy landings, and thereafter there were no more of those excrutiatingly waggish letters. But though I never heard from him again, I heard of him once. I quote the official citation.

"On the morning of June 6 the Landing Craft in which Major Jackson was travelling struck an underwater obstacle and sank some two hundred yards from the shore in rough water, and in an off-shore current Major Jackson, a strong swimmer, not only supported a non-swimmer to the shore, but insisted on returning again and again to rescue others until, becoming exhausted, he was swept out to sea and drowned. At least four men owe their lives to the gallantry of Major Jackson, which was in the highest traditions of the Royal Army Medical Corps."

He was always a good swimmer at school. It was the thing he did best.

I wrote to Jason a couple of times but received no reply.

And then in the autumn I was sent to France and was away for several months, and had other things to think about.

". . . GOOD FRIENDS WHO HAVE
HELPED YOU . . ."

I CANNOT be sure of exactly when I returned to England, but
it was in the depth of winter, because I remember the bitterness of the cold at Versailles just before I left, and sitting in
an office in my greatcoat, and trying to get a stove to burn
with no fuel but paper (which was plentiful) and huge
chunks of wood. I remember, too, that flying bombs were
still falling on London, and that on the day I got back a
V2 rocket landed somewhere out at Harrow.

There was the usual collection of out-of-date letters at
Pearson's headquarters. One, however, was only a few days
old, and it said that Mrs. Grayson would be At Home the
following evening between six-thirty and eight at an address
in Eaton Square. At first, I had no idea who Mrs. Grayson
was, nor why she should send me an invitation. But then I
noticed the Eaton Square part of it and realized that this must
be "Kathy," whose party I had attended as the friend of a
friend's friend just after the outbreak of war. Since our only
mutual acquaintances, as far as I knew, were Jerry and Jason,
it occurred to me that she might know Jason's whereabouts,
so the following evening I went to the big house in Eaton
Square.

Jason's whereabouts was Mrs. Grayson's sofa. He was
drinking a champagne cocktail and talking to a plump,
youngish man with thinning hair and a brightly coloured
waistcoat, whose face seemed vaguely familiar. Jason was in

civilian clothes—in fact I was the only man in the room in uniform.

By comparison with Mrs. Grayson's last party this was a very small and intimate affair. There were not more than twenty people present. She came across to me, looking as impressively beautiful as ever, if a trifle fuller-blown, took me by both hands and said, "Darling—how sweet of you to come and how lovely to see you. Now, tell me—which are you?"

I said, "Henry Payne." She at once gave a little squeak of pleasure, and turning, called to Jason, "Darling—*look* who's come! Now you can be happy."

Jason looked round and saw me, immediately jumped up, hesitated and then came across to us rather awkwardly and uncertainly. He was wearing a very smartly cut grey suit, and his hair was plastered down neatly. The effect was not very happy, and produced that faintly bounderish air that I had sometimes noticed before.

Mrs. Grayson was saying, "He kept on badgering me to ask you and I said, 'Darling, of course I'll ask your Henry. But since we don't know in the least where he is, I don't think there's a *chance* that he'll ever get the invitation.'"

I said, "I only got back to England yesterday."

"Well, what a *terrific* piece of luck. Well, there you are, darling—there he is. And don't ever say Kathy doesn't try to make things nice for you."

He may have badgered her ask me, but now I was there his main reaction seemed to be acute embarrassment.

I said, "Well, Jason—how are things?" and he replied, "Oh, very well, thank you. I say, come over and talk to Simon. You remember Simon?"

"Simon? Good heavens—of course it is. Simon Grieves."

Grieves jumped up, wrung me by the hand and squawked, "Why, Henry, darling . . . ! How *much* water under how *many* bridges, my dear! Not since those happy days that were

264

so unmentionably foul! Now, come and sit down between us and tell us all about everything—but everything—except of course about . . ." he waved a hand. "You know."

I said, "Except about what?"

"The unmentionable, my dear. The absurd conflict."

"You mean the war?"

He gave a little gasp of horror. "My dear," he said, laying a hand on my arm. "You're not to know, of course. But that word is *never* mentioned in this house. Is it, Jason?"

Jason smiled faintly but said nothing.

I said, "It was being mentioned enough last time I was here. In fact, at that party there were plenty of people who seemed to be taking charge of the whole thing."

"When was that, Henry?"

"Just after the war broke out."

"Oh yes," said Grieves. "Well, of course that was before my time. But nowadays one and all have had quite enough of it. *Quite* enough. We wait, tensed like greyhounds in the leash, for the end of the whole nonsense and a return to civilized life."

I turned away from him and said, "What's happening to you, Jason?"

He looked down at the floor and said, "Oh—I'm out."

"Out of the Army?"

"Yes."

"For good?"

"Yes. It took a long time, but it came through eventually, a fortnight ago."

"When the powers-that-be *eventually* agreed that Jason had done his share," said Grieves indignantly.

I said, "I'm glad, Jason."

"Oh yes. It was the only thing to do." He raised his eyes to mine and said, "It was my leg you know. I'd had trouble with it before."

"I remember," I said gravely.

"Yes. Well, they couldn't get it right. They kept on giving me medical boards, and then in the end they invalided me out."

"With barely a 'thank you,'" said Grieves. "After all that perilous stuff with aeroplanes."

I said, "Does your leg trouble you now?"

"Not much, really."

There was a pause. I said, "What are you going to do now?"

Jason's eyes had gone back to the floor. "I don't know," he said bitterly. "There isn't very much one *can* do. Anyhow, I'm supposed to rest."

I turned to Grieves and said, "And what are *you* doing?" not because I wanted to know, but because I wanted to stop bothering Jason.

"Well, my dear, since even *Service* doctors agreed that I was *quite* unfit for conflict. I've been able to devote myself to keep some tiny flame of culture going in the darkness."

"What sort of flame?"

"I'm in art publishing."

I looked at him and wondered whether he published art-studies-for-students-twenty-attractive-poses-state-age.

Jason said, "I want another drink," and got up and went away.

Grieves said, "And how do you think our cherub is looking?"

"Jason? He looks fairly well."

"Yes. You can't think what a relief it was to me when he got out of it. He was so brave—so *recklessly* brave—one was always terrified over what he would do next. And anyhow, I think he's fallen on his feet, you know."

He jerked his head towards the side of the room. Jason was just taking another champagne cocktail from a man-servant. As he did so, Mrs. Grayson seized it, took a tiny sip, handed it back to him and put an arm round his waist. She was slightly taller than he.

I said, "Fallen on his feet? How?"

"Our hostess, my dear," said Grieves, lowering his voice. "Absolutely devoted. Head over heels. And so *rich*, Henry."

"He doesn't live with her, does he?"

"A word of many meanings, dear Henry. He doesn't actually *reside* in the *house*. Though I believe *that* has been under discussion. . . ."

Jason came back and said, "Doesn't anybody want another cocktail? They're quite good."

To my relief, Grieves said, "I, said the stoat, with my little throat, *I* need a cocktail," and went off. Jason sat down.

I said, "By the way, you know Jacko's dead?"

"Yes," said Jason. "I heard he was. Farthing's been killed too. He was in the R.A.F."

"Farthing who was head of the House?"

"Yes. I'm sorry he's been killed. He was a good chap."

"Farthing?"

"Yes. I liked him."

This was rather much. I said curtly, "Well, I'm sorry if *anybody's* killed. Frankly, Jason, I can do without Farthing. But I shall miss Jacko."

He said, "Oh yes," rather vaguely.

Grieves came back and squawked, "Make room, children, make room," and sat down between us.

Perhaps because I was neither talking to anybody nor listening, I think I was the first person in the room to hear that queer, angry buzzing in the distance. I said to Grieves, "I know you don't like to hear the war mentioned, but I think I can hear a bit of it coming."

Grieves listened and said, "Oh dear, dear, dear. Yes. It's one of those beastly things. I do *hope* it isn't coming over us. . . ."

Everyone was listening now, and the room was completely silent. The noise was louder and louder, and as far as one could judge, the thing seemed to be coming straight over the house. They always *did see*m to be coming straight over the house.

Kathy said calmly, "Along to that end—away from the glass." The place had big windows and there was only one corner which looked fairly safe from splinters. We crowded into it, most people still clutching their glasses. The noise had risen to a roar that seemed to shake the house. I found myself pressed hard against Simon Grieves's flowery waistcoat and suddenly it all struck me as quite remarkably funny —cowering there in a corner, holding champagne glasses, away from the thing which was too boring to mention.

But at that moment the flying bomb began to splutter, which usually meant that it was coming in at any moment, and as we all instinctively crowded closer, I saw Jason's face. It was dead white and contorted with fear. Kathy had an arm round him, and he was cowering against her. Her face was alert but completely calm. Simon Grieves squeaked, "Oh, the *beastly* thing!" I don't think he was really frightened. Then I realized that the bomb had passed beyond us, still spluttering. We stood there listening to the sound of its engine growing more distant. Then suddenly it cut out. There was a moment's silence and then the distant booming crack.

As we relaxed somebody said, "How appallingly *selfish* one is. One's so amused when it goes over one and lands on somebody else."

Kathy said, "What we all need now is a drink."

After about an hour, I made a move to go, but Kathy would not hear of it. She pressed another drink on me and backed me into a corner and said, "Well—have you made him happy?"

"Jason? I don't know. I was glad to see him."

She was looking at me with the rather bad-tempered eyes, slightly bloodshot.

She said, "He seems to think you do something for him. I don't know why."

"I don't know either."

"Well, do you do anything for him or not?" she said aggressively. "And if so, what? Come on—tell me, George. No. Henry."

"I don't know. I'm very fond of him."

"Like that bloody pansy over there?"

"No," I said. "Not like Simon."

Kathy considered, swaying a trifle on her feet. "Well, I tell you what," she said. "I'm very fond of him too. See?"

"Yes, I see."

"Well, that's all right," she said. "As long as we know where we stand. If you're one of the things he wants, he shall have you. He shall have any damn' thing. Come again on Wednesday."

"I'm afraid I shan't be in London after tomorrow."

"Oh. Well, come again soon. Because we're friends, aren't we, Henry?"

"Of course."

"That's all right, then. And you said you wanted to go. All right, you go. You do just what you like, my dear. . . ." She turned and shouted, "Jason. George is going."

*   *   *   *   *

A few months later the war that had begun with a whimper ended with an atomic bang. Oddly enough, I have no particular recollection of either V.E. day or V.J. day.

I was particularly anxious to get out of the Army quickly because, through Pearson's influence, I had been offered a research studentship in London, and the department wanted me as soon as possible. On a strict interpretation of the regulations, I should not have been demobilized for some time. But the Army was as courteous and reasonable as ever, and before Christmas I was, heaven help us, a retired major, had started my new job, and had taken a flat just off Baker Street which was at once small, unpretentious, and far dearer than I could really afford.

I gave a very small house-warming party, and sent an invitation to Jason at Cheyne Walk. But he neither replied nor came; and it must have been well over a year later that I saw him again. I came home one evening to find him sitting on the stairs outside the front door of the flat. Almost before we were inside he said, "Have you got any money, Henry?"

"A bit. How much do you want?"

"Well, I don't really know. I should think a couple of hundred would do for the moment."

I said, "Heavens no. I don't have that sort of money. I thought you wanted to borrow a quid."

"I wouldn't ask you, but the old lady is being very sticky and I can't raise more than fifty myself."

"There's no harm in *asking* me, Jason, because I simply haven't got it. What do you want it for?"

"Well, Simon's in a mess."

"What sort of a mess?"

"Some horrible youth's been blackmailing him."

"I can believe that. Well, all he's got to do is to go to the police, and they'll handle it without Simon's lily-white name coming into it."

"It isn't like that. This youth's *gone* to the police already."

"Then how can he be blackmailing Simon?"

"I suppose it isn't exactly blackmail——. Anyhow, Simon's got to get out of the country or he'll be arrested."

"He can't go too soon for me."

"But that's the point, Henry. He hasn't got any money."

I said, "Look, Jason—be sensible. Even if I had it, which I haven't, why on earth should I fork out two hundred pounds to keep Simon Grieves out of jail?"

"Well—he's an old friend."

"Not of mine. I can't abide the man and never could. Anyhow, he's had this coming to him for years."

"Old Simon's never done anybody any harm."

"If he hasn't, it isn't for want of trying. Anyhow, for goodness' sake, keep out of it."

"But we can't just let it *happen*," said Jason earnestly. "I mean, he can't help being like he is. Anyhow, the law about this is absolute nonsense."

"I hold no brief for the law, but I hold even less for Simon Grieves. If you want to help somebody, at least let it be somebody a bit more worth while than that."

Jason looked hurt. He said, "I didn't think you'd feel like that about it, Henry. After all, he's an old friend of mine." He said it with the air of a child of ten whose mother has refused to buy it a motor cycle. It irritated me and I said, "Well, if you want to borrow some money for him why not try your pal Kathy? She's got plenty, I gather."

Jason's mouth shut very tightly. "Kathy won't," he said curtly.

"Why not?"

"She doesn't like Simon. Kathy's nice enough with people she likes, but she's got her knife into Simon because he's a friend of mine."

"Can you blame her?"

"I don't see why you're all so down on poor old Simon." He sat in silence for a while. "I don't see whom I can go to now," he said dispiritedly. "I think Arthur Laidlaw would help, because he's always sorry for people who are being persecuted. But of course he's very poor. . . . Look, Henry, couldn't you just lend the money to *me*, and I'll pay you back within six months? After all, you would have if I hadn't told you it was for Simon."

I said, "Jason, I tell you I haven't *got* two hundred pounds. I've only just taken this place and I'm broke."

271

He gave a curt nod as though he didn't believe me and said stiffly, "Then I'm sorry to have troubled you, Henry."

I said, "Well now, forget about that for a moment and tell me what's happening to you. Where are you living?"

Jason hesitated. "Mostly at Cheyne Walk."

"Are you doing anything?"

"Oh—pottering about. I was thinking of starting a market garden."

I said bluntly, "Well, I should think that would be more fun than hanging around with Simon Grieves and Kathy."

I saw him stiffen, and for a moment I thought, and half-hoped, that I had made him angry. But he hesitated and then just said listlessly, "Oh, I don't know."

I said, "How's your godmother?"

"She's all right. Very trying." He got up. "Henry, I'm sorry, but I must go. You see this business about Simon is urgent."

I said, "Jason, for God's sake let it alone."

"Oh no, I couldn't do that," he said coldly. "I'm surprised that you should suggest it."

At the door I said, "We must get together, Jason."

"Yes, of course."

"Only I can never get hold of you. Why not give me a ring here? Any evening. Welbeck 0080."

"Welbeck 0080. I'll remember that."

"You'd better put it down. It isn't in the book yet."

"Oh no," he said politely, "I shall remember it. Goodbye, Henry."

When he had gone I went to the window and watched him as he came out into the street. He took a long time to get down the stairs, and when he appeared he stood for a long time as though uncertain which way to go. Then he started slowly in the direction of Baker Street with lowered head and drooping shoulders, and I knew that this time I had really let him down. There had been plenty of times before when I had made him angry, or when he had felt that I bullied him. But this time I had disappointed him.

He had implored me to buy him the motor cycle, and I had brusquely refused; and with that refusal something of faith and warmth had gone out of the world.

Nothing appeared in the papers about the Simon Grieves affair, and I decided that it had been a false alarm, or that Kathy had relented, or that Jason had "put the bite on the old lady," as he used to describe it, or even that Laidlaw had cashed his savings certificates to save somebody from persecution. Anyhow, I have never seen Grieves nor heard of him since, which has suited me admirably.

Nor, for at least four years, did I see any more of Jason. I rang up Cheyne Walk several times, but he was never in, and on at least one occasion the voice that said he was out was remarkably like his own. After that I gave it up. For some while I half expected to find him sitting on the stairs again some evening. But as the years passed I accepted that the break was final and complete, and was never sure whether I was glad or sorry.

*   *   *   *   *

In 1948 my mother died, and in 1949 I got a lectureship; so that by 1950 I was slightly more prosperous, and moved to a rather bigger flat only a few doors away from the other. I was looking out of the window one very wet evening, just as it was getting dusk, when I saw a figure standing in a doorway on the other side of the street. There was something familiar about it, but it was not until it moved slightly, so that the light fell on its head, that I realized that it was Jason. He was wearing a mackintosh, but despite the pouring rain he was bareheaded.

I was about to open the window and shout to him to come in when I saw him stiffen, stare across the street, and then start to stroll casually away, still looking across the street.

Then he paused, turned, and went back to his doorway. He did the same thing again a few seconds later, and after a while I realized what was happening. The doorway was opposite the entrance to my old flat, and Jason was simply arranging to meet me accidentally.

There was something peculiarly characteristic and rather touching about the whole manœuvre. I put on my coat and went out with the air of a man going on some expedition. He had not expected me from that house, and so had not moved from his doorway, and it took us fifty yards in pouring rain before he could cross the road to my side and I could see him and call, "Why, hallo, Jason!"

In the dim light of the street he looked unchanged, but when I got him inside I could see that the cherubic face was beginning to have lines around its eyes and that the skin had roughened and coarsened, in both texture and colour. The effect was oddly unpleasant, like seeing a middle-aged actress off the stage when one is used to seeing her play twenty-five-year-olds. It came as a shock to me to realize that Jason was now thirty-three.

I knew better than to expect him to tell me what had been happening to him. I merely told him such news as I had, and then talked generalities and waited.

"Henry—I need a job. Do you know anything about getting jobs?"

"What do you want it for? To earn a living or just to keep you amused?"

"Well . . . both really. The old woman's being awfully sticky and trying about money. And anyhow, it would be good for me. I'm sick of just messing about. I'd like to get out and—and be on my own."

"Where are you living now? At Cheyne Walk?"

"Oh no. I haven't been living there for a long time." He hesitated. "I was with Kathy for a bit, but I've packed that in. That's why I want to get a job. I don't want to go back to Cheyne Walk."

"Why did you pack in with Kathy?"

"Well . . . I don't want to say anything against Kathy, because she's been very good to me. But she can be a bit much sometimes."

"I can see that."

"She's so—so *possessive*. You mustn't have any friends or any life of your own. And, of course, she's always been used to having exactly what she wants, and if she doesn't get it she's livid. So I've packed it in."

I said, "Frankly, Jason, I think you're well out of it."

"Oh, I'm sure I am. But now I must have a job."

"Any idea what you want to do?"

"I don't know," he said vaguely. "There must be *something* I could do. After all, everybody else gets jobs—even the dumbest people."

"How about the market garden?"

"I haven't got the money. You need a hell of a lot."

I found myself starting to compose an advertisement, "Unreliable and neurotic retired parachutist, seeks position with prospects. Age 33. No qualifications or experience. . . ."

I said, "What you want is something where you could use your languages."

"Yes. I should like to go abroad. Preferably Italy. I really do speak Wop awfully well. . . ."

I don't know why, but it took me two days to realize that the most likely answer to Jason's problem was Mr. Ironside. Mr. Ironside was an American whom I had met during the war at the Parachute station, and who was now in charge of the London office of a big American travel agency. I had an idea that he also had some control of the offices in most of Western Europe.

Having taken two days to think of Mr. Ironside, I then spent about a fortnight trying to find him, since he was the sort of man who was usually breakfasting in Paris, lunching in Hamburg, and dropping in at Geneva for tea. But eventually he came to rest in London for a few hours, and I was able to put the proposition to him.

It went surprisingly well. Mr. Ironside was not short of staff in Italy, but there was a possibility in Zurich and another in Brussels. He listened respectfully to my account of Jason's war record and my claim for his knowledge of languages and of Europe. Privately, I had a nasty feeling that to turn Jason loose with a lot of time-tables and tell him to work out the details of a journey from Zurich to Madrid would probably be inviting chaos. But I did not say so, and Mr. Ironside did not know Jason. In the end he said, "Well, of course, I can't promise anything, Henry, but from what you say I should think we could probably use your friend. I should *certainly* think we could use him. Now, I've got to go on down to Nice and one or two other places, but when I come back I'd like to meet him, and we'll see, eh?"

This seemed promising, and I was rather disappointed by Jason's reaction to it when I told him, which was simply that he didn't care much for either Zurich or Brussels. He showed no interest in what the job might entail in terms of work, money, or anything else. As he did not seem to have done anything about looking for a job himself since we had met before, I was slightly irritated.

I said, "Well, look, Jason—you said you wanted a job. Here's a chance of one that you might be able to do rather well. If you don't like the sound of it, you've only got to say so."

"Oh no," he said politely. "It's not that, Henry. I'm very grateful to you for taking all the trouble. I should certainly like to see Mr. Ironside."

"Only you're not going to be the easiest of people to fit in, you know."

"No," he said humbly. "I know I'm not."

He was looking at me with the shy, deprecating smile, and I could feel, as I had felt so many times before, that curious veil between us—not an opaque curtain which shut out all sight, but a translucent something that left visible only a dim, undefined shape that might, for all one knew, be laughing or crying.

According to his office's account of his movements, Mr. Ironside must have spent most of the next three weeks in aeroplanes. But he must have found time for other activities, because when he eventually became becalmed in London again he sent for me and his first words were, "Say, Henry—this friend of yours we talked about. You didn't tell me he was a Communist."

I said, "He isn't."

"Well, a fellow traveller then."

"He isn't that either. I don't think he's interested in politics at all."

Mr. Ironside shook his head and said, "That's not my information, Henry." He was a big, slow, soft-spoken, courteous man with bi-focal spectacles, and he was looking at me in a hurt way, as though he felt that I had let him down badly.

I said, "What *is* your information?"

"Well, he fought for the Reds in Spain, didn't he?"

"I don't know if he actually fought, but he certainly went there and helped the Spanish Government against Franco."

Mr. Ironside spread out his hands expressively.

I said, "But surely that doesn't make him a Communist— or even a fellow traveller? Lots of people did that simply because they saw through Fascism before the rest of us did, that's all."

277

"I suppose **you can look** at it that way," said Mr. Ironside without enthusiasm. "But, apart from that, he was mixed up with the Commies here, wasn't he?"

"He was very anti-Fascist and used to go and help break up their meetings. But he was only a kid then. And, anyhow, surely it's not a crime nowadays to have been anti-Fascist?"

"Maybe not. But it's one thing to have been anti-Fascist and another to have been pro-Communist. And my information is that he was tied up with the Commies."

"He had a girl who was a Communist for a while."

Mr. Ironside shrugged his shoulders and spread out his hands again. "Well, there you are. He *was* tied up with them."

I said, "But damn it, Ironside, this is crazy. That girl was killed in the war, doing fine work for the Navy. If she wasn't all right, and straight, and on the right side, who was? You know Jason's own record. They were simply anti-Fascist, which is what the war was *about*. And if they were pro-Russian, so was I and so were you when they were fighting on our side."

"Maybe," said Mr. Ironside rather bitterly; "but that's some time ago."

He sat and stared moodily at his blotter for a long while.

"I don't know," he said at last. "It's a crazy world, Henry. I'm a Democrat myself, and nobody could say I was a witch-hunter or in favour of witch-hunting. But I can tell you this, I could never recommend that we hire a man with a record like that, because I know that if I did, our head office would slap it down, and slap *me* down for suggesting it. You may be right. Your friend may be quite O.K. But he's got the paint on him from that brush, and our policy is that we don't touch them." He shook his head. "You see, Henry, we've got to be careful—particularly in our business where we've got people all over the world, and a lot of them not American nationals. You've only got to get the

whisper going round that we're employing Reds and. . . ."
He shrugged his shoulders expressively.

There was nothing to be done, except to keep one's temper.

I got up and said, "I quite see. I'm sorry to have given you this trouble. It never occurred to me."

"That's quite all right, Henry," he said in his gentle way. "I'd have liked to have helped. But there it is."

At the door Mr. Ironside paused and said, "I don't think you people over here sometimes realize how strong feeling is in American about this."

"I don't think we do."

"And come to that, I don't think *we* understand the way *you* look at it." Mr. Ironside smiled a trifle wryly. "Well, let's hope there'll never come a day when you'll find out that we were right, Henry. But I'm afraid there may."

I rang up Jason and said, "I'm sorry, but I'm afraid the Ironside job has fallen through."

Jason said, "Well, as a matter of fact, it's just as well, because I was just going to ring you to say that I've got a job."

"Fine. Doing what?"

"Selling insurance. I think it might be an awfully good thing for me, don't you?"

"Well . . . it might. What are they paying you?"

"They don't actually pay me a salary, but I get commission on business I arrange."

"I see."

"After all, Henry, I do know a lot of people, and one can talk to them about it. If I could do enough at it I could make a packet. They say they're not interested in anyone who doesn't want to earn at least a thousand a year. Which isn't bad, is it?"

"Very good. If you can get it."

Jason said, "I'd like to come round some time and talk to you about it. It really sounds rather fascinating. I had no idea there were so many different sorts of policies."

They gave him a fortnight's training in how to sell insurance and during that time he came in nearly every evening to tell me what he had been taught. He was sure that I personally ought to take out at least one of each of the things he had to sell. I tried to explain that as a single man with no dependants, I was not the most obvious of prospects; and that anyhow I was insured already. But he continued to gaze at me with earnest grey eyes and to say, "But supposing you were to die suddenly, Henry?" or, "But you see it would give you £4,000 when you were sixty-five, *with profits*." He was at once so boring and so sincere that I sometimes wondered whether, after all, he had not landed in the right job.

My interests were not the only ones he worried about. He discovered, with his usual fascinated surprise, that by using her capital to buy herself a life annuity, Lady Peasmore could considerably increase her income, and that, moreover, he would earn substantial commission by arranging the deal. "So you see, Henry, *everybody* would be better off." It took me some time to explain that if Lady Peasmore bought an annuity she would not then be able to leave her money to him, which I understood she was proposing to do; and that, if he ever found an insurance agent trying to persuade her to buy an annuity, his logical course was to throw the man out of the window at once.

Jason's most exciting discovery, however, was that if he took out a policy *himself*, he could act as the agent and draw the commission on it. He came back positively bubbling with excitement over this, as a man might who had discovered perpetual motion. I was not in a good temper that evening, and I think I really hurt his feelings by suggesting that while he was about it he might as well set up a laundry to take in his own washing and live on the profits. I don't think Jason ever felt that I appreciated the full wonders of insurance.

This sort of thing went on for a fortnight, after which his company turned him loose to sell insurance to an unwarned and unsuspecting world. I had long been resigned to the fact that I should be his first client. I managed to settle for a very small, very cheap whole life policy. I have it still, and when I die somebody will be four hundred pounds better off, purely as the result of Jason's efforts.

After that, I saw little of him for nearly a year, though he used to drop in occasionally. During these months I think he worked really very hard, and did in fact write one or two policies for acquaintances. But I don't think he could ever have lived on what he made, if he had been entirely dependent on it, instead of having a few hundred a year of his own. Even as it was, I gathered that he was living in not very comfortable rooms, and he never invited me to them.

I could not help noticing, on the rare occasions that I saw him, that he was gradually talking less about his work, and with less optimism; and that whereas at the beginning he had tended to drop in for a few minutes and then go bustling off to interview some "prospect," he now liked to stay for as long as I would let him, often quite silently, like a man who does not know where else to go, or why. I was therefore not at all surprised when one evening he suddenly said, "You know, I think I shall chuck up this job."

"Why? Doesn't pay well enough?"

"No. I suppose it would be all right if you could get enough business. But there are such a hell of a lot of people at it. Besides, you need a pull somewhere—with a big firm or something like that."

281

I said, "What will you do, then? Look for something else?"

"I suppose so," he said without enthusiasm. "Though I don't see much what. I suppose you couldn't speak to your pal Ironside again? There might be something there now."

"I honestly don't think he'd be any good, Jason."

"Oh. . . . Well, you see, Henry, I've only got just over three hundred a year of my own. I suppose I could live on that. Lots of people do. But it'd be pretty grim."

I said, "Could you go back to Cheyne Walk?"

"Oh yes. The old lady's always badgering me to. She's always thought it was ridiculous for me to work—her heir and so forth. But she doesn't see that if I'm not going to work she must give me some money, because otherwise there isn't anything to *do*."

"No. Well, I should certainly get another job if you can. I think you'd be happier."

"I suppose so," he said rather doubtfully. "But at the moment all I feel is that I should be happier if I hadn't got to live in those bloody digs." He was silent for a moment. Then he raised his head and said, "Henry—will you tell me something—frankly?"

"What?"

"Do you really think anybody will ever pay me enough to live on? I mean—am I worth it?"

"Of course. It's only a question of finding the right job."

"But *what* job?" he said rather bitterly. "What is there that I can do that anybody's likely really to want? You see I don't know . . . anything. *You* know something. Everybody else knows something. But I don't. Ever since I left school it's—it's all been blind alleys." He frowned in a puzzled way. "It's very odd to have spent sixteen years without learning *anything* useful. I never really see quite how it's happened."

"You've got your languages," I said rather feebly.

"Yes. Except that they're getting very rusty. But I suppose they'd come back."

Thirty-six hours later he rang me up at the laboratory and said, "I say, can I come round and see you this evening?"

"Of course."

"Only I've got a bit of news."

"Good news?"

"Rather. Wonderful. I'm going to marry Kathy."

I suppose I might have thought of that one, but for some reason it had never crossed my mind. After all, as far as I knew he had not seen her for a year. He arrived at about six-thirty, bringing a bottle of champagne, and so excited that at first I thought he had been celebrating already. He was flushed and beaming, and even as we shook hands he gave a sort of little skip of sheer exuberance.

I said, "Well, this is all very sudden and exciting. I didn't even know you and Kathy were still in touch."

"Oh yes. We've seen each other from time to time. I think we both *knew* really."

"What's happened to Kathy's husband?"

"Well, that's rather the point. She's only got her divorce a few months ago. He's been a frightful nuisance, but he's gone at last."

He seized the champagne and started to pull at the wire, "Come on—we must drink to it, Henry."

The cork came out with a bang and the champagne frothed over and spattered on the carpet, and over Jason's trousers. He roared with laughter and said, "God, what a mess! I'm a ship and you're launching me. . . . Glasses, Henry —glasses!"

I fetched some glasses, and we solemnly drank to their happiness. I was finding it rather difficult to know what to say. There was something faintly hysterical about Jason's excitement, and I did not know quite how to handle it

I said, "When are you going to get married?"

"As soon as we can. Probably next week. Nobody'll marry us in church because of Kathy's divorce, so we shall just pop into a registry office. But there'll be a hell of a party after, Henry."

"I'll bet there will."

Jason jumped up and started to walk about the room. "You must come. I mean to the registry office as well as the party. I couldn't get married without you. You must be my best man. Or does one *have* a best man at a registry office? I don't know. Have some more champagne."

"And you'll live at Eaton Square?"

"Well, yes. But there's a country place, too, of course. Anyhow, we're going off for a long time first. I want to go to South America. Have you ever been to South America?"

"No."

"Nor have I. Kathy has. In fact there's practically nowhere that girl hasn't been. She says South America's terrific." He gave another little skip. "My God, Henry, I am lucky."

"No more insurance, eh?"

"No more bloody insurance. Except that I shall make Kathy take out an enormous policy and draw the commission on it. Then I shall stop." He suddenly added gravely, "Of course I shall be very busy looking after Kathy's affairs. She's got interests in all sorts of things."

I had a sudden vision of Kathy's face, and visualized her sitting meek and admiring while Jason explained that she should sell out of Rand Mines and re-invest in Roan Antelope.

I said, "Yes—I suppose if you have as much money as that it takes some handling."

"Oh, a terrific lot. You know all this that I've been learning about insurance will be awfully useful now."

Rather to my relief the champagne, instead of making him more excited, seemed to calm him down. After his second glass he stopped walking about the room, giving little skips and giggling, went and sat down and said earnestly, "I say, Henry, you do think this all right? I mean you don't disapprove or anything?"

"Of course not."

"Only I'm absolutely relying on you to tell me frankly. You're the only person who ever *does* tell me frankly, and I know I do sometimes do damned silly things." He stared at me very solemnly. "You don't think this is damned silly? Because, after all, we're not married yet and. . . ."

I smiled and said, "Oh come, Jason. You wouldn't not get married just because I didn't approve."

"Well . . . I don't know. But there's no reason why it shouldn't work, is there?"

I hesitated and said, "None at all. As long as you're sure you're in love with one another."

"Oh, I think we are. I know Kathy wants to marry me. She's wanted to for a long time."

"And you're sure you want to marry her?"

"Why, yes. Of course. I assume I obviously *should* want to, shouldn't I? I mean, it's a tremendous piece of luck for me."

I said, "The only other thing is to be sure you realize what you're taking on. Kathy's a very rich girl and you're not a very rich chap, and that can be a bit tricky for both parties—unless you get it properly worked out from the start."

"I shall still have my own three hundred, of course."

"Yes. But that won't take you far with the sort of life you'll be leading."

"I suppose not," he said reflectively. "Though there'll be more when the old lady dies."

"There's no earthly reason why it should be a snag," I said hastily. "I only mean that it's a thing to get worked out."

"Oh yes," said Jason soberly. "I quite see that. But I

think it will be all right, you know. Kathy's awfully generous. She doesn't really care about money at all."

He sat for a moment in silence, gazing down at the carpet. Then he suddenly threw up his head and looked at me with the beaming smile that seemed almost to strain his mouth at the corners and said, "By gad, I like the sound of this South American trip, Henry! I've always wanted to go to Chile particularly. It's such a rum *shape*."

I said, "Will you fly, or go by boat?"

* * * * *

There were only four of us at the registry office—Jason, Kathy, myself and a curious, very tall girl known as Herby. We must have been an odd-looking group, for I am over six feet, Herby was as tall as I, and Kathy herself was a big woman, and she was wearing a large mink coat, whereas Jason looked even smaller and younger than usual. I thought I caught a questioning look in the eyes of the clerk, as though he wondered what we were all doing to the poor little chap; and indeed I wondered the same thing myself.

Kathy kissed me warmly when we met and said in a low voice, "It's sweet of you to have come, Henry. It's absolutely *made* the whole thing for the little man." She drew away slightly and said archly, "I wasn't at all sure that you'd *let* him marry me."

I said, "Oh yes. Grandpapa gave his consent."

"Well, I really *will* be good to him, Henry. I promise."

I had never been to a registry office wedding before, and had always assumed that it was a coldly legal affair. But the room was decorated with flowers and the actual ceremony seemed almost as solemn and religious as the church service, which I did not like. It was one thing for Jason to marry Kathy. It was quite another to see him there with his hair plastered down with water, looking like an unusually serious and slightly worn choir boy, solemnly swearing that the union would last till death. Kathy was at once demure and slightly amused by the whole business, and on several occasions I saw her glance at Jason and smile as one might at a child which is behaving well. Herby spent the whole time looking round the room and pursing her lips as though she had been shown into an hotel bedroom and was finding it unsatisfactory.

As soon as it was over Kathy kissed us all in turn, thanked the clerk, and led the way briskly to the street, where her yellow and black Rolls-Royce was waiting. As the chauffeur opened the door she said, "Well, that was very nice. Here comes the bride, Clements. Come along, children, we're wasting good drinking time."

It was only just after half-past three when we reached Eaton Square. The party was not due to start till five-thirty, and in the huge drawing-room servants were still bustling about preparing for it. Kathy took us to what she described as "The Little Room," which was only about twenty-five feet square, and sent for champagne, which we drank out of silver tankards. Kathy said, "There's only one way to give a party, and that's to get on and have a decent drink before the guests arrive. Then you don't dislike them so much."

It struck me that though it might be the way for her to give a party, it was unlikely to be the way for Jason, who could get drunk on half a pint of beer if he was in the mood for it. I think the same thought occurred to Kathy, because about four o'clock she suddenly decided that we must have tea. Tea was accordingly produced and we all sat and looked at buttered toast, tea-cakes, crumpets and pastries. The only person who ate anything, I think, was Herby, whom I remember seeing with a crumpet in one hand and a glass of champagne in the other.

The next hour or so was rather uncomfortable. Jason was in his silent mood and merely sat smiling politely at every-

body without saying anything beyond "Yes" and "No."
Herby was not a talkative girl and, moreover, seemed to be
in a very bad temper. For most of the time Kathy and I
talked about South America.

South America is a big place, but by about five o'clock I
was beginning to run out of things I wanted to ask Kathy
about it, and there were some long silent pauses. I noticed
that Kathy's mouth was beginning to tighten, and that she
was shifting her feet restlessly. She glanced angrily once or
twice at Jason and Herby, and I could see that unless something was done there was going to be an explosion.

But before I could formulate a question about the valley
of the Amazon she turned to Herby and said, "This is the
jolliest funeral I ever knew. What the hell are you sulking
about?"

"I'm not sulking," said Herby sulkily.

"Well, if this is your natural manner, darling, you'd better
take it to the dentist and have it out."

Herby said, "All right. What d'you want me to do? Sing
a comic song?"

They sat and glared at one another in silence for a
moment, and I thought we were in for a real squabble. Then
Jason murmured, "Girls . . . Girls . . . on my wedding
day . . . !" and beamed at both of them. Kathy whipped
round towards him, her face still furious, hesitated, and
then suddenly smiled and said, "No, darling—they shan't
make it horrid for you . . ." and rumpled his hair. Herby
gave a contemptuous grunt and turned away.

The thing that really saved the situation was that though
the party did not start officially till 5.30, people began to
arrive soon after 5. I heard at least half a dozen lots
explaining to Kathy that they *had* to come early so as to be
able to drink her health "before the mob arrived." They
were all fairly hard-bitten types, and they not only drank
her health, but anything else that they could lay their

hands on, with great zeal. By 5.30 there must have been fifty people present, and by six the big room was packed.

It was a peculiar affair—not quite a wedding reception, not quite a cocktail party. Kathy remained near the door and Jason hung about rather uncomfortably just behind her. Kathy greeted the guests as they were announced, and Jason was then presented, though Kathy occasionally forgot about this part of it. My impression was that there were only a dozen or twenty people present whom he had met before, and for my own part there was not a soul I even knew by name.

A large, bald man with a very big stomach came as near to me as the stomach would allow and said confidentially, "Who *is* this little cove that Kathy's married?"

I said, "His name's Jason Pellew."

"Pellew? What's he do?"

"I don't think he does anything."

The bald man considered and then said, "Well, Kathy'll need one that size on each foot," and went away.

At about six-thirty a toast-master-like person called us to order and announced that the cake would be cut. Kathy then cut the cake with great competence and considerable strength of wrist, and a small man, announced as the Viscount Limeton, proposed the health of the bride and bridegroom. Broadly speaking, he said that we all knew Kathy and loved her, that she gave the best parties in England, and that for his part he would be only too happy for her to get married every week if it produced a gloriously happy occasion like this. He concluded by saying that the bridegroom was a very lucky man. I had a strong impression that he referred to Jason as "the bridegroom" because he had forgotten his name. I was at the back of the crowd, and Jason's reply was inaudible to me, and, I think, to most other people. But it was very short and everybody

applauded loudly. The Viscount then led the singing of
"For she's a Jolly Good Fellow" in a key which was quite
beyond most of us.

The arrangement was that the bride and bridegroom
would leave in a charter aircraft at about eight, fly to
Paris, spend the night there, fly on the next day to Milan,
and catch their boat for South America from Genoa. I did
not feel that any of this involved me, and I was not enjoying
the party, so after the cake-cutting and toasting I worked
my way across to Jason and said, "Well, I think I must be
off. Bless you, Jason, and all good luck."

He stared at me rather owlishly for a moment. I think he
was beginning to be slightly drunk. Then he grabbed my
arm and said, "But you can't go yet, Henry. You can't."

I said, "Well, you and Kathy will be going soon yourselves."

"Yes, but you've got to come and see us off. To the airport.
You *must*. It's all arranged."

"Oh come—you don't need me for that."

"But you *must*," he said almost piteously. "You can't just
leave me to go by myself. You *must*, Henry. . . ." He was
gripping my arm so hard that it hurt.

I hesitated and said, "Oh, all right, if you really want me
to."

He looked round the room with a curious, glassy,
frightened stare and said, "I *hate* all these bloody people.
Let's have a drink, Henry."

I said, "You've got one."

"So I have. Anyhow, I hate them."

Kathy came up and said, "Well—the conspirators as usual.
What are you two hatching?"

Jason said, "He *is* coming to see us off."

"Of course he is," said Kathy. "I'm not sure he isn't
coming to Paris, too. Would you like that, darling?"

There was a very sharp edge on that. Jason felt it and smiled rather sheepishly. She patted him on the shoulder and said abruptly, "You'd better go and change. You take much longer than I do." As he started to move away obediently she called after him, "Have a lie down first. You need it."

She looked after him for a moment and then turned to me and said aggressively, "You're coming to the airport and no farther, see?"

I remembered about Kathy at the end of a party, and guessed the sort of thing that was coming.

I said, "I didn't even want to come as far as that."

"Oh yes," she said. "He wanted you and he shall have you. He shall have anything he wants. But only as far as the airport. After that . . ." she waved a hand, ". . . finish. Clements will drive you home," she added with dignity.

"That's very kind of you, but I can probably get a taxi."

"No, you can't. You can't afford it. You can't afford taxis. Clements will drive you anywhere you want to go." She suddenly stared at me and smiled and said, "You see, I've done you in the eye, George."

"Henry."

"That's right, Henry Payne. I apologize, Henry. You see, you couldn't stop him from marrying me."

"I didn't try."

"Of course you did. You're telling lies." She suddenly took my hand and said pathetically, "Why do you have to tell such lies, George? I could be very fond of you if only you didn't tell such lies. I could give you anything. But you tell such lies."

I said, "Look here, Kathy, hadn't you better go and dress?"

"That's quite right," she said. "I must go and dress. But we're friends, aren't we?"

"Of course."

"Then kiss me." She threw her arms round me and kissed

291

me passionately, pressing herself hard against me. We were in the middle of the room and I saw a lot of people grinning. The fat, bald man said, "Hey, steady, Kathy. Wrong chap."

Kathy let go of me and I looked round. "Don't take any notice," she said loudly. "They're only a lot of cadgers. See you in a minute." With that she went out.

Kathy had been married in a mink coat. She went away in a beaver one, which I suppose was her knockabout travelling garment. Jason wore a camel-hair overcoat, which made him look rather like a successful jockey.

The party came thronging down to the door to see us off but no other car accompanied the yellow and black Rolls, which was a relief. As at the registry office, the only other person who came was Herby. I never did know Herby's other name, who or what she was, nor why she was selected for these more intimate moments. If she was a close friend of Kathy's, one would certainly never have thought so, for I never heard them speak a civil word to one another all day. Herby had drunk her way steadily, perseveringly and morosely through the party, and now seemed to have reached a state of completely speechless fury. I only spoke to her once on the way to the airport, to ask her if she had enough room, and she answered with a low snarl. I have often wondered since if she was angry that day about anything in particular, or just chronically angry.

The fresh air on the drive seemed to be good for Jason and Kathy, and by the time we reached the airport they both seemed reasonably sober and normal. As the chauffeur was getting their luggage out of the boot I noticed that Kathy's extremely expensive matched suitcases bore the initials K.P. It took me some moments to realize that K.P. stood for Kathleen Pellew. I had spent most of the day watching Kathy marry Jason, but somehow it had never occurred to me that it had done anything as important to her as to change her name.

Rather to my surprise, and I think to Kathy's, Jason announced that he would go and inquire about the aircraft, and set off purposefully for the Inquiry Office. It was the first sign he had shown of taking charge of anything, and it was not a very successful effort. He was away about a quarter of an hour, and then came back to say that the plane would be ready to take off in about half an hour's time.

Kathy said, "Half an hour? But it was ordered for eight and it's ten past now."

"I know, darling. But they're still fuelling or something."

"Tell them we're in a hurry."

"I have told them. They say that's the quickest they can do."

Kathy's mouth went very thin. She said, "Well, if they think I'm going to sit around in this miserable place for half an hour when I'm paying for a special plane, they're very much mistaken. Where is the man?"

She went storming off, looking very large indeed in the beaver coat. Jason smiled at me rather feebly, sat down, and closed his eyes.

Kathy came back and said, "Take-off in ten minutes. I shall go to the ladies' room. Stay here." She set off. Herby rose silently and trailed after her.

I said, "Now, I wonder how she managed that? Presumably by telling them not to fuss with details like putting petrol in."

As Jason did not reply I turned and looked at him, and saw that he had opened his eyes and was staring straight in front of him as though he had just seen something terrifying. I said, "Hey, are you all right, Jason?"

He turned his head slowly and stared at me in the same frightened way, and said, "My God . . . my leg."

"What's the matter with it?"

"I can feel it coming on. The—the thing I had."

293

I said, "Nonsense. You've just drunk too much champagne."

"No—honestly, Henry. It's going. I can feel it. . . ."

I got up quickly and said, "Stand up."

He rose slowly to his feet and stood swaying slightly, still looking at me with wide, frightened eyes. I said, "Now, walk about."

"I—I can't."

"Yes, you can. You know perfectly well you told me that you could always make it work if you tried hard enough."

I put a hand under his arm and said, "Come on, now, Jason. This is where we came in."

I started to pull him along. He was leaning heavily on me and swinging the leg with an effort of his whole body, in the way I remembered so well.

I said, "Only this time you haven't got to jump out of the bloody thing. You've only got to sit in it with Kathy as far as Paris, and then tomorrow you'll be off to South America, you lucky so-and-so."

He said, "Genoa first."

"Yes, Genoa first. So you'll be able to talk Genoese."

"Yes. I can talk Genoese rather well. At least I could. I expect I've forgotten it now."

He was walking more easily now, and I cautiously let go of his arm.

I said, "All right now?"

"Yes. It's going to go off, I think. . . . You know, you're the only person who's ever been able to get rid of it for me."

"All done by kindness."

"Yes." Jason stopped suddenly and said, "I say, Henry—do you think it can have been Genoa?"

"Think what can have been Genoa?"

"Well, it was a port. They told you it was a port, didn't they?"

I hesitated and said, "You mean Leah?"

"Yes. She was working at a port. Only, don't you see, if it *was* Genoa I might quite easily have met her. Because I was there quite a bit. I might have met her, Henry. That would have been damned funny. '*Scusi, signor agento de Gestapo. . . .*'"

He started to laugh. I saw Kathy and Herby coming back into the hall and said quickly, "Dry up, Jason. Here comes Kathy."

He was still laughing when they joined us but quite quietly. Kathy said, "Hallo, darling, has Henry said something funny? I didn't know he ever said funny things."

A loudspeaker with a very refined accent said, "Will Mrs. Grayson and her party please go to number 3 door. Mrs. Grayson and her party to number 3 door. . . ."

Kathy said, "So I should damn' well think."

The last time we had not stayed to see the plane take off, but had only heard it go roaring overhead when we were back at the Station. But this time we stood, Herby and I, and watched her rise and head away to the south, till one could no longer be sure which were her lights and which were stars. Then we went back to the Rolls-Royce and Clements drove us back to London. It was almost as silent as driving back with Colonel Fry, except that as we turned off the Great West Road Herby suddenly said, "I don't mind telling you that if he thinks he's going to get much out of her, he's wrong. Kathy'll soon see through *him*."

I said, "I'm not sure that there's very much to see, in that sense."

"Well, she'll see through him," said Herby with satisfaction. "He may think she's a fool, but when it comes to a showdown he'll find it's all sewn up, all right."

There was no further conversation except that when we dropped her somewhere in Knightsbridge she said, "Good night," without looking at me, and as though she begrudged it.

* * * * *

"May I speak to Mr. Payne, please?"

"Speaking."

"Oh, hallo, Henry. It's Jason."

"Hallo. Back then? I thought you were going to be away another month."

"Well, we were, but Kathy's got a bit tired of it. You see she's seen it all before."

"How is she?"

"Fine. Look, can you come and dine with us on Friday?"

"That's very kind of you. Where?"

"Oh—Eaton Square. I'll send the car for you."

"There's no need to do that, Jason."

"But of course. Clements will pick you up at your flat at about seven. That all right?"

"Yes."

"Good. Black tie. I say, it will be nice to see you."

"Look, I'm awfully sorry, Henry, but Kathy's had to rush down to the country on business, so I made her take the Rolls, and the other car's in dock. But I've got a cab downstairs if you don't mind. . . ."

"Of course not."

"I thought we'd just go and dine by ourselves at the Majestic, if that suits you?"

"Need we be so grand as that?"

"Well, I know the Majestic's rather a barn, but they know me there. And then we can go round to Green's. Do you know Green's?"

"I've been taken there once."

"I've only just joined. I think it's rather a nice club. Some amusing chaps."

Jason was wearing a dark blue dinner jacket with lighter blue facings and a dark red bow tie. South American sun had burned his face to a brick-red colour, and the skin was still peeling off his forehead.

The head waiter at the Majestic greeted him by name, and he greeted the head waiter by name, and we were shown to his usual table and had a glass of that Manzanilla that Jason had had before, and we would, of course, start with a dozen oysters, and after that what was really good today, and in the end it was, I fancy, something that was not on the menu. The accompanying wine was obvious to all concerned. I am a poor man and it may be that what I was feeling was jealousy. But it did not feel like jealousy. The food was, in fact, very good.

As usual, Jason was not very communicative about South America, but I gathered that he had enjoyed himself and would like to go there again. Chile was not only a rum shape but a very beautiful country, and as Kathy had some interests in Valparaiso it would be easy to run out there some time.

I said, "I'm sorry not to have seen Kathy this evening."

"Yes," said Jason briefly. "I know she's sorry, too. How about a sweet? They usually have a rather good chestnut cream if you ask for it."

He asked for it and got it. He also asked for various other things and got them, including what seemed to me rather a lot of brandy. He eventually signed a bill which I did not see and left a pound note as a tip, and we went on to Green's.

Green's had been much slower to take Jason to its heart than the Majestic. He seemed to me distinctly nervous of the place, and told me several times that he had only just joined. When he asked at the porter's desk if there were letters for him, he was rather curtly asked his name. As we went into the bar Jason said, "What I like about this place is that everybody seems to know everybody else. Some awfully amusing chaps."

The bar was full of what were probably very amusing chaps indeed, and they did appear to know one another. They were standing or sitting in large groups, and the main problem was how to get through them to the bar. On a couple of occasions Jason said, "Hallo, George," or "Hallo, Phillipson," rather shyly, and on each occasion received a rather cool nod in return. It struck me that the blue dinner jacket and the maroon tie were not really helping us.

When we had apologized our way nearly to the bar Jason suddenly said, "Oh—there's Dan Herold," with what seemed relief. I then saw that a considerable section of the bar was taken up by the bald man with the large paunch who had asked me Jason's name at the wedding.

Jason pushed in beside him and said, "Hallo, Dan."

The fat man turned and looked at him and said, "Oh—hallo," without enthusiasm.

"By the way—do you know Henry Payne? Dan Herold."

Herold nodded to me and said, "Evening."

"Have a drink, Dan?"

Herold said, "Well, seeing that it's somebody who can afford it, I'll have a large Old Club brandy." As he said it he gave me a sly wink over Jason's head.

"Good. Will you have the same, Henry?"

I said, "I don't think I will, thanks, Jason."

"Oh, but you must. The Old Club is frightfully good. Three large Old Clubs, please."

Mr. Herold caught my eye and cast his own up to the ceiling with a slight shrug of the shoulders. I don't know why he always picked on me for these confidences.

Herold said, "Well—here's to you. How's her lady-ship?"

"She's fine."

"Well, I'll tell you something," said Herold with a glance at me. "You keep that girl in her place. Stand no nonsense from her, see? What she needs is firm handling."

Jason flushed and said, "I'll tell her you said so, Dan."

"That's right," said Herold. He drank the remainder of his brandy at a gulp. "And give her my love when you see her. Now, if you'll excuse me, I'm going to play bridge."

He turned and thrust his big stomach through the crowd and waddled out of the bar.

Jason said, "He's a character, is Dan."

"Is he?"

"Yes. As a matter of fact it was due to him that I joined this place. Kathy very much wanted me to have a club, so he said he'd put me up for here. I say, this brandy is frightfully good. Have another?"

I said, "No, thank you, Jason, really. I shall have to be going."

"But you can't possibly go yet. It's only ten o'clock."

"I must. I've got some work to do before I go to bed. But don't let me take you away if you want to stay."

He hesitated and said, "Well . . . I think I shall probably hang on for a bit. It's usually more fun a bit later. There really are some awfully amusing chaps. . . ."

At the door I said, "I wonder if you and Kathy would dine with me one night?"

"I'm sure she'd love to, Henry. When?"

"How about Wednesday of next week? Perhaps you'd better ask her?"

"Oh no—I'm sure that would be fine."

"Well, you can ring me if it isn't. Otherwise, say seven at the flat?"

"Thank you very much."

"And thank you for a very good dinner."

"Not at all. I'm only sorry we had to put off going to

Eaton Square. You must come here again. It's really a very nice club when you get to know it."

         *   *   *   *   *

"I say, Henry, this is Jason. I'm most awfully sorry, but I'm afraid we shall have to wash out Wednesday, Kathy isn't very well."

"I'm sorry about that. Anything serious?"

"Oh no. Just that she's a bit under the weather and I think she oughtn't to go out. I'm very sorry."

"That's all right. Would you like to make another date?"

"Well . . . would you mind if we left it open for the moment? So that I can see how she goes on?"

"Of course. Give me a ring when she's better."

"I'll certainly do that. I shall be ringing you anyhow and we'll fix something."

After that there was silence broken only on one occasion about six months later. I was walking past the Majestic one night at about ten o'clock when a party of half a dozen emerged, in evening clothes. I recognized the yellow and black Rolls-Royce and Clements before I recognized them. As I passed I heard Kathy say loudly and irritably, "Darling, I tell you there simply isn't *room*. You'll have to get a taxi or something. What the hell's the good of my buying you a car of your own if you always want to barge in here crushing everybody?"

I walked on without looking back. In a few moments the big car passed me, and in the light of a street lamp I caught a glimpse of Jason's yellow hair in front beside Clements.

         *   *   *   *   *

I took on Mrs. Larner as resident housekeeper in the summer of 1951, and it must have been one of the first things that happened after she came. I remember that it was a very hot night. She met me in the hall as I came into the flat and said, "There's a Mr. Pellew, sir. He said he wanted to wait for you."

I said, "Is there, indeed?" and started for the door of the living-room. Mrs. Larner said, "He asked for a drink, sir, and there wasn't anything in the house but some sherry, so I gave him that. I hope that was right?"

I said, "Yes, of course. Mr. Pellew's an old friend."

I went into the living-room. Jason had taken his jacket off and was sitting in his shirt sleeves in an armchair. To my surprise the bottle of sherry, which had been half full, was still half full. Jason got up with a slight effort and said, "Hallo, Henry. I hope you don't mind my making myself at home. But it's so damned hot."

I said, "Not at all. Nice to see you, Jason. How are you?"

He said, "I'm as well as can be expected, Henry. I say, you didn't mind my asking your housekeeper for a drink, did you? I haven't actually drunk any."

"I see you haven't. Why not?"

"Well, to tell the truth, Henry, when I come to think of it, I've had quite enough to drink already, and I like to be able to take it or leave it."

"I agree. Anyhow, it's lousy sherry. Well, how's everything? How's Kathy?"

Jason smiled and said carefully, "I don't know how Kathy is and I don't bloody well care. All I know is she's gone."

"Gone where?"

"God knows. She's shut up Rockham and shut up Eaton Square and pushed off. So I've left her," he added with dignity. "I was going to anyway." Jason's lips trembled. "Do you know she's even taken my car? Well, she's welcome to it, the bitch. I don't want the bloody thing."

I said, "Wait a minute—let me get this straight. You and Kathy have parted?"

"Yes."

"For good?"

"I wouldn't live with her again if she was the only woman on earth. I'd rather be dead. You won't believe some of the things she's done to me. Nobody would believe it. That's why I didn't drink the sherry, because that's what she wants —to make me into a drunk so that she can get rid of me."

"When did this happen?"

"Well, it's been coming for a long time. I was going to leave her anyway. She shut up Rockham about a month ago and then we had a flaming row and I went and stayed at that bloody place Green's, and then two days ago I went round to Eaton Square and she'd shut it up and gone. I can't even get at my clothes."

"Have you got any money?"

"Of course not. Not a cent. You see, she knew that some ought to have been paid into my account yesterday, so she hasn't paid it in so as to leave me flat. You'll never believe some of it, Henry. . . ."

It went on for several hours. Quite a lot of it I did not understand, since it referred to people and things that I had never heard of. But the general outline was clear enough, and more or less what one might have expected. For the first few months she had encouraged him to be as extravagant as possible—though strictly in ways that amused her, rather than in ways that amused him. She had given him an allowance of two hundred a month, a car, a personal man-servant and so on. She had got him elected to Green's, and opened accounts for him everywhere. But the whole thing had been on a carefully controlled monthly basis, and the car and the accounts had always been in her own name.

Then, growing tired of this comparatively simple game, she had begun to put the screw on, encouraging him to buy things and then refusing to pay for them, and constantly reminding him before her friends that she could take it all away at any time she chose.

In the last phase she seemed to have lost all interest in him, except as a butt and an object of irritation, and whilst insisting that he should come everywhere with her, had encouraged her friends to sneer at him. She had also been openly unfaithful.

It was a nasty story, and often his face was scarlet with shame and humiliation as he told it me. I think there was probably a good deal more and worse, but I heard quite enough.

At the end I said, "Well, I'm extremely sorry, Jason, but quite frankly I'm not very surprised."

"But why did she *do* it to me, Henry?" There were tears in his eyes. "Why did she ever marry me? After all, it was she who wanted us to get married. I couldn't see why she should want to, and of course I knew it might be difficult. You remember you said so. But she kept on saying she loved me, and that money didn't matter, and that it was silly not to marry her just because she was rich. . . ." He paused and then said quietly, "She kept on saying she loved me even after we were married. That's why I stuck it so long, because I thought she did in a queer way. But, of course, she can't ever have done. And I didn't realize that." This was said in a very low voice as he stared down at the carpet, and I realized that though Eaton Square and Rockham and the car and Green's had perhaps had a good deal to do with Jason's marriage, they were not the main things that he had now lost.

I said rather awkwardly, "I think she probably did love you in a way. But she just isn't a person that can go on doing it."

He said, "You really think it might have been that? I wouldn't mind so much if it was. Otherwise I should feel that—that I didn't understand people at all."

There was a long pause. I said, "Well, what happens now?"

"I shall divorce her."

"You can't. You've got to be married three years before you can get a divorce. You've only been married eighteen months."

He looked rather taken aback and said, "Oh. . . . Yes, of course. Well, I don't know that it matters much."

"What matters is where you're going to live and what you're going to live on."

"Yes. I shall have to think about that."

"Have you got a solicitor?"

"I've used Kathy's. Anyhow, what do I want a solicitor for?"

"Well, some of the things she's given you are probably gifts. You may be entitled to them. You'd better go and see a chap I know. Daniels. Very good bloke."

Jason said, "Oh no. I couldn't do that."

"Why not?"

"I couldn't take anything of—of hers."

I said, "I see how you feel, Jason, but after all, she's let you down, and she's got a lot of money and you've got none. I don't see why she shouldn't pay *something* for her fun."

"Oh no," he said without interest. "That's not on. You see that's what she *thinks* will happen. It's what they all think."

"Then what are you going to do? Can you go back to Cheyne Walk?"

"Not very well. . . ." He hesitated. "You see, the old lady doesn't know about Kathy."

"You mean she doesn't know you've parted?"

"No. She doesn't know about our getting married."

"Good God! You never told her?"

"No. I didn't think she'd like it."

"Then what on earth does she think you're doing?"

Jason wrinkled his forehead. "I can't remember," he said helplessly. "But it'll come back to me."

This was a trifle too much for me and I said nothing.

Jason said, "I've still got my own three hundred, of course. The problem is where to live."

He paused and looked at me appealingly. "Just for a few days until I can get things sorted out. All I want is a bed, really. . . ."

I hesitated longer than a kind man would have done, because life at that time was running unusually smoothly and pleasantly. But the thing was clearly inescapable.

I said, "Well, I've got a spare bed here that you could have for a bit."

His face lit up for a moment. Then he said very politely, "That's very kind of you, Henry, but I couldn't dream of troubling you. . . ."

"That's all right. The room's very small, but for what it is, you're welcome to it."

The next day I insisted on making an appointment for him to go and see Daniels. He was very dubious about it. "I don't see what he can *do*, Henry."

I said, "That's why I want you to see him—to find out."

In the end, according to Mrs. Larner, he went off obediently at the appointed time. When I came home in the evening I asked him what Daniels had said. Jason looked me very straight in the eye and said, "Oh, he asked me a lot of questions."

"Does he think he can do anything for you?"

"Well, I can't get a divorce till we've been married three years, of course."

"You knew that before. What else?"

"Nothing much really. He said he'd let me know if he thought of anything."

I guessed what had happened, but I rang Daniels up next day just to make sure, and of course Jason had never appeared. After that I let it go, for in a way he was probably right.

I must say that Jason was very little trouble to have in the flat—almost pathetically so. For the first few days he took so much trouble not to make work for Mrs. Larner that he rather hurt her feelings—even insisting on making his own bed. This phase soon passed, but he was always very tidy and unobtrusive.

I was out all day and saw very little of him except in the evenings and at week-ends; but I heard from Mrs. Larner that he nearly always went out at lunch time, so that she did not have to prepare a meal for him; and several times a week he would be out all the evening. I have no idea where he went or what he did, for I know he no longer used Green's. I think he went out purely to be out of my way.

During this time he never drank at all at the flat, even refusing a glass of beer if I offered it to him. But sometimes when he had been out all the evening I could see that he had been drinking a certain amount—not because he was drunk, but because he was so pathetically anxious that I should not think he was. Nearly always on these occasions he talked a great deal about the past—about things that happened at school, or even before. Sometimes, also, he would tell me about incidents in his life with Kathy. The period of the war he never mentioned.

I can't say that I was really much help to him. I suppose I should have tried to find some way of helping him to put his life together again. But somehow I could never see quite what was going to happen to Jason now; and apart from making a few vague inquiries about possible jobs for him, I did nothing. I seem to have been content to let him stay at the flat, and to talk to me occasionally, and apart from that to let it go, waiting fatalistically for something to happen.

Of course in the end it began to happen. For three weeks, or perhaps a month, he seemed well and reasonably happy— or if he was not, I contrived not to notice it. But then he began to suffer from insomnia, and after that I began to recognize the old pattern only too clearly. Before, he had always breakfasted with me, fully dressed. For perhaps a week, he took to appearing at breakfast in a dressing-gown, and after that he was always still in bed when I left the flat. He no longer went out at lunch time, refused to let Mrs. Larner give him lunch, and would lie in bed all day, awake but scarcely moving, only making a tremendous effort to be up and dressed, or to have gone out, by the time I reached home.

At last even that effort was too much, and I came home one evening to find him still in bed, with Mrs. Larner very worried because he had not moved or eaten all day.

I went into the small bedroom. It was only about eight feet square. He was not in the bed but lying on it in a dressing-gown, and my mind went back to the time in the war when I had made him obey the order to go on the refresher course. He turned his head for a moment and said, "Hallo," and then looked away again.

I sat down on the bed and said, "Look here, Jason, Mrs. Larner says you've been in bed all day."

"Yes."

"Well, that won't do, will it?"

"No," he said listlessly.

"You've got to pull yourself together, my lad."

"Yes." There was a long pause. Then he said in a low voice, "What d'you want me to do?"

I said, "Well, the first thing to do is to get up and wash and have some food. It's no good just living here moping."

"No." He stared in front of him for a while in silence. Then he said, "I'll go if I'm in the way, Henry."

"It's not a question of being in the way. But it isn't good for you."

There was a moment's dead silence and then suddenly he sat bolt upright and screamed, "Well, beat me, then—beat me, the lot of you! That's the only thing that's ever been good for me, isn't it?" He sat there rigid for a moment and then slumped down awkwardly sideways and began to cry with a loud, high, rather formal sobbing noise like a child that is not only heartbroken but angry.

I said sharply, "Jason—stop it."

He stopped at once and lay there looking up at me for a moment. Then he said quietly, "I don't know what to do. I'll do anything you tell me, but I don't know what to do. Tell me what to do."

It had been easy enough before, because there had been orders—impersonal orders, issued by someone else, and one could tell him that he was a soldier, and that he must put on his uniform and obey them. But now he was not a soldier, and there was no uniform, and no orders. I made him get up and wash and dress. While he was doing so, I reflected bitterly that last time I could hand him over to Jacko, and thinking of Jacko reminded me of Parsons.

I got Jason in and sat him down. He was quite quiet now and very meek.

I said, "Look here, Jason, it seems to me that you'll never get anywhere until you're properly fit and getting proper sleep and so on."

He said, "Yes . . ." and hesitated and gave me a quick glance. "I'm not very fit. I haven't told you but—but I'm having trouble with my leg. You know—the thing they invalided me out for."

"I see. Well, I think you ought to go and see a doctor I know. His name's Parsons. He's just round the corner in Welbeck Street."

"Not if he's a trick-cyclist. I tell you, I had half a dozen of them during the war. They never did me any good."

I took a chance and said, "Well, Jason, you asked me to tell you what to do, and I'm *telling* you what to do. Go and see Parsons and talk to him. If you don't like him you needn't go again, and there's no harm done."

"But I haven't got any money," he said weakly. "They charge the earth."

"Parsons isn't that sort of doctor."

He shook his head doubtfully, and I had a vision of a long series of appointments with Parsons that would never be kept.

I said, "Jason—let me put it this way. I'm rather worried about you. Will you go and see Parsons as a favour to me— just to put my mind at rest?"

His head came up and he stared at me for a moment in a startled way. Then slowly a smile spread over his face and he said, "Well, of course, Henry. I mean—it's nonsense to say it's a favour to you, isn't it? After all, it's entirely for my own good. Of course I'll go if you think so."

Parsons always seemed to work about fifteen hours a day. Most of the time was spent at one of the big psychiatric clinics, and it was there that I had met him. For the rest he carried on a private practice in rather shabby rooms in Welbeck Street, where his clients seemed to consist of an odd mixture of countesses and down-and-outs.

I went to see him at eight o'clock one night, and before he was free to see me three patients arrived in the waiting-room; a handsome old man in a frock-coat, a negress with a bandaged head, and an immensely fat woman in black, whose breathing was so asthmatic that she made a noise like kittens mewing in the distance.

I told Parsons very briefly that Jason had broken up while in the Army and had been invalided out, that his marriage had now gone wrong, and that I thought he needed treatment. Parsons nodded and said, "Know anything about his background before that?"

"Yes—a lot. I've known him all my life. Shall I tell you about it?"

"No. I'd rather get it from him. But I may want to check some things with you after."

"If he tells you his father was a missionary and was eaten by cannibals it isn't true."

"Does he tell people that?"

"Sometimes. As a matter of fact his father died in an asylum."

Parsons said, "I'll remember that, Henry. Father not eaten by cannibals. Died insane. Well, when can he come along? I shall want him three times a week for a bit if he can manage it. After that we'll see."

"I think he could come anywhere that you could fit him in. He's not doing anything."

Jason had been to Parsons three or four times before he ever made any comment beyond saying rather cautiously that Parsons seemed a nice chap. Then one evening just after I came home he suddenly said, "Parsons says I can have a drink if I want one."

I said, "Why not? D'you want one now? I think there's some beer."

Jason hesitated. "No, thank you, I don't want one now. But he says I can if I want to. He says I'm not an alcoholic."

"Has anybody ever said you were?"

"No. But that was what Kathy was after."

"I should have thought Kathy and her pals drank so much that they wouldn't notice whether anybody was an alcoholic or not. What does Parsons think about her?"

"He says she sounds a bitch. You know I quite like Parsons.

He's much more straightforward than most trick-cyclists. But he doesn't strike me as very *clever*."

"Why not?"

"Well, I'm sure that you could pull his leg and he'd never spot it. You know, Jackson was like that, too. But most of the Army trick-cyclists were awfully clever. If you told them anything that wasn't true they were on to it like a knife. But anyhow I'm glad he's told me I'm not an alcoholic. I was a bit worried about it."

He went out shortly after, and I bet myself half a crown that he would come home very drunk indeed. But instead he returned completely sober, and spent over an hour telling me the plot of a film which he had been to see.

One Sunday a few days later we went for a walk in the park. It was a damp, soft, windy day in early autumn and the air was full of falling leaves. We stood for a while watching a man training an Alsatian puppy. He would send the dog away about a hundred yards and make it lie down. Then he would wave a hand and it would spring towards him. When it had gone about twenty yards he would hold his hand up and it would lie down again with its ears pricked and its head on one side, waiting for the next wave. I remarked idly that you could see that the dog was having a fine time. Jason said, "Yes. I wish somebody would do that to me."

"Teach you to come when he beckons?"

"Train me. You see, nobody ever has, except for a bit in the Army. And I liked that. It's always a lovely safe feeling when people are telling you what to do and you don't have to think, but just do it."

"I seem to remember your getting very bored with it."

"Oh, of course. But I liked it all the same, because I knew it was good for me." He paused, picked up a leaf and began

311

carefully to shred it off the veins. "But I'm going to be all right, because I'm so lucky."

"Of course you're going to be all right."

"I have had the most tremendous luck, you know. After all there was school, and then I had that grand time in Italy when I was seventeen. And then Cambridge and Spain. . . . And look at the war. I might easily have been killed that time in 1940, before Dunkirk."

It was very unusual for him to mention the war so freely. I said, "Yes. And if it comes to that you easily might not have got away with the Italian job. I don't think Fry thought you would."

"Oh yes. It was only my luck that got me through there. As it was I came through it all without a scratch, and what is more, didn't even lose a friend in the whole thing. Except. . . ." He paused and I glanced at him sharply.

He said, "Except poor Farthing."

"And Jacko."

"That's right. And Jacko." Jason slowly scattered the shredded fragments of leaf. "Of course the Kathy business was unfortunate in a way. But even there I had that trip to South America. Considering I've never learnt things or worked or anything, it's really extraordinary . . . oh hell!"

"What's up?"

"He's taking the Alsatian away."

A leaf had landed exactly on top of Jason's head. It was almost the same colour as his hair. It looked funny, but he did not seem to have noticed it. He said very seriously, "But I would like you to know, Henry, that I do realize how much you've done for me. You couldn't have done more, and whatever happens now it won't be your fault. *Whatever happens.*" He repeated it with great emphasis.

I said, "Why? Is something *going* to happen, Jason?"

312

"Oh no. I'm going to be all right. But I just wanted to tell you."

I said, "You look extremely comic with that leaf on your head."

There was something oddly disturbing about this conversation. It rang hopelessly false. But a little later I saw at least part of the point.

When we were nearly home he said, "Has Parsons rung you up?"

"No."

He gave me a quick, almost secret glance. "He's going to."

"What about?"

"He wants to see you. He asked me if I minded, and I said, of course not." After a moment he added casually, "I expect he wants to talk to you about me."

"Maybe. But psychs. don't talk about their patients much, you know."

"I think that's what he wants."

Parsons rang up on the Monday and asked me to come in at 9 p.m. Knowing Parsons I arrived at 9.15 and Parsons arrived at 9.30.

There was no desk in his consulting-room, but there was a writing bureau at one side, and he had a habit of sitting at it when he was talking to you, so that one had an odd feeling that he was going to start writing a letter at any moment.

He said, "About your friend Pellew. How d'you think he seems?"

"He's a lot better than he was."

"Yes, I think he is. But there's a hell of a lot of stuff there, of course. It isn't going to be easy to get at, and the question is whether it'll serve any good purpose to get at it."

313

I said, "I don't know what you've been doing. He's hardly talked about it at all."

Parsons turned and poked about in the pigeon-holes of the bureau as though looking for the paper and envelope.

He said, "Well, you see, Henry, in my job you get mainly two sorts of people—the ones who've worried without there being any obvious cause for it, and the ones who've worried and have plenty to worry *about*. Now friend Jason's a mixture of the two. He's just separated from his wife, he's got no money, no home and no job. So it's not surprising if he gets depressed and starts having a paralysed leg and generally doesn't want to have anything to do with it all. See?"

"Yes."

"Right. Well, I can deal with that up to a point. All he really needs there is somebody to talk to about it. He's very withdrawn and tense, but I can help him there with injections and so on and then he talks—after a fashion. And when he's done that half a dozen times he's better. We don't hear any more about his paralysed leg and he begins to see he's well out of his marriage, and he even begins to talk a bit about the future. In other words, we've cleared up what was lying about on the surface. Time—one month." Parsons paused and tapped reflectively on his blotter with his fingers.

"But now comes the question. He may have had some bad luck, but most of his troubles have arisen because he's like he is. He's very immature emotionally and very insecure. He's always had a big fantasy life, and it comes out all the time when he's talking to you."

I said, "I warned you about that. He's always been like it."

"Yes. Well, at present he knows what's true and what's fantasy. He just spins yarns and tells lies, and if people believe them it gives him a feeling of power—of being

314

clever and outsmarting people. It's a typical child's trick. But the danger is that with his immaturity and insecurity, if he ever comes up against something tough, as he did in the war, or as he has recently over his marriage, he'll crack up. Finding he can't handle the world he'll withdraw further and further from it into fantasies, until he doesn't know what's real and what isn't. And the end of that's schizophrenia."

I said, "It sounds a pretty grim prospect."

"Well, I'm being frank with you, Henry, because I want you to understand my difficulty. The real Freudian analysts would tell you that the only thing that will help him is a full analysis, maybe over several years. But here he is, age thirty-four, with that background and that heredity. Very withdrawn, very unreliable, not very co-operative. A really full analysis would be a hell of a long and difficult job. It *might* do the trick for him. But in my experience there are about three chances in four that it'd do more harm than good by starting a lot of things that you couldn't finish."

There was a long pause.

"Well, what do you think we'd better do?" I said rather helplessly.

Parsons frowned thoughtfully. "There's a chance that if he could live a normal life—say with a job to do, and friends, and maybe a satisfactory marriage, he might be all right. His trouble is that he feels nobody loves him or ever has. He's fond of you, but you're all mixed up with his father, which doesn't help. Apart from that he doesn't seem ever to have had a normally satisfactory emotional relationship with anybody in the world—man or woman. Though, like most people who are as immature as that, he's mildly bi-sexual."

A thought struck me and I said, "Look—he has told you about Leah, has he?"

"Leah? No. Never mentioned the name."

It was 10.15 when I left. Parsons came down to the door with me and as we passed the waiting-room I caught a glimpse of a man in working-clothes with a muffler, sitting with his cap on his knees. Parsons said, "Well, I'm glad we've had this chat, Henry. I think the only thing to do is just to carry on for a bit and see how we go. But in the meantime —anything you can do to get him out of his shell. A job— friends—girls—a hobby—any damn' thing except being alone and doing nothing. And just one other thing—don't be afraid to let him see that you're fond of him. I mean, don't be too sharp with him. He knows it's all right really, but he's a bit scared of you."

I said, "In fact, don't tell him he must pull himself together and so on?"

"That's it. See, the trouble about telling people like that to pull themselves together is that they're a damned sight *too* pulled together already in some ways, and what they need is to have some of the laces undone. Good night."

* * * * *

I walked the short distance back to the flat. Jason was out. I was tired, and would have liked to go to bed, but I remembered that he had been rather silent and suspicious ever since he had known that I was going to see Parsons, and thought I had better see him before he went to bed, so that he would not feel that something was being arranged behind his back. I sat down in the living-room to wait. I had had a long day and Parsons had depressed me and even irritated me slightly. I had a feeling that he was rather throwing the whole thing back at me instead of providing a solution. I was fond of Jason, but I did not fancy having him on my hands indefinitely. And as for finding him a job or friends or what not, that was easier said than done.

I remember thinking that Parsons was trying to take on altogether too much, with patients still waiting at ten o'clock at night; and that one of the reasons why he was dubious about full analysis for Jason might well be that he simply didn't want a long, tough job.

I must have been sitting there for a quarter of an hour waiting and thinking about it before I saw the letter. It was not on either of the tables or on the mantelshelf but on a shelf of the bookcase in front of the books. I think I knew what it was as soon as I saw it.

DEAR HENRY:

I hope you got on well with Parsons and that this will not upset anything you have arranged. He is a nice man, but I have been thinking about it and do not think a trick-cyclist is really what I need. He keeps telling me to relax and not worry about things, and so I find myself tending not to care about things, instead of pulling myself together and putting them right, which is not good for me and unfair to you because I can't just go on living on you.

I have therefore gone away, and shall not come back until I have got everything right, which I think I must do by myself because I never have, which has been half the trouble.

I am sorry not to have seen you to say good-bye and thank you, but I did not know you would be so late. I realize that I have never paid you anything for my food, but as soon as I have my next quarter's money I will send you a cheque. Please give the enclosed pound to Mrs. Larner with my kindest regards. I can't give it to her myself because she is out.

I think this will be very good for me, as I always do better if I have to discipline myself, and now I know that I am not an alcoholic I shall be quite all right. Again, thank you, and you were not to know that this is what I needed like that time at school. I hope to see you again quite soon.

Yours,

JASON

I ran down the stairs and along to Baker Street. It was after half-past ten, and the traffic was thinning, but the pubs had just turned out and there were plenty of people in the street. I stood for a while looking up and down and watching the buses as they ground up to the stop. Then I realized that I was being silly and that he might easily have been gone two hours. I took a last look at the impersonal street that was full of strangers, and saw a smallish fair man without a hat. But when he came nearer he was a stranger, too, and I turned and went slowly back to the flat.

EPILOGUE

THE JUDGE raised his head and passed his tongue quickly over his lips. It may have been my fancy, but the dark, heavy face, which had looked troubled, now seemed coldly serene. Perhaps in that long moment of reflection, he had found some truth—or some relief in ceasing to pursue it.

"In your statement you have expressed regret, and what little there is to be said in your favour has been ably urged. But the fact remains that nothing the court has heard amounts to a full explanation of this disgraceful behaviour, let alone an excuse for it. Had this been a single isolated offence, or a matter of sudden impulse, it might have been possible to avoid sending you to prison. But it is quite obvious that for a long period you have acted with wilful and planned dishonesty, and with an utter disregard of the rights and interests of any other person. Your record shows that you are not a stupid man, nor one likely to have difficulty in knowing right from wrong. The choice was yours, and you chose to minister to your own petty desires and comforts by robbing others. Society must and shall be protected against this type of monstrous egoism. I take into account your previous good character, your service to your country in time of war, and the fact that, once arrested, you made a frank admission of your crimes. But for the crimes themselves I can find no excuse. In these circumstances the least sentence that I can pass consistent with my duty is that you should go to prison for twelve months."

There was a pause and then he flapped again briefly at the dock. I saw Jason turn, and for a moment—the only moment in the whole affair—his eyes flickered quickly round the court. But he did not see me, and then he had disappeared, and I rose and blundered out of the court. As we went through the hall Parsons said, "Fair enough, I suppose, according to their lights. I thought he might get eighteen months. He wasn't exactly defended with genius, but I'm afraid it wouldn't have made much difference anyhow. It was pretty hopeless from the start."

I said, "Yes. Right from the start."